Matthew pulled her off the ground and jammed her mouth against his own. He had to stop her talking before his brain burst. Her blood seemed to fill his mouth as her lips opened and her tongue ran against his gritted teeth. He wanted her and hated knowing he was not the first. Had Cord been? he wondered. All he could see were her eyes, mocking and hating and aflame with desire.

"Bastard," she gasped, arching against him....

THE
PAGAN
LAND

by

Thomas Marriott

FAWCETT GOLD MEDAL • NEW YORK

THE PAGAN LAND

Published by Fawcett Gold Medal Books, CBS Educational and Professional Publishing, a division of CBS Inc.

ISBN: 0-449-14446-1

Printed in the United States of America

First Fawcett Gold Medal printing: January 1982

10 9 8 7 6 5 4 3 2 1

BOOK ONE

THE ROAD TO SION

To an exile of sad slavery
   has Judah departed,
to settle among pagans,
   with no longer peace;
and in her anguish her pursuers
   overtook her.
The paths to Sion are woebegone...

               LAMENTATIONS

1

He and his father had almost traded blows.

Matthew Eastman clucked softly against the roof of his mouth and pumped his right arm up and down as a signal to the rider coming up behind him. There were scents on the wind and a stillness over the veldt that smelled of wrongness.

He was a day and a night away from the Eastman farm and yet the anger lived on, as vibrant and oppressive as the predawn darkness he had been riding through. His father's blank refusal to allow him to join the Commando because he was "needed" on the farm was based on no logic Matthew could see or understand. Things had been said that could never be taken back by father or son....

Gaika, his mare, was hard-mouthing the bit and fighting the rein as an odd reluctance stiffened her forelegs. Matthew drew in until she settled, waiting for Boie to reach him. The Khoikhoi would scout ahead.

The rising sun spread a blush through the eastern hills dimming the few stars that still showed there. Great dull banks of cumulonimbus rushed solemnly southward toward the Eastman farm, propelled by a dying wind that blew into Matthew's face and brought the scent to him. The familiar terrain was alien in the half-light, rolling away on all sides, a patchwork of muted dulls and darks. Dongas, thorn, and dead ground merged into an anonymous and blind sameness.

The small Khoikhoi reined in beside Matthew, and his foal nuzzled Gaika, whickering softly. Boie blew into her ear to settle her, leaning his small frame along her neck. When he stood back into the saddle his head with its kinky hair barely reached Matthew's shoulder.

A jackal scolded the paling darkness and his mate coughed to silence him. Thunder clattered without lightning and left a harder silence.

Matthew held the foal as Boie dismounted, holding her on a tight rein to stop her from trampling spoor. The veldt turned tan and green under the silver and lead sky as rolling wind tossed the brush like a dry sea and erratic olive shadows chased the clouds. Here and there, the night's hail had gouged rifts in the grass and ripped gullies in the earth.

Boie loped in a wide circle, bowed over, his face almost touching the ground. He crossed and recrossed the trail in a zigzag and returned to the horses when a flight of birds banked sharply away from the ridges above and beyond the mission station at Hendricks's farm.

"They came last night, Nkosi," Boie said, squatting beside an anthill. He pointed to the impression of a bare foot and the pock of a spear shaft under the scurrying ants. Then, almost reluctantly, he stretched his arm to the west, making the finger sign for forty. "See, they came around under the hill so Baas Hendricks see nothing."

"Mount up." Matthew's neck prickled as he swiveled slowly in the saddle, squinting at the horizon.

Kaffirs.

2

Kuba the Xhosa had planned his raid well.

He had hidden his young warriors in the night grass around the corngrowers' farm to wait for the morning when the sun would be at their backs and in the white men's eyes. The weather had been bad, a storm had hailed through the dark hours, and Kuba had prayed to his family gods for deliverance from the lightning and success against the corngrowers' guns. If his fate was death, he wished to go prepared.

Hintza the Xhosa King had declared a spring war against the corngrowers who came from the southern waters with their women and children to build their stone kraals and to wall the land as their own. The old men of Kuba's village spoke of older men who spoke of a time when there were no whites and the Xhosa cattle roamed to the great salt waters with only the small, shy Bushmen for company.

Kuba did not know if he believed such a thing, for it seemed to him that the sight of the corngrowers' wagons was as familiar as giraffe reaching for the sweetest topmost leaves or a pride cutting a fat gnu from the milling herd.

Kuba had seen one of the corngrowers' witchmen; making finger crosses in the air with unliving clay hands and smelling as bad as wet feathers. And he knew their magic books were protected by nothing but empty talk of a living-dead god's son, talk as meaningless as the dark beyond a fire.

A cockerel called the sun into the dawn, and Kuba's men stirred around him, easing the stiffness from their limbs and sucking pebbles to bring saliva to their mouths. Nobody drank before a battle, for water in the belly is bad for wounds.

Smoke rose from the Hendrickses' chimney and horses whinnied in the wooden grain store beside it. Spring flowers showed bright from the borders of a small garden. Kuba again wondered why the corngrowers planted things that could not be eaten.

Two whites, one old and bent, the other a green willow who was not yet a warrior, came from the house and went to ready the horses for work. Kuba saw they had guns and that their white shirts made them clear targets. Later, two more men came out and talked together with a woman as if she were an equal.

Kuba raised his hand to motion his left horn forward when a shrill, warbled birdcall cut the silence. Without turning his head, Kuba knew it was a signal from the lookout on the high ground to the south. A moment later his carrier brought the message: two riders coming from the southwest. One white and the other a Khoikhoi.

The two men standing outside the farmhouse had heard the call too, and were casting about with their hats held out to shield their eyes from the eastern glare. The woman started back to the house, crying out to someone inside, a small girl in a bonnet who came out with long guns for the two men.

Kuba stood up, his chest bared to demonstrate his own bravery. He held his shield high above his head and ordered both horns forward.

3

There were four males at the Hendricks place, Matthew knew. The old man and his three sons. Five, if he counted the priest from London who ran the mission station on the farm. And the women: mother, wife, and daughter.

He and Boie would have to go along the dirt road through a gully to reach the farm, a bad place for ambush. Old Kobus Hendricks had always laughed when the Commando told him so. He thought the priest was all the protection he needed. God help him now, Matthew thought.

God help them all.

He set Gaika forward, away from the farm. If he could get into the high ground above the war party he might just get them in a cross fire. He and Boie took their horses through a kloof into a maze of gullies where strangers would lose their bearings in moments, twisting and turning to the base of a kopje where a rough goat track led sheer to the flat summit.

Matthew heard the shrill birdcall as he dismounted and took his smoothbore from the saddle scabbard, edging to the

8

rim on his stomach as Boie held the horses and watched the back trail. The war party was well organized, Matthew realized grimly as he raised himself up on his elbows and took in the scene below. The Xhosa were moving in fast and he was in time to see the first cracking volley from the two men in the grain store rip into the forward runners. Two went down, then a third, punched down by the heavy four-ounce balls that fragmented on impact.

One of Hendricks's sons fell and was swamped by a ring of Xhosa anxious to blood their spears, cutting down at him long after he was dead. The other boy made the farmhouse and was pulled inside by his mother. The flanking Xhosa were lighting torches and hurling them onto the thatch, into the gunports.

Matthew spat a ball into his smoothbore and ran it out ahead of him, cradling it in against his shoulder as he panned for a target. The Xhosa who directed the attack stood tall in the long grass, beating his men forward with the flat of his spear. Matthew made allowance for windage and bore down on Kuba, trapping the black torso in his sights and, as he breathed out to steady his aim and his bumping heart, squeezing the trigger slowly. The stock bit his shoulder and the long gun reared, blooming black smoke. At the last moment, a warrior rose up before his target and took the ball through his chest. All save Kuba sank from sight.

As Kuba stood alone on the knoll, a sheen of sweat broke out on his body. Death had come close, but he grinned with malice until his warriors again stood upright. It was no man who showed fear to his enemy.

Kuba watched where the shots from the farm fell. A young warrior tottered and spun to fall in his own length, blood marking the earth in a spatter. Another clutched his ruined neck and went down. The two were in against the farm buildings, firing the thatch and cutting at the shutters and doors with their spears. Kuba grunted with satisfaction. The whites' guns could not bear so close to the house. He had found their blind spots.

Satisfied, Kuba ordered four men to follow him. The white man and the Khoikhoi were on the high ground behind the Xhosa, and they must be stopped before they joined the corngrowers at the farm. That would be bad for Kuba's prestige, and the gun the white man carried must be blessed with a magic eye to shoot so far and so accurately. Kuba wanted the gun very badly.

9

Matthew reloaded and drew back from the rim of the high kopje, realizing he was less than no use to the Hendrickses at this range and Boie's short arrows would carry less than a third of the distance. They had to get closer. Back at the horses he found Boie watching the west.

"Nkosi, see beyond the fields."

Matthew looked over the rows of maize and the clumps of peach trees to where far crimson figures showed through their own dust. They were coming in at an oblique angle, distorted by haze. English soldiers. He had heard they patrolled the boundary of the Fish River but had never seen them before, viewing them now with mixed feelings. Although of English stock himself, he knew these red soldiers were ruled from the Cape Colony and felt nothing for the people of the hinterland. Foreign soldiers in a foreign field, who viewed the settlers in much the same light as they did the blacks. Still, now they might just help to save the day.

"Mount up, Boie," ordered Matthew, holstering his gun and swinging into the saddle. "We ride for the farmhouse."

Boie frowned and grinned; he knew as well as Matthew that they had to use the gully road before the Xhosa cut them off. It would be a bad place to be trapped.

As they worked their way back down the winding kloof, sporadic gunfire racketed in the gullies, compounded by echoes, seeming to come from all sides. They crossed a dry wash and turned up into the narrow dirt road fast, galloping into sudden shadow that momentarily blinded them both.

A streak of metal hummed past Matthew's face and chunked into the earth wall.

Warriors were rushing down the slopes, wailing and screaming to spook the horses and unseat the riders. A Xhosa threw himself bodily at Matthew, spear thrusting for his stomach, raking his shirtfront. Gaika reared back and away as her rein was seized close to the bit, pulling the black off balance. The Xhosa grunted through bared teeth, sweat and ocher paint spraying from his forehead, blue crane feathers bobbing as he again lunged up over the saddle. Gaika came down on stiff forelegs and the keen blade bit at Matthew's lower ribs. Somehow he swayed away from the next stab, drawing his long gun.

Boie was turning the foal in a flailing circle, guiding her by her mane as four Xhosa danced around him fanwise, trying for spearthrusts. They were after the man, eager to make the horse a prize. One of them—Matthew recognized him as the

10

leader—broke away and came in on Gaika's flank, grabbing and holding onto her tail.

Matthew sighted at the closest warrior and fired one-handed.

The heavy ball punched through the oxhide shield, took the Xhosa in the throat, and blew bone and feathers in a cloud. The body fell away as Gaika bunched her muscles and kicked out. Her hooves caught Kuba full in the chest, and he was smashed into the gully wall, his heels thrashing as he still yelled orders.

The Xhosa turned from Boie and concentrated on Matthew. His horse was better and they knew his long gun was empty. Matthew warded them off with the smoothbore, swinging it in savage arcs and tiring too quickly. He threw it from him and drew his pistols.

Boie's first arrow pecked into the wrist of the nearest man, pinning it to his thigh. The Xhosa sank to his knees wailing his death chant, sure that death from the poisoned barb would come soon.

Gaika's plunging prevented Matthew from cocking or firing either pistol, and the horse's screams seemed to come from his own torn stomach.

Kuba, triumph on his face, scooped up the smoothbore and brandished it.

Matthew dug his heels into Gaika's flanks and shouted down into her flattened ears. She surged forward and burst through the Xhosa, scattering them like corn dolls. Boie was ahead, low in the saddle, another arrow nocked and trained back at the Xhosa as they tumbled and broke.

Then the horses were in the open ground before the farmhouse.

The grain store was ablaze. The Xhosa had fired the thatch and set light to a heap of dried maize cobs stacked against the door. The heat had driven them back, and they were grouped on the lower slopes of the high ground, ready to spear anyone breaking from cover. When they caught sight of the two horsemen, they came forward in a rush, braving the heat.

One glance told Matthew that there was no hope for the two men and the horses in the grain store. Dark moths of soot spiraled from the fierce updraft in lazy drifts, and smoke rolled across the front of the farmhouse, obscuring the view from the gunports.

Matthew took Gaika through the flames and up onto the stoep before the running Xhosa could cover enough ground

11

to cut him off. A single spear struck the door just as the bolts were drawn and Matthew rode inside with Boie behind him, his ragged clothes smoldering. A wooden tub splintered under the horses' hooves and a pan bowled away across the stone floor.

The women and the girl were pressed against the far wall, guarded by the boy whose fowling piece only fired light birdshot.

"You are welcome in this house, Matthew Eastman," Marina Hendricks said, as though he had come out of the sun for a ladle of cool water. The grandmother, drooling and rigid with shock, muttered psalms and held the little girl's hand for comfort.

Matthew inclined his head and slid from his horse. He ruffled the boy's hair and then with the horses ushered the women into the big kitchen, asking them to keep the mare and her foal quiet.

When they had pulled the heavy table across the door, he and Boie took up station at the shuttered windows to watch the Xhosa as they capered and drummed on their shields. Young Manie Hendricks stood quietly at Matthew's side, the fowling piece firmly pointed at the barred door.

Matthew prayed that the soldiers would see the smoke before the fire ate through the walls.

4

Captain Cornwell had dressed with care to attend the ball Colonel Spenser was giving in honor of the Governor of the Cape, Sir Benjamin D'Urban. His dress tunic, sewn with a newly awarded campaign ribbon, had arrived a bare hour before he had been due to leave. Pleased, Cornwell had settled a large part of his tailor's account and quite unnerved the poor fellow. As his carriage swept him up to the large colonial mansion, Cornwell was agreeably surprised by the expense and ceremony the Colonel had lavished on the occasion.

The long marbled drive was lined with liveried blacks who supported gilt flambeaux to light the way. The soldiers of the 72nd/75th formed a guard of honor before the main entrance, guidons fluttering from their lances. An orchestra played from an ornamental podium on the manicured lawn, while another played for dancing in the ballroom. An army of flunkies skimmed about with drinks trays and a trio of black girls sprayed scented water to freshen the arid night air.

12

As his man handed the reins to an ostler, Cornwell noticed a footman armed with a silver shovel and matching bucket watching for any equestrian ordure that might mar the whiteness of the drive. Cornwell's invitation card was solicited and passed to the Master of Ceremonies, who announced him the moment his foot touched the threshold.

The interior of the mansion was a blaze of candlelight and crystal, fine manners and finer clothes. Cornwell, luxuriating in the contrast between this grandeur and his recent trials up-country, joined the receiving line to await his turn to be greeted formally by his host. He was reminded of Sergeant Coffee and the fiercely loyal 75th who fought with him in the bush against the Kaffir, but then he saw that Katherine Spenser stood beside her father and all such thoughts left him abruptly.

Katherine Spenser wore black the way no widow would dare for fear of being stoned at the graveside. Her bare shoulders rose from a bodice of frogged lace, and her fine-boned face was framed by copper red hair that fell in thick waves to a froth of bows at the small of her back. Cornwell knew that most of the women there were giddy with envy. It was also clear that she well knew her effect on them and consciously played upon it.

Beside her, crusty Colonel James Macadam Spenser had the look of a great white lion who had taught himself to stand upright for the single express purpose of clawing success from other men. His hair glared whiter than his stock, waistcoat, and hose.

It was common knowledge that the huge old man ran the Cape, whoever might head the British political administration, for without his support they could not flourish. He had survived the Dutch East India Company, and was even more entrenched in the Colony now that the British held sway. Hardly a ship could dock in the harbor or a caravan enter the interior without his, albeit clandestine, seal of approval. He had made men and broken more. His brand of tyranny had lasted for so long that it had attained the cynical sufferance of the business community, a kind of respectability in itself. To the merchants he was a gentleman whose handshake meant more than any written contract.

Cornwell felt his hand being taken as the great white head nodded in recognition. "Deuced good to see you, Captain. We are glad to receive you. I've read dispatches and was pleased to see you were decorated. Your wound does not trouble you, I trust?"

"Thank you, Colonel. Too kind as always, but the wound was no more than a scratch."

"Nonsense, you fellows are too self-effacing. My daughter feels much the same, eh, Katherine?"

"If that means I do *not* believe that bravery is its own reward, yes."

Cornwell could scarcely bring himself to meet her frank violet gaze. Damn it, she had the direct stare of a man. He bowed and kissed the back of her wrist to cover a sudden confusion and found himself asking for the privilege of marking her card for a dance. She laughed until he was forced to look into her face.

"I regret not, Captain," she said in her brisk and slightly mocking way. "To fulfill my commitments I should be at the gavotte until next spring."

Cornwell hid his disappointment. "Your servant, ma'am, and yours, sir."

Colonel Spenser was already greeting his next guest, and with less affability, Cornwell noticed with some pleasure, although Katherine's sting would last with him for some time. He moved away across the entrance hall to where an arched colonnade led to the ballroom. Here and there, he nodded to acquaintances and fellow officers whose company he avoided. To waste time talking army on an occasion like this would be nothing short of criminal, especially as he was due to rejoin his regiment within the week. Sergeant Coffee would, no doubt, be relieved to see him when he rejoined the troop in Colesberg.

He took a glass of wine from a passing tray and found it chilled to perfection. To his extreme surprise, there was ice packed around the bottles set in several large coolers. Where on earth did they get it? he wondered, watching Katherine Spenser's back as she dutifully greeted more fawning members of Cape Colony society.

"Hullo, Cornwell. Back from thrashing the old Kaffir, are we?" A tall and thin-faced Captain of hussars was snickering at him, head back to see more clearly through a monocle. He had spilled wine over his white gloves and his complexion was liverish. His name was Chevening, Cornwell remembered, and he had no time for the man. A man who wagered on the outcome of drinking contests and played billiards on

14

horseback wearing a blindfold was not Cornwell's notion of an ideal companion.

As usual, Chevening had drunk his luncheon and was less than steady on his feet, his manner abrasive and overbearing. A notorious duelist, he had killed four men in England and had been banished to the Cape just one jump ahead of the arresting officers. Only the considerable influence of his family kept him in uniform and out of the penal colony on Robben Island. His few admirers were with him now, young and penniless subalterns who were dependent on his generosity and kept him company in his never-ending pursuit of "sport."

Chevening nudged Cornwell, gesturing off with his slopping glass.

"Only one filly here tonight worth giving a canter. That Spenser gel, what? Give a full month's remittance for a dally with that one, by the Lord Harry. All of us would, eh?"

"Not all of us, Chevening." Cornwell stared around into the ring of overheated faces with distaste as his good humor evaporated.

"Pure as a white miter, aren't we?" Chevening's tone was unpleasant.

"If you'll excuse me?" Cornwell moved aside, only to find that the hussar had draped an arm over his shoulder and blocked his path.

"Your attitude would change, Cornwell, if you knew what I knew, and that's a fact. La Belle Katherine's been a bit of a naughty gel. It's all over the Cape. She's taken up with some damned trader fellow, some foundling who's made a fortune from elephant's teeth and the like. He's got some vineyards west of here. I swear I don't know what she'd see in some fellow with grape skins between his toes, d'you?"

Cornwell was incensed. "Keep your infernal gossip to yourself, damn you. You'll oblige me by allowing me to pass."

"Dashed if it ain't the truth, though," said one of the subalterns.

"And you can hold your tongue, sir," Cornwell snapped. "You'd all be well advised to leave the reputation of decent women alone. Why don't you go off and mistreat a horse or two? That's surely more your mark."

Chevening stood back in mock horror. "Gentlemen, I do believe this officer has insulted me. Have you insulted me, Cornwell?"

Cornwell gave him a frozen smile.

"One cannot insult what is already abominable."

15

The hussar's sallow complexion turned pale. Blotched by freckles, it reminded Cornwell of lichen on an old rock. Chevening's eyes were miraculously drained of alcohol.

The orchestra stopped playing a medley abruptly and, after a pause, struck up the national anthem. The Governor had arrived. Discipline brought all the officers to attention as Sir Benjamin D'Urban passed by with Katherine Spenser on his arm, her father escorting the Governor's lady a bare two steps behind.

When Chevening turned his attention back to Cornwell, he was nowhere to be seen.

5

Color Sergeant Coffee spat on the ground and eased his aching shoulders. The burial detail had brought the canvas sacks from the gutted grain store and laid them in the trench. They would never know which of the burghers was which. Hendricks and his sons were unrecognizable. The flames and mutilation had reduced them to charred jigsaw puzzles.

The 75th always got the dirty jobs, it seemed. At least the women were safe and were resting, along with the young Englishman and his Khoikhoi servant, in the shade of the only remaining outbuilding. One of the women, the old one, dribbled and stared with empty eyes at nothing, smiling simply. Coffee shrugged; at least she was alive.

He had four wounded Scots who wouldn't see the sunrise; eleven Hottentots with spear wounds. At least their stoic silence steadied his Highlanders. There was precious little morphine for the pain of his boys. The Hottentots had not been issued any medicine at all; they had instead made up a paste of spit and leaves and cobwebs to coat their wounds with, sitting quietly in rows, quietly rocking in their ragged breechclouts. To them, death was an old friend who must inevitably take them by the hand.

Captain Cornwell was fortunate to have missed this patrol, thought Coffee. There had been no glory to it, no sense of achievement when fighting in this desolate country; only weariness and frustration with no chance of a straight confrontation in a square with flanking cavalry in the classical European manner.

Coffee would have to get one of the women to say some words before he had the grave filled and covered with stones; best coming from kin since the priest who ran the mission had gone off into the veldt to visit his parishioners before the attack. Coffee's scouts had found his body the previous morning, staked out with the ants running where his eyes should have been. To Coffee, a heathen was a heathen, however many Bible stories he might learn by heart and gobble back parrot-fashion. Just like the rice Christians he had seen in India. Untouchables with full bellies and psalms on their lips.

God, for a mouthful of decent whisky.

Straight off the stinking military transports and a forced march into a full field action against the Kaffir for a land that was too stony to plow, fighting in rain that broke your back and washed the powder from the pan; heat and humidity that took your breath and vitality away. At least there had been women in India. Small and olive with eyes dark enough for a man to lose himself in. And established stills when the rum ran out. Coffee spat and found no saliva.

As he walked, he checked the sentries on the high ground. There the Hottentots were formed up in a defensive line behind a wall of grain sacks abutting the supply wagon. Although they marched worse than any straw-foot he had beaten into precision, nevertheless they fought with a fierce grace Coffee could only admire.

He tugged his jacket smooth and, with his pace stick square under his arm, turned the shaded corner of the outbuilding. The wilting Highlander picket straightened at the sight of the Color Sergeant's shadow.

"All right, lad," said Coffee, halting. "Anybody can die at attention. Just you keep your eyes where them Xhosa is lying. You've seen what they can do to a tender young hide."

"Aye, Sergeant."

"Step off a way then, lad. I want a word with the ladies."

"Heat's a bastard, ain't it, Sarge?"

"That it may be, but it ain't for you to comment, right?"

The boy dared to lick the sweat from his grin as he moved out of earshot to stare off into the brilliant hills.

Coffee found Mrs. Hendricks and touched a finger to his pith helmet. She held herself and her grief well, he thought, a self-sufficient woman of about thirty and still handsome in a sun-bleached and wholesome way.

"Ma'am, begging your pardon. We're ready for you ladies. There's the Lord's words to be spoken and better coming from one of you, them being your own departed and all."

The woman inclined her head.

"Thank you, Sergeant. If you'll give us a little more time.

17

My mother..." She motioned toward the old woman propped up against a mud wall, still holding onto the little girl's hand.

"I'll call the Englishman, ma'am. He'll want to be there at the graveside with you. You just come along when your other ladies are ready."

Coffee saluted and backed away from the forlorn group and found Matthew Eastman near what had been the east wall of the main house. His shirt was unbuttoned to the waist and he had bound linen around his slashed ribs. He had refused a measure of morphine, even though his lean young face was lined with fatigue and pain.

Coffee said, "Mr. Eastman, letting an orderly dress that wound proper wouldn't come amiss now, would it?"

Matthew's look was distant.

"Save your medicines for your men, Sergeant. It's a clean cut and I'll live. That's if we leave here now."

Cocky young snappers these farm lads, Coffee thought sourly. Nothing like Warwickshire lads of his age in the old country. This one couldn't be more than eighteen or nineteen and nothing to his name but his shirt and his boots, yet he talks back like a London blade with an income of a thousand a year. Not that the likes of them had the tallow and wick to stand on a burning stoep and cover his patrol's run for the farm. That took more than guineas and a crest.

"These ladies was lucky, you and your Khoikhoi happening by like that," said Coffee.

There might have been a smile on Matthew's face under the soot and sweat and the long, matted hair when he said, "Luck?"

"Can't do nothing without it, lad."

"Luck is something you make. When d'you plan to move out?" Matthew buttoned his bloody shirt as he stood to watch the sky for weather, his movements spare and controlled.

"The burial party's about to muster. Then there's the question of the sore wounded."

"Sore dead if you stay here," Matthew cut in. "And you with them. Throw away anything you don't need, empty the supply wagon and use it for your wounded. And pick a short prayer for the graveside."

"That's your advice is it, sir?" Coffee asked with heavy sarcasm. He eased his pith helmet back and frowned at the small Khoikhoi, who grinned back without understanding half of what the Sergeant said in his strange accent.

"If you want it. How are your mounts?"

18

"Enough for the troopers…."

"If you put the women and the Hendricks boy in the wagon with your wounded, you'll only have to get horses for the Hottentots. Those Totties aren't what you'd call good-conditioned."

"Nothing," snapped Coffee, banging dust from a sleeve, "is good-conditioned in this bloody territory. I'm letting the Hendrickses' livestock loose. Damned if I'll jeopardize my command for a few bulls riddled with rinderpest. We ain't drovers, Eastman."

Matthew's big frame momentarily blocked Coffee's view of the fourteen black bodies sprawled around the farmhouse as he swung to point across the veldt.

"There's a Commando group just north of here, joined up with a laager of about eighty wagons. We were heading there when this happened. The wagoners are mostly traders, but their company is better than nothing. You're only thirty and there're fifteen thousand hostile kaffirs in this area. You can rest your men at the laager, and leave the women there when you go on."

"North, eh?" Coffee scratched his reddened chin with a calloused finger. Another week of patrolling and he would be heading north anyway. Captain Cornwell would be rejoining his men at Colesberg, the frontier town just south of the Orange River. Within the next five weeks, all twelve patrol groups would reassemble in the dusty town. The Captain would no doubt be carrying fresh orders from the Cape.

Coffee nodded. "Seems there's no choice." He stamped both feet and sent up a swirl of red dust. "Let's bury these Dutchmen."

The old woman with empty eyes had started to scream.

6

Kuba watched the young warrior dying of the Khoikhoi poison.

Although the man had cut Boie's arrow from his arm himself, it had done no good. His chanting stopped when his tongue filled his mouth and yellow scum formed on his lips. He was a roundhead, a young warrior with no experience, his first and last time at war. True, he had been bold in the fight, had braved the shooting and speared his white through the soft parts between the legs to make death come slowly with pain. But now his own muscles jumped in spasm and his eyes saw only fear. He did not deserve a death thrust and Kuba would have left him to die alone, but the horse kick troubled him; one of his ribs was broken.

Kuba rested and considered what to do next. The red soldiers and their blacks had come too quickly and fought too well. His party was either scattered or dead, and Kuba had only five veterans left, and they were watching the trail against surprise.

Kuba admired the long gun he had taken from the white horseman, its solid feel and the patterns on the stock. An armadillo man on a horse was killing a snake with legs that had fire in its mouth. Kuba had never seen a white man like the one on the metal picture, and he thought he must be a god whose magic helped the lead balls kill enemies.

The roundhead gave one last great shudder and stiffened in death.

Kuba looked at him as if he were already part of the earth. The young men did not last long; they broke like green vines. Kuba worked his shoulder as he stood up and found that the pain in his chest was not too bad. He also knew that he could not run as fast as the other veterans when the time came to move on. They would show their teeth and taunt him for his ragged breathing, jealous of the fine gun he carried; saying that only a calf-boy with sun sickness would discard a good shield for a gun that would not shoot. They might even try to kill him if he lost his strength and speed.

Kuba would not let that happen. He would slip away when the sun had gone below the edge of the world and would make his own raid.

There were too many whites and red soldiers to the north where the river called the Fish ran, even a circle of wagons from one of the white kraals on the edge of the salt waters. Kuba would go to the south and steal cattle for himself alone. He knew his cunning was big enough, and maybe he could kill a white man for the lead balls and the burning powder that would make the musket shoot.

When darkness fell, Kuba set off toward the Eastman farm.

7

Matthew Eastman had searched the ash of the burned grain store and had found the Hendrickses' guns. They were still warm to the touch and much of their wooden parts had been burned away. He cleaned and stripped the mechanism of the best piece and fitted a spare stock from the tackle room. When he had primed and loaded the gun, he test-fired it at a circling vulture, ripping the bird out of the sky. The entire burial party swiveled in his direction, the psalms dying on their lips as he reloaded, ignoring them. Coffee hurried down to him.

"Kaffir, lad?"

"No." Matthew sighted off at a second vulture that was climbing a thermal, tracking it then lowering the musket without firing. "I'll pay the widow Hendricks what this gun's worth. Coin'll be more use now her man's gone."

Coffee stared at him. Up to that moment he had seen nothing but piety from these colonials, especially the Dutch, but there was a coldness about this young Englishman he had only experienced with Hessian mercenaries.

"You ought to have some respect, lad."

"To the living first."

Matthew mounted and, the gun across his lap, sat looking down at Coffee and waiting for Boie to ride in beside him. The Khoikhoi was watching the hills with the edges of his eyes, searching for movement.

"Those women need to say their last prayers, Eastman," said Coffee.

Matthew's face was grim. "When there's time, I'll say my words. Right now there's not much daylight left, and I don't plan moving at dusk when those Xhosa can pick us off in the poor light. If you don't get your people on the trail in the next few minutes, you'll all die wondering how it all came about. And that's gospel enough for any man."

"That's a brisk way of getting it said," Coffee offered without heat.

"No time for anything else." Matthew gestured off toward Coffee's native contingent. "You'll lose your Totties too, if you don't get some victuals inside them. I know their dialect and it's what they're saying. They're not much for fighting when their spines are showing through their bellies. Give them meat if you can, mealies if you can't, but do it fast. They'll eat on the run."

Coffee took hold of Gaika's rein as Matthew began backing around him. "Eastman," he said, "I'd take it as a favor if you and your black was to travel with us. There's strength in numbers and it seems you know the country. Mark the trail for us."

Matthew lifted his hat to run fingers through his hair, letting a long breath out through his nose. He seemed to be damning the whole world with his mouth closed. Coffee watched him watching all around, weighing and calculating.

"Think of the women, lad. What those heathens would do to them."

Matthew laughed then and his face was transformed. He looked no more than his nineteen years, smoke-gray eyes filled with sudden light, white even teeth biting as he grinned. He spoke to the Khoikhoi in rapid patois and then Boie was laughing too, bobbing in his saddle.

Coffee waited. There was nothing else to do.

"Ach, man," Matthew finally said. "You know nothing. The Xhosa respect women; it's you and me they want to butcher. And that flagbearer with his fine feathers. His red coat would make a fine trophy for the King's kraal. Big *mouti.*"

Coffee nodded in silence, holding his temper, conscious of the sweat running out of his mustache.

"All right," Matthew said. "We'll stay with you. Best tell your stragglers to keep up. You were tracked by a big party, and they'll be trying to get ahead of us. Just pray the merchants' laager hasn't moved on, *and* that the Commando is still on this side of the river. The Xhosa don't like the taste of their lead."

"I thank you, lad," Coffee said, as if saying his thanks hurt his mouth. He dropped Gaika's rein.

Matthew's eyes became veiled and remote, all humor gone.

"Five minutes" was all he said.

8

Katherine Spenser danced well enough to consider her private affairs without the added imposition of keeping time while the Governor guided her around the floor. A permanent smile was the only response his rhetorical conversation required. The glittering room spun past, all the faces and furnishings a rich blur with no focus and no meaning.

Last evening's storm had not cleared the air. The atmosphere, sweetly scented with jasmine, weighed oppressively. A heavy sheen of perspiration glazed the Governor's forehead, and Katherine thought that any moment a droplet would form at the end of his nose and drop onto the front of her dress. The notion of his stuttering embarrassment made her laugh suddenly. The sound was rich and full and carried across the ballroom to Captain Cornwell. He caught her eye, and she saw the start of a slow and elegant bow before he was obscured by the whirling pillars.

It could be that he was different from the usual crowd of young officers. God knows there was little enough to distinguish between the hordes of socially polished and deadly dull subalterns who infested the withdrawing rooms of the Cape. Their commissions were bought and paid for, their experience of life governed by the strictures of public schools, the formal manners of the parlor, and the baser pleasures found in the gaming halls. Katherine instinctively knew Cornwell was worthy of more consideration than most of the young woodcocks she continually stumbled over, and thought she might keep him in mind as a suitable escort, should any future occasion demand one.

The waltz ended and Sir Benjamin D'Urban leaned forward from the waist. "Most enjoyable, Miss Spenser. But I see I have kept you from the young men too long." He was looking past her at an approaching hussar.

"Your Excellency, Miss Spenser." Captain Chevening waved a crumpled card. "My dance, I believe, Miss Spenser."

At a glance Katherine took in the wine-stained gloves and also noted the sourness of Chevening's breath. This particular honorable and drunken son of a peer of the realm would be better off sleeping under the nearest tree until his legs were strong enough to carry him back to the barracks.

"I'm sure the Captain will forgive me," she said. "I am fatigued and wish to sit this one out."

Chevening blinked. Kennaway, McClure, and all the other subalterns were watching him, and he had a dozen guineas riding on her acceptance. What did the gel think she was playing at? She was cutting him in the middle of the dance floor as if he were some minion. A touch of the spur was called for. He took her arm.

"Come," he said. "I've waited like a gentleman."

"And that is where the similarity ends. Good night, Captain."

Chevening's hand tightened around her arm. By God, she was going to do it, humiliate him in front of everyone. "Not good enough for you, madam?" He leaned in to speak in a loud, carrying whisper. "Not like that trader fellow, eh?"

The sound of the blow clapped around the room, a flat, dead slap that brought silence like a shroud. Stunned faces

23

claimed the horizon as Katherine blindly gathered her skirts and left the ballroom, her awareness returning as the night air touched her face and whistled in her nostrils.

"Too much to drink, unforgivable in the circumstances ...severe discipline... should be recalled..." A gentle voice, troubled, sympathetic.

Katherine knew that Hugh Cornwell stood behind her, shielding her distress from the curious eyes of those gathered at the long french windows, gossiping behind their fans.

From the balcony where Katherine and Cornwell stood, the night glowed with light and dancing insects, moths and fireflies. The calls of nightjars sounded. Behind them, a low hum of conversation had started and the musicians had struck up with a lively waltz.

"You're trembling, Miss Spenser. I'll send for a wrap...."

Katherine spun on Cornwell, her color high, fury burning her cheeks. "I am not cold, Captain. Please consider your duty done if you wish to rejoin your noble friends."

"Duty, Miss Spenser?" He raised an eyebrow and lowered one lid. "I, like you, seem to have few friends here."

Katherine faltered, seeing her error of assumption. "Nevertheless...I thank you. But I'll not explain what happened in there. You'll gain no gossip from me."

"I can guess all I need to, and Chevening will long have cause to remember this night. Gossip is for those who gossip. I save all my spice to tell my horse; he at least is discreet."

Katherine ignored the attempt to lighten her mood. She had no interest in Chevening's fate. Cord Laidler was out beyond the fireflies, waiting for her with his hard belly and hands that brought her brilliantly alive....Cord would be amused by tonight if word got to him. Katherine was not ready for that to happen. Somebody knew and had made their liaison public.

The word must have been passed anonymously through private channels, for to make such an allegation in public would most surely have brought the full weight of her father's enmity to bear on the informant. Even to Katherine, the situation was as distasteful as a piece of bad Italian opera, with more sour humor than quality of wit. But to break with Cord Laidler now was beyond her strength, even though the association was bound to cost her her elevated position in Cape society. The only question left was whether it mattered to her or not.

*　*　*

She had been out from England barely a year when she had first seen Cord Laidler. Cape Town was still a strange and exotic place, a mixed bag of people, differing nationalities, languages, colors, and religions. Malay vendors hawked their wares, stridently demanding the custom of passing matelots, parasoled matrons, tightly suited Huguenots; small and quicksilver Hottentots offered to sell what they had stolen hours before, their crude barrows heaped with watermelon and pomegranate, peaches and mealies; diminutive Bantu women sold posies of rock daisies, sorrel, and Cape forget-me-not.

The smells and life of it all went to her head.

The fun of the morning stroll with her father had been broken by a train of sixteen wagons that rumbled into the main thoroughfare, causing heads to turn and stare. Cord had been driving the lead wagon and the sight of him had been as physical as a blow.

"Good day, Colonel Spenser." He swept off his hat and bowed from the driving box. He spoke loudly, Katherine noticed, sweat dripping from his matted hair, his grin wide and challenging. He addressed her father, but his eyes were full on Katherine.

"Cord Laidler. And we thought you were dead."

"I am sorry to disappoint you, Colonel. I am, as you see, not dead, although a good many tuskers are." His coiled bullwhip took in the prime ivory under the lashed hides.

Katherine laughed aloud at the sudden color in her father's face and at the set of his mustache as a dark vein throbbed in his temple. The antipathy between the two men could almost be tasted. At last, she remembered thinking, a man with enough grit to outface her father, the first she had seen dare. A man who would ask before taking and take anyway, whatever the answer. Cord's eyes found hers and held them until she flushed.

"I'm hardly dressed for formal introductions, Colonel, so I'll forgo the pleasure of knowing your daughter at present. There'll be another time." Laidler's whip had cut forward with a curl and a snap, and the wagons rolled away.

"There must be an emperor's ransom in those carts. Who is that man?"

"Hardly a gentleman, Katherine. I have had dealings with him in the past, and frankly, I regret it."

"Does that mean he bested you?"

Colonel Spenser rapped the ground with his cane. "You

will not be meeting that man again, socially or otherwise. Put him from your mind. He will never present his card at our door."

After that, it had taken Katherine surprisingly little time to find out all there was to know about Philip McCord Laidler.

He had been fostered out by his parents into the care of old Mrs. Bezuidenhout, whose small vineyard of twenty acres was in the richest winegrowing area of the Cape. She had known nothing of distilling, content to sell her crop by weight and to live modestly on the small income, warming her arthritis in the sun. Cord had stayed with her until he was fourteen, running off to live in the squalor and privation of the dockland area. There he learned to lead the free-spending foreign sailors to the best whorehouses, how to cut purses, to use the knife and the belaying pin, and how to guide the safest route to the interior for those deserting the hard shipboard discipline. He learned to separate gold dust from the sawdust beneath the gambling tables, whom to sell it to for the best price, how to siphon wine from a barrel without breaking the seal, to steal food, and to hide his money. When he had saved enough, he bought himself a pistol and wore it in his belt, a London-made dueling piece that fired true and symbolized his determination to rip a fortune from the raw colony of the Cape.

When Mrs. Bezuidenhout died, he inherited the house and the vineyard. He set himself to learn all there was to know about the wine and spirit trade, all the while taking commission from the prostitutes and English silver from the matelots with a taste for his overpriced *brandewyn*. To fugitives he sold wagons that had the knack of falling apart on the outskirts of town.

Little by little, and secretly, he bought up land around the Bezuidenhout holding from the vintners who left to travel north into the interior to avoid the stringent monopolies imposed by the corrupt officials in Colonel Spenser's pocket.

Then, using judicious bribery, he bought a minimum wine export franchise from the Cape authorities. He had long known that self-confidence and assurance would convince lesser men to give him what he wanted. At this point he found himself dealing directly with the one man he could never hope to bluff, Colonel Spenser. But, as luck would have it, by bending the rules, seemingly to suit himself, the Colonel had unwittingly allowed Cord an almost total monopoly for the export of wine from the Cape.

26

Philosophically, Colonel Spenser had accepted a percentage of the profits as they grew year by year, until his promotion to the Civil Service had placed him outside the sphere of influence governing Cord's vineyards. By then, Cord Laidler no longer needed him.

The ivory, sold in England and Holland, had made him wealthy.

Katherine had chosen a Friday to visit him, the one day he stayed at his homestead to pay his Khoikhoi field-workers. He was dropping the last coin into the last calloused palm when she arrived, a slender vignette against the glare, sitting a horse few men could have handled, a big roan with a knowing eye.

"Miss Spenser, an honor."

She showed none of the near panic she felt as he walked across to help her from the saddle, his grin wide and getting wider.

"May I ask what brings you so far down the mountain?"

If he had expected a lame and improbable answer, he was disappointed.

"Since it is all too obvious that you shun our way of life, Mr. Laidler," she replied levelly, "I thought it just as well to see what it was that so fascinated you about your own."

Fire and ice, he thought, no answer ready. He turned her horse and tied it in the shade of the cottage stoep, taking trouble with the knot. Katherine smiled at the sweat line on the spine of his shirt. That makes us even, she told herself silently, seeing how good he looked clean-shaven, his face square and strong under the bleached mane of hair. There was no one like him in the society that surrounded her, those pale and mannered men who stammered at her.

"I have little to offer a lady," Cord said, opening the door of the cottage, standing aside for her to pass inside, "except shade and cool water."

She strode into the dark interior with its low ceiling and heavy horsehair furniture. Crudely inked maps covered a rustic table, all of them crawling notations in Cord's cramped hand. She glanced at them.

"Layouts of your holdings, Mr. Laidler?"

"How do you..."

"You forget, my father is a military man. I can at least tell east from west and north from south. You seem to own a good deal of land around here."

Cord took her riding crop and hat and she shook her hair

down around her shoulders with unconscious grace. He wanted to touch her and she seemed to know.

"I would say some twelve thousand acres," she added.

"Do you always guess with such accuracy?"

She laughed to see him frowning at her. "You are naïve, Mr. Laidler. There is but one topic of conversation at most dinner parties. And that topic is you. They are afraid that you will eventually hold a monopoly...."

"Afraid? I already do. And there's nothing any of those weak-bellied parsons' sons can do about it."

"Good," Katherine said lightly.

Cord felt blood darken his face. "You approve?"

"Why not? It is your right as much as any man's."

"Those are not exactly your father's sentiments. You can tell him from me..."

"Mr. Laidler," Katherine snapped, "I am his daughter. Not his spokeswoman. You had best remember that." She was aware that he believed she had come to twist his tail for her own perverse amusement, using the visit as raw material for anecdotes with which she could amuse her drawing-room intimates. Through his eyes she could see herself as the superior bitch he considered her; his jaw clamped closed and tensed in the event that she was about to laugh at him.

"Sit down," he said. "I'll have the boys draw some water."

"I'll stand if you please. Is that brandy? I'll take a glass." She gestured toward an earthenware jar on a table beside the single window.

Cord poured two generous measures of the peach brew. Later, she discovered, he made it for his field-workers and it was rough, without vintage. He watched her gulp at hers and gag when it bit at the back of her throat. The raw fumes rose into her nose and watered her eyes. She drained the mugful and stared solemnly at his mouth.

"You may kiss me," she said.

Cord dared not laugh, dared not take too deep a breath. She was absurd; her simple directness was outside his experience. Even the most hardened whores tended to simper and play coy. The hint of a smile would wound her pride and she would be gone.

Cord took her by the shoulders and pulled her toward him, driving her lips apart with his own. She did not pull away as he had expected, but flowed in against him, tongue questing, hips moving against his thighs. Her back muscles jumped under his hands as they ran down to cup her buttocks.

28

He wanted to draw back her head to look into her eyes. Her teeth raked his lips as she broke away to draw breath. He lifted her chin and saw she had ridden fifteen miles for this, and whatever her motive, she knew precisely what she was doing. His fingers stumbled over the hooks and buttons of her riding skirt, wondering what the old bastard her father would say if he knew Cord Laidler had his hands on his only daughter. Her hands found him and he stiffened under her kneading. Nothing else mattered then, there were no more questions and to hell with Spenser. He lifted her onto the couch and found he was the first to enter her.

The fact registered itself, calmly divorced from the confusion of small sounds and movements she made under him, the crisp explosions of breath against his face as she bucked and lunged, the wild spasms as she rode up to her first climax. A small and faraway cry tore from her as she swept over the crest and was left sated and limp and dewed by exertion.

Propped above her and still rampant, Cord waited. He meant to take her on a second and longer journey, this time to a joint ecstasy. His teeth were bared in a savage grin of self-congratulation and some astonishment, hardly able to comprehend his luck.

They were together whenever she could get away, and when they loved, it was all-consuming: it drained them so completely of affection that they would part almost like strangers. Sometimes she would come to him in his waterfront warehouse where they rolled on dusty sacking surrounded by soured barrels, and she would go home rumpled and reeking of wine.

They were lucky; they had kept their secret for almost eighteen months, until tonight.

Katherine was on the terrace outside the ballroom, and nobody in the mansion seemed to be watching her. They most certainly would have been if anybody had overheard Chevening and whispered the same into her father's ear.

Beside her, Hugh Cornwell was briefly illuminated as he drew on a small cheroot. His silence was easy, his presence reassuring. Katherine had to get away and find Cord. The question she shyly put to Cornwell brought a quizzical smile to his lips, and for a stunned moment, she thought she had misjudged him. Then he shut one eye in the exaggerated wink of a conspirator.

Fifteen minutes later, Cornwell's carriage drew them

away from the graceful gables and porticoes of the Colonel's mansion.

9

The light was turning pink before dying. Long shadows reached out across the tawny murram to confuse the eye in the tangles of thorn and sansevieria along the ridge above the wide and shallow valley.

Below, a brown dust haze hung over the laager of wagons, and the whistles and bawling of herders and stock came up to Matthew and Boie on the wind that swept across the Zuurveld from the northern ranges. The valley walls rose in harsh splendor, eroded and timeless, highlighting the impermanence of the double ring of wagons on the valley floor.

Matthew sagged with pain and fatigue. His keen eye found the Cuthberts' wagon in the inner ring, brighter than those of the other itinerant peddlers who traveled in train from place to place, selling or bartering thread and needles, muskets and hides, wooden churns and copper pans. Down there, Matthew knew, Dutchman bargained with Scot, Huguenot with Catholic, all of them trading beads or home-brewed brandy with the Xhosa or Hottentots for their thin animals.

Usually he enjoyed the carnival atmosphere, but he felt no lightness now, not even at the thought of seeing Elise Cuthbert.

Matthew fired into the air and the flat bark rattled in the crags like summer thunder. Behind him, Sergeant Coffee's column breasted the rim of the valley to straggle down the inverse slope to the river.

Through the milling cattle came a group of mounted Boer Commando, riding hard to where Matthew waited. Boie, looking to the rear, could make out the nearest band of hostile Xhosa squatting under their shields on the darkening flatland. They would surround the valley in the coming darkness and keep the laager awake with their calls and threats.

Coffee had set himself ramrod straight in the saddle as an example to his men, dressing the Highlanders' line so that they rode into the laager with some semblance of Aldershot pomp with a bandsman playing a regimental tune on his fife despite cracked lips. The Hottentot contingent broke into a trot and then a run, a drink from the river more meaningful than British military pride.

The Commando brought up sharp all around Matthew and

Boie, their homespun and battered felt hats drab against the passing red tunics.

The leader of the Commando, a big old man with silver hair and a full red beard, clasped Matthew's hand, pumping his arm with vigor, the fringes of his buckskin jacket jumping. He was Abraham de Villiers, a third-generation Dutch farmer, known and respected throughout the Zuurveld.

"Menheer de Villiers," greeted Matthew. "It is good to see you."

"And you, Matthew. Your father and brother are well?"

"They are well."

"Good, good. But I see you bring us *rooinek* soldiers. Tell us, do they come to fight or to *talk* as they usually do?"

Matthew shrugged away the barb. Although good-humored, it struck home too well for comfort.

"You must ask them."

Abraham de Villiers laughed his big laugh. "I will, boy. I will."

His son Dirk, who was small and dark and quick, laughed differently, leaning on his pommel. His beard and hair curled close to his head and the chest hair inside his shirt was a black pelt. He nudged his horse in against Gaika, his narrow blue eyes locked on Matthew's face. He tapped Matthew's chest with his bullwhip.

"But *I* ask you, Eastman. Those are your people, the British. Or do you deny the land of your father?"

Matthew's face was taut and pale when he looked past Dirk to old Abraham.

"Your son has no manners, menheer. He was that way at school when he couldn't make out the words in his primer."

Dirk spat close to Gaika's forehooves.

"Words and books. For girls and thieving Government clerks. It's the men of books who bring us Cape law, paid for with British silver; who tax us for the pleasure of starving on our own land. Land we can't work because they made us give up our slaves. What do such cockroaches know of a farmer's life? Nothing!"

"It's the same for all of us." Matthew was impassive.

"The same, Eastman?" Dirk slapped his thigh with the bullwhip. "*I* ride with the Commando while you sit at home, hiding under your father's beard. The same for you? I don't think so."

Abraham's voice cracked hard. "Enough, Dirk. You shame your own father with your wild talk. Apologize."

31

"To this?" Dirk grin-sneered across his horse's neck. "To this *dassie?*" He wheeled his black and spurred away into the gathering night.

Barely in control of his own anger, Abraham's face grew seamed as he watched Matthew's fury mottle his neck and jaws, the big knuckles white on the rein.

"I ask your forgiveness, Matthew. Accept my word, you may name the punishment for his rudeness."

Matthew shook his head from side to side, his eyes hooded. "No, it will happen again and again until there is blood between us."

"Yes," Abraham agreed. "It has been that way since you were children. Will you say why?"

"No." Matthew did not know himself, did not care. The issue must be shrugged away. "This is more important. The Hendricks men are all dead save for young Manie. The soldiers have him and the women safe, but all their supplies were burned with the men and all the buildings are gone. They will need your help."

"May God strike the Xhosa," said one of the men who had lost his farm and family three days before.

"Hendricks trusted too much in the priest from the London Missionary Society," said Abraham. "I told him, we all did."

"The priest died too." Matthew cupped his forehead. "And slower. He'll cause no more mischief. Ach, these outsiders."

"You talk like one of us, boy. Your father would think otherwise, I've no doubt."

Matthew showed no expression.

"Probably, menheer, as in most other things;" adding after a pause, "I'll be at the Cuthberts' wagon if you want me."

"I'll ride with you," Abraham offered, careful to demonstrate there was no rift between the two families.

The other riders peeled away to patrol the perimeter of the valley. The smell of wood fires and broiling meat grew stronger as they rode slowly toward the laager where the storm clouds churned dark against the darker jet of the far hills.

Abraham's sigh broke the silence between them and when he spoke, it was as if he talked to himself. "I am tired, you know that? We, our people, have fought the Xhosa for fifty years. Every year they return, stronger and in greater numbers, whilst we ..." He sighed again. "We grow fewer and rebuild our farms with less and less. I'm glad the soldiers are here, *if* they fight Hintza and don't placate him with our cattle and British silver. We've lost too much for too long. Dirk is right about one thing, things *must* change."

Matthew agreed. His family too had suffered.

"Our slaves were taken from us by legislation made up by men who have never seen a black man, and these same civil servants paid us a pittance in compensation. But is that all? No, the compensation can only be paid in London. I for one still wait to see this money. Maybe my sons will build my headstone with it, if they aren't too old themselves."

They passed through the outer ring of wagons where the talk was low and the children sat without playing. There seemed to be no laughter left in the world, for many of these families had had their farms razed to the ground in the recent raids.

Abraham studied the sky and tested the wind with a raised wet finger.

"It will storm again, maybe hail," he said with certainty. "At least that will keep the kaffirs under their shields until it passes. Some of us will be able to sleep tonight."

Matthew said, "Coffee, the British Sergeant, told me that this campaign against Hintza is the biggest yet. They will capture or kill him, break his power, and burn his kraal. The way Coffee put it was, 'We shall sow salt in his fields.' We both have enough Bible for that quotation, menheer."

Abraham cleared his throat. "And," he said harshly, "there will be peace until next spring. Then the British soldiers will have gone and another Xhosa will make himself king. Nothing will change for us, Matthew. The British care nothing for the interior, so long as the Cape is safe and their sea route to India is open. They fear the French for their sea power, the Russians for their armies. Us? Us they despise. So long as they have their gold and spice trade, they will keep their command of the seas. We, the true people of this land, fit nowhere in their scheme of things."

Matthew was touched by something outside himself, something he barely understood, feeling more than he could explain in words; a threat to all the things he hated and yet held dear. His family, the farm, all of it. "What will you do, menheer?"

De Villiers's face was lost in the shadows of his hat and his voice could have come from anywhere. "We will trek," he said simply.

"Away from the Cape, from the Zuurveld?" Matthew's
33

mouth was dry and his side hurt. He brought Gaika to a standstill, distant firelight flickering in his eyes.

"Yes, my boy. Think on it, Matthew. You are a second son, and I say this for your ears only. You won't inherit your father's estate unless, and God forbid, your brother Edward should be taken before his time. And Matthew, he is a young bull, not so much older than you, and with many decades left to him. He also has a wife with hips for childbearing, so he will be blessed with many sons. Think about these things, Matthew, when the time comes for us to trek. What holds you here, eh? Unless I am mistaken, the veldt is in your blood."

Matthew nodded. It had always been so, from his earliest memory. Edward cared for the farm as if it were his own. No man had ever sired two such different sons as Edward and himself; Edward was the true son of John Eastman, made from the same stamp. Tall and stooped and slow to smile, he even walked like Pa. At the age of only twenty-three, four years older than Matthew, he thought only of crops and rain, rinderpest and lambing. He was already a man settled in the land and saw no horizons beyond the farm's boundary. He was *set*, thought Matthew.

Old Abraham tipped his hat and wheeled his horse around. No more talk was necessary. He could see the restlessness in the Eastman boy's shoulders, the tension in his jaws, in the big hands so sure on his mare's rein. His people would need men like Matthew Eastman when they trekked north; a man who could keep his own counsel and was sure in a fight.

"I wish you *gooie nag*, Matthew." A chill of wonder touched Abraham's spine as he headed out into the darkness to join the patrolling Commando. What he had seen for the briefest moment in Matthew's face was more than an ordinary man's dream.

10

Elise looked at herself in the mirror, a tiny furrow of concentration between her luminous blue eyes as she smiled and pouted and bared her teeth, frowning at her command of expression critically. It was important to use one's face prettily.

The mirror was real glass in an oblong wooden frame. True, it was cracked across one corner and the silvering had flaked along the break, but it was nonetheless a real glass mirror. The other girls on the train had to make do with highly polished pan backs or make out their reflections in still water.

In the cramped living quarters of the wagon, Elise Cuthbert built on the promises she had made herself through her short life. One day she would have an oval silver mirror, one with a long handle decorated with bows and cupids. Matthew would buy her a Geneva watch and a chatelaine pin engraved with sprays of flowers and a vermicelli border. Then yards of Cluny lace and real French curl plumes, a silk-patterned parasol and a hat made of best-quality picot chip braid.

Elise bit her lips to make them redder and teased the yellow curls over her ears. Matthew was late. She expelled her breath in a light hiss of irritation. If he didn't come soon...But no, she would have to forgive him prettily but not too quickly. There was time to change him. There were a great many things she would have to teach Matthew Eastman when they were married.

11

Matthew paused outside the firelight to watch Harry Cuthbert as he worked over the bullet molds. The last few months had not been kind to Elise's father. He was heavier in the body and more of his freckled scalp showed through the thinning grizzled hair. His face had thickened and coarsened and his eyes were almost lost in the craze of concentration lines. His big veined hands had lost none of their sureness as he sprinkled steel splinters into the molds, pouring hot metal carefully so that the shrapnel would be encased inside perfect lead balls. They must fire true and fragment on impact with the target and not before. Fired close, they would open up a rib cage like a rotten barrel.

Martha, his wife, was at the rear of the wagon where she used the side of a hammer to tack the lid onto a barrel of nails. About her on the yellowing grass were crates and boxes of trade goods in various stages of repacking. Although her angular body was still firm, her cheeks were gaunt, the hollows around her eyes deeper, and gray streaked her carefully combed hair. She looked to have slept badly and jerked every time a Xhosa called from the darkening bush.

Matthew stepped forward and Martha turned to see the

dried blood on his torn shirtfront. The hammer fell from her hand. "Harry, Matthew's hurt."

Harry was peering through the pungent fumes of the setting lead, then he was up and sitting Matthew on a backless stool as Martha brought a tallow lamp to see more clearly.

"It's nothing. Boie patched it up."

"Ach," Martha scolded. "Who knows where that brown scarecrow has had his hands. This country will be the death of us all." Her smile was brittle and belied the hostility in her eyes. "Harry, where's the balsam?"

"Where's Elise?" Matthew asked.

"She's somewhere around." Martha sounded vague. "I don't want her to see this. Hold still, boy." She teased the pad of dirty linen away from the jagged cut and poured brandy over it. Matthew hissed as the world made a single slow revolution.

"You'll live." Harry handed him a plate of food. "What happened?"

Matthew told them about the morning attack between mouthfuls of boiled mutton and corn bread.

"I must meet this Sergeant Coffee," said Harry. "You say he travels north to Colesberg? That's a journey I envy no man, soldier or not."

Abraham de Villiers's implacable words, *"We will trek,"* came back to Matthew. Where would the Boers trek but north, north across the mighty Orange River and beyond?

The Kommissie Trek had already sent out their scouts, men who had returned with stories beyond common belief. Unlike mariners of old, they did not fill the void of the unknown Central Plateau with dragons and mythical beasts; they went to see for themselves. It was good land, they said, greener than the Cape, with lush pastures where a man could roam as free as the quagga and the ostrich. There was limitless lumber to build homesteads, water that ran clean and clear, more game than the *volk* could eat in a hundred generations. And the land ran never-ending from the Kalahari to the Zoutpansberg, and on to the haunting beauty of Natalland.

"...and another thing," Harry was saying, tamping tobacco into his pipe, "all the burghers and their Commando are staying here in laager until the Xhosa decide to retreat."

Matthew heard Martha's sharp intake of breath when he said, "That could take weeks. Three, maybe four."

"You're right." Harry set a lit splinter to his pipe. "But the talk of trekking north keeps them here as much as anything."

"They cackle like cockerels from morning till night." Martha sounded bitter. "Blind stupidity. They'll lose their children and all they own...."

"Hush, Martha. The elders have enough troubles...."

"And what about us, husband? Will we also stay in this forsaken place surrounded by savages?"

"Matthew?" Harry breathed smoke.

"We'll travel back to the farm as we always do," Matthew said quietly.

"Is it safe, Matthew, really safe?"

"The Xhosa won't trouble us. They'll stay here until they've stolen enough cattle, then take them back across the Fish River. There'd be no profit in attacking us."

Martha Cuthbert would have preferred to travel straight back to Port Elizabeth, rather than go via the Eastman farm. She thanked the Lord that this was their last journey to the interior. Now that their modest store in Port Elizabeth prospered, safe from Kaffir raids, it was no longer necessary to make the journey into the veldt to sell their hardware, gun parts, and patent medicines. Let others take the profits and the accompanying risks. They had no more need of the burghers' business, and besides, it was high time Elise took a part in the thriving social life of Port Elizabeth. It was time she opened her eyes to the existence of other young men, saw the opportunities for a good marriage, which were open to her. To forget farmers....

"That's settled then," Harry said. "Come, Matthew, we'll search Sergeant Coffee out." He looked impatient when Matthew asked again about his daughter. "She'll be here when we get back." He winked at his wife, who affected not to see.

"We should be ready to travel soon," said Matthew. He set down his plate and stood up, testing his re-dressed wound. "This bad weather will help us."

"My thinking exactly." Harry knocked out his pipe.

"Tonight?" Martha turned shrill, whirling with her arms out, staring with horror at the clutter of boxes and barrels.

"The morning will be soon enough." Matthew hid his disappointment at not seeing Elise. "We leave at dawn."

12

Kuba lay shivering under an outcrop of rock.

Lashed by hail and the abrasive wind, he prayed through chattering teeth. *Help me, great Mwari, keep me strong and safe from your winds and the biting forked fire from the clouds.* Lightning sheeted around his shelter, crackling with raw power. The night sky between the flashes was full of dark afterimages of fearful things.

Kuba had walked and jogged a great distance and his head pounded. The air he breathed smelled burned and was bitter to his tongue. He shouted prayers to his family gods to ward off the spirits of the night who could reach into a man's throat and steal his soul.

Despite his fear, Kuba kept his body between the hail and the long gun. It must not get wet, and he resolved he would never return to his kraal without the gun and the lead balls it spat.

13

Harry Cuthbert and Matthew found Sergeant Coffee walking the horses before he allowed them to be watered. His ginger-and-salt mustache bristled when a Highlander was clumsy with a saddle gall, causing his horse to rear and snap as the soldier backed away, slipping on the stony riverbed.

"All my life," Coffee said, half to himself, "I've been around horses and boys. No sooner do I get them acquainted with each other's faults than one will go lame and the other'll get himself bought out by his widowed mother. There may be a shortage of lads and horses, but it's my temper that don't lengthen, and that's a fact, gentlemen."

"You've taken some knocks," Harry observed after he had been introduced by Matthew.

"Had worse, Mr. Cuthbert, had worse."

Matthew paddled out to the army horse and stopped it from churning the water to a muddy boil.

Coffee approved with a grunt. "The brush was alive with the black baskets when we came up on the Hendricks farm. Never really saw them after that but the once when they came up in a rush on the stragglers, much like young Eastman must've told it. I shall have to smarten up the Totties'

38

bayonet drill when we get to Colesberg. Show them how to feint around a shield and spit a Kaffir as neat as a paid bill."

Coffee had bivouacked his men upstream of the Hottentots because of the latter's dubious toilet habits, hobbling the horses between the two parties. There was enough sickness among his men without the added scourge of cholera.

"We're leaving in the morning," said Matthew as he handed the gentled horse to Coffee.

"And how many wagons would that be, then?" Coffee felt obliged to ask.

"Two." Matthew saw a quick frown crease the Sergeant's forehead.

"A long journey and a dangerous one for a small party," Coffee told Harry. "No offense, but wouldn't it be safer to wait in laager rather than travel south alone? This area's under martial law, not that that seems to mean much to you people."

"It doesn't. We're used to making our own way and our own decisions," Harry said as the rising wind drove a cold, light rain into their faces. "You soldiers came too late to teach old hounds new ways."

Coffee looked toward Matthew. "Young dogs too."

"In the old country, Matthew would be a boy, ready to listen to his elders. Here, and make no mistake about it, he's a man."

"I'll not argue, Mr. Cuthbert. I saw him fight those blacks."

"Then you know." Harry offered his hand and Coffee took it.

"Good luck, Mr. Cuthbert. Goodbye, Eastman."

Matthew was reluctant to leave the tall, rawboned English soldier without some remark. "Your helmet would serve you better if it looked less like a full moon."

"Meaning what?"

"Dye it with mimosa bark. You'll be less of a target."

Matthew and Harry were almost at the ring of outer wagons when Coffee's laugh reached them. Harry stopped in his tracks.

"Strange humor, these soldiers," he said, and Matthew smiled in the darkness.

Huddled against the rain, the Xhosa beat their assegais against their shields, a rhythmic crescendo of sound.

"Katherine."

Cord Laidler had burst through the cottage door and seen her slumped on the horsehair couch. Whatever he had been engaged in through the long night, sleep had not been on the agenda. His face was drawn beneath two days of beard and he smelled of alcohol.

"I've been waiting since before midnight," Katherine said, shielding her eyes against the glare from the opened door.

The cottage lapsed into dusk as Cord closed the door at his back. He crossed to the stove and poured stewed coffee into a mug. "You've been here all night?" he asked, seeing her discarded ball gown lying over a chairback, incongruously delicate in the roughly furnished room.

"I had to talk to you."

"How did you come here?" Cord asked. "This coffee is filthy."

"I was escorted by carriage. An officer of the 75th brought me."

"A night alone on that old couch hasn't impaired your temper. I take it you were alone?"

Katherine nodded. "Unlike you, it seems."

Cord's laugh was short and cruel. "I leave for the hunt in a few hours, you know that. Was I not to taste the pleasures of civilization before I take to the bush?" He dropped onto the sofa. "Come and sit by me. What did you have to talk to me about, hmm?"

"I think I was compromised last evening." She told him about Chevening, the slap, Cornwell's gallantry. It all seemed far away and of little importance.

"Chevening, yes, I seem to remember relieving him of a thousand guineas at the tables. Damn it, I still have his note for the same. I'll have my seconds deliver it with a request for payment or the chance of satisfaction. He'll back down of course." Cord's eyes danced.

"Will he? Cord, he's notorious...."

"My dear Katherine, I've outshot the fool before, why do you think he went after you and your lily-white reputation. Always take the second target when you can't hit the bull."

"This is serious, Cord."

"No it isn't. Remember who I am. I'm the social leper, the Uitlander who has nothing but wealth and no pedigree. Chevening couldn't face me on the field of honor, I'm not a gentleman. But he'll pay all the same. Put him from your mind."

"I am nevertheless compromised."

"Of course, you stayed out all night. Well, that can't be undone quite so easily, can it? I can't help you there at all."

"No." Katherine was miserable.

Cord drew her to him casually. "I thought not to see you before I left, but since you are here..."

He smelled of stale sweat and whisky, of seawater and sweet perfume. His mouth closed over hers and she strained to meet his kiss, letting all her worries melt; none of it mattered....

The sound of an approaching carriage barely interested her; Cord's tongue seemed to be filling her head. She was losing herself in her pounding blood when Colonel Spenser's roar beat through the walls and parted them.

"Well I'll be damned for a poacher, the old bastard dares to show his face here." Cord had tucked in his shirt and was out through the door before she realized whom he was speaking of and whose voice boomed from outside. She got into her dress and buttoned herself up as best she could and went to stand on the stoep beside Cord, who drew her to him, smiling and insolent.

"Greet your father, Katherine."

Colonel Spenser breathed as raggedly as his blown horses. His face was as white as his hair and his eyes were darker than plums. At the sight of Katherine he nodded as though confirming something to himself. Without preamble he said, "Laidler, I know you are due to leave soon for another ivory hunt. My daughter will naturally remain here in Cape Town. If when you return, you still feel anything for Katherine, I am obliged to say you are permitted to leave your card at my residence. I will then invite you to call to pay your respects."

Katherine gnawed her lip, scarcely believing her ears. Cord was genuinely amused. "I see. You would see that as the only honorable course under the circumstances?"

"I would, sir. I do."

"My dear Colonel, I don't need your permission for anything. There might have been a time when I should have been honored to cross your threshold, but not now. You see, I have crossed your daughter's, and that was much more to my liking."

The two men measured each other in the buzzing heat, as

41

flies worried the horses and the baked earth gave off its bitter fragrance.

"I can think of no words to describe your infamous conduct, sir."

"Can't you? I can think of several for yours, Colonel."

"Damn you, sir!"

"And damn you, sir. You see, Katherine, your father cannot take satisfaction. Like Chevening, he can only bluster and pay his bills."

"This interview is at an end," growled Spenser. "You will never see my daughter again. Come, Katherine."

"Am I not to be consulted?" Katherine flared.

"No, madam, you are not."

Cord drew Katherine closer. "In this situation, it is you who are at a disadvantage, Colonel. A gentleman would have accepted your offer and spent the rest of his life trying not to act the rotter. I am no gentleman, and never intend to be."

"Then you are a fool, sir. My daughter and I will leave you to your moneygrubbing."

Cord toyed with the bow on Katherine's shoulder.

"I am not a child, Father. I shall leave when I am ready, and not before."

A fleck of saliva trembled on the Colonel's mouth and Cord feigned a yawn.

Spenser said, "I warn you," and his voice was very old.

"Ah," Cord was awake again. "The threat. But it was only a matter of time, wasn't it? We both know you would never have had me at your table, don't we?"

"I'll break you, Laidler. I have documentary proof of your dishonesty. I have Mason's signed affidavit...."

"Mason?" Cord rocked with unholy glee. "That fat little man who clerks for the harbor master? Let me tell *you* about Mason, Colonel. It's very simple, and the documentary evidence you mention will see you behind bars as well as myself. I bribed Mason to get your countersignature on my bills of lading for last year's crop. I made a handsome profit, and it was worth the fifty guineas and the price of the lady I commissioned to entertain our Mr. Mason. By God, he needs some diversion, married to that wormwood figurehead of a wife."

"I'll see you broken, back with your own kind, running with the rats under the jetties," sneered the Colonel, his back straighter.

Cord's face was no longer handsome. His voice came from deep within him. "If you choose to discredit me, I should probably have to return to the waterfront. But"—Cord pulled Katherine's head up by the hair—"I'll take her with me. Katherine would be an asset to me down there; she'd please the eye of any lusty sailor with silver in his pocket."

Colonel Spenser reared in his seat and raised his whip.

"*Think*, Colonel. And don't make the mistake of disbelieving me."

The Colonel slashed at his horses and turned his carriage in its own length, his wheels skipping the ruts. A silence gathered in his wake and lasted a long time.

"That was cruel," Katherine said finally, freeing herself from Cord's embrace. "So very cruel."

"Not so much cruel as necessary," he answered as she moved out of reach. "No man threatens me lightly. I meant every word."

"You cannot treat me like some piece of merchandise. I am not one of your waterfront whores."

For an instant they faced each other, crouched and snarling like animals. Cord straightened first; he found and lit a cigar and blew smoke from a corner of his mouth.

"I own you, Katherine," he said calmly. "I own you as surely as if I traded you for coin. Know it, and accept it. We're as alike as two fingers in a fist."

"No!" She shouted the lie, knowing the truth.

"If your father's sensible, nothing will happen. My arrest would cost him very dearly. His position, wealth, everything. We should probably share a cell together. I don't think the weather on Robben Island is terribly clement; he'd hate it. Our plans can stand as they are; you'll join me in three months' time in Colesberg, and we'll marry as we planned. Isn't that what you want?"

"I, no, sometimes...I don't know."

"I do."

"Then take me with you now."

"There are certain places I cannot take you, certain things I don't want you to see, ever. We'll meet in Colesberg when my Griquas bring up the supply wagons. Not before." Cord shoved into the cottage and the door smashed closed against the frame. Katherine lowered herself to the stoep, gripping her knees as tears and sweat streaked her face. *Let it not be so*, she prayed, *let me not belong to him so totally*, and knew it was useless. She did.

It would only be a matter of time before she followed him inside.

15

The rain caught them again on the second day, only two hours from the Eastman farm.

The clouds rolled darker and darker, boiling violet with black undersides; lowering until the overcast was all around the wagons, solid with oppressive humidity. Sounds died still-born under the heel of the sky. The horses trudged with hunched shoulders and flattened ears.

Thunder drumrolled in from the north and lightning chattered to light fragments of the far high ground, bright and fierce and sharp. A deeper turmoil seemed to rise out of the earth itself, surfing in at them like troglodyte cavalry, rain spears shafting down in a sudden solid wall that stole the vista, smashing into the soil and churning it to boiling ocher soup.

Matthew sat on a medicine chest in the confines of the Cuthberts' wagon with Elise close to him. Martha and Harry were up on the driving box, working the ox team between them. Matthew could see Boie through the rear flaps of the canvas sail, hard put to keep Gaika on rein as his own foal sidestepped under him.

For the first time, Matthew and Elise had been left alone together. Throughout the journey, Martha had contrived to keep them apart, finding small chores for Elise, impatient when Matthew did not volunteer to take the driving over for her husband, until Harry, with uncharacteristic brusqueness, had told her to join him on the driving box, ignoring her protests.

Elise sighed prettily, just as she had practiced in her mirror. "How much longer, Matthew?"

"If we don't hit mud drifts, two hours, no more."

"Oh, I hate all this discomfort. I wish I hadn't come now. Ma said I should have stayed behind, and I wish now I had. It's so cold and...uncomfortable. I'm tired of being jostled." A petulant frown lowered her eyebrows and drew her mouth into a tight line.

"Why did you come?" Matthew had taken her hand and was surprised to find it warm, wondering why women said what they did not mean.

"Why? To see you, of course."

"I'm due to come up to Port Elizabeth next month. You

could have waited until then if you hate coming out here in the winter...."

"I should have, but you see how Ma is behaving. She's turned against you, Matthew. I don't know, I think she doesn't want us to marry...."

"She doesn't." Matthew drew his coat collar up against drops of rainwater that ran down his neck from a leak in the canvas.

"Well, I don't care. When you come to Port Elizabeth, you'll see. The shop's getting too much for Pa all by himself. When we're married you can come and run it with him. Then you see, she'll..."

Matthew stood abruptly and crushed his hat against the hooped canvas. "I'm no shopkeeper, Elise. We've been through this, and I thought you understood. I have plans...." Standing, he was conscious of her delicate, almost fragile features, the smallness of her bones, and the swell of her bosom. But for her furious expression and the set of her mouth he would have lifted and hugged her.

"But I thought that was before..." Her eyes brimmed with tears.

"Don't cry, girl. Listen, because we have to settle this thing. I won't tend store, and I won't live on the coast in a town. I'm a farmer and a hunter, I need the veldt and the mountains, and I've never said different. The country to the north of here is going begging for anyone who wants to take it. Free land, Elise, and we can take what we want, if you'll come with me. I meant to tell you just as soon as I'd told Pa and Edward. I'm trekking, Elise, leaving the Zuurveld and traveling north."

"You've been talking to de Villiers and Dirk."

"I've talked to Abraham, yes, not so much to Dirk, we don't...Anyway, that's no matter. What's important is we can't fight for a living here any more."

Elise drew back when he reached for her hands. "And what will your father say when you tell him?"

Matthew was puzzled by a petty note of satisfaction in the question. "Pa's old; he wants all his family around him, even me. Edward and Becky will give him grandchildren and I won't matter any more."

"He won't let you go, and neither will I," said Elise.

Christ, she sounds triumphant, thought Matthew.

"And what about me?" she asked. "D'you really expect me to trek off to live with kaffirs and lice and filth? Look at the

45

Hendricks family. They say old Mrs. Hendricks has gone mad with shock."

"They died *here*. For a farm with no water and bad soil. Like my pa they dug and fenced and fought drought and hail and frost. And Xhosa. That's no life for a man and his family." Matthew caught Elise as the wagon dipped in a rut and held her until the crazy teetering stopped. Man, there was so much softness under his hands, and she had been a part of his life for as long as he could remember. His pa and Harry had even picked out the names of their grandchildren. Only Martha had kept out of what she called their *brandewyn* chatter. She had always wanted more for her daughter, much, much more....

"We'll marry, Elise, and go north, eh?"

She raised an arm as though to strike him, and held the pose for a long time. When she spoke, it was as if he had become a stranger.

"Go to your horse. The rain is turning to hail."

To punctuate her remark, Boie yelled as ice rattled on his head and shoulders.

Matthew felt nothing as he emerged into the holocaust of sound and movement. He saw only the girl, her body taut, her fist clenched whitely at her side. And in her eyes, an expression he didn't want to interpret.

16

Kuba saw the old men before he saw the bull. He did not know that the tall and gaunt white man was Matthew Eastman's father, or that the wizened little Khoikhoi at his side had sired Boie.

Kuba had been resting when he heard them coming through the brush, making noise as if they beat for game. His broken rib was a sharp tooth inside the skin of his chest and the swelling around it gray and painful. Kuba sank to the ground under a wait-along thorn and let the two men pass by. The white man carried a long gun and Kuba knew he could not outcast the old Khoikhoi's arrows.

The Xhosa could see eight good cows in the waist of the kloof and thought they must have been hobbled there by the corngrower; it was a trick he had heard they used to stop strays from wandering away from their lands. These cows must be strays, for Kuba had seen farmhouse smoke four miles off. The two men were going into the thicker growth where the kloof narrowed, hurrying now because of the driving rain. Why they would do such a thing puzzled Kuba, for there was no real shelter and rain was pouring down the rock face. Then all became clear; something snorted and pawed the ground out of Kuba's sight, beyond where the men had gone. Ayee, a bull. Kuba knew the animal would be casting about with a lowered head, his back close to the rock wall, nervous and ready to use his horns. The Xhosa also knew the bull would not be taken easily; farm animals went wild quickly in the bush if they learned to survive fast enough. When he had been a herdboy he had tried to bring such beasts out of narrow passes like this one. Kuba lay still and would not look at the men for fear of attracting their attention.

They were in the dripping undergrowth when he raised up, and the wind brought the scent of the bull and the white man to him, the one rank and powerful, the other as unpleasant as the stink of a wet ostrich.

Kuba squatted on his haunches and thought deeply. If he could spear the white man, the Khoikhoi might run away. Or, if he could get the long gun, he could shoot them both. The eight cows, a good bull, and a second gun would be a great prize and would bring him much honor. They would sing of Kuba's raid in all the kraals of the Xhosa.

He bowed out from under the thorn and began to sidle down the rocky wall. The rocks were proud of the thin soil and many were in loose tumbles, ready to start a slide at any time. He trod cautiously, inching closer to the floor of the kloof, aiming to keep upwind of the cows and to use them for cover.

Kuba reached the frightened animals and crouched in the rain with their bawling all around him, their hides shivering under the streaming rain. Thunder rolled around the rim of the kloof and the light faded to an oppressive dullness. Kuba laid the gun beside him to free his spear arm for the only cast he might get, and set himself to wait.

The men called to each other in a language he did not understand, but the urgency of their words was clear.

"He runs, Baas John."

"Stand aside, Jakob. Let him run."

The bull burst from cover in a rush and slid in a half circle, corrected, and swung his tail in angry flicks. His small eyes were red and cramped. He bellowed and ran at the cows, bursting through them, close to Kuba. The cows scattered with clumsy jumps and the two men came out of the cover to see Kuba and the bull in the same instant.

John Eastman unslung his gun, and rain sheeted from his hat as his head came up to sight. The old Khoikhoi reached for an arrow.

A cow blundered into Kuba and hurled him into the mud. When he fell, the rib cut through his chest and his spear flew off somewhere out of his view. He arched over himself and managed to find his feet in the sucking mud, only to see the long gun bearing down on him. He made a grab for Matthew's musket, caught it up, and, turning, leapt for the wall of the kloof.

A rock near his face grew a dry scar and fragments peppered him. The sound of the gun was as big as a thunderball in his head. He climbed faster, moving erratically to spoil the enemy's aim.

Ayee, the pain was eating his strength.

A pumice rock loomed and Kuba made for it, spilling shale behind him. His right foot caught a cleft and he was up alongside the rock. A heave, and he was behind it. An arrow drowned itself in the mud.

Kuba leaned back against the rough and wet surface, his body alive with reaction as he looked for a sheltered path to the upper ground. Under his feet the mud was running liquid, spilling from the pumice overhang in two brown spouts. Kuba set a foot against the rock and made ready to jump over the rim of the gully and lose himself in the brush.

As he launched himself forward, the rock tipped away from him and he was dropping after it, falling loosely in a rattle of shale and larger stones. Kuba felt his legs break as the rock smashed into others and the whole face dragged into movement, grinding down into the kloof. The falling seemed to go on forever and then it was over.

Kuba lay on his back with no pain, his head on one side. There was no feeling at all, just a detached curiosity. The old Khoikhoi was in Kuba's line of sight, and the Xhosa watched him throwing rocks aside wildly, pulling at something that was limp and turned out to be the body of the corngrower. The Khoikhoi freed the white from the rockslide and laid him on the muddy open ground. The white man's hat fell away from the slack face and blood ran pink from the crushed skull, watered by the rain.

Kuba showed his teeth at the sight. He and the stone god had killed an enemy after all.

48

Kuba was still grinning when the Khoikhoi came to finish him.

17

The storm swept in over the Eastman farm as a black pall.

Edward Eastman and his field hands abandoned the irrigation ditch they had been reinforcing and made for shelter—the Khoikhoi to their huts where smoke curled sullenly in the thatch, and Edward through the gate and into the forecourt before the farmhouse. He unsaddled and dried off his horse in the barn, gave it feed, and dashed into the house. By then the hailstones were clattering in the great oak by the gate and bounding across the courtyard to form glistening drifts. Filled with concern for the young wheat in the fields and the fat-tailed sheep in the pasture, Edward tore the homestead door open and crashed it shut behind him.

Rebecca was leveling the house musket only inches away from his head, her knuckle white on the trigger. It was a long moment before she let it fall, just long enough to remind her husband he had broken the rule that they all lived by: to call out before entering the house. It had been drummed into them from the time they could walk.

"Sorry." Edward spread his arms in contrition. "You wouldn't have heard me anyway, not with the noise of the storm and all. Does my wife have a kiss for me?"

Still frowning, Rebecca chastely pecked his cold cheek and colored when he patted her rump; Edward was not usually given to demonstrations of that sort. It was probably because they had the house to themselves, a rare occurrence. Rebecca had only the houseboys for company during the day; Edward, Matthew, and their father took their midday meal in a twist of linen usually, for a journey back to the farmhouse for a food break took too many precious daylight hours.

"Pa isn't back?" Edward stripped off his sodden coat and followed his wife into the living room.

"No. I wish he'd taken the horses, but you know your pa, stubborn. He and Jakob thought they'd find those strays better on foot."

"He's right. The ground's too broken on that quarter to use a horse properly. They have rawhide shields with them and they'll shelter until the hail stops. My head's ringing with it." Edward stood before the fire and his breeches

49

steamed. His hair, darker than Matthew's, lay in damp tangles around his thin, serious face.

When he was dry and warm enough, he eased himself into the hide chair by the fireplace and filled his pipe from a slipper of tobacco as Rebecca moved around the room, anxious that everything should be ready for the Cuthberts' arrival. There was a light flush on her cheeks and she wore a heavy apron to protect her one good dress.

Dear Becky, Edward thought, had she imagined her life would be like this when he had asked her to marry him? He recalled the first time he had seen her outside the Port Elizabeth Dutch Reformed Church, standing demurely beside her father, Dominee le Roux, as he bid good day to his congregation.

The Dominee had been a man of strength and courage. Born of French Huguenot immigrant parents, he had been brought up to austere Calvinism. His was a strong belief and he tempered it with kindness and humanity. Unlike most Calvinist ministers, the Dominee did not hold with the notion, in some cases a conviction, that the Boers were a chosen people. That, like the Jews fleeing out of Pharoah's land into the wilderness, they were alone and stood against the barbarian hordes to the north. The Dominee had felt no desire to condemn outright, as so many had done, first the East India Company, and now more recently, the British, for their handling of the tiny colony. Rather he had believed both sides could be brought together under God and strove to that end.

Becky's mother had been a cheerful, utterly uncomplicated woman of Dutch origin, and Becky was like her in most ways, but not altogether without her father's stubborn spirit over moral matters. Occasionally, at night, she and Edward would talk of those early days, saying how wonderful it would have been had her parents lived to see them married. A few more days...how long had it been? Edward could scarcely remember now, but it could not have been more than a week before the wedding was due to take place when a neighbour had ridden in with the news that the le Roux wagon had been found overturned and that both the Dominee and his wife were dead.

Edward had done his best to reconcile Becky's grief, but when the three Eastmans had appeared in Port Elizabeth for her parents' funeral, it was to John Eastman that Becky had instinctively turned. The tears she had shed in John Eastman's arms, were the last Edward had seen.

And now, four years later, the plump girl had become a comfortably pretty wife. Becky would never be beautiful as Elise was beautiful. For Edward, her true attraction lay in the calm gray eyes and her uncanny ability to reach him in all his moods. Her calming presence had even had an effect on his naturally reserved father. John Eastman had taken to lingering over breakfast, and to returning home earlier in the evenings. He too had been without the company of a woman for far too long, and he had become devoted to his daughter-in-law.

"Will there be trouble tonight?" Rebecca asked Edward, opening the yellow-wood shutters to peer out briefly.

"Isn't there always with Matthew and Pa? Neither one will bend."

"But is Pa right in this?" Rebecca hesitated. "I sometimes think it would be better if Matthew was allowed to travel with the Commando. He's so...restless. If your pa gave his blessing..."

"That will never happen." Edward was short, tired of the eternal squabbles.

Rebecca loved both father and son, and the growing bitterness between Matthew and John troubled her deeply.

"And there's Elise, Becky. Her mother has brought her up to expect more than she's any right to expect as a farmer's wife." Edward bit on his pipe as though he had said too much.

"She'd learn to become content."

"Would she?" Edward did not think so. He was suddenly on his feet and reached for the house musket. "I hear horses." Standing Rebecca away from the door, he went out onto the stoep with the gun cocked.

By the time Matthew had organized the outspanned wagons and oxen and seen to the stabling of the horses, the Cuthberts were seated and drinking hot coffee around the roaring fire. Matthew caught Elise's eye, but her gaze faltered and she turned away from him, her face expressionless save for a puckered lower lip.

"Hey, *boet.*" Matthew touched Edward's shoulder, unwilling to pursue matters. Women had their own way of working around to the things they held important; let Elise sleep on it. "Where's Pa?"

Edward glanced at Rebecca; he too was thinking that it was high time their father was back, but he wanted his wife's

51

carefree mood to last a little longer. Company meant so much to her.

"Ach, Matthew, he'll be here soon. If he isn't, we'll send some of the boys out to hurry him along. The old man knows better than to go far in this weather."

"*Old* man?" Harry Cuthbert bristled. "We're of an age, your father and I, so let's hear no more about our great number of years."

Rebecca laughed. "Hey now, Oom Harry..."

"Never mind the hey now....Let me tell you boys what kind of a man your father is. There was a time when hail, fire, and Lucifer's brimstone wouldn't have stopped him from something he'd set his mind on. Your mother, God rest her, knew better than to argue with him; he made this farm and saw you both dressed and fed even when there was little enough for them, let alone you. He brooked no argument."

"Then he hasn't changed at all, has he?" Martha Cuthbert said, too much of an edge to her voice. "Stubborn and mulish, like all the Eastmans."

"Mother," warned Harry, seeing his wife flush, knowing she had gone too far—her words meant for Matthew more than his father.

Rebecca paled as she watched the exchange. The two families only had this one night together and already discords were apparent. What, she wondered, had happened on the trail. It was clear it had something to do with Matthew and Elise, for they were at opposite ends of the room and the dispute had spread to include Harry and Martha. Mrs. Cuthbert had always been plainspoken, but her reproofs were always couched in milder language and she had never openly criticized John Eastman before. Edward did not seem to notice; he glared into the fire and listened through the wind for his father.

The hail raged in the thatch as ironwood logs threw up bright flames in the hearth, lashing the fireback with sparks when the odd hailstone dropped down the chimney. The tallow candles painted soft hues into their faces, adding luster to the women's hair. The warm room smelled of seasoned mutton and sugared pumpkin, of buttered corncobs and sweet potato and the heavy tang of Cape wine.

Harry drew his pipe alight and tried to lighten the atmosphere, planning to talk sternly to Martha in private. She was a good woman, but she was too forward, too direct with

52

her remarks. He wanted it the way it had always been between the families, always should be. He slapped Edward's arm.

"A tot of *brandewyn* then, Edward," he suggested, his face flushed from heat and discomfort. "Or should we wait for your pa? *Magtig,* I thought he'd ..."

Matthew, sitting close to the door, heard the soft thumping sound from outside and held up a hand to silence Harry. It sounded like a small animal mewing for attention. Edward heard it then and lurched to his feet. Matthew stopped him with: "Stay where you are, *boet.* I'll see who it is."

The big old house gathered another layer of quiet and Edward felt a knot cramp his chest as Matthew threw the door wide. Matthew's cry was drowned by wind and rolling thunder as Jakob took a step into the room, and another, his knees buckling under the weight of John Eastman.

"Baas," croaked Jakob, barely able to articulate through frozen lips, his hair stiff with frost, rime on his lashes as he stared mournfully up at Matthew. "I bring Nkosi."

Nobody moved for a long, bleak moment, then Rebecca screamed, "Come in! Bring him inside, Jakob!" She bit on her fingertips to keep her teeth still.

John Eastman's face stared with dead eyes, the blood frozen in jagged runs down his long slack jaw. The guttering candles threw no light into the depressed wound at the side of his head.

"I bring Nkosi," Jakob said again into the shouting silence, as snow feathered around his head and shoulders.

Matthew kicked the door shut and gently took the body from the small Khoikhoi. Rebecca led Jakob to the fire as the men eased John Eastman's body onto the sofa.

"Oh God," murmured Martha. "Look at his head."

Matthew quelled a rush of nausea as he breathed down into the dead face, willing life into the still thing that barely resembled the man he knew, the father he needed to explain all manner of things to. His hand stroked hair sodden with melting blood and ice and saw the thick red on his palm without true comprehension. In a bare moment his world had twisted to form a dark and senseless place where there was no kindness and no chance to show his father what he felt for him despite their deep differences of opinion. Someone, some*thing* had taken that opportunity from him, had denied him the chance to explain to the autocrat who had lived inside that smashed face what his roused anger and clenched fists had meant.

Martha and Harry were pulling him away and he shrugged them off easily. Elise was trying not to see the body or Matthew's shock, and Rebecca held onto Edward as though she feared he would fall and draw her down with him.

Matthew said what everybody knew and would not accept. "Pa's dead."

Jakob's arms were outstretched as though he still carried his master's body, his brown pebble eyes dull with fatigue. Harry squeezed his lids closed and blinked them open in rapid succession as if his actions would somehow change the scene. Martha did nothing as Elise clung to her.

"How did it happen?" Matthew asked Jakob, not wanting to know. The small old Khoikhoi spoke of the bull and the rain and the Xhosa warrior, planting his words like seeds in a painful furrow.

Xhosa. The word drummed in Matthew's mind. *Xhosa.* God damn them one and all for black savages.

"Where are the horses?" Edward had found his voice.

"I bring Nkosi like this." Jakob held out his arms.

"You carried him?" Rebecca whispered. "All the way from the high kloof?"

"I bring Nkosi," Jakob repeated.

Nobody moved or spoke and the candles and firelight gave the dead man's face an unnatural glow.

Matthew felt the room shrink about him and knew he could not stay inside for another minute. He threw himself outside into the torn night and ran to fall against the great live oak in the courtyard where he punished his fists against the trunk, asking for a forgiveness he would never receive this side of judgment.

18

Elias eased the small, high-wheeled buggy through Market Street, his face blacker than usual, his lower lip jutting and purple, the long horsewhip clenched in his ham of a fist and ready to lash the first trader who so much as glanced twice at the woman he followed. Outside he was menacing and furious, inside he quaked. The Baas Colonel would have his hide nailed to a cross if he ever found out what Elias had allowed the Missie to bully him into.

Here she was walking unescorted down Market Street with the trash and pickings of a hundred nations, stepping along high and fine across the littered cobbles between the stalls as if she were in some garden that smelled of roses instead of in a place that stank of bad fish and unwashed humanity. And her a lady from the fort, not some doxy from Fish Street. Ach, some of them wouldn't even come here without their pimps or a pistol in their skirts. Elias kept the horse moving and prayed heartily for deliverance. If she hadn't found out about him and that indentured housemaid who had whelped a yellow baby, Elias could have refused to bring her here. But she had and he had no choice but to obey her.

Katherine Spenser took a deep breath of the market smells and quickened her step, knowing how Elias felt and enjoying it. His indiscretion would be used against him whenever she pleased from now on. She loved the freedom of this place, the thrust and vigor of the people who lied and sold and bought after heated bargaining. It was all so different from the muted hills of Sussex and the desultory summers in London. Here on the Cape all the smells and colors assaulted the senses with a bludgeon. The stinks were high and the fragrances heady. The fish stalls were bright with stripes of gold and green and the fiery reds of mullet. The blooms were violently white or crimson and the birds' plumage was glaring and glossy. The circling seabirds were bold and noisy and the talk of the peddlers and the traders was loud with insult and salted with oaths. The skins were charcoal and freckled, blue-black and darkly tanned. The stalls were heaped with fruit and bread and simmering stews; rough wines and beers; flour and sugar and a hundred different shelled beans; okra and yams and fat pumpkins with skins like saurians and centers like wet orange silk. Old women dragged children by the arm and beat the traders down by farthings; men repaired shoes and saddles and swore on the efficacy of their patent medicine. Nguni women offered their unglazed pottery and the men their pagan carving in a great babble of cheerful dishonesty. There were sailors who ogled and more who staggered from a surfeit of locally brewed liquor.

It was inexpensively brewed and almost certainly lethal in large quantities, probably bought from Cord Laidler, thought Katherine. "Give them what they want," she could hear him drawl. "I don't hold a knife to their throats. If I didn't supply it, somebody else would. And that is all there is to that." Damn him and his arrogance. His absence was both a physical and psychic ache. He had been gone three weeks and he expected her to wait out the full three months. It could not be borne, would not be borne. Katherine would do what she could, which was why she walked in this market unescorted.

"Miss Spenser?" The voice came from an unexpected quarter and startled Katherine out of her daydream, adding a perfect touch of startled surprise, something she might otherwise have been required to feign. She tilted her parasol to shield her eyes from the sun and to give her time to recognize first the uniform and then the face.

"Miss Spenser," Captain Cornwell said again. "This is a...an unexpected pleasure."

Katherine looked at his insignia. "Captain..."

"Cornwell, Miss Spenser. Hugh Cornwell."

Katherine stifled an inward smile, fearing it might show on her face, seeing his disappointment at her lack of recognition. He was too much of a gentleman to remind her of their last meeting, but, standing there in the fierce heat and jostled by the crowd, she could have hugged him. It had worked; she had achieved what she had set out to do and learning his routine had been well worth the trouble. Katherine lowered her lashes.

"Captain Cornwell. How feeble of me not to have remembered you and your great kindness."

Elias was crouched on the box, ready to spring the length of the horse if Cornwell moved a finger. He glared at the tall officer without recognition and stored his features away should the Baas Colonel demand a description. Like all whites who wore the red coat, he was young and his features were all sharp angles under the pale skin. His hair was like bleached sand.

"Not at all," Cornwell was saying gallantly. "There's no reason why you should remember. Quite understandable. What brings you out on such a hot afternoon, may I ask? And to a place...like this?"

Katherine unleashed her thousand-guinea smile.

"I am not unescorted, Captain. As you will see." She dipped her parasol at Elias, who dipped his head and raised his hat, his glare still in place. "Like you, however, Elias disapproves."

"I see that. Perhaps it would please your man more if I were to offer to accompany you?"

"Have you no soldierly duties, Captain? No riots to quell, no men to inspect?"

"None whatsoever, Miss Spenser. I leave to rejoin my command in two weeks, but until then I enjoy the privileges of

56

a convalescent line officer. Which in military terms means idling about hoping to be of service to ladies like yourself."

"You will forget your boredom once you go up-country, Captain. Then you will remember the comforts available at the fort more kindly." Katherine walked in the direction of Long Street, assuming Cornwell would keep at her side without the benefit of a straight answer.

"On the contrary," said Cornwell, smoothly keeping pace with her mannish stride. "Enforced idleness weighs heavily, so heavily, in fact, that I have applied for an earlier departure."

"And has your application been successful?" Katherine's mouth was suddenly dry and her step faltered.

Cornwell took her arm firmly above the elbow.

"These cobbles are devilish slippery. The answer is no; Colonel Robertson was not inclined to amend my orders. That would involve paperwork in triplicate—more than one could expect from a senior officer whose main preoccupation is with his dancing master." He laughed with irony without removing the sting from his words. It was well known that Colonel Robertson thought of nothing but the ballroom and the ladies since his rich and aged wife had died, leaving him wealthy and fancy-free.

"Altogether too much," Katherine agreed, her smile no less forced. She had suffered from the Colonel's straw feet and thought that two weeks was an interminable time to wait.

They reached and turned into Long Street, leaving the noise and bustle behind the first row of fine houses. Two old men read the colony's only newspaper, the *South African Commercial Advertiser,* and a water carrier jogged down the center of the street without spilling a drop from his brimming buckets.

"I understand your destination is Colesberg, Captain." Katherine laughed and spun her parasol at his mystified expression. "The Colonel talks, Captain, rather better than he waltzes. It was of no moment to discover where you were being sent. It was only the idle curiosity of a grateful lady who is interested in a gallant officer who did show her great kindness and see her through a difficult . . . evening."

"You flatter me," Cornwell said despite his unease. "Yes, I travel to Colesberg, and as lightly and quickly as I am able. Ball and powder is not a commodity I should like to have fall into Kaffir hands."

"I don't understand such matters, but I do believe your journey would take you the best part of two months, would it not? Others have told me that the country is not parkland."

"I find you well informed, Miss Spenser. So well informed, in fact, that I do believe you know the names of my men and the age of my horse."

"Hardly, Captain."

"I think otherwise, Miss Spenser."

"That remark," said Katherine, "smacks of an arrogance I did not believe you capable of. Indeed, I do not have to flatter you, you do that very well for yourself."

"Indeed." Cornwell stopped in his tracks and forced Katherine to face him. He knew now that their meeting had not been accidental, and anger vied with the need to know why she had sought him out. His words sought to sting. "I hate to be the one to disillusion you, madam, but I happen to be the only officer traveling with the troop. There is no other, so whoever you are *interested* in will not be in my party. You seem to have been wasting your time with me; your quarry is obviously elsewhere. Now, if you will tell me where I may conveniently escort you, I shall leave you there with pleasure."

"Were I a man I should shoot you dead, Captain." Katherine smiled, her eyes snapping, her manner cool. "I have no interest in this officer you have invented; I am not one who follows the colors like some romantic who sees the uniform and feathers rather than the man. You malign me, sir."

Cornwell affected indifference. "For that," he said, "I apologize."

"Far too lightly, Captain. I do not intend to make it that easy for you. Unlike a gentleman, I do not have to be perfectly mannered. However, I do plead guilty to being far too direct with you. I should have employed much more subtlety; you are more intelligent than I had supposed. I apologize to myself for that error of calculation, but I do not forgive you for your crass assumption that I vapor after some pretty lieutenant of horse, when you must know I could choose whom I pleased from the cream of society. Don't look so shocked, Captain. If your intention was to insult me, you have succeeded."

Cornwell was distracted. No woman of quality had ever spoken to him like that before. If Katherine had been a man, Cornwell would have drawn his glove across the fellow's jaw and killed him before seconds in some quiet field.

"Madam, I intended no such thing."

"Yes you did, Hugh Cornwell, and quite rightly. But we'll put that aside if you will be of service to me as you offered earlier." Katherine looked directly into his eyes, daring him not to act the gentleman.

"And in what way would that be, Miss Spenser?" Cornwell asked stiffly, wondering what was coming and conscious of Elias, who was glowering from the buggy.

"Very simply. I wish to accompany your troop to Colesberg."

"Riding sidesaddle on a tortoise, I suppose."

"If that's what it takes, yes."

"By heaven, you're serious."

"Totally, sir. You will find I have little humor and less patience. You will take me?"

Cornwell was smiling despite his irritation.

"Of course not."

"Will you explain yourself, sir? I had thought I was talking to a man who was capable of looking after himself in the hinterland. I must have been mistaken. It seems I have confided in a blowhard." Katherine's face was white and her eyes flashed and narrowed with contempt.

Cornwell stiffened and fury burned his cheeks.

"Since you have presented this bold face of yours, madam, I take the liberty of replying in a like vein. You are too forward and very naïve if you believe I'll roll over like Punch's dog Toby for your selfish whims. Nobody can deny you are a very beautiful woman, and I am sure that half the regiment would risk their commission for one of your smaller smiles. But you are also willful and headstrong, and you clearly care little for the welfare of others. I don't believe you would think twice of asking your father to strip me of rank and favor if it suited you. I'm sure he'd do it over an after-dinner cigar and have forgotten the incident by the time he reached for the port."

Katherine nodded, her face sober. "Splendid, you do have spirit after all. That means I should be quite safe if I placed myself in your hands. You have my solemn promise I'll neither slow your progress nor ask to be treated any differently from any of your men."

"Weren't you listening at all? The veldt is no place for a woman of your...class. You have no idea of the dangers we should have to face."

"I can sit a horse and shoot as well as any man."

"Riding sidesaddle smothered in petticoats, I suppose."

"In Godiva's hair if that was what it took," said Katherine. "But I think men's clothing would be better-suited to the arduous country you describe."

Cornwell summoned Elias with a jerk of his forearm.

"Take your mistress home."

"Yes*sah!*" said the delighted black giant. "C'mon now, Mizz Spenser."

Katherine held out her hand to be helped into the buggy.

"We will discuss details on Friday, Captain. I'm sure we shall be able to slip away from Mrs. Kruger's dull dinner party early."

"Mrs. Kruger? How the devil did you know I'd be..."

"But I know everything there is to know about you. I shouldn't take Mrs. Kruger's flattery too seriously; she is beating the woods for an eligible suitor. Her plain but delightful daughter Sophie is almost twenty-three and her dowry would more than make up for her lack of charm. I'm sure her squint doesn't become apparent until she gets tired."

Cornwell's jaw threatened to drop onto his chest as Katherine rose up into the buggy and seated herself without his help.

"Until Friday then. Drive on, Elias."

"Yes'm." Elias clucked and the horse took off down the street, leaving Cornwell casting about for answers to his dilemma. Katherine Spenser was quite unique in his experience and she was obviously set on throwing herself at this fellow Laidler who was no gentleman and thought little of those who were. Would she really carry out her threat to travel up-country and tear the last of her reputation to threads?

19

The last three weeks of the military campaign saw the Xhosa driven back across the Fish River and into the high desolated lands beyond. The army burned Hintza's kraal and the chief himself was shot as he tried to escape from Captain Smith's column. Hintza's death brought apoplexy to the missionary zealots of Exeter Hall and rejoicing to the Cape farmers.

The Governor, Sir Benjamin D'Urban, proclaimed a new province between the old frontier and the River Kei, named it Adelaide, and ordered a capital built on the left bank of the Buffalo River. The red soldiers patrolled far and fast, burning Kaffir crops and capturing cattle. Some of the settlers rebuilt with their meager resources, but already the slow trickle of wagons had begun to travel north. The Boers were trekking and no force on earth could stop them, not even the assurance that the newly appointed Xhosa chiefs were suing for peace.

During the weeks following the heavy seasonal rains, the Eastman farm grew green from the sky-borne nourishment. The ewes dropped fat lambs, the wheat grew straight, and the life-giving maize was rich and heavy. Edward and Rebecca wondered at their good fortune; the harvest was the best they had known and the Khoikhoi sang as they worked in the fields. The family had laid John Eastman to rest beneath a tall and gnarled kokerboom, a tree, as legend had it, that would live forever.

Matthew worked each day until he fell. His body became teak whipcord and his hair grew down his back. He spoke little and answered less, working as though total physical effort gave him some kind of absolution. Boie was his shadow and made him rest at noon, saw he drank from the waterskin, and curried Gaika when Matthew ignored her. Rebecca would steal into his room to take his clothes for washing and mending and he never noticed.

Finally, when his condition had become the worry of the entire farm, Jakob and Boie led him to where his father had died and left him there in the long morning shadows to make his peace. When he came back to where they waited on the rim of the high kloof, the sun was past its zenith and he swung into his saddle without a word or a sideways glance at father or son. There was a great calm about him, a clearness of eye that had not been there since his father's death, and he carried the rusted smoothbore he had lost to Kuba the Xhosa. Matthew had found the warrior where he had fallen, half-buried by the rock fall, his skull picked clean by white ants. He had labored to build a cairn over the bones so that they would not be scattered and Kuba would go to his ancestors with his spirit whole.

Two days later, Matthew left the farm and traveled in the direction of Port Elizabeth. Boie tracked him for two days before he was able to circle ahead of him in the night. When Matthew awoke, a fire was lit and meat roasted on a spit. Boie stood outlined against a saffron sky and grinned as he threw a crisp shadow across Matthew's sleepy face. He held out a leather flask and a saddlebag for Matthew to see.

"Water, spare ball, and powder," he said. "It is good, Nkosi?"

"It is good, my friend," said Matthew, turning a yawn into a smile.

They ate together in the early haze and Matthew found himself singing a barbaric song that told of a warrior's lust for a girl who counted his valor by the skulls of his enemies and the manes of the lions he had slain. The words could have been about Elise and himself and they made Matthew laugh for the first time in too long. He had made up his mind and time was running short.

20

Port Elizabeth had changed.

Many of the narrow streets and alleys had gone, torn down and replaced with double-fronted clapboard buildings, and the elevated wooden sidewalks were lined with young trees. Old men smoked on benches in the shade and matrons bustled with purpose. A water cart damped the baked streets to lay the dust, and sailors who smelled of tar and shag lounged with tankards by the waterside bars. Spars and rigging rose above the roofs, and seabirds screamed as they spiraled through the shrouds. There was noise and busyness everywhere.

Where a harness store had been, a gang of sweating blacks tore at a pile of rubble in a cloud of choking brown dust. A sign nailed across the gap announced the building of an extension to the adjacent hotel.

Matthew dismounted and walked Gaika, oblivious of the horse smell and trail sweat on him. He passed an assayer's office where men gathered around the tariff board, arguing and stabbing blunt fingers at their newspapers. A fat man with a green shade over his green cigar watched from the doorway and waited to buy at his prices. A lumber wagon rolled past, then an elegant carriage, the woman inside breathing through a scented handkerchief. The man at the reins wore livery and a small Chinese dog yapped from the backseat.

Matthew was pleased that Boie had stayed camped in the bush; all this noise and bustle would have made the small Khoikhoi nervous. Gaika rolled her eyes as two drunken men insulted each other under a saloon awning, slopping beer on their boots and slurring their Dutch.

"Hey, you!"

Matthew swung toward the close, loud voice.

A big, dusty man in black stood in the middle of the road, and a teamster yelled at him from over his ox team as he took avoiding action. Casually and without effort, the man in black hefted a hundredweight sack from one shoulder to the other, big teeth showing through his beard, hair hanging long from beneath his bush hat.

"Here, you boy, earn a schilling?"

"I'm not for hire, mister," snapped Matthew, bristling. "Keep your schilling."

"Nou ja." The man in black stepped away from the hooves of a wagon team and dropped the sack at Matthew's feet. "Then maybe I can help you. You look lost. What's your name?"

"Matthew Eastman, and I'm not lost."

"Klyn." The other man grinned, stretching his back muscles and offering his hand. Matthew took it hesitantly.

"I'm on my way to the Cuthbert store. You?"

"I'm passing the store," Matthew answered vaguely.

"Good. Here, help me get this sack over your saddle. Grab the other end."

Matthew gripped the rough hemp and let it drop. Klyn looked up from his stoop showing even more teeth.

"Too heavy, neh?"

Matthew frowned. The man was a lunatic. "Why should I help you, man?"

"Because we're going to the same place, Matthew Eastman."

"The Cuthberts don't need your corn, man."

"It's *my* corn. I'll store it with Menheer Cuthbert until it is time." Klyn winked. "Now, if you please..."

"You trek?" Matthew asked.

"Ach, all these questions, boy." Klyn reached again for his end of the sack. "You're too young for such things. Your father would take a *sjambok* to you if..."

Matthew's fist took Klyn full in the mouth and pain numbed his arm as his knuckles split.

Klyn's hat flew away and he sat heavily in the dust, blinking with bewilderment as he explored his mashed lip with his fingers. He stared at Matthew for a long time before climbing to his feet and spitting in the dust. Matthew had crouched and circled away, his fists clenched and raised, ready to give an account of himself. A crowd gathered from nowhere and began giving conflicting advice. Both the young men were big and there was the prospect of a good fight.

Klyn shook his head and retrieved his hat. "I'll fight you, man," he said slowly, "when you tell me just what we're fighting about."

Matthew had no way of telling him. The blinding anger had flared and died away, leaving him unsure and contrite. He had struck this stranger over an imagined slight to his father's memory.

The crowd parted as a storekeeper in an apron shouldered through them, setting himself between Klyn and Matthew. It was Harry Cuthbert and he was bawling at the crowd, "Go home, wastrels. Mumpers. Go, find honest work." He punched Matthew in the chest. "You two! What is this? Ha?"

"Menheer Cuthbert," Klyn started.

"Enough. Matthew, you? Brawling?"

"Menheer, if you'll listen..." Klyn started again.

"A fight, that's what it was. That isn't blood on your hand, Matthew? And that lip isn't split, Klyn? *Dassie,* you won't whistle for a week."

"I apologize." Matthew offered his hand around Harry.

"Accepted," Klyn said around his tongue.

"All right, both of you. Into the store," Harry ordered. There was a mutter of disappointment from the onlookers. "Go home before I cut off your credit—ask your wives how they'd like that!" The crowd began to melt as if it had never been.

"You carry the sack. I'll find your horse," Klyn said and was gone.

When Matthew dropped the sack of corn inside the store, he knew he had somehow done penance for the blow; it had been a long walk.

The Cuthbert store had two long windows with a double central door. One window was dressed with women's clothes, fans, hats, and shoes; all townwear. The other was piled with imported teas and spices, biscuits and chocolate in boxes as frivolous as the hats. Inside were harnesses and wheels, rims and bolts of cloth, canvas, hardware, and gleaming rows of china with delicate Oriental patterns. A guncase flanked hooked sides of beef and strips of biltong hung in white gauze sacks. A grocery counter stretched down one side and it was where Martha usually served. Whole cheeses and barrels of hardtack stood in the cool at the rear, and the rafters were hung with saddles, hides, and yokes. The air was heavy with leather, soap, new varnish, spice, and hemp.

Matthew lifted the sack again and followed Harry to a small storeroom at the far end of the store where he placed it in line with others in the confined space, trekboer's provisions, enough to keep a man alive on the veldt for months.

"So, this Klyn is really trekking?" said Matthew.

"He's crazier than you are. He plans to join this Hendrik Potgieter across the Orange River."

"A good plan. Did you get the supplies I wrote for, Harry?"

"Over there, marked with your name." Harry scrubbed his freckled head with the palm of his hand, taking a first good look at Matthew. He was slimmer in the hip and bigger at the shoulder, his features fined down to a manly leanness.

Abruptly, Klyn was there, using one side of his mouth to smile.

"Your horse is at the rail. You'll drink with me soon, eh, menheer?" His laugh racketed around the beams and he had crashed the door closed before Matthew could answer. He found he liked the man.

When Harry had closed the store, he and Matthew walked to the Cuthberts' house. Having settled Gaika in the small rear stable and washed up at the pump, Matthew went into the living room. There were new French china figures on the side furniture and a heavy Indian carpet woven with blooms and vines that never grew in any garden. The dark glass furniture was stark against the whitewashed walls.

Matthew caught a glimpse of Elise in the kitchen. A lock of hair had strayed across her face as she concentrated over the stove. She seemed even more delicate than he remembered, pale from being indoors so much, a damp bloom on her cheeks from the heat of the fire.

Harry talked about his business. "It grows every day, Matthew. The port is full of money. Craftsmen earn good wages from all this new building, and they spend them in stores like mine. There are chandeliers from England in one of the saloons, and one burns a hundred candles a night. Imagine that, and I know because I supply the candles." Harry chuckled. "I've milled the lumber and built a warehouse on the dock for a Bristol shipping firm; ach, there is money everywhere. But I tell you, it's all too much for one man. I need a young man to help me, somebody I can trust, somebody who's *family*."

Matthew felt cramped in the small, neat house with its juxtaposed furniture and useless ornamentation. "We heard you were doing well. Most of the farmers couldn't afford to trade with you now; you were right to stop the trips to the Zuurveld. Things are bad there."

"Aye, the future's here, Matthew." Harry pointed at the floor.

Martha bustled in with a tray of cooled lemon water and coffee.

"You seem well, Matthew," she said as she poured coffee into fragile cups on tiny saucers. "Elise will show herself when her biscuits are baked. We hear the farm does well, praise be."

"Edward and Becky are pleased." It was all Matthew could say.

"We're *all* pleased." Martha passed him a cup of coffee and it sat on his palm like a toy. Martha's eyes were dark in her drawn face, and she nervously avoided Matthew's steady gaze when he said, "You know why I've come."

"There's time for that later," she said with flicking eyes that would not settle.

"No, now."

"Ach, patience, Matthew. She's not eighteen yet. You can't expect a girl to decide something so important as . . . marriage without a good deal of thought. We're living right and decently now, and it's taken us a long time. I . . . I won't see my child go hungry or thirsty . . . or waste herself up-country with a boy who cannot guarantee her the basics, let alone a decent . . ."

"Martha!" Harry came close to shouting.

"Say what you have to, Aunt Martha, I want to know what you think."

"I'm not your aunt." Martha slashed the air as though pushing Matthew from the house. "It's just . . . we've nothing against you, boy. We've been as one family all our lives. We love you like a son, Harry and I." She took air through her nostrils and they were white. "But I brought Elise up for something better, Matthew, something more than you can offer."

"Mother?" Elise stood in the doorway, smoothing the skirt of her dress. Matthew climbed to his feet, his face set.

"He's still determined to trek," Harry told her sadly.

"Well?" Elise asked. "Is that true, Matthew?"

"Yes, and I want you to come with me as my wife."

66

Elise took a pace backward.

"Listen to me, Elise, not them. I mean to join up with Potgieter's party. The de Villiers family's going, all of them, and Klyn. If we travel with the main body we'll have all the protection we need."

Elise opened and closed her mouth slowly, as though the air had turned solid in her throat. "No," she said.

Harry ran a thumb around the bowl of his pipe. "You could live well here, Matthew. There are doctors, schools...."

"No, Harry." Matthew kept his eyes on Elise. She could not bear looking at him any more. She flung herself from the room and her heels drummed up the uncarpeted stairs. A door slammed. Light from the window burned the features from a portrait on the wall and Harry showed less expression. Martha's stare was coldly triumphant.

"There," she said softly, "now you know how things are."

Neither of them moved as Matthew walked from the house and turned toward the waterfront.

21

The residential section of Port Elizabeth withdrew behind closed shutters and bolted doors early, whereas the waterfront area defied the night with torches and braziers and music. One building with a flimsy balcony had smiling women at every window. Fiddlers stamped and concertinas piped. A barber shaved men and trimmed beards on the street; inside his shop he pulled molars and lanced boils.

In the drinking houses, beer was drawn from the oak and brandy was sold by the mug. Wine came in black bottles and the milky native brew was there for those who could only pay in farthings. Lascars and drovers drank with farmers and shipping clerks.

The saloon with the most competitive prices was a long marquee with a ramshackle wooden frontage; a row of rough planks laid across soured barrels served as a bar. The owner was a morose Dutchman who had lost his farm the year before through neglect, a severe outbreak of rinderpest, and an even more severe confrontation with the Government tax collector. The Dutchman had won the site and the canvas arm-wrestling with a drunken shipwright from Bristol.

The Dutchman had plans for laying a wooden floor that would keep, dreams of a long and ornate mirror that would not. His bank was the money belt at his waist, and he settled all arguments with a beer paddle.

Klyn was hunched over a corner table, watching a thin woman in feathers struggle through a romantic song, using every key but the right one. The Mauritian violinist rolled his eyes and scraped on to the end. Klyn drained the rough wine from his mug and listened. The talk around the place was a ragged surf interspersed with rocks of coarse laughter. He had eaten two whole cracked lobsters and a tureen of bouillabaisse and drunk two bottles of new wine.

He tipped the black bottle and his mug remained empty. As he raised his fist to drum for service, a green Cape bottle was banged down on the table in front of him.

Klyn took his time looking up, and when he did, he hissed painfully through his bruised lips. Matthew loomed at his side, swaying slightly, his hat over one shoulder and his shirt-tail outside his trousers. Wild-eyed, Gaika stood behind him on a short rein. From the corner of his eye, Klyn saw the Dutchman start his slow approach from the end of the bar just as the feathered woman coughed into silence to no applause.

"Do you always bring your horse into saloons?" Klyn used Matthew's hanging shirt to pull him down into a chair.

Matthew nodded solemnly. *"Brandewyn,"* he explained, as though it meant something profound. The green bottle he held by the neck was empty.

"Are you buying, Matthew?" asked Klyn, his hand raised to the Dutchman, who hovered over their table, his beer paddle poised.

"Cert'nly." Matthew dug into his pocket and rooted around with two fingers. "With this," he said, and tossed a ring onto the table. The setting was delicate, the stones small. Klyn appraised it without moving and addressed the Dutchman without lifting his head.

"Jakobson, we have a prince with us who wishes to buy the finest in your kingdom. His wealth lies on the table."

"Glass," grunted Jakobson.

"Philistine," Matthew muttered. "We'll go down the street and barter with gentlemen."

"Ha," snorted Jakobson. "And take your damned horse with you."

"You have no breeding," Matthew told him, and Klyn's smile widened.

"And you have no credit," Jakobson countered.

Matthew noticed the gold chain across the Dutchman's waistcoat. He grabbed at it and had a turnip watch in his hand. The beer paddle went back and started down in a vicious sweep. Klyn caught the heavy wrist and held it as Matthew smiled sleepily into Jakobson's face.

"Glass," he said. "Diamonds cut glass, neh?"

"That's my watch, you hyena!" Jakobson bawled.

"Matthew..." Klyn was too late. Matthew took up the ring and ripped it across the face of the watch, turning it so that Jakobson could see the clean scar across its glass face.

The Dutchman ripped his arm free of Klyn's grip and took a roundhouse swing at Matthew's head, roaring deep in his belly, spittle gathering at the corners of his open mouth.

Gaika reared at the noise and pulled Matthew over the side of the chair and saved his head from splitting open like a melon. The Dutchman was off balance when Klyn rammed the table forward into his middle. The paddle continued its swing and struck the back of a matelot's head, splaying his hair. He fell forward across his table, scattering drinks.

Gaika stopped backing when her rump came up against one of the poles supporting the marquee. Matthew used her rein to pull himself upright, completely disoriented. The woman who couldn't sing began to laugh when Jakobson went down, taking five of the matelot's friends with him. The Mauritian put his violin in its case and slid with it under the bar. A small man jumped on Matthew's back and tried to bite off his ear; hurt, Matthew jerked both elbows back and the small man was pitchforked into a farmer's lap. The farmer swung his tankard and knocked him to the floor.

Klyn hit a drover who was aiming a bottle at his head.

Pulling Gaika after him, Matthew moved unsteadily toward the struggling Dutchman, who was tearing sailors from him. When he saw Matthew, Jakobson lunged for him, dragging bodies in his wake. Matthew held out the watch and Jakobson tore it from his hand, drawing back an enormous fist. A chair broke across Jakobson's shoulders, and shaking himself like a wet bull, Jakobson reached for the nearest throat and raised the chair wielder from the floor. Matthew patted Gaika's neck, showing the mare his ring.

"Bought it for the prettiest girl in Port Elizabeth," he murmured.

Klyn swore in Dutch and forgave himself in English. He caught Matthew's arm and dragged him toward the entrance.

At the door, he turned and shouted, "Soldiers! The King's men!"

The tableau froze. Startled faces raised themselves from the melee as the two men and the horse hurried into the street.

Matthew had started to sing.

22

Waves heaved under the pilings of the jetty, a lazy swell heavy with salt and disturbed sand. Hemp warps creaked as the trading ships shifted around, black water slapping their tarred beams.

Matthew crouched with both hands pressed to his temples, his vision a kaleidoscope of sharp and painful colors. His stomach had nothing more to offer his contracting throat. His tongue ran raw against his jumping teeth, as swollen as an old bull toad.

Klyn was holding him over the water to save him from soiling himself or falling in, now and then splashing seawater into Matthew's face and massaging the knotted muscles above his shoulder blades.

"Matthew Eastman," he said, "you have tasted the waters of Sodom. In anger and on an empty stomach. *Magtig,* I don't envy you. My first time was bad enough for me to remember it clearly. I drank sacramental wine in the apple store of the friars' mission. I was fourteen, and I remember it was the reddest drink I had ever seen. The Predikant was sent for and he beat me with a birch rod, but I only felt the wine in my head. It wasn't until the day after that the weals he had raised on my rump troubled me. My voice broke at the same time. Ach, I never knew if it was the wine or the beating that made my balls drop."

Matthew half-turned and slid down onto his backside. He squinted at Klyn's bulk, his face a gray smudge in the light of the watch lamps.

"You talk too much, my friend."

Klyn nodded cheerfully. "True. Come, you must walk." He took Matthew by the armpits and held him until he could balance on his heels. They walked leaning against each other from the clumping jetty boards to the water-slicked cobbles.

Klyn unhitched Gaika and led her back to Matthew, who hitched his elbow around the pommel and staggered after as Klyn led him out of the waterfront. Beer and grilling fish assaulted Matthew's nostrils and fingers of nausea curled in his stomach.

At the livery stable, Klyn hammered on the door until a sleepy and ragged Bantu opened up and brought out his horse, a spirited gray with dappled haunches. Matthew watched drearily as Klyn saddled him, recognizing a fine animal despite his wretched condition.

"His name is Pallas," Klyn said with pride. "He has the strength and speed to girdle the earth. I spoil him badly and he expects it. Come, *vriend,* I will ride you to your camp."

He helped Matthew onto Gaika's back, hooking his boots into the stirrups. Matthew's limbs shivered with a life of their own, and each step Gaika took drove a nail into his head.

They left the town and rode in moonlight across the endless grass where sparse trees raked the stars with crooked monochrome fingers. Jackals laughed cynically in the distance and a soft wind stirred the air, bringing the scent of warm grass and wild mimosa.

From a knoll two miles on, Boie's banked fire beckoned like a red and flickering finger. A male lion coughed from far off and a nighthawk screamed before plummeting.

"This land is too tame now," Klyn said. "The game is thin and even the lions are moving north. I tell you, I've seen many changes since my boyhood, and much has gone in that short span. When did you last see zebra or quagga in numbers, eh? Wildebeest used to run here like black rivers. Ostrich were as numerous as the rocks...."

"When do you leave?" Matthew asked abruptly.

"One week, maybe two."

"I've still got so much to do before I can pull out."

Klyn brought Pallas up sharply. "You?"

Matthew focused on the other man with difficulty. He nodded and instantly regretted it.

"You trek alone?"

"Alone, yes." Elise was a thorn in Matthew's chest. "There was...but that doesn't matter now. I plan to join up with Hendrik Potgieter, I know people in his party."

"Then you will have to travel fast, *vriend.* They have already left and every day draws them away from you. And from me."

"I'll find them." There was sudden strength in Matthew's voice.

Klyn barked a laugh. "I believe you will, and I shall be just ahead of you."

71

They rode in silence for several furlongs, considering. Then Matthew said softly, "My road has always been my own."

"You're your own man. That's clear," Klyn agreed, adding, "As I am."

"Yes."

Boie's fire winked out as they rode into a hollow, forced into single file between raking thorn where mammals rustled. Something screamed as it was taken by a predator, and a stone skipped from Pallas's hooves when he took the steep rise to higher ground. Gaika followed more surely.

"What can you achieve in two weeks?"

"Everything." The word tasted rich and seemed to scale the fur from Matthew's tongue. He straightened in the saddle. "In two weeks I'll be ready to go."

"Then we trek together," Klyn suggested.

"We trek!" Matthew shouted.

Their laughter brought Boie out of his doze, his bow nocked and drawn in one fluid motion.

23

Old Jakob's face fell into hollows and gullies when Boie told him he wished to trek with Nkosi Matthew. The old man's face was the color of the mud wall behind him, his eyes glittered in deep sockets, and his head rested on the thin wrists hanging over his bony knees. His woman saw him accept that his son was now a man, that it was time for him to leave the family house to follow his chosen master, just as Jakob had chosen to serve John Eastman. They were free men, these small Khoikhoi, and they followed masters of their own choosing. It was fitting that Boie should go with the son of Nkosi John.

Jakob touched his son on the forehead in an ancient blessing and it was decided. Boie stepped back from his father and allowed his mother to approach him. She took his face between her creamy palms and brushed each of his eyes with her lips. Returning to her place by the fire that was never allowed to die, she dabbed wood ash on her cheeks as a sign of mourning for the child who had become a man.

There was grief in Boie's joy, for no father lived forever, and he did not know if he would travel this way again.

Edward and Rebecca had accepted Matthew's decision without question. He had not mentioned Elise and they would not ask, so clear was the pain he carried around with him.

The far country was the best place for him; staying he would have rotted like a windfall.

"The farm is yours, *boet*," Matthew told them both. "All I want are two of the wagons and all the supplies you can spare. Boie will collect all my gear from the Cuthbert store."

"Take all you want, Matthew. It's half yours anyway. We've had a good season and there's more than enough for the winter. Pick the best ox teams. You'll need them. Dried meat, grain, anything. And remember, there will always be a place here for you, should you ever want to come back."

"I won't, Edward. But I thank you."

There was much to be done.

The oxen were fattened and kept rested. The best wagons were strengthened and fitted with new hoops. Storage boxes and water barrels were pegged along the sides, spare rims and wheels slung beneath a new wagon bed. The women made new canvas sails and the young girls wove large reed mats for bedding and awnings. The men made a table and a *riempie* chair that would fold flat, ventilated chicken cages. They filled barrels with gunpowder. The Khoikhoi men in the kraal made a new bow for Boie, a supple and powerful weapon, a quiver of ironhead arrows that flew true and far. They loaded dried corn and meal, salt, cheeses, great slabs of salted beef, and a small chest of medicines. They hung game in the sun for biltong and the girls beat leather for pouches, water skins, and *veldschoene*. They made unglazed earthenware in their beehive kilns.

Then it was all done, and on a day that dawned bright and cloudless, Matthew snaked his long rawhide whip above the ears of the leading ox team and the wagons began to roll north.

Edward and Rebecca stood on the stoep with Edward smiling as he crushed his wife's hand, trembling with the effort of keeping his emotions in check. He had promised himself that the leave-taking would be a happy affair with no undue show of grief. Matthew had come alive again after the long and dark months of his private mourning and now was not the time for tears. Rebecca also smiled and waved gaily, almost glad to see the going of the brother-in-law she barely understood.

In the still, early morning chill, Jakob too stood watching, his eyes on his son Boie, who sat small and erect in the second wagon, staring ahead. Eight other young Khoikhoi padded along beside the wagons and Jakob knew their fathers would be watching them out of sight, all of them wondering if they would see any of them again. Such things were unanswerable puzzles best not to be considered by men. It was all in the hands of the great Mwari, and he would make a sign if he chose. Jakob turned away. It was written. He would ask Nkosizana Edward for a sacrificial goat, bleed the animal over the sacred stones, and feed the flesh to his people. The bones would be buried as though they were a person. The white man's gods were powerful, he knew, they brought all manner of strange and wonderful things from across the salt waters. But who would deny a father the right to seek protection for his only son from the gods beyond the clouds and from those beneath the crust of the earth?

BOOK TWO

1

Matthew invariably took the lead.

He rode in the first wagon and left the second in charge of Boie. The other eight boys divided the rest of the duties between them, two ranging far ahead to scout the trail and marking the way with stone cairns or blazed trees.

The land changed with every passing mile. Flat and undulating grassland would roll on seemingly forever, only to fall suddenly into sheer ravines where the sun never penetrated, or rose gradually into wooded hills, both beautiful and impenetrable.

Rivers and streams came and went their meandering ways and it was common to cross the same river many times by simply traveling a straight line. The rivers were as different as their courses; there was rock and shale, mud and sand, and stagnant outfalls where mosquitoes clouded in the fever trees and stinking gases bubbled out of the muddy wallows. The men drank where their animals drank and crossed where they crossed.

They were bitten and tormented by stinging insects, burned by the sun, and nipped by sharp frosts, their muscles hardened from clearing acres of boulders from the oxen's path. They choked in dust storms and lost blood to river leeches. They grew hard and patient and watchful, and after four weeks of trekking, they remembered incidents rather than days.

There was the time of the stealing boy.

He had been dragged into the fireglow by Abba, Klyn's senior Khoikhoi. He was a thin and snarling figure with the stink of starvation on him, naked and filthy and savage. Abba sucked on fingers slashed by the boy's stone knife.

Matthew talked to the boy until he got answers, making him a present of biltong that he would neither eat nor give back.

Matthew made a sound of disgust and turned to Klyn. "He's a Fingo. His people have been driven from their land by the Xhosa. They have no weapons, so they can't hunt. He last ate three days ago. He caught a land snail and ate it raw." Matthew threw food into a sack and hung it from his saddle, mounting and pulling the boy up behind him. "You coming?"

Klyn nodded and followed on Pallas.

They found the Fingoes huddled around a dung fire in a hollow by a brackish pool, three men and seven women, two of the mothers with dying children, all of them too apathetic to run away. Matthew gave them food from the sack and two steel knives.

Klyn hunkered down near one of the men and made him talk until he was breathless. By the time Matthew had distributed the food, he had his story. Matthew had no idea Klyn knew their language and meant to ask him about it. Klyn was full of surprises.

"They think," said Klyn, "that Hintza lives on as a malignant spirit, more terrible than when he was alive. Hintza ordered the death of all Fingoes and when the Xhosa crops failed, Hintza's warriors began eating these people. Caked them in mud and roasted them over slow fires. The children first, then the parents. This man says they made a great sport of it...." Klyn broke off and would say nothing more. Matthew shivered as they rode away under the warm stars.

There was the time of the hanged giraffe.

It was up against a tree, reaching for a topmost branch where the leaves were young and sweet. Its head was caught between intersecting branches and it had strangled. Jackals had opened it up and eaten all the vitals they could reach. Its legs hung from an open hide rib cage, horribly alive from a distance.

There was the time of the dead family.

The smoke had shown on the horizon all morning, a thin straight plume from a chimney. They had come upon a house in a clearing at midmorning. The roof was made of grass sods over a framework of poles, and the walls were dried mud with slits for windows. A warped greenwood door swung idly on its frame, and a dead horse lay bloated in front of the corral.

Matthew and Klyn had fanned the boys out to check for sign as they went into the house with cocked guns. It was one room with a single hearth and a small section screened off by a blanket nailed to a beam. Matthew moved the blanket aside with the barrel of his gun.

The woman lay on the bed with flies on her face. Her clothes were in disarray, one breast out of her bodice and her legs obscenely open. She had been used many times before her throat was cut through. Klyn watched Matthew force himself to touch her and rearrange her clothes decently.

The man was wedged in the recess by the fireplace, half-covered by an overturned table. He had been shot at close quarters, his shirt blackened around the hole in his chest. His pockets had been turned out, the few shelves ransacked, broken earthenware all over the floor.

Matthew saw it all through someone else's eyes. When he found the doll with a broken head lying beside the small girl at the back of the house, he went off into the bush and vomited. It was a long time before he stumbled back and let Boie report to him.

"There were maybe five, Nkosi. They took a wagon and four oxen. One is lame and the load is light, the ruts are not deep."

"Who, Boie?" Matthew snarled. "Which tribe?"

"Tribe?" Klyn had come out to join them. "Renegades, man. White men. They belong nowhere and are less than men. Those people were murdered by people of our color. This family couldn't go on, they had begun trekking but they lost most of their oxen and the child became ill. They had that horse in the corral and two oxen left. Enough corn to last another month. The man wrote all in the fly of his Bible. Look."

Matthew took the brassbound book but had no need to read the dead man's words. "We must dig a grave and bury them deep. Do it between us, you understand, Klyn? Alone. You and me."

Klyn's jaw was lumped and jumping with a useless fury. "Yes."

They dug deep into the stony earth and laid the family together under the house door and piled with rocks that no jackals could disturb.

Klyn read from the Bible as Matthew hammered a cross into the cairn, using more strength than was necessary.

Klyn closed the Bible and said, "They were Calvinists, Matthew. They wouldn't seek revenge."

"No? What about you?"

"Two against five? That's the reality of our situation. Would you have our blacks do our killing for us?" Klyn left Matthew searching for an answer he could not find. The memory of that day stayed with them for a long time.

Then there was the time Matthew discovered Klyn's gift of magic.

They had passed many small kraals where only women and children and old men showed themselves, waving shyly from their fields of stunted corn. The British army had chased most of the warriors into the high ground.

Klyn seemed to know every tribe by name and could make himself understood in most dialects. He was patient and cheerful and answered all of Matthew's questions save those about himself. After weeks of traveling side by side, Matthew found he knew no more about Klyn than he had the day they set out.

They seemed to have traveled great distances, but in fact had just traversed the upper reaches of the Kat River.

Barking dogs warned of their approach to a rambling Nguni kraal.

The huts were built in a semicircle and a brushwood cattle byre boxed the open end of the arc. Thin goats wandered aimlessly on the packed earth compound and chickens pecked as the people gathered to watch them approach.

Matthew was easing his smoothbore from its scabbard when Klyn stopped him with: "I know these people."

"How?"

"Because, my *rooinek vriend,* I've been here before. Drop your horse back behind me." Klyn spurred Pallas forward, raising his hand in the symbolic gesture of peace. The tribe flowed apart and the clan chief was there, an old man with spear and shield, careless strokes of paint lining his cheeks and forehead. He spoke and Klyn answered him with a series of clicks and grunts and flowing vowels. The chief made a long reply and Klyn dismounted, signaling Matthew to do the same. All three men spat on their palms and clasped hands as Klyn seemed to inquire about the health of the chief's thousand relatives and the history of all his ancestors back to the first black Adam.

Klyn said over his shoulder, "His breath is like a midden, but he is a great chief. Or so he says, which is much the same thing. We are invited to the fire to eat."

They sat on skins beside the chief's stool, and Matthew understood nothing of the talk, content to watch the strange and hospitable people serve food with great ritual.

"They knew my father well," Klyn said, turning quickly to pay a flowery compliment to the chief, giving Matthew no chance to ask how this was so.

They ate sorghum and pumpkin, calabashes, beans, and coco yam. There were great wedges of watermelon and clay goblets that the woman filled with beer.

"A great honor, Matthew," said Klyn, nudging him. "Show it. This is their sacrificial beer."

"Whom do they sacrifice?"

Klyn laughed. "Not whom, what. An animal, what else? We're not important enough to warrrant a maiden at the stake. Look around; all I can see are chickens and goats. Not a cow or a calf anywhere. We shall have to make the chief a great gift."

Matthew was suspicious. "How great?"

"They need rain," said Klyn. "To make rain they must sacrifice more than an old billy. That is a pauper's gift to the heavens. A proud clan such as this must give the best they have, you understand?"

"Or the best we have, is that it, Klyn?"

But Klyn was no longer listening; he held his hands wide and began a speech that included the earth and the sky and, Matthew suspected, the shades of the grottoes beneath. The chief's face was rigid with respect, his eyes alive with alcohol. The subchiefs used their elbows on each other and Matthew had the uneasy feeling that his stock and wagons might no longer be his property.

Klyn stopped talking and a drum started to boom at the setting sun, resonant with power. The medicine man came from the shadows with pouches and gourds, threw powder into the fire, and wet the ground with beer before crouching to draw symbols in the muddy patch.

"Now we can get started, Matthew. I must ask you to bring me that bull of mine that's losing weight. It still looks better than it should, although I doubt it'll last through the Drakensberg Mountains. And Matthew, smile as you go. If we don't give them that one, they'll probably have to steal a better one." Klyn held out his goblet to be filled by a heavy girl with a high giggle, lighting his pipe one-handed.

When Matthew led the beast into the kraal, it was greeted with warbles and cries from the women, a single jubilant shout from the men. Small hide drums set up complicated rhythms and gourds clacked. A row of girls sat swaying from the hip, slapping their oiled thighs.

A great shout went up when the chief dispatched the bull with a sweep of his broad hunting knife. Then the butchering began. The chief took his place on his stool, arms running with blood. He emptied a full goblet in a single draft.

Klyn winked solemnly and laughed loudly. The chief laughed too.

"What's he laughing at?"

"He laughs because I laugh; it's their way of being polite, my stiff-necked Englishman. Smile, you ostrich, or he'll be insulted."

Matthew grinned weakly and pounded Klyn on the back, gesturing at the chief, who showed his gums in appreciation of this obscure joke. Children sidled up and stroked Matthew's hair and clothes, wondering at his gray eyes. He drank hugely with no effect, earning even greater respect from the glassy-eyed chief.

Spitted hunks of meat sizzled in the fires. Fat ran and turned the flames blue. Men stamped in circling groups, stabbing the night with their spears. A wispy lavender haze had firmed into small puffs of cumulonimbus clouds on the eastern horizon in an otherwise black and windless night.

"How long does this go on for?" Matthew asked.

"Sometimes for days, until it rains."

"Rains? We haven't seen a spit in three weeks. What happens if it doesn't?"

"It will."

"Klyn, you don't believe that."

"On the contrary, I've seen it."

"Hah," snorted Matthew.

"Would you wager Gaika against Pallas that it won't?"

For once, Klyn seemed not to be joking. Matthew shook his head.

A wooden platter heaped with the best cuts of meat was offered to the trekkers. Klyn deliberated and then took the heart. He rubbed it against his lips and threw it into the fire. The chief grunted happily.

"Pick a small piece, Matthew, one of the sweetmeats, and do as I did. Go on, and keep a straight face."

Matthew kissed his shred of offal and threw it into the fire. A yellow jet of flame shot into the air with a roar.

The drums dropped in volume and the men sat to eat. A finger of breeze stirred the fire, laying Matthew's hair across his face. The first fat drops of rain fell less than twenty minutes later.

They left with gifts of native tobacco after much hand-touching, handshaking, and arm-slapping. The beer and music still drummed in their heads as they stumbled sleepily and not a little drunkenly to their horses.

"I saw it and I still don't believe it," Matthew said, as they rode back to the wagons through the downpour.

"My father was never reconciled," Klyn said heavily.

"Mine wouldn't have understood either. Where is he now, your father?"

"Dead," Klyn replied flatly, as he dismounted, his face toward Pallas as he uncinched the saddle. He dropped the saddle by the fire and squatted with his back to it. "Killed with my mother. By the Mfengu."

The flickering firelight, spluttering in the rain, danced in Klyn's expressionless eyes.

"I didn't know."

"How could you?" Klyn slid onto his back and dropped his hat over his eyes. "Let's sleep." One day he would tell Matthew about his parents, how they had taken their missionary zeal out to the Mfengu clans and died over slow fires for their trouble. Why should the kaffirs want God? Had there been anything but savagery behind the laughing and drunken eyes of the old Nguni chief? What use could he make of brotherly love in a territory where only the strong and the quick survived? Klyn made a sour face under his hat, hearing Matthew make his bed with the rain drumming on the reed awning. It seemed suddenly fitting that two fatherless sons should travel together into the unknown across the Orange River. So far it had been easy, perhaps too easy.

It couldn't last.

2

It rained for a week and stormed for two days more. Matthew would have been grateful if Klyn's magic had been less potent. They made less than fifteen miles in the mud during that time.

3

"Aye, she has the stomach for adversity, that one," Corporal Fry said glumly, eyeing his superior officer with some caution. Damned if he thought he'd live to see the day Captain Cornwell would do anything as *unsoldierly* as this. As if it wasn't bad enough that she was a woman, but the besom was the only daughter of Colonel Spenser. Damned if he understood any of it.

Hugh Cornwell had to admit that he had been wrong about Miss Spenser's ability to keep up with the patrol, and he just admitted as much to his dour Corporal, Henry Fry, with some amusement and not a little admiration. After three weeks on the veldt, Katherine Spenser had yet to complain or ask a favor.

"Never seen anything like it, by God!" Cornwell said with grudging pleasure.

At the outset his men had watched critically as she learned to cope with the physical stress of traveling in column. Her skin reddened under her broad felt hat, angry mosquito bites welted every inch of her bare flesh, and her lips, chafed dry in the heat and dust, swelled and split. Dehydrated, she hallucinated for much of the time during the first hard days of fast riding and slid from the saddle at dusk, barely able to wrap herself in her horse blanket before she had fallen into a fitful sleep. Sometimes she had to be awakened and made to eat.

The soldiers shook their heads. It could not be long before she pleaded to travel in the wagon; they remembered how hard it had been for them in their early straw-foot days. None of the eight cavalrymen was impervious to her presence; she may have lolled like a scarecrow with tumbled hair and her features may have been ravaged by bites and trail dust, but she was all woman and white at that. They had gambled on how long she would last and nobody had bet past the first week. After that she toughened and began to ride more easily, holding herself erect and guiding her mount with a sureness they could not fault.

Only then did they rummage in their saddlebags, Ben Cobbin for an extra blanket, Arthur Deakin for a precious tin of foul-smelling insect repellent, Dick Chambers for his currycomb and ointment for a saddle gall on her horse's back. Howard Daley shared his affection for and rare knowledge of the endless veldt; and finally, Corporal Henry Fry capitulated by stitching a broken seam in her riding boot.

None of them would know what those early days had cost her, Katherine thought grimly, nor would they guess how close she had been to giving up. If only they hadn't watched her all the time as they whispered among themselves. Cornwell too. No pity, no kind words. He had struck a bargain with Katherine and had carried out his promise to the letter. She would have died rather than admit to her desire to give up, death being the lesser choice in her mind.

Katherine spurred her horse to catch Captain Cornwell and Corporal Fry at the head of the small column. A high rock kloof had risen before them and the towering overhangs rose either side of a narrow pass choked by rubble and fallen rock. The forward scouts rolled their eyes and used their hands to show that the wagons could pass through. Just. To skirt the massive outcrop would take four days they could ill afford.

They bound the horses' hooves with rags and made hide sandals for the oxen and moved into the shadowed pass, knowing that a sharp noise could bring tons of rock down onto their heads. The horses' hooves sent up clopping echoes and the wagon wheels ground solemn thunder between the confining walls. They were an hour traveling the first third of a mile, sweating in the dark chill. Cornwell sent Katherine ahead with Corporal Fry, knowing that she could outrun any fall that overtook the main column. He could not and would not abandon the wagons himself, preferring to take his chances with them rather than face a charge of dereliction of duty.

Each hour passed more slowly than the last and they moved on, guided through the darkness by flickering reed torches. They were in the last stretch, with daylight a blinding white wedge ahead of them, when the clattering started above them and flints began to rattle and bounce among them, sharp splinters with razored edges. Dust turned the wagon sails gray and filled the air with a choking brown swirl. The horses whinnied and coughed as the oxen bawled, plodding stoically under their yokes. The men bit the inside of their mouths and would not look back at the stew of rock and dust that poured down behind them, yearning for the open spaces beyond the tantalizing glimpses of the kloof mouth.

Katherine's mount reacted before she did, trembling between her thighs as the first tremors heralded more massive vibrations that built into a consuming and monumental roar that rolled in from their rear to batter their senses and move the ground in a slow and sickening roll. Rock scaled from the unseen summit and both faces seemed to be in motion, grinding down to crush them between thousands of tons of solid stone. Katherine reset her hat and held her horse on a tight rein, refusing to run from the landslide, and Hugh Cornwell hunched inside his collar.

The roaring struck them like fists, battering their senses. They all listened for the stone hammer that would smear them with massive indifference, launch them into a black vacuum....

Then they were streaming out into the afternoon sun where brazen shafts of sunlight cut through the dusty brown veil that boiled from the dark kloof, all of them coughing filth from clogged throats, trying not to draw attention to themselves and their fear.

"Are you all right, Miss Spenser?" Captain Cornwell was a brown scarecrow with pink eyes and he saw that Katherine's hands refused to stop shaking on the reins, her face ashen under streaked dust.

"Yes... I shouldn't like to do..." She could not go on with her thought.

"None of us would; you aren't alone."

Great wonders, was that a compliment, a word of kindness? Katherine wondered, seeing his hair turn to muddy plaits as the sweat burst from his scalp.

"Permission to speak, sir," Corporal Fry had whacked some red back into his coat and tartan showed through the dust on his bonnet.

"Corporal?"

"May I suggest we send the boys out? No way of knowing who'd have heard that racket. It'd carry for miles."

Cornwell stiffened his back and quartered the savannah with narrowed eyes. "Xhosa, Corporal?" he asked, forgetting Katherine's presence.

Corporal Fry licked his lips pink, unwilling to say more.

"Well, Corporal?"

"Precaution, sir. Them black baskets... begging the lady's pardon."

Cornwell did not hesitate.

"Very well, order them out."

Henry Fry saluted smartly, turned his horse about, and galloped back to the wagon.

"It's more than a precaution, isn't it?" asked Katherine, thinking of more than a bath and soap. "I've never seen a Xhosa."

Cornwell made himself smile through caked lips.

"Then let me assure you, Miss Spenser, I shall do everything in my power to ensure that you never do."

She picked up the game, surprised to see her hands no longer shook.

"Too kind, Captain. Whatever would Papa say to your gallantry?"

"At this precise moment, I would prefer not to think about that. Please oblige me by keeping close to the wagon."

Corporal Fry's barked orders had galvanized the small troop, and the Khoikhoi scouts were at full gallop, fanning out on three sides. Cornwell left Katherine with a formal nod and she waited for the wagon to draw abreast of her, smiling at Howard Daley, who drove the team. At nineteen he was the youngest man in the troop.

"Corporal Fry's orders are for you to keep close until the scouts report back."

Katherine set her horse to pace the wagon and saw that there was a dusty little collection of flowers, twigs, and corms in a basket on the seat beside him.

"What do you have there?"

"I'm making a collection, miss, learning as we go along, you might say. The boys bring me things." Daley bubbled with enthusiasm, the slow haul through the kloof forgotten. "They think it's a game; well, it is, really. But look, see this?" He held up a thick twig, "They call this *kanna,* and the natives chew it because it tastes good. It takes pain away as well."

Katherine showed surprise.

"A medicine that tastes good? Are you sure they're telling you the truth?"

"Oh yes, miss, I've tried it, you see. Not on myself, on Jobe, he's the boy who spells me on the wagon, you know? He had toothache."

"And it worked?"

"More than that, he kept the other boys up half the night with his singing."

"So that was what all the noise was about."

"Yes, miss. I also have wild rosemary, which is good for stomach aches, and cat-herb..."

"You should have been a botanist, Mr. Daley, not a soldier." Daley turned pink and dropped his eyes. Katherine quickly said, "I'm sorry, it really is none of my business."

"There weren't no money for book learning, miss. There were seven of us and I was the fifth son. It was either the mills or the army. There's no shame in being poor, but it do mean it takes the choice out of a situation. Captain Cornwell says he'll get me some tuition after this tour's over, and then he'll see about getting me into the army college. I've got some writing, but it needs some working on. I read steady but a bit slow and the books the Captain lends me are awful heavy going sometimes."

"I can imagine," said Katherine, seeing another side of Hugh Cornwell she had not suspected was there.

"Have you read Euclid, miss?" asked Daley.

"No, and anybody who has is far cleverer than I will ever be."

"Then it's no bad thing my being slow about making out the words then?" Daley asked in a rush, pinker than ever.

"None at all," Katherine said gently. "You must read to me if you will. I'm sure Euclid would benefit me too."

"Be proud to, miss, if you'll overlook the stumbles...."

"We'll stumble together."

Howard Daley snaked his long rawhide whip out over the oxen in a delicate move that cracked close to the lead animal's ear. The pace picked up imperceptibly as the late afternoon sun closed them around with shimmering false horizons.

4

Matthew opened his eyes as though they had never been closed.

Klyn was shaking him, his smoothbore in his hand, a brace of horse pistols at his waist, his nose flaring and his eyes wary. Matthew had a sound picture in his head before he made his feet; from beyond the sighing grass and over the hum of insects came the sound of men. A watery moon sailed through ragged cloud and silvered the night with erratic detail.

They had outspanned on sloping ground below woodland and there was light in the trees, flickering and dim. Matthew strapped on his knife and pistols and loaded his long gun. Boie and Abba had already spread the boys in a defensive line and Klyn was checking the animals' hobbles. He came back to Matthew and said:

"I don't like it, *boet*. They could be trying to draw us into the trees, to split us into two parties. We'd be easy meat if they did."

Boie trotted up in time to hear what was said.

"There is no sign this side of the trees, Nkosi. Abba has seen tracks of wagons over the pass above the wood. Fresh, maybe today's."

Matthew yawned with tension.

"We'll have to risk going down," he said. "Klyn, if we have Tembi and the boys give us covering fire from here, they can watch the downslope at the same time. Anybody coming from that direction will have a quarter of a mile of open ground to cross. We could be back long before they got into range, neh?"

Klyn was thinking of the people who may have been ambushed down the hill and nodded slowly once.

"All right, *boet*," he said simply. "We'll take Abba and Boie with us. I prefer their eyes to mine."

"We'll go down in line and circle when we get to the trees. You go right and I'll go left. Yes?"

They moved down and into the trees, avoiding the falls of dead wood and skirting the bushes of parasite thorn, ducking and listening and moving on. Klyn and Abba melted into the night and Matthew followed Boie's noiseless tread, wishing he had the Khoikhoi's agility. The firelight flickered ahead of them from an open space in the trees and there was laughter and cries of pain, tiny cries that raised the hair on Matthew's neck. Boie swiveled his hand from the wrist, signaling caution before he folded almost double and moved on with his bow across his chest. Matthew cocked his smoothbore and followed.

The clearing opened before them, a natural depression with a rock and sand floor surrounded on three sides by the trees. There was a wide path out onto open veldt on the fourth side and it was guarded by two Mfengu warriors armed with army-issue muskets, their backs turned on the wagons halted in the clearing.

Boie touched Matthew, then opened and closed the fingers of one hand four times to indicate twenty warriors. Matthew thought that Klyn must come up on the flank of the sentries and turned his attention to the Mfengu in the clearing.

Three of them were throwing barrels and boxes from the wagons and a fourth hit a tin with a rock. There was a picture of a peach on the label. A small case burst open and tiny bottles rolled out. A Mfengu smashed the neck from one and swallowed the contents. Then he spat and made a face as attar of roses filled the air. Ball and black powder had spilled from the barrels.

There were bodies near a wood fire and one of them still wore his red coat, his back pierced by arrows. Captain Hugh Cornwell lay over a cask, his hair scorched by fire and an assegai through his spine. His naked feet had no toes on them and he had been opened up to let his spirit free. The other bodies had been disfigured in a like manner and had been thrown in a heap out of the way.

Several Mfengu were grouped around the lead wagon and

Matthew's brain seemed to soar in a hot and roaring mist when he saw what was amusing them. A survivor had been forced into a kneeling position, both arms spread out and tied to the underside of the wagon struts. The shaft of a black arrow protruded from the right shoulder.

Boie leaned in to whisper, pointing to the hollow between his own chest and shoulder.

"There is an arrow here, Nkosi," he said. "They twist it so...." His hand revolved as if winding a key.

The Mfengu who worked the arrow rocked on his haunches as he caused the tortured man to give out harsh moans and sipping cries, his own chest swollen with laughter.

Where was Klyn? Matthew's face ran with hot ice as he sighted along his musket at the group to the left of the tortured figure, calculating the spread of the four-ounce fragmentation ball, knowing he must hit at least six of the warriors with the blast. The arrow was rammed home again and the figure reared, skimming his hat away and releasing a thick mane of red hair. God Almighty, a woman!

Matthew squeezed off his shot and ran through his own smoke before it had cleared, and the men were still toppling when he reached the Mfengu who worked the arrow. The man was rising when Matthew smashed his jaw with a swing of his gun butt and broke his neck with a second blow. Guns exploded all around him and powder stank along with the warrior's musk and the disemboweled bodies. Boie's arrows found marks with a burr and a faint tick.

Matthew picked out a painted face near the woman and blew it to red ruin with his pistol. She has violet eyes, he was thinking in the sweat and the fear and the stench. Violet. A body flailed into him and he tripped over a dying man to sprawl in the sand. An assegai gouged the ground near his face and he rolled aside to bring his back in beside the rear wagon wheel, drawing his second pistol and firing into the press of black bodies. A Mfengu fell across his legs, spitting the last of his life onto Matthew's chest. He booted the body away and saw Klyn spit a man on his own spear with a great lift of his shoulders, throwing him bodily into the fire where he threw up sparks and died, a maverick nerve jerking his leg. Then Klyn was parrying another spear thrust with his forearm, and his fist drove the Mfengu to the ground. Abba shot a man from Klyn's back and knifed another who tried to run.

Boie shot a warrior zigzagging for the trees and it was over.

There was the sigh of the trees and the crackle of the fire, the far howl of a wild dog.

They went from body to body to cut every throat, taking no chances, and Abba and Boie dragged the corpses away for the jackals to find. Klyn rolled the barrels of gunpowder away from the fire and found several of them were dangerously hot. Matthew went to the woman and cut the rawhide from her wrists. She stared up at him, her pupils dark with shock, pearls of perspiration forming on her forehead and rolling down to streak her dusty face. She was very beautiful despite her filthy condition, and Matthew was shy of touching her, feeling clumsy in her presence. He somehow lifted her onto her buckling legs and held her awkwardly, uncertain what to do with her.

Klyn had lit an unbroken lamp and had cleared the tailgate of the second wagon.

"Bring her over here, *boet*," he shouted, seeing Matthew's hesitation. "Over here, you *dassie*, before she bleeds to death."

Matthew took the woman up in his arms, feeling her back jump with reaction as he took her step by careful step to the tailgate and eased her down onto the blanket Klyn had spread there. Klyn worked the shirt away from the wound and had the lamp brought in closer. Dark blood welled around the shaft and it was obvious it had struck deep.

Klyn clucked and said, "It has gone in as far as your shoulder blade, lady. If it is pulled out it will tear badly and perhaps sever an artery. It must..." he broke off, conscious of the woman's eyes on him, knowing she was aware of what must be done.

The woman coughed and Matthew gave her a drink from a waterskin.

"I know," she said calmly, "it has to go through. They're all dead, I suppose. The soldiers?"

"Were any of them kin?" asked Matthew.

"Brothers all," said the woman sourly. "There was a young boy, Daley..." She caught her breath as the thread of pain closed her throat. "Please...find him. His eye..."

"Later, first we must tend to you," Klyn insisted.

"You look," the woman told Matthew, leaving no room for argument.

Matthew and Boie searched the run of stone and thickets on the edge of the trees and followed bloodsign through the

90

thorn. The boy lay at the end of twenty feet of flattened grass and blood-spattered scrub. The spear was still in his eye socket and he had died in agony. His hands were full of dried flowers.

Matthew went back and shook his head.

"Would it have been quick?"

"Yes," lied Matthew.

"That's something, that's something...."

Klyn cut in.

"And you'll join them if that shaft doesn't come out. It'll hurt like the devil, but it has to be done," he said cheerfully.

Katherine Spenser looked directly at Matthew. "You do it."

Klyn interpreted her look of defiant courage correctly and his tension exploded in loud laughter.

"You heard the lady, Matthew. Get it out."

They eased her into a sitting position and Matthew grasped the shaft as Klyn supported her.

"Push clean, *kerel.*"

Matthew pushed hard as the woman's body arched and the barbed head cut out through her back. A scream died in her throat as she slipped into oblivion.

"She's passed out," said Klyn. "Good thing too. Now let's patch this up and get back to the wagons."

5

The redheaded woman slept long into the day on the *katel* in Matthew's wagon. Klyn's wagons were packed, the oxen inspanned and ready to travel. Matthew drank coffee and stopped himself from lifting the flap of canvas to see how the woman fared. She shifted uneasily once or twice in her sleep, murmured words that drifted into long mews of pain, then the ragged breathing and long periods of silence.

Anxious to be doing something, Klyn had ridden out for game, unable to bear the shuffling and listless boys and the camp in its state of suspended animation. Matthew, on the other hand, still lived with the memory of the previous night, more real in the present sunlight than it had been at the time. Klyn was right, he had acted like a demented bobbe-jaan, cursing and swelled up with angry blood, killing like an executioner in a Roman arena. Boie seemed to have grown a head taller with pride for his lion of a Nkosi. The other boys were deferring to him without question, even Abba, who was

91

five years his senior, called him *abenzansi* and offered him the first cut of biltong to break the fast. Lord, thought Matthew with a guilty-proud squirm, there would be praise songs about it next.

The woman fumbled with the *riempie* knots of the canvas sail and slowly climbed down from the wagon, squinting into the sun, a blanket around her shoulders. Matthew offered his arm for the final step down and she accepted with a distant nod of her head.

She squatted on a mat by the fire.

"How do you feel?" Matthew asked, knuckling his unshaven chin.

"Stiff," she said. "And thirsty."

Boie poured coffee into a mug and gave it to Matthew to hand to her. She made a small sound of pleasure.

"There's biltong," Matthew offered. "And mealie biscuits."

She held out her empty mug. "Just more coffee."

She was even more beautiful in the daylight to Matthew's eye, her skin gilded a light bronze, the whites around her violet pupils as pale as porcelain. Her mouth was generous over small and perfect teeth, and she had a man's direct gaze under the tumbled red hair. The long hands had strength and elegance despite the raw stripes around her wrists.

For no reason at all, Elise was suddenly between them. Matthew rose abruptly to throw boxes onto the tailgate, to haul the *katel* bed from under the awning and lash it beneath the wagon bed.

"Hey," the woman called softly.

When he came close enough to touch, she said, "Your name is Matthew, isn't it?"

"Matthew Eastman," he answered, wondering if he should add a title when he addressed her, wondering also why he was thinking this way.

"Thank you for saving my life, Matthew Eastman."

"We were lucky...surprise..." There were no words.

"Please stay a moment," she said as he made to move off. "Look, I may not look or sound it, but I am grateful, believe me. I ought to introduce myself, I am..."

"I know who you are. There were papers in the soldier's wagon. We brought them with us."

"You are surely the most incurious man I have ever met. I don't think I like it." Katherine ran her tongue between her lips, pointing the tip at him, mocking him with her whole body.

"Where were you heading when we..."

"Ah," she interrupted. "A direct question at last. Well, Matthew Eastman, I shall tell you when I've had a chance to clean myself up." She lifted a corner of the blanket to peer at her shoulder. "I see you've put some sort of gauze on this. Is there any more?"

"Yes. I'll heat some water and soak the dressing off. You must be careful not to open the wound."

"Such solicitude. Pay no mind to my sharp tongue. It won't be a pretty scar, will it? I shall have to cover it with a corsage when I wear a low-bodiced dress."

You're alive, damn your silly face, Matthew wanted to shout at her, alive and not stinking with sores and dysentery, a chattel to any Mfengu woman who wanted to beat you out to hoe her fields for her. To live on scraps like the village dogs if they let you get a look in. He swallowed his words. If Katherine noticed anything she gave no sign.

"Did you rescue any of my clothes? No? Well, these breeches will do until we reach somewhere civilized. But, if you could loan me a shirt...?"

"I could ride back for your dresses...."

"You would ride for nothing. There are only shirts and breeches. My clothes are waiting in Colesberg." Katherine used her hand like a fan. "There, you tricked me into telling you my destination before I was ready. Just you help me back to the wagon."

"Colesberg is where we're headed," said Matthew, helping her to her feet and leading her. If he expected delight or surprise from the woman he was to be disappointed.

She merely said, "Of course, all trekkers do."

6

Matthew and Klyn watched her eat, her small teeth tearing at the meat without pause, hungrily and catlike. She had swept her hair back from most of her face with her one good hand and one of Matthew's shirts was knotted about her face, her right arm cradled in a sling of white flannel.

Klyn was unashamedly fascinated by her, and he watched her openly. Like Matthew, he had never seen a woman in trousers before. She appeared almost naked to them, the buckskin tight across her belly and hips, moving over her lower frame like a second skin. She did not even walk like other women, striding about freely with purpose in her veldschoene, unconscious of the effect she was having on the two men.

"Why don't you sit down?" Matthew asked. Another strange thing, she ate walking about, never still.

"After weeks of sitting a cavalry saddle I like to use my feet," she replied simply, saying it all.

"While you eat?" said Klyn, watching the boys watching her overtly.

"Why not? That's why we're here up-country, isn't it? No rules. No laws."

"No laws," Matthew echoed, grinning. "You're right. Only the laws we make up ourselves, right, Klyn?"

"Right." Klyn stopped gnawing a beef knuckle. "And my first law is that Miss Katherine Spenser will now and forever be known as Kit."

"Kit?" Katherine looked at each man in turn. "What kind of a name is that?"

Matthew became bold and amused by Klyn's lead.

"Your name. I'm Matthew, he's Klyn, and you are Kit. No one is called Katherine out here."

She studied them both for a moment with a curiously serious air. Then she laughed, tossing a bone into the fire.

"Quite right. But you'll excuse me if I don't respond to that name for at least ten minutes."

7

After thirteen days of traveling, they reacted variously to the news that Colesberg was directly ahead. Klyn clapped Abba on the shoulder, beaming all about him and yelling encouragement to his oxen, who did no more than flick their ears and strain patiently under his bullwhip while he thought of talk and drink and perhaps a pretty woman or two. Matthew's smile did not reach his eyes. He did not look at Kit riding on Gaika, but frowned blankly ahead. Kit said nothing, made no sign one way or the other of what Colesberg might mean to her.

Matthew was soured by the prospect of Colesberg because it would take Kit away from him, and he was no longer stirred by the Orange River and what lay beyond it. This teasing and self-knowing woman who gave nothing away, who conducted herself with an insolent disregard for the conventions of others, had turned his face from distant horizons as surely as if she had him bridled and bitted. He felt both fool and neuter, wanting desperately to reach and hold her, to keep her at his side as the northern vistas rolled forever under their wheels.

Matthew moved his head as if he shook water from his ears.

He saw Edward, Becky, and old Jakob under the big oak on the farm and was suddenly hungry for the old, tame, and familiar things. Elise appeared before him, just a pink smudge of a face, and he could not remember what she really looked like. Just the tears and the recriminations of the last meeting. Nothing ahead and nothing behind, nothing to hold him, nothing to pull him on. He slumped on the driving box and left the oxen to find their own way.

Kit did not sleep in the wagon as she usually did. She curled up on a reed mat outside the spill of the firelight, watching the stars, her thumb between her teeth. She ate what was brought her and would not be drawn into the usual campfire discussion. Her sharp and useful comments were missed, as was her quick way of recognizing the nub of any problem and describing a solution in simple and precise language.

When she drifted into sleep, she was back with the Mfengu racing through the half-awake soldiers, killing them before a shot could be fired. Hugh Cornwell was rousing her, his eyes glittering in his calm face, showing acceptance of the inevitable rather than defeat or fear. As he was telling her to run and hide, the assegai found its mark, transfixing him and killing his voice. He fell slowly, his arm still outstretched toward the outer darkness where he had meant her to take refuge. Then she had been punched backward and an arrow grew from her shoulder, making her scream before she could guard her mouth with her fist.

Howard Daley had staggered past her, a black shaft growing from an eye socket, his bare feet tracking through the grass like lost pink puppies. He went into the trees and was followed by two blacks.

She was hauled upright and made to watch the Mfengu cut the life from the wounded then open them up to free the life forces. Then they had worked the arrow and the night had lost everything of meaning save the great shocks of pain....

Kit came awake as the camp settled down about her; the fire was dying and the men had taken to their mats to sleep. She shifted position and retucked her blanket, finding no comfort in the knowledge that Cord was half a day's ride away. He would be furious she had not honored their arrangement, which pointed up the difference between him and this Matthew Eastman. Both possessed an unassailable maleness that was incredibly attractive to her, but whereas Matthew would claw an empire from the new lands across the Orange River, the blood and sweat he spilled being his own, Cord would take an empire, and cheerfully sacrifice anybody who could not stay the pace or got in his way. Including, Kit suspected, herself. She slept on that sobering thought, and when she awoke in the morning, her black, introspective mood had lifted.

She discarded the sling and hummed a wordless song as she helped pack some of the lighter things into the wagons.

By the time the sun burned off the early haze and had stretched long morning shadows, the wagons had traveled almost two miles. As they progressed through the scrub and brush, the ground was more and more tracked and scarred by wheels and churning hooves, the mute testament of many wagons. Ahead, the blue Drakensbergs rose to cut the bluer sky where cirrus clouds feathered, dry-brushing the upper sky.

Kit rode apart and kept her own counsel. Matthew glowered blindly from his lurching wagon as Klyn swore happily in Dutch, his singing whip urging speed from his boys and his stock.

Abba, riding lead, called back from the rise ahead, pointing over the brow and circling his spear above his head.

Kit spurred her horse forward at a gallop and Boie brought Gaika up for Matthew, taking Nkosi's place on the wagon. Matthew dropped into the saddle and set the mare after Kit, passing Klyn, who bawled happily and tunelessly. Kit did not look at Matthew as he pulled in beside her; her eyes were locked on the town below them.

Clapboard and canvas buildings rambled either side of a single broad street choked with people and carts where dust rose in a permanent ocher pall. A collection of native huts stood off to the east, leaning together in a tired huddle, alive with shouting children running naked. The tall gables of a neat and well-built *kerk* rose from the western end of the town, strangely permanent against the stock pens and circles of wagons.

"It looks like a dirty painting," Kit said in a monotone.

"Will there...*is* there someone to meet you?" Matthew's

96

question was gruff. He could barely accept the notion that this ugly shambles of a town could part him from her.

"There is someone...." Kit hesitated, looking at him for the first time. She had a sudden urge to be close to him, to stand in against his body and let the strength and size of him blot out everything else.

"Yes," she said. "There is someone."

Matthew let out his breath as he heard Klyn coming at full gallop on Pallas. Of course there had to be someone, he reasoned; some lord or other, some damned blueblood with more servants and acres than he had sheep. "The boys will outspan the animals and make camp," he said. "Let's go on in."

They spurred their horses down the slope.

Riding carefully past the hovels made from mud, packing cases, and hammered tin, they skirted a stinking open midden and a dung heap as tall as a hut. This was the native quarter and there was sickness there, boils and open sores a common sight. Beggars with twisted limbs wailed their misfortune, offering gourds to catch any thrown small coins. Many of them were Fingo, some Bantu, sad refugees from the lands of the Xhosa, Mfengu, and Zulu.

Matthew led the way through the squalor and they threaded their way between wagons and carts and loaded packhorses, all in constant motion. The atmosphere was brash and friendly and urgent.

They passed a grain store where men bargained over plump hempen sacks in a haze of chaff, the great brass scales sawing up and down almost constantly, prices and weights called and logged by a bluff man white with flour.

A Frenchman drummed custom as his natives hammered metal into bowls and knives on the earth behind him. Men played cards in the shaded interior of a clapboard saloon, quaffing great schooners of beer. Various dialects came at them in bursts, mostly incomprehensible. They came to a general store sandwiched between a saloon and Colesberg's only hotel, advertising clean beds in bold letters and clean straw for the less wealthy.

Nobody so much as glanced at the trio as they reined in. Without warning, Kit slid from her horse and removed her hat, shaking her hair out in a cloud around her face.

All the talk in her vicinity stopped, the bearded burghers staring as though she were an apparition sent to tempt them from the narrow track of piety. They bit on their pipestems and forgot to breathe smoke.

Kit threw her head back and glared about her until she spotted a small tousled boy and she smiled at him brilliantly. The boy moved back uncertainly and cast about for a parent to hide behind. Klyn touched Kit's arm to draw her off but she shrugged him away.

"Have you been here long, boy?"

Speechless, the boy nodded in a fury of shyness.

"Then you know who comes and goes, eh?"

"J...Ja, mevrou," the boy stammered.

Matthew dismounted while Klyn fumbled for his pipe.

"Do you know a man called Laidler, *kereljie?* Menheer Cord Laidler?"

The boy looked blank and flustered.

"We'll find him inside the hotel," Matthew said. "Come...."

"Menheer Laidler?" a tall farmer in homespun cut in. He leaned away from a post and spoke in guttural Dutch. *"Ja, I know this man."*

Kit replied in the same language. "Thank you, menheer. Could you tell me where he is, where I can find him?"

The man shrugged, running a thumb through his beard, looking around at his neighbors and friends before answering. "I will tell him I have seen you," he said with a distant dignity.

"I thank you again, menheer," Kit said coolly, handing two small coins to the boy with no answers.

Matthew took her elbow. "Now that you've caused your stir, perhaps you'll put on your hat and follow me." He turned on his heel and shouldered his way through the crowd around the store entrance before she could react or answer to the contrary. Klyn flipped her hat over her eyes a moment before she was taken out of his reach, and followed at a more leisurely pace. Matthew was already deep in conversation with a group of burghers when Klyn crossed the stoep and elbowed his way inside the hot and dim store.

"Yes, today," Matthew was saying. "Our wagons are outspanned in the valley. We need news of Potgieter and his trek."

"He may not come through here, *kerel,*" said a burgher with a livid facial scar. "He may go straight north to Alleman's Drift."

"Potgieter left the Tarka area weeks ago," said another man. "More than fifty wagons. Ach, they were the lucky ones.

98

Many who have reached Colesberg cannot go on. Their stock has been lost to the banditti, sickness; their wagons are beyond repair, their money has gone. Many reasons. Some have lost everything to their servants who have betrayed a lifetime's trust, stealing everything. There is lawlessness everywhere." He sighed. "Others have lost their will to go on. Those with Potgieter are lucky, they have God on their side."

"He has many men. Good weapons," said a youth with old eyes.

"Half of *them* would be his sons," somebody laughed without malice. It was a well-known fact that Hendrik Potgieter was the father of an immense family.

"Better if they are," an old man with a blind white eye said. "They will be lions to a man."

"This town was empty when Sarel Cilliers's party left three weeks ago."

Matthew found Klyn when he turned. "We've missed them. Potgieter might not be coming through here, and Sarel Cilliers has already left."

Klyn used his height to make his voice carry.

"Does anyone know where they're planning to meet? The two wagon trains will be joining forces."

"The Blesberg, that's what Menheer Cilliers said," offered the old man.

"The Blesberg," said Matthew. "That's the mountain the vultures and rabbits have given a white hat, isn't it?"

Kit looked up at him and looked away, forcing her interest elsewhere.

Klyn said, "It's in the land of the Baralong clans. They call it Thaba Nchu."

The scarred man produced a rough, much-fingered map and pointed out an area between the Orange and the Vaal rivers, south of the settlement of Winburg. "The Kommissie Trek reports it somewhere here...." His rough finger traced the route on the greasy parchment.

Klyn nodded solemnly. "It seems, my friend, we must shake ourselves if we are to catch up with Menheer Cilliers. The country we have just come through is an Eden compared to what we are now about to face. Come, let's..."

He was interrupted by a commotion at the door. A man barged through the crowd and stood splay-legged for a moment, searching the gloom with narrowed eyes.

"Cord," whispered Kit.

He wore a fringed coat, gold against the ivory of his im-

99

maculate corduroy waistcoat and trousers, black hunting boots, and a soft white shirt with steel buttons. His hair was the bronze of spun molasses, swept back to the nape and tied with a bow. His hard yellow eyes were flecked with hazel, his nose was thinly hooked with delicately flaring nostrils, and his wide mouth was set in a square jaw. He wore a pair of matched pistols in a black belt at his waist, the butts forward.

He strode over to Kit, ripped her hat away, and pulled her up onto his mouth, kissing her brutally.

Matthew's chest contracted and his hands made themselves fists.

"That," Klyn said mildly, "has probably opened the wound again."

The burghers shuffled and coughed and growled in a low cheer as Cord's face parted from Kit's. Her eyes had lost focus and her breath came in a gasp from between her swollen and parted lips.

"Katherine, by God. I didn't think the fool who said you were here was anything but a foolish drunk. Let me look at you. I should beat your pretty hide for coming here...."

"Cord, please." Kit placed her fingers on his mouth, turning her head aside. "You have these gentlemen to thank for my safe arrival."

"What?" He could not tear his eyes from her face.

"This is Matthew Eastman, and this, Menheer Klyn. Philip McCord Laidler. They saved my life."

Cord raised his head and looked at the two trekkers for the first time, assessing them coldly with hard-eyed calculation. His eyes settled on Matthew, recognizing a rival and perhaps an enemy. "What happened?" His voice was thick with heat.

"A Mfengu raiding party," said Matthew. He was a head taller than Laidler and saw that fact register itself in the flecked, angry eyes.

"Christ in his heaven, Katherine," Cord said furiously, "I should..."

"You should thank these men for my life."

"And thank you for putting yourself at risk in the first place, I suppose."

"All *right!*" Kit's voice matched his for strength. "I was slightly hurt when the kaffirs killed the army patrol. I was traveling with Captain Cornwell and his men.... I thought I'd be safe enough in their company."

"Cornwell? My Saviour, woman! There're over a hundred and fifty men assembled here waiting for Cornwell."

Coffee, Matthew thought with surprise. Of course, Sergeant Coffee must be here with the troops.

Cord's yellow gaze took him and Klyn in again, his voice a bare shade more civil. "You have done me an immeasurable service it seems, gentlemen. I shall not forget it and I thank you both. And now, if you will excuse us? Your servant, sirs."

Holding Kit close against his side, he turned and walked out of the silent store into the blazing afternoon.

Klyn hooked a restraining arm around Matthew's shoulders as he made a move to follow, holding him back. It hurt Klyn to see the agony of loss in the other man's eyes, suddenly realizing just how much the woman had come to mean to his friend. It was clear he must get Matthew on the trail again just as soon as it was humanly possible. If they lingered, this might conceivably be journey's end for their joint dreams.

8

Colesberg had seen the end of many dreams.

Families were decimated by illness and misfortune. Mothers, sisters, and brothers died of the coughing sickness, wasting to nothing in weeks, dying as they gasped for breath. Crosses formed a small white copse on the hill north of town.

Wagons disintegrated in the dry heat, desiccated and riddled by white ants. Men gave up hope, became bitter, stealing from their neighbors when their own meager resources were gone. Many took their guns to the high veldt and turned outlaw, running with the growing bands of banditti who ravaged the weaker trains. Cattle and men disappeared overnight, drifting into the no-man's-land between the Sneeuwberg Mountains and the Orange River. Bones bleached in the dry vastness and the vultures flapped glossy wings over stinking carrion under an indifferent sky.

The Mfengu raided constantly, cutting cattle and sheep from the dwindling herds, leaving the trekkers with less and less.

But somehow the trekboers survived as an integrated group, their stoic faith and courage keeping them together, sharing their all with the less fortunate among them. They were a hardy people with the Almighty most surely at their side. These were the Chosen and they must prevail against the tribes of Ham as the Bible predicted they must. Services at the Colesberg *kerk* overflowed into the street where whole families knelt to pray in the dust.

Colesberg grew fat on their misfortune.

Matthew and Klyn made their preparations to travel on surrounded by these people, both of them impressed by their rough kindness and their inherent fortitude. The Boers may have turned their collective back on the mainstream of European culture, their vision narrowed by strict adherence to Old Testament ethics, but there was always coffee for a stranger, and prayers for his good fortune. Their manner was brusque, their philosophy rustic, but they treated with the land like the prophets of Israel, fighting the elements and their enemies with a strong right arm and a simple, abiding faith.

Matthew watched Klyn as he dealt with them, buying well with the small amount of money they had pooled. Their stock grew, for there were many who were anxious to sell. There were times, Matthew knew, when Klyn would have overpaid the patriarchs he bargained with, but it was they who would only accept a fair price for their animals. Ruin may face them, but to trade fairly was more important, to be able to kneel at the *kerk* with a clear conscience far outweighed any consideration of unreasonable profit.

Matthew's cages were soon noisy with kakoek hens, and Boie, now armed with a musket, guarded eighty head of cattle as they fattened on lush grass. A hundred and fifty sheep joined them over the next few days.

Matthew and the boys replaced the disselboom shafts, adding another sail of waterproofed canvas to the hoops of the wagons. The long days of trading and preparation, the nights of planning, swept past like so many blurring playing cards.

Klyn seemed to have forgotten that Kit had ever existed. He was in constant motion, talking stock and routes and weather and water, the miles that could be traveled in any given day, laughing rather than drawing breath.

For Matthew it was different. He did what was necessary, but his concentration was abstracted by the image of violet eyes under a mane of red hair. He listened for any mention of her name, any grain of information about the man Laidler. He was too proud to ask directly; all he knew was what Sergeant Coffee had told him when he had visited the army compound outside town.

Leaving Klyn with the wagons, Matthew had taken the tin box of papers they had salvaged from Captain Cornwell's wagon and sought an interview with Sergeant Coffee. He found the soldiers bivouacked on the western edge of town, ridge tents in neat rows under the British Jack and inside a hedge of mopani thorn.

A sentry took him to the officer's tent where Sergeant Coffee greeted him with warm solemnity. "Right good to see you again, Mr. Eastman, but for the circumstances...."

They shook hands and sat under the rapping canvas, silent while an orderly served them with mugs of army-issue tea. Then Matthew handed over the tin box and described the circumstances under which he had come by it. Coffee, despite his craggy professionalism, and his stated views of the officer class, was touched by Cornwell's death much more than he would have cared to admit.

When Matthew had finished, Coffee said, "I thank you for giving the lads and the captain a decent burial, and for saying the words, Mr. Eastman. Seems we're bound by killings, you and me. Captain Cornwell was a good soldier and a gentleman, if you get my meaning. I'll have to write up a report and have you sign alongside it."

Matthew said he would be glad to.

"This woman." Coffee stopped writing longhand. "This Miss Spenser? She wouldn't by any chance be Colonel Spenser's daughter?"

Matthew said she was.

"Irregular, that side of it; don't know what the Captain was thinking of. Was he following Colonel Spenser's orders, bringing her up here?"

"No chance, I'd say. Look, when you've met the lady you'll know how she could talk Satan into Gabriel's shift."

"So I've heard. There's always talk about quality skirts on the Cape." Coffee wrote more of his careful copperplate, keeping his thoughts to himself. He had to play things along right to keep the Captain's record clean. "You setting out for the north, lad?" he asked over the scratching quill.

"In a few days. We aim to catch up with Cilliers's party."

"You'll have to move fast to do that. By rights, I ought to stop you, but how in the world could I do that? There's naught we can do for you once you cross the Orange, you know. That's bad country and we've no jurisdiction, I'm glad to say. If you get through the Mfengu and the Xhosa you'll come up against the Matabele and the like. Still, you look set to do it."

"We are."

"There's others besides, you know. Them Griquas for some.

Ever seen a Griqua? I got a pair chained up here for causing a public affray."

"No," said Matthew.

Coffee almost smiled. "Drunk as sacks, belong to Laidler. They was shooting out the *O*'s in a saloon sign. The Boers don't like them at the best of times, call them Bastaards, and like to see them on their way as fast as they can. To me they are just half-breeds, like the Anglos in India. They get their money and they drink it away, sort of natural to them."

"You know Laidler, then?" Matthew spoke without inflection. Coffee's eyebrows lifted out of alignment.

"Know him? Bless you, he's one of the biggest men on the Cape. There's more than a hundred that jumps when he growls. He's got one of the biggest estates down there. Vineyards, bottling plant, mill, and cooperage. Has some ships too, I hear tell, and he's building a fine house in the Rhynveld Valley. A mansion. A fellow who made a friend of that one would be well placed for favors."

"What's he doing up here?"

"He hunts, lad. Ivory. That's what got him started, that and some sharp trading with Colonel Spenser...."

"Colonel Spenser and Laidler?" Matthew exclaimed despite himself.

"You seem surprised, but that was a while back. There's bad blood between them now. For a time their feuding split the merchants and the military down the middle."

"Miss Spenser was met by this...Laidler. They seem to know each other...well."

"Was she now." Coffee pursed his lips and scratched his mustache. "If she was traveling without her father's permission, it'll be bad for Captain Cornwell's record. It's like as not the story will be that money changed hands between the Captain and Laidler. Damn." Coffee nibbled one horn of his mustache and brooded out at the compound. A working party stamped past with shovels over their shoulders, horses champed as they were curried, and sentries marked post with shouts. Coffee came out of his reverie to say, "A dead man can't defend his reputation, so how am I going to couch my dispatch? Spenser will chew on his bones rather than eat his own cowcake." He was talking about Cornwell.

"Kit...." Matthew faltered. "Miss Spenser knows her own mind."

"And everybody else's it seems. A like pair, her and Laidler."

Matthew stopped himself from making a firm denial of that.

Coffee pulled a battered timepiece from his shirt. "Time I let Laidler's blacks go. Come and look at them. A sight, even out here."

They walked past a row of hobbled horses and a steaming field kitchen. A square of thorn quartered an area of beaten earth where a single stake had been driven into the ground. Two men sat against it, chained at the ankle. They wore greasy skin suits sewn with beads and gold amulets. Their long, kinky hair was tied in plaits and bound with gold wire. One of them had an ivory snuffbox fixed to his extended earlobe. Insolent and somehow proud, they watched Matthew and Coffee pass the sentry and approach them, their teeth bared.

"We go now, baas?" one grinned, offering a fettered boot.

"Corporal of the Guard," called Coffee, his pace stick tapping the ground.

"Sar'nt."

One of the Griquas spat in the dust as close to Coffee's boot as he dared. Coffee's stick jabbed him in the neck, pinning his head against the stake, forcing his eyes up into the sun.

"Now listen, you greasy half-black," Coffee said quietly, a saw in his voice. "One of my lads got himself a boot in the slats taking you two in. I don't take kindly to that. If I ever have sight of your ugly faces before you go back into the bush with your Baas Laidler, I shall shoot you both against the nearest wall. If I don't hang you. You want to hang from a tree for the buzzards, take just one drink, that's all. Just one."

"Baas Laidler don't let us die like dogs," said the Griqua, squinting at Coffee outlined against the glare, a green pallor under his skin. The pace stick drew a ring around his throat.

"Your Baas Laidler has made his point as forcible as he can," said Coffee. "I know he looks after his people, even pariahs like you. *But,* and this is where he gets off, he don't tell a Sergeant of the King's colors nothing he don't want to hear. Take that back to him, Bastaard. Until he's big enough to tear down that Jack yonder, he'll dance to my tune, and that could be at a rope's end between you two miserable specimens."

The Corporal unlocked the fetters and the Griquas got stiffly to their feet to make crosses on the detention sheet the Corporal held for them.

"Our guns, red soldier."

"Confiscated to pay your fines, Bastaard. Seems Baas Laidler figures to take the price of them out of your purses or your hides." Coffee jerked his stick at the gate, dismissing them.

The Griquas trudged away without looking back. Coffee shook his head after them, drawing a meaningless scribble in the dirt at his feet.

"Ugly pair, eh, lad? There're bands of itinerants like them all over the Drakensberg. Watch out for the likes when you're trekking. They run with renegade whites in the shanties along the river. They'll steal from Christian and Matabele alike. Cattle, powder, or rum. They ain't so nice about handling women neither."

Matthew was reminded of the dead family killed by white renegades he and Klyn had found in the hut on the trail and told Coffee.

"Then you know."

"Seems I do."

"At least those two serve a man who doesn't need to truck with that sort. Laidler would hang them himself if they or any of his boys so much as looked like stealing a twist of shag. He's known for never losing a servant or a clothespeg. He's that hard and that fair. When exactly are you pulling out?"

"Three or four days."

"Then I wish you well," said Coffee, offering his hand. "I hope you find what you're looking for on the high veldt. You people are leaving quietly; a peaceful secession, and I can admire that. They don't seem to care too much either, on the Cape. For what it's worth, lad, I think they're losing the best."

"Maybe we'll meet again."

"If God wills, and then under happier circumstances. Good luck, lad. Me, I'll still go on with the same old problems. Boys and horses, horses and boys."

"Would you have it any other way?" Matthew forced a laugh.

"Not on your life, laddie. Not on your life."

9

The lamps were lit and the sun was a dying ball beyond the fly-screened hotel windows.

Kit brushed her hair idly as Cord Laidler talked with two of his Khoikhoi scouts. Their musk overcame the scent of the wilting flowers arranged in bowls around the room. Their dusty boots had left a trail on the expensive carpet, and the maid's mouth was a thin line of disapproval.

Cord lounged on an overstuffed chesterfield, giving rapid instructions in the Khoikhoi dialect. He was talking about the ivory hunt, the last he would make before returning to the Cape.

Kit breathed perfume from a glass stopper. Master and man stank alike on the trail, but in the stifling humidity of the hotel room, it was different and hard to bear.

Even in repose, Cord gave off an air of commanding arrogance, ready to tear down the world and remake it to his liking. He would never be satisfied with what he had, always reached for more, insatiably. She had seen it the first time they had met, and recognized the same flaw in herself, the same overweening appetite for the unattainable.

"You will report to me in the morning at first light." Cord stood and went to the window, turning his back on the two men. They backed hastily from the room.

"We leave a day early, Katherine. Which means that the Dominee must come tomorrow and do whatever he has to do."

Kit nodded although a splinter of doubt sharpened her tone. "We could wait until we come back...."

"Oh no." Cord tipped a brandy decanter over a tall glass. "If the hunt is as successful as I plan, we'll bypass this dull stinkhole and head straight for the Cape. No, Katherine, we'll marry as planned."

Kit rose, the blood pounding in her hurt shoulder. Over the last four nights, Cord had demonstrated an unmanageable and savage appetite. He had pawed her body like a predator, intimately and possessively. In the heat of passion her lust had equaled his, and even now, feeling sick and giddy, she would have given herself to him if he gave the slightest sign of desire. This self-knowledge humbled and weakened her, adding to her growing irritation.

"Ah, it slipped my mind. You have a visitor." Cord skimmed a square of cream card at her. It sailed onto the chair she had just vacated and she saw it was a plain card with the hotel crest on it.

A name was written there, the big and round characters of a man little used to writing. Matthew Eastman. She had to read it twice before the name registered.

"Cord, this is..."

"I know who it is. It's that brave young rustic who saved your honor."

"Shall we have him up here?"

Cord stayed at the window. "I've thanked him once. Would you have me offer him money? If he's trekking with the other fools he'll have little enough. How much do you think you're worth, Katherine?" Kit stared at him coldly as he swallowed brandy and grinned with the lower half of his face. "Still the grand lady, Katherine? Forgive me, I misjudged your response to my humor. You see your heroic herder and offer him whatever reward you think fit. He deserves a great deal for bringing you safe to me. Tell him Cord Laidler is eternally bound to him for his valor and gallantry." He bowed unsteadily.

"You're drunk," Kit observed stiffly.

"Just enough, my lady, just enough. You'll feel my weight tonight."

"That we will discuss later."

The closing door cut his booming laugh in half.

Kit smoothed her hair and dress and walked slowly down the stairs to the half-landing where she paused to watch the lobby. It was empty but for Matthew and the desk clerk, and the trekker seemed as out of place as a tree in a ballroom. Kit swept down the last flight of stairs and watched his gaze drawn toward her.

"Kit?"

He had never seen her in a dress, she realized. And she had never seen him without the dark growth of ragged hair on his face.

"You look...different."

"And you, Matthew." She pretended to study him. "Without the beard I see you are a most handsome young man."

Matthew was lost in a gathering silence.

"Come, let's walk outside for a moment. This is not a place for old friends to meet and talk."

Outside, Kit took his arm, grateful for the cool evening air scented by the pitch flares that lit the street.

"We're leaving in the morning," Matthew said abruptly. "We've bought some good stock, the wagons are ready, and...well, I've just come to say goodbye."

Most of the frontages were dark and guttering lamplight bled through few of the windows. After the frenetic bustle of the day there was a sudden, rare quiet over the town.

"How is your shoulder?"

"Healing nicely...." Kit stopped walking and turned to face him. In the half-light her hair was dull copper, her eyes almost black. The corners of her mouth turned up and bared white eyeteeth. "I was going to ask you to take care of yourself, but that really isn't necessary, is it? You'll survive the final trump, I think."

"Will you marry him?" Matthew asked bluntly.

"Yes. Just as you will marry your little girl, the one you left behind."

"Elise? How did you know? Did Klyn—?"

"Of course not; you told me yourself. It's in your eyes. You love her."

"I thought so once."

"Think so again, Matthew. It's best you do."

"When I met you it changed."

"No, my dear, nothing changed. Believe that," Kit said firmly. "Say goodbye to Klyn for me, Matthew. Now I must go back."

"Not yet." Matthew caught at her and she was against him, her mouth caught by his, her tongue running alive between his teeth. They clung for a breathless moment before her head twisted aside and her cheek rested against his shirt-front.

"Don't leave....I...I'm sorry," he stumbled.

"Don't be."

Kit disengaged herself, looking hard into his face. Then, deliberately, like a sightless person imprinting a shape and a thousand textures on her memory, she ran her hands over his loins and chest.

"I'll see you again, Matthew Eastman," she said. "Remember me."

Then she was gone.

10

The going was hard and slow.

The long drought had baked the earth, crazing it into hard scales separated by cracks and fissures. The brush and thorn were brittle, seared black by the sun's anvil. Vultures panted under spread wings, too hot to squabble over carrion. The lizards stayed buried until nightfall.

Bush fires were a constant hazard. One spark from a pipe, a flint skittering from beneath a hoof could have started an inferno with nowhere to run for sanctuary. The wild game suffered badly, dying in their hundreds, mummified by the intense heat before decay could start. Water holes dried up and the animals fled north, driven toward water by instinct. The rarefied air lost its heat at night and the cold burned as hard as the midday sun.

Matthew and Klyn sweated all day and shivered under their blankets at night. They lost weight and suffered from dehydration, their tongues furring and swelling in their mouths until they could hardly talk. They ate salt by the spoonful and rubbed animal grease into their skin to salve the burns. Their lips split and split again, causing them to converse in sign. Their beards and hair grew long and matted and their boys walked beneath their shields, complaining of sunburn.

They traveled during the cool of the day, resting up before the sun reached its zenith. They moved from water to water, resting often, staying for days where the grass was good.

They posted their guards around the animals and no longer raced toward the bleat of a terrified sheep. Whichever predator had struck, there was never a trace of the victim. When they dared, they lit fires around the herd and prayed the flames would keep the big cats away.

They built thorn kraals around their wagons whenever they stopped, for a hungry cat would take a man if it could. Lions stayed away, but the leopard and the lynx were always with them. They watched for amber eyes beyond the firelight, heard the coughs of anger from the outer darkness.

Each night, they tallied the animals and discussed the day, listening patiently to their boys' minor troubles, giving judgment where necessary.

There was no time to think of what they had left behind. They thought only of reaching the great Orange River, of crossing the hard country as quickly as possible.

The way was ahead.

11

They sensed it before they saw it.

They stood motionless, boys and stock and men, halted by no command, watching the way ahead grow out of the night.

They had started in darkness and had traveled through the quickening dawn to the edge of a depression ringed by kopjes and stunted mopani trees. Mist hugged the ground and the milky ghosts of mountains haunted the lower sky.

The oxen lowed into a wistful silence, muzzles close to the bitterly scented ground, smelling water off to the north. The stars faded into the paling sky as the first golden rays fingered the high ground and turned the distant mountains blue.

The ground mists burned away without a flurry and the ground sloped away and down to the banks of a river flanked by stands of willows. Cicadas began to shrill in the grass and a flock of cranes beat slowly out of the west.

Matthew took a step and then another, ran a few paces and turned to see Klyn half-erect over Pallas's saddle, a leg dangling, eyes fixed on the river.

Matthew gathered himself and vaulted into Gaika's saddle, bringing her head up and around. He rode up to Klyn and hit him hard on the bicep. "Yes?" he asked in a plume of his own breath.

"Yes." Klyn was positive.

"Yes!" Matthew shouted. "Yes!"

The boys began an impromptu jig. Boie fired his gun into the air, driving the groundbirds upward in a squalling frenzy. The sheep butted around and ran in rings. The oxen made for the water, following the trail of clods thrown up by Pallas and Gaika. Klyn's boys beat their shields, drumming for their gods.

Matthew tasted sudden bile when he brought Gaika up short at the bank. Klyn reined in and the two men stared with disbelief at the river as it swept furiously between two sheer banks. It was a heaving expanse of copper water with no real shallows, swollen and dimpled by a vicious, twisting undertow.

The early sun shimmered along the far shoreline, silvering the whitecaps breaking over the crowns of submerged rocks. A wild duck plumped into the water, bobbed up, and was borne past at running pace, spinning slowly.

It was not possible. Here was the mighty Orange River and there was no way of crossing with their stock and wagons. Matthew sat in a misery of impotent fury.

Klyn had dismounted and was walking beneath the willows that trailed their lower branches in the water. He was kicking the ground, slashing at the reeds, his head down between hunched shoulders. Matthew set Gaika's head to the west and jogged slowly to where Klyn was savaging the undergrowth. He was weary of the whole damnable trek and wanted to share his disillusion with Klyn. Perhaps they

111

should crack a jug and damn the whole venture as they drank themselves stupid.

Klyn straightened with a shout, flinging an arm up against Gaika's chest. Startled, the mare reared and threw Matthew in an arc over her rump. He struck the ground with his shoulder and the side of his neck.

Winded and furious, Matthew scrambled to his feet and was downed again as Gaika backed into him. A rock grazed his face and another numbed his hipbone. Klyn was jigging about, mad words showering from his opened mouth as he beat his thighs with clenched fists.

Matthew rolled from under his mare's dancing hooves, found his feet, and spat grass and seeds from his mouth. Klyn pranced on like a madman and Matthew thought he must knock him down and truss him up before he injured himself with his lunatic actions.

"See!" Klyn bawled. "Look around!" He waved a handful of whipping strands. "Rawhide, Matthew. *Riempie!*"

"I'm not blind, man. So *what?*"

"So what, *boet?* Look: Cilliers was here, man. Cilliers. See there, stripped willow branches. There, in that clearing, the stumps of the trees they felled. There, a broken disselboom shaft. They were here. Cilliers was here!"

Matthew saw what Klyn had seen and understood. He nodded slowly, recognizing the marks of construction sites, the discarded branches and the leather strips. He looked out over the wild spate of the river, working it out in his mind.

"They stripped their wagons," he said, the idea growing. "They built rafts and floated them across. Think of it, fifty wagons or more. God alone knows how many head of stock. Children, mothers, hens and sheep and milch cows. They took them all over...."

Klyn spat on his hands and mimed a swinging ax. "If they did it, so can we, neh?"

There was no other way and there was no time to delay.

They set Abba and his boys to felling the Babylonian willows and to stripping the branches. Boie's party made plaited ropes from the spare canvas and hide thongs to lash the rafts together. Matthew and Klyn unloaded the wagons and dismantled them. The first raft was ready by nightfall and they worked by the light of tallow candles to complete a second by the following dawn.

Matthew drew in the sand at first light.

"We must pass a rope to the other side," he told the assembled boys. "Tie it to the raft so that it can be towed across. Another rope fixed to this side of the river will bring it back. The first load will be the oxen; we will need their strength to pull the rafts with the wagons aboard. As one raft goes across, the other can be loaded up. That way, we can cut the crossing time in half."

He leaned back on his haunches and looked out over the tumbling water to the bleached winter grassland of the Drakensberg Mountains beyond. Waterfowl clamored from upstream and the warm scent of wild flowers rode on the breeze that stirred the willows around them. Klyn's black clothes were rusty in the clear light.

"Which of us goes across to fasten the first rope, *boet?*"

"I'll kiss the ground for you," said Matthew, walking over to Gaika.

Klyn stared at the stubborn set of Matthew's mouth and the way he held himself, much like a fighter squaring for a winner-take-all contest. It was a stance he had come to know well.

He tried though. "It is me who must go, *boet.*"

Matthew's voice had no inflection, no warmth. "You're too heavy. You don't swim all that well, either. In that torrent you wouldn't stand a chance. There's no choice."

"I swim like a crocodile and Pallas can carry a regiment." Klyn snarled, hating the truth.

Matthew mounted up and smiled briefly. "Liar."

Klyn nodded gravely. "True," he said. "But no other man could tell me that to my face."

"No other man could *find* your face."

"Also true."

Matthew made three turns of the rope around his waist and tied the end to his pommel, then he urged Gaika down to the water's edge.

"Give her her head, Matthew. Don't let her panic."

Matthew spurred the mare down the bank, angling her into the current. She shied as the chill water closed over her hindquarters and immediately her feet lost the river bottom in a swirl of mud and pebbles. The undertow dragged both horse and rider sideways and down, and for a single, eternal moment, both disappeared beneath the surface.

Sweating and waiting, Klyn played the plaited canvas rope through his hands and the line of boys behind him followed his lead, seeing the swell of his great neck as he held his breath.

The rope swung downriver with the current, slackening as the undertow died on a reef and man and beast fought to regain the surface. There was a tight-lipped silence, then, in a great upsurge of spray, first Gaika's, then Matthew's head broke the rolling pillows of brown water.

Boie cried out in high pitch as Klyn took up tension on the rope, hand over hand, bawling for the boys to follow suit, all of them hauling like madmen.

For Matthew, the time underwater was a long ordeal where he forgot the land and the reasons for striving upward. The cold blindness took first his notions of up and down and then his will to fight for them. The struggling mare was an irritation and his own identity seemed to shrink to nothing, replaced by an indifference for survival that bordered on a need to accept that the outcome rested with a force he no longer cared to control. He was shrinking inside the negative brownness and longing to open his mouth to swallow infinity and rest.

Then they were bursting into the sun-warmed air and Matthew was trying to breathe for Gaika and himself, pumping reassurance to the mare through his thigh muscles.

Easy, he thought, meaning, fight, you stupid horse.

Water sprayed from Gaika's nostrils and mane as she gained her equilibrium and swam hard for the land. Matthew's ears sang from the pressure and cold, his lungs raw from constriction.

With infinite slowness the far bank closed and the tempo of the river speeded up as it churned against the rocky banks. A whole drowned tree swept past, its roots clogged with earth, its branches heavy with yellowed leaves, an unconcerned grebe perched on the trunk, billing its breast feathers.

The sight was reassuring. Matthew lay on the water and gripped the saddle pommel with both hands, giving Gaika full rein, watching her head and neck bow and plunge ahead of him. So long as he held on and did not add his full weight to her back, she could make the far bank, he knew. He wanted to look back at Klyn and dared not, fearing that if he took his eyes from the land ahead he would be swept away.

Gaika's front hooves skittered on shale, bit, then slid away as a freshet of current pushed her back into deeper water.

The mare surged with the current. Again she touched land, gathered herself, and struck into the mud. With a low snort she heaved herself up and out onto a shelf of firm ground, high-stepping onto crisp grass like a new colt feeling its legs.

114

Matthew was scraped over rock and grass and he released his grip from the rope around the pommel when his fingers had solved the mystery of the swollen knots. He fell into stubble and dried gorse and the sun struck steam from his clothes.

The blue-white sky beat clean above him and the earth under his aching belly was unmoving and reassuringly hard. He spat brackish water and remained sprawled on his face until Gaika whinnied close to his face.

Then he climbed to his knees, bowed forward, and solemnly kissed the ground. When he made his feet and threw two great handfuls of earth into the air, the veldt erupted with the sounds of relieved joy from across the river.

12

There was a stillness over the great kraal of the Matabele.

Mzilikazi, the Great Bull Elephant, King of a Thousand Impi, had ordered a killing day, a day when the witchmen would make great *mouti,* magic that would cleanse and strengthen the tribe, weaken their enemies, make the warriors fierce and the women fertile.

It was written in the earth and stones of the centuries.

The old men and women marked for death had been gathered in bonds by the precipice at the end of the kraal. They stood waiting to be clubbed and thrown to the vultures. The vultures were the adopted children of Mzilikazi, the King. His own people were dogs beneath his heel and were proud to serve such a powerful king even though they might become fodder for his adopted children.

The unmarried girls sat in rows before the huts circling the central compound. Their eyes were lowered and their small maidenhead spears rested on their thighs, held lightly between crossed fingers. The regiments of the impi stood in silent lines curving out from the raised throne; the King on his throne was the bull's head and the impi were its horns. The Snakes, the Ill-Tempered, the Sticks, the Bees, and the Invincibles—all the regiments were waiting for the King to signal the start of the clubbing.

Mzilikazi sat in state in the morning sun, pondering as horsehair fans kept the swarms of flies from his great drum of a belly.

Prostrate on the beaten earth before him was Jakot, one of his scouts. Jakot's nose touched the ground; his message was delivered and he knew that his own belly might be opened in public as a punishment for bearing bad news.

Jakot had drawn an ocher Earth Mother symbol beneath his loincloth as protection. It was a bad death, to lie screaming as the dogs ate your living entrails. He had laughed from the ranks of the impi to see others die this way, fighting the mongrels for their own stomachs, but now he wondered what he had found so amusing about such life-and-death scrambles. Jakot trembled and tried not to sneeze.

Mzilikazi looked at the severed white heads lying by his feet, their beards matted with their own blood, their light blue eyes frozen open. They were corngrowers from across the mountains and they had come to the land of the Matabele without permission, and had compounded their crime by hunting.

Mzilikazi kicked a skin over the blind faces so as not to look at them any more. They offended him. The heads would be thrown into a midden where his warriors would defecate on them and bind their souls to the earth.

The scout Jakot was the third to bring him reports of white men coming in strength. There might be more than he knew and these men were as bad as the Zulu or the Griqua *bandetiiri* who crossed the Vaal River to steal his cattle and women and to trap his game unlawfully.

It was no easy thing to rule this land, taken by force from the Bantu, held now by force of arms. Of all his river boundaries, the Vaal was the most sensitive. His impi held the Limpopo, the Crocodile, and the Molopo easily, but the Vaal was different. All his veterans could lose themselves in the gullies, kloofs, and tributaries there. It was bad country, where the Matabele themselves sickened and died if they stayed too long, almost as bad as the Limpopo where flies and mosquitoes swarmed and cattle died of the wasting sickness.

Mzilikazi measured his vast kingdom by the days his warriors took to march around it. The fact that his territory covered thirty thousand square miles meant nothing to him. Ruling it was another matter entirely. It was a heavy burden and there could be no weakness in him. That was why he had ordered this purge of the old and infirm. The tribe must stay young and strong.

He addressed the scout: "Where is this Bastaard you brought?"

116

"Lord Elephant, he lies in the dust outside the sacred ground of your kraal," said Jakot, sweating into the earth.

"He lives, dog?"

"Aye, Lord. He loses blood from the side—a thrust as he was taken."

Mzilikazi turned to his chief witchman. "Have the Griqua flogged and brought before me," he said, raising his knob-kerrie as a signal. A long sigh went up from the assembled warriors. The killing would now begin.

The first old man was brained and flung from the ledge, to break open on the rocks below like a rotten yam.

The impi stamped, roared *"Bayete!"* and rattled spear against shield as the women keened and beat their open palms on the ground. As the executioners moved methodically down the line with their hardwood clubs, beef and ale were brought to the King, who drank steadily without wiping off his mouth. Blowflies gathered on the platters and clouded over the bloody killing ground. Vultures sailed in from the southern heights to drop squabbling on the fresh corpses. Bloodstink, sweat, and smoke formed an evil pall over the kraal.

When the killing was done the Griqua was dragged naked before Mzilikazi and thrown down before him, his head held by a wooden yoke. There were fresh stripes across his legs and torso and his nostrils bled where a gold ornament had been torn away. As he rolled onto his side to avoid a kick, Mzilikazi noted a crusted, weeping *iKlwa* wound below his third rib. The witchman capered, clacked tortoise shells, and flicked pinches of crimson dust into the Griqua's ruined face. He gave a last piercing ululating cry and left a hard quiet as sudden as a spearthrust. All eyes turned to the King.

Mzilikazi saw that the prisoner's wits were still his own and had not flown into the wind away from the pain. The Griqua's breath was as ragged as torn cloth and Mzilikazi smiled for sport.

"You know our ways, half-man. You must die. How will it be?"

The Griqua did not hesitate. "The assegai."

Without needing to look, Jakot the scout knew that the prisoner's wounds festered and that he would die in agony anyway. He also knew the Griqua did not merit a quick death from a stabbing spear. Too honorable and too clean. He listened to the King's words.

"That cannot be," Mzilikazi said. "You came to my land
117

to steal elephant's teeth. The spear is for warriors and you are a thief. You are for the dogs, the slow fire, or for the women to play with. Any of those would be just."

"No, Lord Elephant," the Griqua pleaded. "I did only what my master bid me do. I did not hunt the elephant for myself, but for Baas Laidler. He is your enemy, not me. I did only what a true servant should do, obey."

"You lie, half-man. Your master, this Laidler, is a white and not of your kind. His blood is clay-water and a good dog does not serve a chalk jackal. Choose."

"I am a prince among my people," panted the Griqua, showing courage. "I have royal blood. I will die with dignity."

"No," Mzilikazi said with quiet enjoyment. "You will just die."

The Griqua screamed until a blow smashed his mouth. As he arched back against the yoke which held him, the witch-man opened his suppurating wound with a single slash. He was dragged away with the women mobbing around, jabbing at him with their stone knives. He was tied to a spit and carried bodily to the killing ground where a charcoal pit was being kindled.

If the women were not too eager, he would last long into the night.

Mzilikazi put him from his mind and summoned his chief induna, Mkalipi.

"This dog," he said, brushing his foot against Jakot's head, "is one that I gave you."

"Yes, Lord."

"He is offal."

"Truly, Lord. Let me kill him for you. No man should offend his king."

"That is so, but did he not find these whites and slay them for his king?"

"That is also true, Lord. He has washed his spear many times for you, *Bayete*. But as you say with wisdom, he is stinking offal."

"But he is still a king's offal. Better than a warrior's meat."

"Yes, Lord."

"Then he is yours again. I want his spear red. Take him."

Jakot backed away on hands and knees until he lost himself in the ranks of the impi. He was trembling. That night he would offer a goat to the Earth Mother, and many whites would die for Mzilikazi the great King of the Heavens, the

Bull Elephant of the Matabele, the Great Lion's Paw. Around him the regiments roared with approval as spear crashed on shield and their stamping feet shook the earth. *"Bayete. Bayete, nkosi enkulu—* Great King!"

"With respect, Lord, that was well done," said Mkalipi when silence fell.

"It was needed. They will fight better for it. And fight they will," Mzilikazi said dourly. "Listen now to my words. There are three parties of these whites that we know about. Two have stock and women and children with them. The other is led by a man who comes only for ivory. I know this man. The last time he came we were not able to overcome him, for our spears were pointed at Zulu hearts. This time we will destroy him and the yellow men who serve him."

"Aye, Lord."

"These others, these corngrowers, are worse yet. They come to stay. They look for land in my land, for cattle among my herds. They would take our women and boys to serve them under the yoke. It is their way. But I tell you this: *we will rid the land of this plague!*"

"I hear, Lord. Tell me what I must do?"

"You will make war on these white men and kill all their men and boys. You will take all their young women and girls and bring them here to be my women. Their beasts shall be my beasts, their wagons shall be as mine to use. You, Mkalipi, will do these things."

"They are done, Lord."

"Leave their bodies where they fall, for the carrion eaters, as we did with the Sotho and their many tribes. Let their bones be testament to those who wish to follow and face my spears. Now go!"

The women began to chant as the impi regiments moved off to receive their orders, already mourning for those who would not return. Returning heroes should not face tears.

Mzilikazi sat without moving until the stamping heels no longer shook the earth. The idea of the white women serving him seemed good, but the thought of their colorless bodies soured his digestion. They must have sinned badly in their graves, these clay people, to have been spat back through the stone teeth of the old mud father.

It was better to sin in this life than the next, he decided.

13

They had the wagons across by midafternoon, just before the current strengthened, running a foot higher than the previous day. They lost too many sheep. The animals had reached the center of the river before they panicked, pulled free of their hobbles, and tumbled into the broiling water. Fifty of them had gone in as many seconds, swept away and gone before they reached the bend in the river. After that, they crossed the animals blindfolded and in smaller numbers.

It was past midnight before Klyn crossed with the last of the cattle, stumbling with fatigue as he jumped ashore. Without a word he threw himself down beside the fire and slept on his face until the following noon.

When Matthew himself awoke, the wagons were reassembled and reloaded, and only Abba and Boie were on their feet, facing outward toward the north, guarding the camp.

The air was still and a crane stalked fish on the far bank. The river was a marmalade surge dappled with gold, and the Drakensberg range was azure and cobalt against a white-hot and endless sky.

Matthew's staleness joined with the tart fragrance of the earth in his nostrils as he roused himself and found himself some food, wolfing down mealie cakes and coffee as though they were his first breakfast in a century. He squatted by the fire and grinned at Klyn, who slept like a dead crusader.

A good man to face any danger with, thought Matthew, tearing at biltong with his teeth. We have done so much, he and I; but for him I might have moldered away back in Colesberg, mooning over a woman with red hair who belongs to another man; that's if I'd ever left the farm in the first place. Ach, we will build empires, he and I. We will raise a thousand children with golden skins and great appetites. Between us we will populate half the unknown continent and grow old to the laughter of a hundred thousand grandchildren.

Then Matthew rose and drew back his foot, aiming deliberately.

He kicked Klyn hard in the side.

"Wake up, you idle *dassie*. The day's half gone."

14

Eight mornings later, they heard the gunfire.

The small popping sounds echoed between the kopjes, rattling and fading to the southwest. Boie was scouting far ahead of the train and he came back to the wagons at nightfall, his foal lathered and coughing with exhaustion. Boie's throat was gummed closed by thirst and it was many minutes before he could talk coherently. They were careful not to give him too much water at once.

"Hunters," he said finally. "Six of them, Nkosi. They wear the big hats and trousers to here." Boie marked a line above his ankle. "They have two horses for each man. No wagons."

"Doppers,"* said Klyn. "They must be outriders for Cilliers's train."

"There is wagon spoor, Nkosi. Half a day there, where the iron arrow always points. They part so." Boie made a V in the air. "Maybe ten days old."

"They've split up?" asked Klyn. "Why would they do that?"

Matthew did not know. "To find grazing maybe. They may well have three or four thousand head with them. It would take a lot of veldt to feed that number at this time of the year. The ground will give up very little until spring, neh?"

"Could be, *boet*." Klyn was not convinced.

"There is other sign." Boie took a deep draft of water and ran a flat palm off toward the southwest. "Many feet without shoes, and men's droppings. As many as our sheep have legs."

"Bantu?" asked Matthew.

"No, Nkosi. I find monkey fur in the thorn. Some white hairs from a cow's tail. Many warriors."

"Matabele." Klyn's face was hard, his voice remote. "The Xhosa are like sick women beside them. Pray that they welcome us, *boet*. Once they come, they'll fight until they win or die."

"Boie," said Matthew. "There was shooting. Was that the Doppers hunting?"

Boie shook his head. "No, Nkosi, that was shooting from where the wagons were. Here." Again he indicated the southwest.

Doppers. Religious sect of trekking Boers.

121

"Sweet Jesus," Matthew murmured. "I wonder if the Doppers heard as well?"

"There may be nothing to know." Klyn's expression denied his words.

"Is that what you think?"

Klyn reached for his gun and checked the priming.

"I don't want to think. I know in my water there's been a massacre. Those guns would have gone on longer if there'd been a straight fight."

"Then we must travel now," Matthew said, checking his pistols. "We can't wait for morning. Look, Klyn, I'll go on ahead and..."

"No, *boet*. Not this time."

"Look...."

"The river was yours, Matthew, this is mine, neh? You swim and I'll track. I'd send Abba or Boie because they're better than both of us, but if there're any survivors, they'll shoot the first black face they see."

"Straws, we'll draw for it."

"Unless you think you can knock me down with your fists, shut up," Klyn said quietly, seriously angry.

Matthew was forced to shrug and accept.

"Better. Maybe I'll catch up with the Doppers or cross the wagons that turned off. I'll leave sign as I go, so keep the boys riding a sweep as you come on. A cairn of stones to the right of the trail means go east, to the left, veer west. An arrow means straight on."

"And to stop?"

"You'll see my body plain enough."

15

The calf the witchman sacrificed had a raddled liver and augured nothing; neither could there be a purification.

Mkalipi was pleased and strove not to show it. Now his decision alone would guide the impi, not some sign the witchmen read in entrails. How could a baby cow know more about strategy than he did? Foolishness for old matrons and beardless boys. Signs did not kill whites. Spears and cunning did. Where he could, Mkalipi would attack at night when the *iKlwa* was surer than a gun. He sent the witchmen back to Mzilikazi with that message and hoped the King would not interfere.

Mkalipi did not wait for a reply. He split his force into

three regiments. He sent the first northeast to the river, the second to the west where the white ivory hunter was camped, and personally led the third regiment due east to the high ground overlooking the Vaal River. That was where most of the whites would be and most of the cattle would be taken. Mkalipi planned to kill with profit, to take the vast herds back to Mzilikazi and become his only right arm, raised above all the other indunas.

16

Klyn came out of the veldt with the sun at his back and lost his profile in the glare. He had seen the wagon from the high ground and had come on to the river with great caution. It stood in the middle of the wide and sluggish stretch of water that was the Vaal. No oxen were yoked to the shaft and the loose canvas slapped against the hoops. Rusty stains smeared the sideboards and something half-submerged rolled lazily in against the front wheel, dipped, and floated out again as the wind played with it. A solitary boot stood sentinel on the foreshore.

Klyn watched from the bank until the silence screamed at him.

Employing patience, even when his was exhausted, Klyn hobbled Pallas in a gully where the grass was sweet and no worrying scents would reach him. A whinny now could cost him his life.

He lay on the shadowed side of a rise for another long count and then slid backward onto the lower slopes, moving crabwise out into the river.

The man in the water was face down and his mutilated back showed through his ribboned shirt. Klyn caught him up by the armpits and dragged him to the southern bank where he turned the body face up and used thumb and forefinger to close the hating eyes.

He found a man and a woman where they had fallen together, back to back. She had a spear through her left breast which had lodged in her rib cage so firmly Klyn could not pull it out. When he crossed her hands he found them blackened by powder burns. She must have taken many Matabele with her, he thought.

A boy who might have been ten or eleven lay beside the dying fire, slumped and small and calm, much as though he slept until the fatal thrust in his chest had healed. There were some women huddled under a baobab tree where they had been used and killed and mutilated. Klyn began to bring them all together for burial, for although sense told him to leave them where they lay, his faith urged otherwise.

He was looking around for a shovel when he saw the dust coming from the east. Pallas was too far away and there was nowhere safe under the trees. He waded out into the river and climbed into the wagon where he lay on a mattress, one eye to a chink in the boards, his smoothbore and pistols beside him, lead balls between his teeth and his powder flask close to hand.

The cloud of dust eddied and died in a depression about a quarter of a mile away and there was another long pause when nothing happened.

Klyn longed for water. The slap of the river as it swilled around the wheel spokes heightened his thirst. He closed off that part of his mind and waited.

Then, suddenly, and for no reason he understood, his skin prickled. Was it something he had heard or smelled? He did not know, it was just something.

There was a scrape from somewhere below his belly, deep in the wagon bed, a small mouse's sound. Were they already beneath the wagon, waiting to spear him through a gap in the boards? Christ. He was too desiccated to sweat.

Klyn eased the corner of the mattress back, a pistol cocked and pointed. From the space between two chests, a small, pale face looked up into his. Eyes as big as blue sunflowers, a grubby thumb in a tiny pink mouth. Another snuggled lower, too frightened to do anything but stare and silently hiccup.

"God Almighty," he whispered. "Girl children."

The elder girl held her sister close and her mouth trembled into a smile that would not sustain itself.

Klyn made a conscious effort to keep the ferocity out of his face.

"We have to stay quiet," he said. "It's a game. We stay very quiet. Can you play that game?"

The girl stroked her sister's tangled hair and gave him a single, grave nod.

"Good, we start now." Klyn let the mattress fall back and considered the prize that silence might bring them all. Life for silence. The chance for the children to grow and grow old

124

in exchange for silence. Death was a hell of a forfeit in this new game the girls were playing....

The dust cloud was on the move again. He could make out two columns, moving in a pincer to north and south, circling his position. He was downwind and no sound carried to him.

Perhaps if he made off downriver he could draw them away from the wagon? If there were only a few he might hold them off from where he was.

He was still working on the problem when the first horseman came out of the trees at a walk and halted just beyond the drop of shadow, a clear and clean target except for his face, which was lost under the brim of his broad felt hat. He could have been anybody.

Probably is, thought Klyn, a slick of sweat on the bridge of his nose, wondering if he was thinking straight. He gathered his smoothbore along his body and eased back the hammer very, very slowly, still playing the silence game.

The rider spurred his horse out across the flats and into the water; it was clear he had read the tracks of the dead man's heels where Klyn had dragged him up the bank. He eased his horse to a standstill and whistled around two fingers, the warble of a lilac roller. Then, deliberately and without haste, he reversed his smoothbore and slid it down into his saddle scabbard.

Hooves drummed from the opposite bank and four riders splashed into the water and fanned out all around the wagon.

Klyn ran his smoothbore out over the sideboard, drawing a bead on the first man. "Hold," he shouted. "Stay where you are."

The lead rider tagged his rein and raised his hands palms showing, kneeing his horse so that it came on toward Klyn at its own pace. As he came, the rider swept off his hat to show his face, his hawk's features calm and pleasant, his manner relaxed.

"Easy, *vriend,* put up your gun," he said. "My name is Johannes Krige. Come, *kerel,* we are friends."

Klyn laughed and took deep breaths. He lowered the hammer on his gun and withdrew it, suddenly anxious to let the children out into the light.

"The game is over," he said as he peeled back the mattress. "The game is over...."

17

It would be the last stand, Cord Laidler promised himself.

Three more days to get upwind of the last standing herd and take the tusks. Time enough for the last big kill and be gone before the Matabele could get too close.

Mzilikazi's impi were at least four days' march away, he reckoned, and there were concentrations of trekking Boers in between. Let them take the brunt with their guns and Bibles, and give him time to make his kill. The Dutch were looking for paradise and Cord was certain the Matabele would oblige by dispatching them with some alacrity. Yes, those bull tusks were safely his.

He had already sent most of his wagons back, and they would be across the Vaal before Mzilikazi's forward scouts could locate them. Once across the river they would head directly for the Cape.

The five wagons he was keeping with him would travel fast and light, and, by having the foresight to have fresh ox teams outspanned along his return route, he could travel for twelve hours at a stretch. He would outwit Mzilikazi yet again. In many ways though, thought Laidler, it was a pity he wouldn't have the opportunity to look into the black King's face as he drew a bead. A great pity, what a trophy his head would make.

He watched Katherine sit her horse as though she were in a public park with cool drinks and a parasol a fingersnap away. She had dropped four bulls and a cow like a veteran, wet-thumbing her foresight between shots like a cadet at the butts.

His wife. His woman.

Cord Laidler was suddenly anxious for nightfall.

18

The Blesberg mountain had grown out of the horizon many days before, calling them on to laager in its shadow. The basalt and indigo mountain reared up starkly, its white guano hat shimmering.

Matthew and Klyn pushed their spans as hard as they dared, wanting speed, yet anxious to preserve their animals' condition. Krige and his men stayed with them until they were twenty miles from the great camp, then they rode ahead to report to Potgieter, and to compare their findings with other scouting parties. They had also taken the two girls with them to find homes with other families, and both Matthew and Klyn found themselves extremely reluctant to see them go; they had become fond of the children in the brief time they had been with them, and hoped they were young enough to forget the horrors they had witnessed on the Vaal when their family had been cut down all around them.

When they outspanned for the night, Klyn and Matthew talked.

"We could not have asked for more," Klyn said with satisfaction. "To find that Cilliers and Potgieter have joined forces is almost too good to be true, *boet*. Now there will be no more straying off to be cut down by the Matabele. It was a hard lesson learned the hard way, but at least it has been learned early, neh?"

"And the children will be safe," said Matthew. "But Klyn, I thought the Matabele never used our women badly. What you told me about the Vaal, that was bad."

"It was bad." Klyn raked at the fire. "We buried eleven burghers, four women, and two children. There were other children in the party, but we never found them. Two of the women had been...used." Sparks rushed up past his angry face. "It shows us that Mzilikazi fears us, and rightly."

Matthew saw Kit lying splayed and bloody in his mind's eye and shivered. "What kind of men are the Matabele? Killing children."

"Mzilikazi is a Zulu and has made this new nation of his by being ruthless. It is what the kaffirs understand, what they have come to expect from a great king. To keep his power, Mzilikazi must kill all those who oppose or slight him. Just to be accused of treason is enough to deserve the death penalty. He kills the women and girls in his seraglio if they so much as squabble among themselves. One of his wives ran away with one of his indunas. Mzilikazi had them brought back to him and the man was killed on the spot. The woman would have been disemboweled or put to the stake but for the intervention of a white missionary Mzilikazi keeps with him. This man pleaded for her life and the King promised not to lay a hand on her. The missionary went away, thinking he had stayed Mzilikazi's hand. When he returned some days later, he found that the wife had been sealed up in her hut and left to starve to death. Mzilikazi saw nothing wrong with that and could not understand why the missionary was upset

127

by his action. You see, the King knew the woman must die, and his way would have been more humane. The missionary never interfered again."

Matthew spat into the fire in disgust.

"Understand Mzilikazi before you condemn him, *boet*. He must kill to remain strong. To show mercy would weaken his grip on his people. Remember that and come to terms with it; we weren't invited here, and his warriors will be waiting for us," Klyn warned before rolling himself into his blanket and dropping off to sleep with his usual ease.

Matthew watched the flames long into the night.

As they neared the great laager outspanned beneath the Blesberg, they saw that the surrounding countryside was thick with wagons and stock. The second wave of trekkers had joined the forerunners who had retreated from their isolated positions north of the Vaal River. Even the most independently spirited Boer recognized the need for a concerted joint stand against the marauding Matabele. Maroko, chief of the Baralong clans, also feared Mzilikazi, and he welcomed the trekkers into his kingdom, seeing them as powerful allies against his stronger enemy.

The Dopper sect headed by Hendrik Potgieter and his ally, Sarel Cilliers, had drawn up their wagons together and apart from the other burghers, pasturing their animals on the lush slopes well away from the other groups. Matthew and Klyn outspanned alongside their laager and went in search of Krige, who had promised to speak to his leader about them.

When they rode into the laager they found themselves in the middle of a prayer meeting, the whole train kneeling around a Predikant in silence as they listened to him preach. When his sermon was over, the women and children sang together, filling the slopes and gullies with sweet sound.

Matthew and Klyn were met with smiles and invitations of hospitality from all sides. Matrons offered coffee and a seat in the shade, and men in moleskin jackets and wide straw hats pumped their hands as they offered food, clothing, help of any kind. Klyn had the art of refusing the overwhelming kindness with a grace that could not offend.

They found Krige beside an open-sided canvas awning stretched between two wagons where many elders were gathered over maps on a collapsible trestle table.

He greeted them warmly and explained, "The elders are talking with the section leaders. They are deciding the next move and will take the rest of the day. Like all our people, they talk long and argue much, but once the decision's made, it's made. Then nothing will change their minds."

"Which one is Potgieter?" asked Matthew.

Krige pointed to a tall, thin man in a brown nankeen jacket and short broadcloth trousers. His eyes were blue and bright and set in deep sockets, a scrubby beard fringed his long chin. He was long-armed and his great gnarled hands hung below his knees.

"And the one next to him is Sarel Cilliers."

"Him?" Klyn could not help laughing.

"Him," Krige repeated, amused.

Cilliers was as short and as stout as Potgieter was tall and cadaverous. His face was pink melon and he held his Bible at high port over his comfortable stomach. He was bare inches over five feet in height.

"He doesn't look much, eh?" said Krige. "But consider, he is an elder at thirty-five, and has the reputation of being a ferocious fighter. Ask the kaffirs, they know his ability well. It simply proves you cannot tell the vintage of the wine from the outside of the barrel, neh?"

"You surely can't," Klyn agreed. "I have heard..."

A strong old voice at his side made him start and whirl around.

"Matthew, *seun! Welkom!*" Abraham de Villiers brushed Klyn aside and grasped Matthew's hands in his. *"Welkom,"* he said again. "But where is your family?"

"I'm alone, menheer. This is Klyn; we travel together."

"Klyn, eh?" The old man appraised the big man as he tried to crush his knuckles. Klyn squeezed back and old Abraham withdrew his fingers to flex life back into them. "A strong one, good. We need you, Klyn. *Welkom.*" He turned on Matthew. "But where is your father?"

"Pa is dead. Edward runs the farm now."

"Your father...well, we were good friends. Sad news, boy. But to see you, Matthew, makes my heart glad. We need these young men, *nie so*, Johannes? Even this English puppy."

Matthew stiffened, his color rising.

"He is truly welcome," said Krige.

Abraham butted Matthew's jaw with the heel of his hand. "Not changed, you see, Johannes? Still all bristles and anger. Tell me, Klyn, how did you live on the trail with this man?"

Klyn grinned. "With great forbearance, menheer."

"You have seen Dirk, no?"

129

Matthew said he had not.

"Then I will ask him to find you. If I remember rightly, he still owes you an apology. Now, forgive me, I must go and talk of heavier things with these talkers." De Villiers ducked beneath the awning, greeting the men who gathered there around the table, shaking hands formally.

Klyn jerked his head at the elders. "When they've talked, what will they decide, Menheer Krige?"

"Go and rest, *kerels,* don't bother your heads with such things."

"No, menheer," Matthew interrupted. "We have come a long way to know."

"Very well, it is simple, I think. Potgieter has just got back from the Zoutpansberg, south of the Limpopo River; he's been searching for van Rensburg's party. Van Rensburg was following the river to see if it led to Delgoa Bay. It's unhealthy country up there; I know because I went through there two years ago. The flies killed our horses and made us all sick with the shaking vomits. We barely got out with our skins intact and most of us were afoot. Potgieter found no sign of them and he believes van Rensburg's party perished to a man. It is a blow; we've lost too many families who've gone off alone. With that in mind, Potgieter will want to take our people to a place we can defend, and once there, fight the Matabele to the death."

Klyn made a gesture both dismissive and impatient. "Good Lord preserve our souls, man. Is he quite sane? How many men can he muster? A hundred? Two? We must surely be outnumbered by a hundred to one."

Krige looked weary. "What choice is there? There have been attacks on our people all along the river boundary. Cilliers knows this as well as anyone, and he will want to push north in strength, get other groups to join us. He knows in his heart they will not, as does Potgieter. But if we stay here all the momentum will be lost. So," he sighed heavily. "They will discourse and disagree, back and forth, forth and back... and *then* they will agree."

"Agree to do what?"

"Agree to agree."

"Krige, menheer, that makes no sense," Matthew growled.

"To them it does." Krige dredged up a smile. "They will go together and make their stand."

"And you, will you take your family into such a battle?"

"*Ja,* Matthew, I will. We are destined to inherit this land.

130

If we must take it by force, then we must and we shall. God's mercy will defend us."

There was nothing more to be said. Matthew looked around at the women bustling about the cooking fires, the chattering children, the men sitting over their afternoon pipes, the lowing and bleating stock a comfortable backdrop. It did not take much to imagine what carnage Mzilikazi's impi could wreak if they swept out of the hills. He stood chilled by the thought.

"Two such fine-looking bachelors," said Krige. "See how the heads are turning? Even my own daughter finds you of interest."

Matthew came back into the sunlight with an effort. Klyn was already trading smiles with a girl shelling peas over a caldron.

"That's my daughter, Herrie, Matthew. Perhaps I will invite you both to eat with us," said Krige, watching the interplay with interest.

"I should be honored," Klyn said promptly, slapping dust from his frayed lapels and rubbing his toecaps against the back of his trousers.

"One of us must stay with the wagons," said Matthew, taking the hint, tipping his hat and walking quickly away. Klyn had moved in to help with the peapodding.

Matthew left the laager and walked up the rising slope to a kopje where he sat himself down to stare out over the massing sheep, his pipe cold in his mouth. The Doppers' wagons were a frail ring of canvas and painted wood and he counted forty gloomily. The Doppers could not raise more than sixty fighting men, he decided. Sixty against the Matabele thousands.

The veldt stretched endlessly in all directions save for the Blesberg at his back and was light to the west where the late sun hung before dipping below the horizon. Matthew did not know whom he was really afraid for, them or himself. Courage was not a constant thing, he knew, it came and went much like the humors. Nobody was always happy, nobody continually sad, and no mother's son was heroically inclined from sunup to sundown.

As the light fell, the fires brightened and became stuttering gems on the purpling plain, and it was night before he climbed stiffly to his feet and went down to his wagons. Boie served him and he picked at the food on his tin plate with no appetite. The mealie biscuits tasted of chaff, the coffee of mud. He scarcely noticed when Boie took his plate and fork away,

131

staring blindly into the snapping log fire as he drew on his pipe.

Matthew had no idea how much time had passed when the soft cut and thump of a horse came easing out of the darkness. He sensed Boie and Abba either side of him, their guns bearing as they watched for the rider to show himself. The horse came into the firelight and halted as its reins were dropped over its head. The rider leaned forward over his pommel, a rhinoceros quirt stroking the dun's withers.

"Is there coffee for a friend?" asked a strangely familiar voice from under the shadowing hat.

"Step down, *vriend*," Matthew said automatically.

The man slid from the saddle onto the balls of his feet and circled until the fire was between him and Matthew. His hat swept from his head and hard, lean features sneer-smiled through the sparks. It was Dirk. Matthew stayed where he was, aware of a chilling anger sweating up his spine and drying the roof of his mouth. Dirk hunkered down, reached for a mug, and filled it from the pot, sipping the scalding liquid noisily.

"Well," he sneered softly. "If I hadn't seen it with my own eyes, I'd have been tempted to call my pa a liar."

Matthew said nothing and showed less.

Dirk snorted into the mug, eyeing the wagons, the outspanned team, the silent and watchful boys, calculating. "If I hadn't seen it..." He shook his head.

Matthew brought his palms together, lacing his fingers so that the knuckles became white diamonds of bone. A white haze of fury made him blind. Keep talking, you..., he thought; there was no word bad enough for what he felt. He just knew he had waited a long time for this meeting.

"I see the Cuthbert girl isn't with you. Elise, isn't it?" asked Dirk, knowing her name full well. "Seems best, considering the stories I've heard about you. I even heard tell of you from a Bastaard."

Matthew took the taunt, the implied insult, and waited.

"This Bastaard..."

"Griqua," Matthew heard himself say before he could bite it off.

"If you like." Dirk shrugged. "This *Griqua* came looking for help two days ago. You'll find this interesting, Eastman. Seems he was with a hunting party from the Cape, after ivory. Did well too, till the Matabele caught up with them. The kaffirs lay in ambush around their advance ox teams and

132

swamped them when they tried to inspan. They didn't have a chance, gutted where they stood. Couldn't have been more than thirty miles from here...."

"Go on." Matthew's hands separated into separate fists.

"Oh, you are interested then?" Dirk was playing a long line.

"I'm interested."

"There was a woman in the party. Well, that's what this Griqua said, but you can't trust them half-men to tell the truth from a groundnut. Will you send for Elise, or is that over? Pretty little thing...."

"The woman, de Villiers."

The brilliant sneering smile was back on Dirk's face. Nerves jumped along Matthew's jawline and the big artery in his neck had swollen.

"Ah," Dirk said. "So that's how it is. I told the Bastaard there was nothing we could do for him. Maybe she got away even though her man was hurt, who knows? We have our own to consider, the *straf* Commando doesn't ride for Uitlanders. I kicked the Bastaard's arse out into the veldt." He was laughing when Matthew stepped through the fire and hit him full in the face. Dirk flailed back onto one knee and an elbow. Boie's gun cocked as he shook his head and spat blood onto the ground.

"No," Matthew ordered.

Dirk got to his feet slowly, his face ugly. "You'll die for that, *rooinek*. I'll cut you into strips." He reached for his bullwhip and straightened it out with a jerk of his forearm.

Matthew stood frozen, watching for the lash to reach out for him. But there was no crack, no pain, just Dirk straining to free his arm from the man behind him. Then he was lifted up and advanced into the firelight, his feet off the ground and Klyn's head growing over his trapped shoulders.

"Gooie aand," Klyn said amiably, releasing Dirk and retaining the bullwhip. "Introduce me, Matthew."

Dirk staggered in a half circle, turning so that he had both Matthew and Klyn in view.

"Aaahh." Klyn snapped his fingers. "You'll be this Dirk. Not much like your father, aré you, bantam? For shame, boy, using this on an unarmed man after you've accepted his hospitality." He hefted the whip to test its balance and flexibility. "Now, you both want to bruise hide, so, we'll have it done right. Abba, build up the fire, let a man see the work to be done."

"Yes, baas." The Khoikhoi threw logs into the flames, topping out with cow chips and kindling.

"Take off your pistols, de Villiers, and the knife." Klyn made the whip snap. "I'll slice the fingers from your thumbs if you reach too quickly, you hear?" The whip licked up a log and laid it at Dirk's feet, then took the lid from the coffeepot and set it spinning on the rush mat by the fire. His point was made and Dirk shed his weapons.

"Set to then," said Klyn.

Dirk launched himself forward, butting low, taking Matthew in the stomach. Winded and surprised, Matthew elbowed Dirk across the bridge of his nose, blinding him with his own tears. They went down in a tangle, rolling from side to side, punching for kidney and groin. As they flailed apart and scrambled upright, Klyn lit his pipe and Boie jumped up and down on the spot.

Dirk hunched his shoulders and kicked high, planning to fold Matthew in half. Matthew skipped away and caught the heel as it lashed past his face, twisting and pushing. Dirk's supporting leg came off the ground and he fell onto his shoulders and the back of his head, biting through his tongue.

Matthew should have waited, but his caution had gone in a red mist. He rushed in to pull Dirk to his feet, crowding in to deliver hard body punches. He took a left to the eye and another to the chest before driving a short left between Dirk's eyes, all his force behind it. Dirk staggered until a right crossed his jaw, then he dropped like a sack of water, his heels slapping loosely on the turf.

"Not bad," murmured Klyn.

Dirk was somehow up on one knee, trying for a defensive crouch, his eyes glassy. Matthew drew off a meaty swing into Dirk's neck. With a groan that wasted away, Dirk slid into sprawling unconsciousness.

They both looked as though they had been trampled by wildebeest. Dirk's right hand wouldn't close around his mug and Matthew sipped with one side of his mouth.

Klyn tipped a bottle of *brandewyn* with no trouble, full of talk and devoid of sympathy as he goosed both men.

"Dirk de Villiers," he crowed. "Canaries will lose their voices when you pass their cages. Your horse won't know you. And you, Matthew, your eyebrow will heal crooked. Even laughing, you will frown. I tell you, the elders will use you both as kaffir-scarers. Whole regiments will run at the sight of you. Look at you, a pair of witchman's frightmasks." He drank deeply.

"What *is* his name?" mumbled Dirk. Making the apology had hurt more than all his other cuts and bruises.

"Klyn," said Matthew.

"Shut up, Klyn."

"Is that the way to speak to a man who saved you both from murder?"

"Shut up, Dirk is right."

"You hit good, *rooinek*. We will fight again, I enjoyed it." Dirk carefully rinsed his mouth with brandy.

"Anytime," said Matthew, not to be outdone. The stars swam and revolved when he tried to look at them.

"I'll be ready."

"You *dassies!*" Klyn exploded. "Save your energy for the Matabele. They'll give you enough fight for two lifetimes. When we cross the Vaal with Potgieter and Cilliers, they'll be waiting."

"You two mean to travel with us?" Dirk looked surprised.

"In Krige's section. I fixed it with him over dinner. *Magtig,* that daughter of his is a fine cook."

"And a pretty girl, ready for marriage. Careful, man, she'll trap you with your stomach." Dirk laughed and hurt his mouth.

"The stomach is bigger than the trap," said Matthew as Klyn colored up. "When do they pull out for the north?"

"Tomorrow."

"Ah." Matthew squeezed his eyes closed, fighting the alcohol. He had to think, make a decision.

Klyn squeezed his knee. "You don't have to say anything, *boet*. I know the Laidler wagons were ambushed. I heard Dirk talking."

Dirk hiccuped and swayed on his log.

Matthew opened one eye and massaged his temple. "Then you know what I have to do. I'll catch up with you. I'll take one of the string horses and Gaika, travel light. The wagons won't make more than ten miles a day. I'll cover three times that and be back before you know it."

"You're going out there alone?" Dirk was astonished. "Man, you'll never make it. That country makes fools of the best of us. If the kaffirs don't eat you, the Griquas will kill you for your horse. *If* you don't starve to death in some blind kloof. Give it up."

"I'll make it," Matthew said shortly.

135

"Tell him he's a fool, Klyn."

"Better to talk to a rock. Anyway, I'm going with him."

"No, Klyn, no you're not."

"I am, *boet,* I've worked it out. The boys can take the wagons on with the main trek. They're better *voorloopers* than we are anyway. Dirk is right about one thing; no one man can get through that country alone."

Dirk swallowed hard and tipped the bottle.

"Damned right. There're Griqua bandits up there, whole townships of them. They even say Mantatisi's Wild Cat people still raid along the rim of the valley, and they're cannibals. Mzilikazi has his patrols out there as well. Take my word, forget the woman. She's probably dead by now, or decorating some Bastaard's bed...."

Matthew got to his feet. "There's no discussion."

Dirk smashed a swollen fist down onto his thigh. "We need your *guns,* man," he shouted hoarsely. "You've seen how few we are. To go off and die like this is useless. Take a look at those people down there. Is this woman worth all their lives?"

Klyn began pulling on his jacket. "The sooner we start, the better."

"All *right.*" Dirk sat straight. "All right. I'll see your wagons through safely. I'll even beat your boys to keep them obedient. But I tell you, if you don't come back, I'll find your bones and piss on your grave."

19

The forest stretched away behind, and on both sides of them when they stopped at the mouth of a pass to eat and to rest.

For eight long days they had walked, ridden, and hacked their way through the crowding trees, hardly ever seeing the sun through the tangled canopy.

The unshod horses were footsore and plagued by flies, and Klyn had an ulcer on his thigh that would not heal. As they squatted in the first open ground they had seen in over a week, they could hear the rush of the Marico River beyond the high point of the kloof.

Their grain was all but gone and they used their hats to collect water from the trickles between the rocks. They were eating the last of their biltong.

Matthew had become increasingly withdrawn and impatient, and even-tempered Klyn was short on words. The two

136

Khoikhoi kept their own counsel as they scouted the way ahead as tireless and as uncomplaining as ever.

Matthew was slumped against a rock and he enviously watched Klyn napping beneath his hat with Pallas's rein tied to his ankle, his smoothbore under his right hand. Matthew recognized the enormous debt he owed the big Dutchman. A full-blooded brother could have done no more. Compared to Edward, he was a giant of filial regard and compassion.

A widow bird swooped in and banked away shyly, calling shrill as she disappeared into the trees. Matthew crossed to Gaika and put a hand over her muzzle to stop her whinnying, his gun across his forearm as Klyn came out of sleep in a surge, setting himself at Matthew's side, listening for what had alarmed the bird. Alarmed lizards scampered away over the warm rocks, flicking from sight beneath the curtains of ivy. Pallas's ears swiveled and he butted Klyn, feeling the tension in the men and wanting to share it. Klyn hushed him and waited.

Boie came out of the rocks followed closely by Abba, and both of them panted from the fast climb. Matthew offered the precious inch of water in the crown of his hat to Boie, who grinned and refused it.

"I have filled my belly from the river, Nkosi. It runs sweet."

"How far?"

"One horse hour, then half more, walking." Boie made a trident with his middle fingers. "The river splits so, three *poorts*. Big valleys. There is camp spoor, old, with many tracks all around."

"What do you think, Klyn?"

"We'll take a look, neh?"

"Baas," said Abba. "Men were there. Wearing clothes like yours. With horses. Not trekkers, these ones. They have faces—" He broke off to draw a ring in the air around his head, leaving it at that.

Matthew had one foot in the stirrup. "Guns, Abba?"

"Many guns. Long, like yours, and small ones at the waist."

"Christ," said Klyn. "Griquas."

Matthew rose up into his saddle looking troubled. "Probably renegades, too."

"At least they won't take much tracking. Think, Matthew," said Klyn. "If she..." He deliberately avoided using Kit's name. "If she *did* get away from the Matabele, she had to fort up somewhere. Why not with them? A lot of Laidler's

137

men were Griquas; doesn't it stand to reason he would head for where he was known?"

"It makes sense," Matthew agreed.

"But remember, *boet*." Klyn settled himself on Pallas and tied his spare horse behind. "The chance of her being alive is remote."

It was the first time Klyn had voiced what they both knew was a distinct possibility, and Matthew understood why he had chosen this moment to do so. He's letting me down in stages, he thought. How could he explain he *knew* Kit was alive? His body told him so; the desolating realization of her unbeing had not touched his knowing heart. He would have known, she had been made for him ... he would have *known*.

They found the burned shells of the Laidler wagons in a circle of blackened grass. The wheel rims had gone and the ironwork had been stripped for salvage. Everything movable and useful had been gleaned.

Boie led Matthew to a point overlooking the dead ground where the Matabele must have waited. It had been easy for them. In a gully they found the remains of a body, just the smaller bones and shreds of cheap cloth; lesser predators and white ants had taken the rest.

A hundred yards on were the rotted carcasses of oxen, discarded brandy kegs, and a leather legging.

A crumb of white glass gleamed from beneath a low bush. Matthew dispossessed the mamba living there to retrieve it, hooking it out with his gunstock. A small crystal stopper jammed in the collar of the broken bottle neck. When held to the nose it was still vaguely perfumed.

Matthew turned away grimly. She had been here.

They watched the settlement for two hours before they went in.

Matthew and Klyn rode with the string horses behind them as Abba and Boie took the point. They kept their pace leisurely as they approached the main entrance across open ground, the sun at their backs. Eyes watched them coming from hidden vantage points and shrill whistles heralded their approach.

They looked front and kept moving.

The beaten trail widened out slowly and the ground changed from shale to scrub grass. Ironwood stakes had been driven into the earth to form a barricade, the tops burned to points. A center section of the barricade could be raised and lowered by a winch and was open, guarded by a single man who lounged in the gap, watching them approach. On either side, empty corrals baked in the sun.

When the horses trotted onto the wooden bridge over a dry moat, the guard leaned off a post, cocking and raising his piece, training it between Matthew and Klyn. If it were loaded with fragmentation shot, he could have taken them both out of their saddles with one blast. Boie measured his knife throw, watching the muscles around the guard's eyes. There would not be much of a warning.

Klyn eased Pallas to a stop and scratched his beard as though for lice, all the while trying to spot the other guns that must be covering them. He snapped his nails together, breaking the back of a nonexistent flea, and flicked it from him, keeping the guard's attention on himself. Matthew let Gaika sidestep a little, so that the space between himself and Klyn was a shade wider.

"Good day, friend," he said. "Can a man buy a little grain, a tot or two of brandy, maybe some female companionship?"

The guard worked a tobacco quid into the side of his jaw and streamed juice at the ground, taking in the state of the horses, how the four men were armed, the bulk of their saddle packs, the marks of travel on their clothes. His face was lumpy and seamed with grime, his hair scraped back in an unkempt cue and held at the nape by a patterned band. A single gold ring hung from his right earlobe. He sucked in his cheeks and spat more juice near Gaika's fetlocks.

"Maybe, maybe not," he drawled.

"Easy," Matthew soothed Gaika. "Well, maybe is maybe and the day's wasting."

"Yours maybe, English," said the guard, showing brown teeth. "You carrying silver?"

Matthew just looked at him.

"We pay our way." Klyn seemed to have found another foreigner in his beard.

"Dutch, eh? You show a lot of canvas seeing as how there's only the two of you. Not counting your boys."

"Seems old Cord was wrong about these people," Matthew said mildly.

The guard left his quid where it was, trying to read their faces. "Cord? Cord who?"

Klyn laughed. "If you have to ask, Portogee, you don't

know him. That means you ain't long off the galleys at Delgoa Bay. Bet you still have the lash stripes on your back."

"You've got names, Dutchy. Say 'em."

"To your chief, Portogee. Not to the likes of you."

There was a hot momentary silence. The Portuguese guard looked sullen and discomfited. Then he showed his teeth again, smiling with an ugly show of bad humor.

"All right, Dutchy, come ahead. There's no mistaking where you'll end up. Me, I'll be here to see what state you're in if you ride out. *If*, mark you." The brown teeth were bared as the musket pointed itself at the ground. "I'd wish you luck, but where's the sense in waste?"

Klyn led the way past him and they passed through the gap in the palisade. A muddle of tents and shacks lay before them, ringed by a second palisade. Beyond was a row of clapboard frontages with a squat stone building at the far end. Chickens pecked in the dust and dogs lolled where there was shadow. There was a stagnant smell of wrongness over everything.

Three Griquas pumped at the bellows of a forge as a white smith beat sparks from a warped axle. There were wagon hoops in a pile under a rattan lean-to. Klyn noted their burned and blacked appearance and was gratified to see that Matthew had worked out their significance for himself. They must have come from Laidler's wagons.

They passed wattle huts. A chained baboon picked at its fur as it perched on a chairback. Exotic birds fluttered in a cage and a drunk lay on his back under a wagon heaped with half-cured skins. A naked black woman pounded meal with a wooden pestle, her breasts jigging violently.

They crossed a bridge over a dry wash where black and yellow children watched scorpions fight.

A line of saddled horses were hitched before the stone building. Men sat in groups along the uneven stoep watching them approach. Mostly they were Griquas, with one or two whites among them.

Klyn edged Pallas into a space at the rail and stepped down, drawing his long gun from its scabbard and stepping up onto the stoep. Matthew stayed mounted until Boie and Abba had reined in beside him.

"You two stay here with the horses," he said in a voice that carried. "Use your guns if you have to. Understand?"

"Yes, Nkosi." And, "Yes, baas."

Matthew dismounted. He hooked his coat back from his
140

pistols and clumped up to stand beside Klyn. Klyn stepped to the doorway and waited until his eyes had accustomed themselves to the interior dimness. Inside, somebody picked at an untuned piano.

"Well, *boet*," he said cheerfully. "Let's get that drink."

There were rough benches inside the door, cuspidors chained beneath them; knife-cut graffiti scored the plastered walls. The floor was planked and strewn with sand.

The bar was pegged timber resting on barrels, and mutton-fat candles lit the bottles on the back bar where a crudely painted nude reclined in a warped gold frame.

A Bantu filled tankards from a stone jar and serviced a gambling school at a corner table. There was a show of cards and coin chinked on the baize covering. The piano fell silent as the picker turned to see who had entered.

"If the bottles aren't for show, man, we'll toast the lady," said Klyn, leering pointedly at the nude.

The Griqua behind the bar was ugly and heavily muscled. He poured two mean measures of *brandewyn* and pushed them across the bar. "We got women if you like them yellow," he said. "Black if that's your taste. None of these dogs is too particular what bitches they sniffs."

Klyn swallowed his measure in one gulp and set his glass on the bar. "I'm different, Griqua. A man should stick to his own in some things. If that's all you can offer, I'll say thanks and no offense."

"All the same to me, Dutchman." The Griqua poured again, eyeing Matthew. "Your friend don't say much."

"Trailing does that to some men. I make up for him," Klyn explained.

A big man at the gaming table scraped his chair back and raked money into his hat. The bridge of his nose had been flattened and his mouth was scarred into a permanent grin that showed two teeth. He was one of those men who were always beaded with sweat. He wiped his palms on his nankeen waistcoat, his petrified grin saying nothing.

Matthew watched intently as he ducked from the room, somehow knowing he and Klyn would not have long to wait. He kept to the center of the bar where he could see everybody and the spill of light from the opened door. As long as the sunlit oblong remained unshadowed, nobody could backshoot him. Sweat crawled down his spine to collect in the hollow of his back. His hands felt swollen and clumsy.

Klyn asked for a refill.

141

"Doesn't he drink either?" the Griqua asked, bottle poised.

"When the mood takes him, *vriend*. Best to leave him alone."

The Griqua poured a shot, corked the bottle, thumbed a nostril, and palmed his shirtfront, leaving a damp smear. His hands dropped below the counter and started to explore a shelf. Klyn threw his drink back and his smoothbore angled up to cover the man's movement. He winked at the Griqua as the nervous hands came up onto the bar and stayed there.

The back door opened slowly, held ajar by a ragged Bantu who watched for somebody's approach along a corridor. A figure bulked through the gap in a swish of silk, heels making gritty ticks on the sanded floor. The feathers in her hair bobbed as she walked over to a chair on a small dais and settled her huge frame into it with a grunt of exertion.

Matthew blinked with disbelief at the sight, momentarily disconcerted. She could have been any age, chins wobbling as she drew breath, huge breasts heaving under her frilled bodice. Her hands were curiously small and fine, unnatural at the ends of her heavy arms. She clicked open a fan and cooled her flushed face, pouched eyes busy. The sweating man with the permanent smile came out of somewhere and stood at her side.

"You want something, Miss Mattie?" he asked, his manner noticeably servile.

"Wine from the cooler. And a cigar."

"By the Pope's beard, her voice is deeper than mine," said Klyn.

"You heard Miss Mattie," said the sweating man.

The Griqua took a bottle from a brass container and filled a crystal glass to the brim. Then he took a cheroot from an ornate humidor and lit it from a candle. The woman swallowed wine and smoke and twin plumes trickled from her nostrils.

Klyn and Matthew watched her openly.

"And tell them to drink with me, Samuel," she told the sweating man.

"Honored, madam," said Klyn.

"By God, manners yet." Miss Mattie giggled and broke wind. "If you can lie as prettily, I'll have trouble deciding what you're all about." She took a long look at Matthew. "I said both of them, Samuel."

"He's got one that's untouched here," whined the Griqua at the bar.

"Out!" said Miss Mattie. "Samuel, you serve."

Samuel watched the other Griqua scuttle away and took his place.

"You," said Miss Mattie, addressing Matthew directly. "Are you a man, or a boy with long legs?"

"Answer Miss Mattie," said Samuel.

"I'll drink with you," Matthew said quietly. "When the man in the back takes his gun off me."

The woman barked a laugh and called out a rapid stream of dialect. "Suit you better, Mr. Longlegs?"

"And Samuel could step away from the bar gun."

"By God, boy, you'll be rifling my petticoats next."

Klyn grinned at that. "That would be my pleasure, Miss Mattie."

"Samuel, bring that bottle over here and find some clean glasses."

Samuel sidled down the bar and rummaged in a cupboard. Matthew leaned over the bar and brought a twin-barreled dueling piece into view. It was cocked and loaded. He blew the powder from the pan and tucked it into his belt. Then he took up his drink and drained it.

Miss Mattie clapped her hands. "I like you boys, like you a lot. What's your pleasure, Dutchman?"

"We'll take *brandewyn*," Klyn said, twisting a chair under him, forearm along the backrest, long gun across his knees. Matthew edged his back against a solid timber upright, watching the doors back and front.

Miss Mattie's hennaed ringlets bobbed as she shook her head. She wiggled her tiny fingers and bit off smoke. "Boy, don't fret so much. One word from me and there'd be fifty kaffirs in here, ready to bite your balls off with their bare teeth. Take my word. If I wanted that, would I set myself so close to you boys?"

Matthew stayed where he was and Miss Mattie sighed. Up close, her skin was oily, peach fuzz on her top lip, her teeth misshapen and stained, her scent defeated by an underlying rankness.

"All right," she said finally, all trace of mildness gone. "You mentioned a name. I want to know how you came by it."

"Well, we didn't steal it," said Klyn.

"Where is he?" Matthew demanded.

Miss Mattie drew her bulk back, her eyes narrowing with an unnamed threat. "Boy," she warned.

"Cord Laidler. Where is he?"

"Well." Miss Mattie decided to be amused once more. "That's a name that comes expensive. Every damned bobbin has a price in this foul backwater. Even me, boy, but I'd take some buying. A lady don't get by in a stinkhole by smelling of violets. I set the price and I don't haggle. What's it worth to you?"

Matthew spoke slowly and deliberately. "It's worth killing you, old woman. And the fat yellowback behind the bar. If he tries for that carver in his boot, Klyn'll shoot his head off."

"Samuel!" The woman's voice was as hard as a rapping knuckle.

The Griqua straightened slowly, running wet.

Klyn reached over to pat Miss Mattie's hand. "Madam, you have a price in mind. Shall we discuss it?"

Ash spilled over the flounces of her dress and she ignored it, smiling coldly. "I see you have business acumen, as well as manners."

"I can afford to with him beside me."

"You're the talker, Dutchman. Will he pay the price he can afford?"

"Ask him."

"That true, boy?" The question was a soft hiss of anticipation.

Matthew nodded.

"Then it's settled. We'll drink on it."

They all watched Samuel pour and then they drank. Samuel watched Miss Mattie shake her head when Klyn reached for the silver pouch inside his coat, her features set in a false simper. Like the heat grin of a lizard, he thought as she said, "Nobody mentioned money, Dutchman."

A blowfly droned and settled to clean its mask. The other side of the Griqua's mouth curved.

Miss Mattie sipped wine. "All your friend has to do is fight Samuel here. Barefist."

Before Klyn could say or do anything, Matthew was unhooking his pistols and removing his jacket. Miss Mattie drew on her cigar and Samuel cracked his knuckles as he came around the bar and squared up in front of Matthew. As they moved around each other, Matthew found himself thinking of irrelevant things. The first blow caught him on the forehead and brought his concentration back to the work in hand, sending him into a ducking swing from the waist as he countered a second punch and took a kick on the thigh that was meant for his scrotum. He made a forward shuffle and shouldered into the big belly, his right elbow sinking deep into shirtfront, his left fist cutting into Samuel's right eye. Samuel's arms flailed as he drove in looking to use his superior weight, to smother Matthew's longer reach.

Matthew took long sidesteps, snapping out stinging lefts to the face, ears, and chin, anything to unsettle the heavier man. Then there was a chair swinging up from the floor and he was rolling under it, trying for space, trying to keep on his feet. He was down and Samuel was over him stomping at his head. Matthew kicked upward into the soft parts between the Griqua's legs and saw his mouth snap open wide before pain roared crimson as a heel gouged his temple.

Rolling again and coming up short against the bar barrels.

The Griqua halted, swaying, a hand over his crotch, the other pulling a knife from his boot top, raking the air with it.

Matthew was all slowness and dizziness, pulling himself along and up the bar, balancing himself to avoid the darting blade. As Samuel feinted and maneuvered for a thrust, the knife seemed to absorb all the light in the room.

The rough bar plank was hard in the small of Matthew's back.

Samuel hunched and set himself for a final, stabbing punch.

Matthew watched him with an almost clinical detachment, moving a moment before the knife came in, both hands bearing down on Samuel's elbow joint, pulling it down onto his rising knee. The knife buried itself into a barrel and Samuel's cry of pain was high and loud. Matthew laced his hands into a double fist and swung at the face teetering before him. Samuel lost all his breath in a long and tired sigh, his limbs slackened, and he dropped on his side, over onto his back, and his one good eye rolled white.

Matthew gulped air and focused on the room with difficulty. The men at the card table were a waxen tableau and Miss Mattie was a tawdry doll in a soiled dress and scuffed velvet shoes. The air tasted of bile and the muzzle of Klyn's smoothbore had lost itself in the ruffles of the bloated woman's waist.

Matthew took up his pistols and buckled them on with hands that had too many knuckles and joints. He wanted to

145

wash the blood away, to lie down and sleep. He held onto a chairback and stayed on his feet, glaring at Miss Mattie, who seemed to be seeing him for the first time.

"Damnation, boy," she said. "I've seen that buck of mine kill five men and cripple double again. I never thought to see him bested. He'll never walk as straight again, I think you busted his pride." She snapped her fingers. "Some of you take this carcass out of here."

Three men skirted Matthew and the card table and dragged Samuel out into the sunlight.

"There's a shack out back. Canvas roof, yellow-wood door. In there." Miss Mattie dismissed them with an impatient wave.

"You'll not mind showing us," Klyn said. "Can you make it, *boet?*"

"I can make it."

"Taking no chances, eh, Dutchman? What harm could an old woman do to you? I'm all alone...." She pushed herself out of the chair and the gun followed her.

"Madam, you'll favor me by please shutting your mouth. My people have never held life cheap, but, may God forgive me, you are less than a cockroach. You threw that man away for your own gratification. What would you have done if my brother there had lost?"

"He didn't, Dutchman. Be grateful."

"Answer, woman!"

"All right!" Miss Mattie's features hardened under the caked powder. "He would have been staked out over an anthill with you beside him. And I tell you, I wouldn't have lost a wink of sleep, there's no room here for sentiment. And don't think you fooled me; you came for the woman, not Cord Laidler. He's finished. And so are you, Dutchman. There're four hundred men in this settlement, and they all do what I tell them, *me*. One shout, just one, and—"

Klyn's fist described a short arc and Miss Mattie's chins shook as she fell into Matthew's arms. Coins chimed as the card table went over and the men scattered.

Klyn kicked the rear door open, standing to one side. The men there froze when they saw the woman lolling in Matthew's arms, his pistol against her jaw. Without a word they laid their guns on the floor and kicked them aside.

Matthew beckoned to the Portuguese with the gold earring. "You, Portogee, go out front and tell your friends we have the woman. One shot or spit when we start walking and I'll kill her."

"Still showing canvas, eh, English?"

"Tell them, *vriend*. One sneeze..." Klyn's tone turned the man's complexion a malarial yellow. He scuttled off and the other men filed out into the saloon. Matthew and Klyn went through the rear door and locked it behind them.

They found themselves in a small compound surrounded by a mud wall. A shack formed part of the west wall and the canvas awning bellied in the light wind. Abba and Boie had the horses lined up by an opening in the north wall, their guns trained toward the front of the saloon.

Boie motioned Matthew on as Klyn held back to cover the rear door. Matthew manhandled the gross woman inside the shack. The cramped interior was lit by a single candle and the stench was overpowering. Matthew squinted, trying to make out details as he swallowed his nausea. There was a pallet of straw and rags in one corner and an unmoving figure lay there, one leg raised over a firkin and wrapped in make-shift bandages. A thin figure kneeled beside the pallet in a shapeless dress, her face hidden by tangled hair.

"Kit?" He could make out the smudge of a face as it turned, the eyes huge as she took him in. A long moment passed before she made a faltering attempt to stand. Beside her, flies crowded a foul bucket.

"Matthew? Is it you?"

Matthew dropped Miss Mattie onto her face and she groaned as he trod on her hand. He stepped in and gathered Kit to him, not caring if she smelled like a midden as she burrowed against him, over tiredness and over fear, sobbing as he crushed her to him. He held her until she had almost cried herself out, then Klyn's musket boomed from outside and they heard his rammer rattle in the bore as the horses danced on the packed earth.

"Come on, Kit, we must go."

"No." Kit was pulling Matthew to the pallet. "Help him, for God's sake, help him, *please?*"

Matthew allowed her to push him into a kneel and he parted the dressing from Laidler's wound, almost recoiling from the running and septic wound. The whole knee and upper thigh were a grayish salmon color. Cord raised his head and murmured something feverish before falling back into oblivion. Matthew wondered what he was supposed to do except leave the man to die in peace.

147

"The kaffirs trapped us, Matthew. They were all over and the spear went through his leg as he pulled me up behind him. He was pinned to the saddle. The riding tore his whole leg apart...." Kit gagged on the memory and hugged herself to Matthew, now and then drawing back to touch his face and clothes with bloodless fingers. The story came out in jerks and stumbles. The horse had run until it dropped. She had rolled clear but Cord had gone under the horse and when she had pulled him out the spear had broken off. They had used the leather cinches to tourniquet Cord's leg and walked. She did not know for how long, the days and nights melted together, and then they were here at the settlement. Miss Mattie had brought them inside and been kind until she learned about the tuskers they had shot. Then she had wanted a share. That had escalated to the whole kill when she realized how badly off Cord had been. Kit said:

"She knew Cord from the Cape; he had set her up there in the early days, she was one of his madams on the strip below the waterfront. She promised to get doctors if Cord would only tell where the ivory was, but he wouldn't.... Then he got delirious and she started to work on me. Did I know? I didn't, Matthew...."

Miss Mattie started to swear in low snarls. Matthew twisted around and laid a boot across her neck. She gaped and fell silent, breath hissing between her teeth.

Kit sobbed. "She made Samuel hurt him and then me...so badly, I...Then she said she would give me to the Griquas, tie me to a bar and let them..."

Matthew held her wet face against his chest, brutal with caring.

"Hurry it up, *boet!*" Klyn yelled from outside.

"They're both here," Matthew shouted back. "We're coming out." He turned to Kit. "Can you ride?"

"Yes...but Cord..."

"I'll take him across my saddle. Listen, Kit, you have to ride double with her." He jerked a thumb down at Miss Mattie. "You up behind. Here's my knife, take it. If she tries anything, anything at all, you must kill her. Can you do it?"

Kit looked at the fat woman for a long moment and her shudder became a nod. "I'll kill her for you, Matthew. For all of us. I've dreamed of it. It's all that's kept me alive."

"Only if it needs to be done, Kit. You hear that, Miss Mattie?"

148

All he got were obscenities in reply; it was enough, he could see she understood where she stood.

Matthew tied his smoothbore along Cord's leg as a splint and carried him outside to lay him over his saddle. Then he took Miss Mattie out and set her on one of the string horses, lashing her wrists to the pommel and tying her legs beneath the animal so that Kit could mount behind her and work the reins. He mounted Gaika and pulled the unconscious Cord across his thighs.

"What was the shooting, Klyn?" he asked, ready to move out.

"A stray head," said Klyn. "It went away faster than it showed." He sounded comfortable and ready for anything. "Ready?" He moved Pallas out without waiting for a reply.

The light had turned to brass and there could only have been an hour of daylight left as they filed out of the alley. They passed Samuel, who lay face down on the stoep in a sprawl. A chicken pecked at something near his head. Wind stirred dust devils between the shabby buildings and a loose shutter swung against a frame.

Men lurked beyond the tents, pacing them on foot on both sides of the road. The naked black woman had left her food to burn over a dying fire and the forge stood idle. As they crossed the bridge the children and the scorpions had gone from the wash. The horses clumped over the boards and spread out in line as they approached the outer palings. Klyn counted heads in the watchtowers and Matthew watched the rear for any move against them. There were none.

Klyn reined the column in and said, "They'll try to split us at the gate. They probably think to jump Kit as she goes through, catch her on the drawbridge and close the gate with us on the inside, neh?"

New sweat broke out along Matthew's spine. It made sense. He was working angles when Boie swung in beside him.

"Nkosi, me and Abba go first. Then you bring Missie and the woman."

"Wait." Matthew needed to think.

"It's the only way," urged Klyn.

"I don't..." Matthew got no further. The two Khoikhoi spurred their mounts and rushed at the gates. One moment they were in the saddles, the next they weren't. What seemed to be two riderless horses went through the narrow gap and a wasted cross-fire smoke bloomed across the animals' backs.

149

Boie fired from beneath his horse's neck and a man flailed out over the palings to fall into the dry moat. Abba's gun went off and there was a multiple scream.

"*Now!*" Klyn urged Pallas forward, slapping at Kit's horse. Matthew was behind them, a bare hoof fall to their rear. Shots came from behind him but the gate did not fall to block them in. As he went through the gap, Matthew fired both pistols at where he judged the platforms were and was gratified to see a man fall over himself as his musket threw itself away. Then they were through the gate and running for the open savannah and it was over. They were through.

20

The white stallion nudged Mkalipi the induna, wanting more of the sweet grass from the wicker basket. Mkalipi pushed him away and stifled a yawn, bored by the ceremony going on around him.

The witchmen were making their puzzles of colored earth, building tiny pyramids of sand which they then halved or holed with quick movements of palm and thumb. Charcoal fires burned in clay pots all around the mysteries and they threw up brown and red smoke as pigment was added from the *mouti* bags. The spirit drums were sounded as the luck and the courage of the warriors of the Great Elephant were considered. Knuckle bones were rapped against polished tortoise shells and then cast onto the sand squares to be read by the row of clay figures wet with goat's blood.

Mkalipi watched the time-honored ritual and was interested despite himself.

One of the witchmen brushed the bones with a widow-bird fan and sang ancient words as he used his gourd rattle. He left three bones from his first cast where they lay, scooped up the others, and threw again. These fell to form a rough square and a witchman sprinkled more blood on the clay images.

The square of bones would represent the corngrowers' wagons, thought Mkalipi, the three other bones will be our impi. If two more impi bones fell in the right place, it would mean that his regiments were bound to surround the enemy in the classic head and loins manner of the sacred bull. No witchman worth anything more than a kick and a curse failed to make that cast, thought Mkalipi. He took a handful of grass from the basket and fed it to the white stallion. The velvet lips tickled the palm of his outstretched hand.

The bones scattered from the witchman's hand and fell as they should, committing the Bees and the Invincibles to the horns of the coming attack, just as Mkalipi knew that they must. He yawned again. It was of no real consequence; there were only a handful of whites in the square of wagons, his scouts had counted forty guns. Mkalipi had five thousand warriors and he knew it would be over quick although he wondered how many of them would have the opportunity to wash their spears in honor of Mzilikazi, the Great King.

What was more pleasant to contemplate was the huge bounty he would take back to the royal kraal. The scouts had reported that the corngrowers' animals were a living blanket over the land, and there would be five animals for every one of his men, maybe more, nobody had ever tried to count that high before. It would take a hundred goat boys seven suns and seven moons to cut all the notches into the tally sticks. The Great Elephant, Mzilikazi, would have to show enormous pleasure when he saw the huge bounty Mkalipi meant to bring him. There would be a month of feasting and much of it would be in Mkalipi's honor.

There would be sorghum and barley beer, and the rare luxury of spitted meat; perhaps a marriage dance for the bachelor regiment, the Snakes, if they showed great valor and did well. The Snakes were all men in their thirtieth spring, a good age to marry. In one year, there might be a thousand new babies in the kraals, and all the boy children could form the nucleus of a new regiment.

Mkalipi prayed that there would not be too many girl children to be exposed on the hillsides for the hyenas. The Matabele could steal all the women they needed from the neighboring vassal tribes, and it made no sense to feed and protect girl children for fourteen years until they were ready for their first fruiting. They were only a drain on the food reserves of the tribe. Better to expose them at birth and have the mothers try again for man children.

In that, as in most things, Mzilikazi was right.

Mkalipi drew in the dust by his stool with the haft of his *iKlwa*.

He drew the Vaal River and the flat-topped hill in front of it, marking where its southern edge abutted the river. Then he drew in the laager of wagons. They made a C around the top of the hill with the open side of the C facing the sheer fall to the river. His warriors would not cross the river and scale the cliff. Mkalipi would attack on the other three sides in the classic way. It was written in blood on the sand and must be so.

He would bring all his impi out of the north in a great show of strength, and his warriors would stay silent until he ordered them to give one great shout in concert. That would be something to chill the corngrowers' hearts and set their children crying. Then his warriors would drum on their shields and sing throughout the night and tire the whites with feints and noise. His impi would insult them by showing off their bigger penises and say what they would do with the women and girl children when the wagons were burning and the men speared.

He would see that the corngrowers thirsted and hungered. He would probe for weakness and offer to parley. If he could trap their leaders in the open and kill them, the rest would lay down their weapons. Was it not true that no white ever fought with courage when there was no hope? Did not the missionary say that it is best to turn your face to your enemy for a second blow?

But then, had not Mzilikazi said these corngrowers were different? Were they not deluded into thinking they were the Chosen Ones of their invisible God? Mkalipi had no doubt that they were deluded, for he had seen them die as other men died; their shirts held no magic power to turn an *iKlwa* from the heart. His impi would tear the thorn barriers from before their wagons, would pull the guns from their clay hands and kill them all.

Mkalipi looked up from his diagram. The head witchman was offering him a gourd of warm calf's blood. Mkalipi took it in his right hand and stood up on the mound where he could be seen by the impi. The drumming stopped and the chanting ended in a great shout, then the only sound came from the spitting charcoal fires.

Mkalipi walked between the sand patterns to the square of bones that was the laager of wagons. He offered the gourd to the cardinal points of the compass and poured blood into the square. Not a drop spattered near the impi bones. The magic was complete.

All the dying would be inside the laager.

Matthew had covered their retreat and kept the Griquas away until nightfall, slipping away when he could no longer see to shoot.

He caught up with the rest of the party on a flat peak overlooking the triple fork of the Marico River. The river creamed below them, silver and white and turbulent, and the forests stretched away to the south, blacker than the sky. The cooking fires of the Griqua settlement flickered bronze on the valley walls to the north and the broken land between was a mottled tumble of iron and blue.

Klyn had found a wide and shallow depression of rock where a spring filled a basin and ran on to cascade from the sheer western face of the peak, pluming down into the river below. A keen wind cut the air, gusted through the fissures and rocks, wailing like forgotten demons.

The boys watered the horses and found shelter for Kit and Cord beneath an overhang. Miss Mattie was tied hand and foot and propped where she could be seen. She lay like a loose bundle of tattered frills and she had lost a shoe. Kit patiently kept Cord covered with blankets as he tossed and shivered in fever. Matthew and Klyn climbed to the northern rim and watched the trail.

"We're not in a good position," Matthew observed. "Those Griquas know this country and we don't. They're probably laughing about that right now. They know we have to cross the river and strike east, and they'll be waiting for us. We can't even make a run for it with Laidler in his condition. If he could talk, he'd probably know a way out of here."

"We can hold these heights against an army," said Klyn.

"Without food? For three or four days maybe; then we'll be too damned weak to hold our guns. One of us has to stay and hold the crest until the others have crossed the river and got well into the trees. It'll take the Griquas a full day to skirt the base of this peak and come in from all sides. By that time, I'd be gone."

"Ach, man, always you, eh?"

Matthew squinted off into the darkness.

"That's out," Klyn snarled. "We stay together."

"And die together?" Matthew leaned far out over the edge of the peak and studied the far terrain, ignoring Klyn's protests. He drew back and said, "Come on."

153

Klyn followed him back to the central depression and watched as he heaped brush and dry branches inside a ring of stones. As he lit the kindling he began to sing at the top of his voice. The dry timber caught and threw great tongues of flame into the updraft. Waves of sudden heat took the chill from the peak and Miss Mattie crawled to the fire to warm her shackled hands.

"Sing," Matthew bellowed. "Sing up, Klyn. The louder the better."

"Have you gone mad, you *dassie?* You'll rouse every Matabele and Griqua in the territory. They'll be fighting each other for the privilege of cutting your throat." Klyn made a move to kick the fire apart.

Matthew blocked him. "I want the Griquas to see the fire, to know exactly where we are. They'll know we can't make a move until daylight and they'll work on surrounding us and starving us out. You see?"

"No."

"Boie, more wood for the fire. Cover me, Klyn." Matthew started back along the draw toward the crest with the exasperated Klyn behind him mumbling about crazy *rooineks* with addled brains and less sense than they were born with. As they dropped to their stomachs at the top and edged to the rim, Matthew fired into the night and ducked back. The shot racketed echoes down along the dark valley and there was an immediate response, bright flashes from the lower slopes as muskets cracked, and the air around them was alive with spattering lead.

Klyn's hat was jerked from his head and hung from its drawstring.

Matthew reloaded fast. "Can you hear me down there?" he called.

A single shot whined off into the night and a long pause followed.

"They must have been working up all the time," said Klyn, watching for a target.

"How many gunflashes did you count, Klyn?"

"Twelve, maybe fourteen. Why, where the hell is this leading us?"

"You hear me down there?"

"We hear you," somebody called.

"Is Samuel there?"

Muted voices argued, a fist struck a palm, then gruffly, "I'm here."

154

"Boie, bring the woman up here," Matthew yelled. "You want to trade, Samuel?"

"I got to kill you, English." The voice was thick, the diction slurred, hatred giving it force and venom.

"Maybe, Samuel, but she's coming up here. Best tell your boys not to fire. Wouldn't do either of us any good if they put a bullet in her old belly, would it?"

"You die, English," said Samuel, sounding both near and far, but he gave the order.

"I know you have to try, Samuel. You hear her coming?"

Boie came up, shoving Miss Mattie ahead of him. She slid and stumbled and complained, which suited Matthew's purpose perfectly; she could be heard all over the mountainside. When she reached the rim she had lost her second shoe. Matthew pulled the bulky figure below the skyline, now clearly outlined by the towering fire.

"She's here, Samuel."

Boots were scrabbling and a powder horn clanked on a rockface.

"They're still climbing, *boet*."

"I know it. Let them hear you, Miss Mattie," snarled Matthew.

"You hear me, Miss Mattie?" said Samuel.

"You still alive, Samuel?"

"I got to be, Miss Mattie. Who else going to get you down from there?"

Matthew pushed the woman into plain sight, holding her by the hair. "You see her, Samuel?"

"I see her, English."

"Then ease your triggers." Matthew pulled the woman back, clamping a hand over her mouth. She had the sense to do nothing but breathe.

"They're circling," said Klyn. "They might have second thoughts about rushing us now."

"Until first light," Matthew agreed. Then, "Samuel, we'll talk at dawn. One move from your people before then, and she goes over the edge. Pull them back, Griqua, or you'll have to catch her. *Verstaan?*"

Samuel gave orders and said, "We going down, English."

Matthew took Miss Mattie down to the fire, where she spread her hands gratefully. Abba had gathered enough timber to burn through the night and Matthew took him aside to whisper another set of orders. Abba nodded and went off to pack and saddle the horses. Matthew toed Miss Mattie, jerking her gaze from the fire. He threw her a horse blanket.

"Take off your dress and put this on." His tone brooked no argument, and minutes later he was back up with Klyn, pulling something behind him.

"They've withdrawn to the first slope. I threw a brand over to check," Klyn reported.

"Good. Here, prop this up so that the satin shows." Matthew passed him the dress stuffed with brush. "Then follow me down, you too, Boie."

The whole party was mounted when they climbed back down to the encampment.

Klyn slapped his forehead. "You don't plan to take the horses down the cliff path at *night*."

"Don't worry." Matthew forced a smile. "I'll hold your bridle."

"You'll hold *my* bridle. Damn your red neck...."

Miss Mattie used all her body to scream. "You mad English bastard. I can't go down there. I'll fall, I can't stand heights. I'm an old—"

Matthew gathered the blanket at her throat, choking her off, his face close to hers. "You'll sit your horse and hold your tongue or I'll throw you off the cliff myself. Decide. Either way, you go down."

Miss Mattie drooled and rocked herself, hating Matthew with every inch of her being. Kit listened to all the talk, hardly taking it all in. Was any of this worth it? she wondered dully. She had to see that Cord lived, but all this effort seemed... too much for so little a thing as her own well-being. If they would only let Cord sleep and get well. They made so much noise. Klyn was blindfolding the horses and she had no idea why. The banked fire spat a million sparks at the moon and she wished she could see Cord's face as he lay over Matthew's saddle. Was he still awake, would he smother from all the jogging?

With the party in line behind him, Matthew led Gaika down the narrow defile three hundred feet above the boiling river.

They were lost in the trees four miles to the south when Samuel reached the dress.

156

22

It was Cord who finally said what the other men had been thinking.

They had ridden due south after crossing the Marico River, then had struck east along the river basin, keeping to the rocky banks to cover their tracks. Boie had made a long circuit to the south and laid a false trail to confuse the pursuing Griquas, and had cut their trail as he doubled back to catch up with Matthew three days later.

They lived on the fish Abba speared and ate it raw to avoid lighting fires and saved their grain for the horses. The river water was sweet and they gathered wild fruit where they could. They rode for four hours and walked for four more, rested through the hottest hours of the day and rode through the cool of the dusk and the early hours of darkness.

It was during the fifth evening halt that Cord became lucid.

He raised himself from the litter they had built for him and saw them all for the first time. His thigh had swollen to three times its normal size, the knee as round as a wild melon. Kit was away at the river, cleaning herself up as best she could.

"Eastman," he called hoarsely.

Matthew came out of his doze and saw the tawny eyes on him, clear in the drawn and sallow face. The wound was uncovered and midges swirled around it.

The boys exchanged veiled glances. Klyn watched from under his hat brim and Miss Mattie stopped cleaning her nails with a thorn.

Matthew crossed to where Laidler lay and squatted beside him.

"It's got to be drawn and cauterized," Cord stated baldly. "And damned fast. I won't last another day if it isn't done right now." He saw Matthew's hesitation and his lip curled. "Give me the knife, man. I'll do it myself if you haven't the stomach."

Matthew was thinking how it would be if Cord died and left Kit ... he caught himself and masked his thoughts, knowing nothing had shown in his face. She was Cord's woman and he had no rights, no claim. She had not spoken more than three words to him since they had left the stinking shack at the Griqua settlement....

157

The wasted fingers gripped his wrist with surprising strength.

"The knife, man. Light a fire and heat it...." Cord's teeth clamped on the pain. "...open it up."

"Hell." Klyn was suddenly standing there. "I'll do it. Abba, light a fire."

Miss Mattie laughed aloud, an unpleasant staccato, knowing what a fire might mean to Samuel and the following Griquas; they could *smell* smoke four miles away. She and Cord traded stares until he was dragged down by the fever. Klyn wedged his knife between two fire stones, the blade deep in the heart of the flames. He tied his belt high on Cord's thigh and used his pistol as a tourniquet.

"Turn that and hold it as tight as you can when I make the incision," he told Matthew. "There must be three pints of pus in there." He looked at Cord. "He's out again. Let's do it before he comes to."

The knife went in and gobs of foulness welled out as Matthew bore down on the pistol. The stench of corruption blended with the smell of braised flesh. Klyn pressed upward from the knee with both hands, trying not to breathe as stuff spattered his face and forearms.

Cord came back and strained upward against the men working on him. Boie and Abba moved in to hold his chest and head, forcing a spoon down his throat to stop him swallowing his tongue. The sound that came from his mouth was high and almost inhuman when Klyn poured *brandewyn* into the open weeping trench.

Cries and stumbling came from the river.

"Kit. Christ," Klyn swore. "Keep her away, Matthew. Now."

Cord gave another hoarse scream as he fought the dark mists.

"Go, damn you. Abba, take the strain on the tourniquet."

Matthew found himself running toward the river down the whipping confusion of the animal trail, blinded by the sudden darkness. He was on a bend when Kit cannoned into him, her arms flailing as she fought to pass him. He trapped her arms, lifted her bodily from the ground. She freed a hand and he tried to avoid her raking nails. She bit and clawed and her legs twined around his, tripping him. They fell heavily together and Kit was eeling out from under him. A bare heel caught him across the bridge of his nose.

He caught her dress, trapped an ankle, and threw her onto

her back, levering his body over hers. Still she fought him, knee and elbow, head and fist. He was telling her things, talking, hardly knowing what he said, hard put to make sense. She spat in his face and still he talked, dimly aware of shouting from the camp.

His weight finally told and she lay under him, rigid and panting.

He brushed her damp hair from her forehead and talked on, softly. She heard nothing, saw nothing, her body in constant spasm.

Boie grew out of the undergrowth. "Nkosi, the Missie woman gone. She take horse, cut hobbles on horse, and go. Baas Klyn say we go and bring her back. You stay here, he say."

"Bloody woman," Matthew swore. "Yes, yes, go on."

Boie ducked his head and was gone.

Kit came back from far places, her limbs losing tension. Matthew helped her to her feet and led her back to camp, where Cord lay still, breathing deeply and evenly, the new dressing very white against his flesh. The trees muffled the silence and muted the river. A single tear gleamed on Kit's cheek.

"He's bitten through his lips," she said.

"They'll heal...."

She whirled on him, her face naked with pain. "Why did you come? Why did you have to come? Damn you and your insufferable interest in me. Cord could have died in that place. I could have died in that place. They could have used me and killed me and it would all have been over now. Why did you have to come?"

"Why?" Matthew stared at her, aware of a numbing fury building inside him. "You're asking me *why?*"

Kit spread her hands out over Cord's body. "Anything would have been better than this. Look at him. This is what is left of my husband. This isn't how I want him. Nor how he would want himself."

"Stop it, Kit."

"Stop it? You stop me, Matthew Eastman. You're so damned good at saving me, stop me. How do you know I want to be saved? What have you planned for the rest of my life? By any man's law you have the right to take me and my life and do what you want with it. I belong to you, don't I? Like some animal you pulled from a bog. You want me that much, do you?" She dragged the loose neck of her dress down to

159

show a pale breast. "Enough to put your friends in jeopardy, bring them into this wilderness for my sake? Enough to get them all killed for *this?*" She had one arm out of its sleeve and her torso was bared. "Here, it's yours, take it."

The flat of Matthew's hand sent her sprawling sideways, her long legs thrashing in the flickering uncertain light. She glared up at him, the tip of her tongue flicking the rill of blood from her lower lip and tasting it.

"You'll never be a Cord Laidler, Matthew Eastman. Even like this he's more man than you. He'd have taken me by now. What will you do?" She came up onto a knee and blood splashed on her chin. "Groan in the dark and make love to dreams?"

Matthew pulled her off the ground and jammed her mouth against his own. He had to stop her talking before his brain burst. Her blood seemed to fill his mouth as her lips opened and her tongue ran against his gritted teeth. He wanted her and hated knowing he was not the first. Had Cord been? he wondered. All he could see were her eyes, mocking and hating and aflame with desire.

"Bastard," she gasped, arching against him, her nails raking at his back, pulling at his shirt. Her dress had fallen down about her waist and he trapped it with a boot as he stepped forward with Kit held to him, kneeling down and laying her on his bedroll. His shirt came over his head and he pulled at his belt one-handed.

She tore herself from his mouth and her hands were against his chest, resisting him. "Don't. No." Her eyes were frightened and clear of the previous mad light. *"No!"* she snarled as he kneed her flanks wide. *"No!"*

"Yes," he insisted, too lost in her nakedness to pull back as he might have under different circumstances. He eased into her, hearing a sound that could have been pain or pleasure. Her hands were weakening and he bore in, pushing his chest down onto hers, drawing himself higher into her, moving slowly while she kept rigid control of her body; then faster and more urgently as her limbs softened and embraced him, drawing him closer and deeper. Her hands rose to his face and drew his lips down onto her breast.

"Matthew." The sigh could have been defeat or exhilaration. Her hips arched to meet his and her fists tattooed his back as she found the path to her climax, willing him to join her, calling him after her with jerking cries. Then she was

160

shuddering, hips twisting down and away, and she was limp under him as he found his own release.

It was a long time before either of them moved and Kit trembled as the night air touched her body.

On the other side of the fire, Cord Laidler's tawny eyes ceased watching and closed to let reality go. He had seen enough of it.

23

Sigwe the Matabele had not given the signal to start.

The young men were ranged in two columns on either side of the smooth slope, all of them greased with mutton fat and naked but for loincloths. No ornaments or beads or bracelets, just three *iKlwa* each. They waited for Sigwe to roll the target log, squinting up at him through the glare. Old Sigwe showed his gums and his one black tooth; behind him were the men with whips, ready to lash the backs of any incompetents. These were the warriors of the Ill-Tempered, and they relished beating the younger Snakes, as much as they enjoyed taunting them for their virginity. As bachelors the Snakes could not marry until they had washed their spears for Mzilikazi, which was why they must learn to kill with the *iKlwa* and not miss either a thrust or a cast.

There was bad blood between the Ill-Tempered and the Snakes impi and their kraals were built far apart to stop them from fighting among themselves. Mzilikazi fostered this rivalry, for it made the impi vie fiercely for honor in the field. The Ill-Tempered would punish the Snakes during war games and the young Snakes would cuckold the Ill-Tempered whenever they could. The year before, a group of Snakes had been surprised as they lay with the wives of the other impi. There had been blood spilled then and it could easily have escalated had not Mzilikazi intervened. He punished the women for tempting the men, burying some of them alive with broken limbs, and impaling two of the men on sharpened stakes. The widowed men were then drafted into the bachelor regiment. Honor had been satisfied all around.

Sigwe kicked the log down the slope.

It rolled slowly at first, gaining momentum as it went. The Snakes began their casts. Spears bit into the hardwood log and others chunked into the earth at either side. The Ill-Tempered moved in to wield their flails.

Sigwe started a second log into the milling warriors and

they danced aside or leapt over it, stabbing down with their spears. One miss was a flogging and two could mean death. A Snake slipped on the polished ground and his leg skidded beneath the second log, breaking below the knee. He bit on his pain and drove his spear into the wood.

Sigwe had him dragged aside, but the warrior clawed his way to his feet and hopped back to throw his last spear at the third log and it went home cleanly. Sigwe made a note to supply the goat the young man would be obliged to give the witchman for treatment. It would take great magic to expel the bad spirits from the broken limb.

Howls rose as the floggings began in earnest. It was good, Sigwe thought. The Snakes must fear the flails more than the guns of the whites.

There would be no cowards in Sigwe's impi.

24

Klyn had lied to Matthew for the first and, he hoped, for the last time.

Boie had picked Miss Mattie's tracks up at first light a quarter mile from a dogleg in the river. He had found where she had sheltered during the dark hours, a tall acacia tree growing from the thin soil above a kloof. How the fat old woman had shinned up the tree had puzzled the little Khoi-khoi when he climbed the tree himself. There was also fur in the upper branches, which meant that a leopard had used it recently. Who knew, Boie had told Klyn when they had met up later, she might well have shared the acacia with the animal, the sign was very recent. She had followed the river, crossing and recrossing it using the many fords that abounded there. Her feet were cut and she had left marks of her moon-time where she had made water in the shallows.

They had caught up with her at the dogleg where a thick stand of reeds grew from a spit of mud. She sat with her feet in the water combing her hair with her fingers, and waiting for the forty horsemen who came down a narrow defile less than a mile from her. Klyn had realized the uselessness of pursuing her farther. All he and Boie could do was watch to see if the Griquas collected her and turned back, or more importantly, continued to hunt the trekkers. They moved up into the high ground and watched the Griquas reach Miss Mattie. Klyn could have knocked Samuel from his horse with his pistol, but there was no need. After a few words, Miss

Mattie made them turn back for the settlement, but not before she made a chilling prediction.

"Samuel," she told the sweating Griqua. "They're dead already. The Matabele are massing along the Vaal. Mzilikazi has drawn his line and won't let a dung beetle cross it. Those fools will ride straight into five regiments of hell-raising kaffirs bent on cutting the nose from every white face they see. Let old Mzilikazi do our work for us. Samuel, you look like you was stomped by a bull. Let's go home and put some grease on those cuts."

"Yes, ma'am, Miss Mattie."

When the Griquas had ridden away, Klyn and Abba had made their way back to the camp and told Matthew they had not found any sign of the woman but that they had seen Griqua horsemen. It was the only way they knew of keeping up their pace without favoring Laidler too much. They both believed he was as good as dead, and his welfare could not come before that of the rest of them.

They had traveled through the rest of that day and rested where the Marico River ran through faults in the valley floor, silting and widening as the terrain flattened out into a modest delta of mudflat and swamp. Sacred ibis and spoonbills fished the reeded silt under the stands of fever trees, not a place to linger long, for at nights the midges and mosquitoes swarmed into the air and made life unbearable.

The surrounding forest petered out as folds of rising rock bellied up through the thin soil and formed low and undulating bald hills. A dry Kalahari wind drew moisture into the thermals rising from the high ground and drove the forming cloud eastward across the savannah.

Klyn hummed a profanity and wiped off his mouth.

The brackish water by a salt lick at the dead end of the draw had slaked the horses' thirst, but had left an aftertaste in his own mouth; the sulphurous tang of ancient eggs. It would have been better to have dug down to the stone bedrock where the water was fresher, but there was not the time for such luxuries.

To Klyn, there never seemed to be time for anything. He felt he had been in the saddle all winter and now spring was here. Was he to ride through this season and into high summer without a pause?

A man should make the time to watch the earth's changes. Watch the young shoots finger up through last year's stalks and throw out leaves, to bud and flower; to cover the winter's

163

dryness with the gold, lilac, and salmon of daisies, the blue of cornflower, periwinkle, and bellflower, the singing yellows of button flowers. God knew spring lasted for such a short time.

To be able to sit on your own stoep, with your woman close, and think together about future things with absolute certainty; to breathe tobacco into the evening light and digest the day's labor, to savor the night to come; to wait for the woman to make the sign that she was ready to leave the day behind, the wordless way of showing she wanted her man. Johannes Krige's daughter, Herrie, would be like that. Strong and careful and warm. She would bake and cosset and fill a man's bed with simple carnality; she would blush when her rump was slapped, be modest in company, sing clearly at the *kerk* on Sundays....

Klyn shook himself. There would be time for that, he promised himself, the rest of his long life, but first...

Matthew sat a yard away, sharpening the flint of his smoothbore before setting it back into the jaws of the lock. Klyn scratched the edge of the ulcer on his thigh. It itched like the devil now that it healed. Klyn had said nothing to Matthew about the wrong things he noticed now that he was back. There was a new tension between Matthew and Kit. Somehow a more disturbing dimension had been added to their relationship, a tenuous thing that defied analysis. Klyn did not care for it. He saw the glaring sensuality beneath the diffidence they affected for each other. It lived just as fiercely in Laidler's fevered face and glowed in the eyes set deep in dark sockets. Whatever Cord knew or thought he knew, it kept him alive despite the stink of gangrene that was on him.

With their share of good fortune, they might get him to Potgieter's laager within the next couple of days. That might not be soon enough, although Klyn saw no point in stating the obvious; it would achieve precisely nothing.

"Klyn, are you certain about the Griquas, that they are probably still following?" Matthew asked.

"Possible, Matthew, possible." Klyn took up his own long gun and inspected the bore. "If they come on too fast they might land in the Matabele's lap before we do."

Matthew nodded somberly. "That's if they're traveling east as we are. We'll have to ride hard to keep ahead of them." He glanced at Laidler and back at Klyn, who said:

"There can be no letup, *boet*. Not for him, not for us."

"Griqua or Matabele. Not much of a choice, is it?"

"Yes there is. The Matabele can run fifty miles in a day and fight a battle at the end of it. Maybe we should turn about and face the Griquas, eh?" Klyn smiled to take the edge away.

"Laidler doesn't stand much of a chance, does he?" Matthew could have been blushing. Klyn pretended to ignore his friend's rising color. Certain things had taken on a real meaning. So, Matthew had dipped his beak into forbidden honey and wanted the sweetness without the stings from the bees of conscience.

"As you say, *boet. Something's* keeping that man alive though." Klyn went off to relieve Abba at the lookout.

Matthew watched him go. He knew what kept Laidler alive.

25

Gaika had her nose deep in a succulent bush, tearing leaves from the branches and pulling them into her mouth with sideways movements of her teeth. Kit punched her in the side to stop her taking too much air into her stomach.

Gaika snorted and her flanks heaved. Kit tightened the cinch another notch and blew hair from her face. One more pull, just one more notch, and the saddle would be seated right. She waited for the mare to swallow air, ready to bring her knee up and to surprise more breath out of her.

Away from the river, the humidity was dramatically lower, the high veldt drowsed under an infinity of sky, and Kit was grateful for that. She thought of bathing in hot water, of making suds with scented soap.

Cord lay in the dappled shade of sansevieria overhanging the rock wall. More often now he had knowing periods and his head followed every move that Kit made. He maintained an impenetrable silence and never voiced the questions crowding his face, even when Kit fed or cleansed him. He listened to the forced brightness in her voice when she changed his dressing, and saw what she tried to conceal when she looked at his wasted limbs.

He was watching her now as she kneed the last wind from Eastman's mare and tightened the cinch to her satisfaction. He was reminded of the jogging rhythm of pain, mile after aching mile, slung on the litter between two horses, sabered by agony.

Better to have died, as Katherine had said. Much better.

Kit! How he despised Eastman's use of the diminutive of his wife's name. He made her sound like some Lascar's drab. He found himself regarding the acid green leaves of a thicket of euphorbia. If only he could reach it, he thought deliriously, cut it open, and rub the poisonous milky juice into his wound. Anything to stop the recurring nightmare of Katherine's body under Eastman's as they joined in a continual erotic conjunction in the dark and pink mists behind his eyelids. The more he squeezed his eyes closed, the clearer the images became, the more obscene their movements....

Cord fell asleep trying to clench his fists.

Kit had insisted as she always did that she take her turn as lookout, and she took the narrow trail to the top of the outcrop whose crest was dominated by a rock shaped like a many-fingered fist. As she climbed, she passed a pair of mature kokerbooms, their trunks glowing like gilded paper in the afternoon sun. When she had sent Boie down she eased her body out along the thumb of the granite fist and stared out over spreading fields of flax to the aching chrome horizon. She had wrapped the long gun Klyn had given her in a saddle blanket to stop the metal parts from burning her hands. She laid six one-ounce slugs in the curve of her powder horn and buried her waterskin deep in the shade of a young tamarisk tree. Kit passed her time counting centuries.

At the end of the first one hundred she started another. At three hundred she would wet her mouth and not before. Her head pounded inside her taut scalp and the skin of her shoulders was dry and scaly to the touch. The sun burned through her dress as though it had no substance.

She was in the low thirties of her fifth hundred when smudgy figures shivered in column in the boiling middle distance, perhaps two miles from her vantage point. Cattle and men, women, and children. A whole tribe on the move. She was in two minds whether or not to summon one of the men when Klyn lowered his bulk alongside her, cupping his eyes to cut down the glare.

"How long have they been there?"

"A few minutes, no longer. I can't read expressions at this distance, but from the way they're moving along, I'd say they were very, very frightened. You see how the men are flanking the rear? I think they fear an attack from behind."

Klyn grunted. "Good assessment. Do you see any smoke to the west?"

"Not in this haze." Kit tried to match Klyn's calm. "What do you think?"

"I think I don't like it." Klyn buried his fingers in his beard. "We'll have to stay here until we know for certain what has flushed them like so many headless quail."

"It's the Matabele, isn't it?" Kit whispered. "Those people are running from the Matabele."

Klyn said yes, he thought so. "But we must be sure. I'll send the boys out when the sun loses some heat."

Kit twisted up on an elbow, squarely facing Klyn. Her gaze drew his eyes to hers.

"That means we lose another day, the rest of this one at least."

"It does."

"What does that do to Cord's chances?" Kit's lips barely moved.

"It doesn't improve them, but you know that. Why have me say it?"

"Because it has to be said. Don't act the Dutch buffalo with me, Klyn, I'll not stand for it. I know you to be an educated man. Those books in your wagon and the way you've worked on Cord tell me a great deal about you. Quite the surgeon." Kit turned back onto her stomach and smoothed her hair about her ears. "To save you asking, yes, I've been through your chest. I've read your letters and your journal. Never put anything past a determined and curious woman."

"I never will again," said Klyn, coldly amused by her confession.

"Will he die?"

"When I went into his leg I would have given him twelve hours at the most. Now I think he could live with gangrene in his heart and a cancer in his brain. He's living for something outside himself, something unhealthy. I don't know what happened when I was away chasing Miss Mattie. I don't know, but I can guess. Your husband has taken hold of life and intends to use it badly. Do you understand me, Mrs. Laidler? He is diseased twice over."

Kit paled as his words bored at her.

"Down there," Klyn jerked his chin in the direction of the camp, "I have a friend and I am here for him, him alone. Only in that regard are you and your husband included in my concern for our well-being. Does that make my attitude clear to you?"

"Not for me. Not for Cord. Is that it?"

"Yes, Mrs. Laidler. That is precisely it."

"So, I am no longer Kit."

"No, Mrs. Laidler, you ceased being that the day you married in Colesberg. I sometimes wish we had been too late to save you from the Mfengu. Then we should be with Potgieter and Cilliers, dying or living for a cause you and your kind would not understand."

"I might have...once," Kit supposed.

"I doubt that."

"You're a hard man, Klyn."

"You have to know. One of us has to use honesty."

The fleeing tribe had passed into the western haze and the terrain below was a blistering, empty void. They watched it side by side and yet apart. Both of them felt the loss of something fine. Kit washed her mouth from her waterskin.

"Matthew says you're fond of a girl you met, a daughter of one of the trekkers."

Klyn refused a drink, shading his eyes as though they were the source of his exhaustion. He did not move or speak for many seconds.

He finally said, "Yes, there is a girl I shall marry. We shared a meal only once, but I may well love her. I think I do." The words tasted strange in his mouth.

"Then can't you understand how I..."

"No!" he snapped. "What you're doing is quite different. You're no Herrie Krige. You have no love for either Matthew or your husband. Your love is only for yourself. You take or are taken, it is your way. It makes no difference to you if Laidler lives or dies, own up to it. You'll take your pleasure as widow or wife."

"Matthew would kill you if you said that in front of him."

"He would try."

"And if I repeat what you have just said?"

"Somebody would most surely die, Mrs. Laidler."

"I won't, I swear I won't."

"Do you? Try it anyway, you might get us all killed," Klyn said, kneeling up.

"Help me, damn you!"

"How can I?" Klyn asked, backing down from the slope. "It's already too late."

26

A solitary quiver tree stood sentinel near the entrance of the deserted kraal of fifty huts. The Bakwena clan, who had inhabited these parts for generations, had fled, driving their precious animals before them. Mzilikazi's impi were on the move and the Bakwena knew that wherever his impi journeyed, they were on a mission of conquest or retribution.

The Matabele scouts moved down through the misty cornfields and up to the kraal entrance with little caution. There were ten of them and they were dressed in karosses and civet-fur kilts. A single black circle marked their oxhide shields and showed them to be an advance guard of the Invincibles. They had run twenty miles since noon and were ten miles ahead of the main impi, heading for Potgieter's laager.

There was a wispy ground mist in the late light, a curling veil of pale vapor over the abandoned mealie fields. A dog scratched itself inside the outer *isango* hedge, ears pricking each time a goat bleated from off in the rock cairn where the Bakwena had driven them the previous night.

A hawk hovered in the darkening sky, watching for mammals in the corn, patient and silent. Without warning, her wings folded and she dropped, braked inches from the ground, snatched, and rose again, a young doe in her talons. She swooped over the rocks north of the kraal and dropped the rabbit to its death. Then she settled on the corpse and began to feed, her golden eyes alert.

The dog breathed the scent of strangers and skulked away.

The Invincibles went from hut to hut and found they were all empty save one, where an old man lay in a coma on the floor. The Matabele ignored him, searching for grain pits or any stored or hidden food. There should be much, for the fleeing Bakwena had taken little with them in their panic to get away.

One of the scouts touched the Earth Mother symbol on his groin and gathered the other men around him.

"We are smiled on," he said. "There is enough here for all our men. Grain, beer, and meat. Mkalipi will praise us."

"Your luck is good for all of us, Jakot," said one called Sihayo. "You have survived the Great King's foot on your neck. Your belly is unscratched. Now this fat kraal. The Invincibles will fight with full bellies tomorrow."

Jakot's face lost its humor. "To speak of a man's luck is a bad thing, Sihayo. You will go and bring the goats here. You will milk the shes yourself. *All of them*. I will go to the Lord Mkalipi and tell him of this place."

Jakot held his *iKlwa* at guard, ready to defend his order.

Sihayo's eyes dulled. He nodded, accepting the task of a lowly herdboy without question. It was fitting, for he had spoken without thought. If Jakot died badly in battle, it would be his fault and his family would lose their wealth to placate the spirits.

Jakot tasted his luck on his tongue and decided it was not too soured by Sihayo's thoughtless remarks. The others saluted him with raised spears as he started back toward the main column. All their luck lived with Jakot and they respected him for it.

The dog had crept into the rocks and lay panting with thirst. In the darkness just downwind of the dog, the shadowy figure of Boie backed down the slope and set off across the open veldt where he was joined by Abba, who had been watching the main force of the Invincibles.

They had much to relate to Nkosi and the baas, and they ran for an hour without pause.

27

Cord's dream was there again, a haunting thing.

It came from outside himself in the brightness and heat where the others lived despite him; their voices discussed him as a burden they must carry, a thing on a litter whose back knew every strap and knot between the poles, knew every gait the litter horses used to cover ground.

If he cleared the mists and opened his heavy lids, he might see and hear himself discussed, learn when they would hoist him back between two horses where he was punched full of pain with every hoof fall. There was less of him every day to fight back, more and more of the consuming thing that came from behind the pain to possess the shell of his body.

Cord forced himself into awareness and listened to the monochrome figures argue in the moonlight. It would be so easy to die and to leave them bickering, but he would not. He found a way inside the bandages and dug his fingers into the wound. With the pain came the recognition of why he must stay. None of them heard his gasp of agony.

Eastman was talking. "You heard the boys, Kit. The Ma-

170

tabele will stay at the Bakwena kraal until first light. We must leave before then and circle around so that we can get ahead of them. That gives us three more hours of rest. The horses need it, I need it. We'll leave then, and not before. We can't afford to confront the Matabele out here. We wouldn't stand a chance."

"And Cord will die. Tell him, Klyn."

"Matthew is right," Klyn sounded short-tempered and Cord wondered why.

"What about Cord?"

"A rest will do him some good."

"He'd rest forever if you two had your way. Both of you!" Kit snarled, teeth bared.

She protests too much, thought Cord. So, that means her conscience is biting her; how she hates to be caught out by her own conflicting interests. Poor Katherine, she wants me the way I was, not as I am now, and she wants the trekker's body without his troublesome habit of doing things his way. Domination or servitude? The classic dilemma of a woman like Katherine. Was that what he meant? Cord was not certain, it was difficult to follow any line of reasoning. He was taking the simplistic view because it was all his failing energy would allow.

He drifted and came back with a jolt.

Survive, he told himself. *Survive*. Consider that and nothing else. *Yet*.

Kit said, "We leave now."

Eastman had lain himself on his blanket and covered his face with his hat. "In three hours. Get some sleep."

Cord wiped bile from his lips. Katherine screamed "Bastards" and he found pleasure in her venom before he drifted away.

28

The scouts had told Mkalipi true.

He sat his white stallion and studied the trekkers' wagons drawn up on the top of the hill. Lanterns showed between the canvas humps, a circle of guttering pinheads against the night sky. Thorn had been packed beneath the wagon beds and between the wagons themselves. Hides had been lashed to the wooden sides to guard against fire and to cover any hand- or footholds. One of the wagons had been fitted with timber skis and could be swung to make an entrance. One side of the hill fell sheer to the river and the other three slopes had been cleared of vegetation so there was no cover for Mkalipi's advancing impi from the moment they showed themselves on the open plain and moved to the attack. Mkalipi did not mind, it was a good killing ground. The sixty wagons were so few and seemed so frail at the top of the bald hill.

Mkalipi ordered the Invincibles into the dead ground facing the hill, the Sticks and the Bees ranged either side of them. When the Snakes and the Ill-Tempered arrived, he would make them the horns of the bull, to east and west of the head and loins.

Mkalipi was glad he had force-marched his regiments through the night and the heat of the day and not stayed at the Bakwena kraal, as Jakot had suggested. Soldiers should fight and keep lean, not sleep under cover with full bellies. Did not the lioness kill best on hunger? When her belly was full she slept in the sun like an old bitch and let her cubs pull her tail, and any herdboy could drive her away with a sling.

After tomorrow, Mkalipi thought, they would call this place Mkalipi's Hill and sing of it for a hundred generations. His face might be lost, but his name would live on in traditional praise songs.

What more could a man ask for his sons and his sons' sons?

29

Cord's laughter rode with them.

It was a continual babble punctuated by shouted orders in English, Dutch, and Sotho. In his mind, elephants died in numberless stands to make him ivory-rich a thousand times over. He beat his Griquas, bribed officials, and drove into Kit's body between gouts of fevered laughter. More than once he brought his mounts to a halt with a harsh command, almost pulling Klyn from his saddle.

They rode the open ground, keeping the Vaal River on their right, following the trekkers' spoor through the new spring growth. By midday, they had begun to straggle and had to stop to bunch up again.

Ahead of them was a rolling plain that fell in a long slope to the river and rose in sudden folds to the higher ground toward the east. The passage of the Matabele was clearly

172

marked in the grass, a snaking trail more than a hundred yards wide.

Drumming came to them on the changing wind.

They cantered up the slope of the first rise, across a saddle of stone and scrub grass, and up a second steeper gradient. Here the terrain was broken and scored by overgrown fissures, and the drums seemed to come up at them from every kloof and pothole. Nesting groundbirds flew from under their horses, clattering into the sky with harsh cries of protest.

They picked through the mopani and mimosa thorn to where a shale fall gave them access to the brow of the last hill. The men and boys dismounted to pull the horses up the slide one at a time. It was hard, sweating work. The horses balked and fought the reins, as their hooves slid from beneath them on the treacherous gravel.

What they saw when they all reached the crest took away what little breath they had left.

A wide plain swept away to the north and east, and on the southern side, a hill rose before the silver ribbon of the Vaal River. Potgieter's wagons ringed the summit of the hill and looked like a circle of toys peopled by tiny dolls. Cattle, sheep, and goats were spread all over the plain, running and milling as the swelling drums beat dull fists at the skies.

Kit's face paled and Klyn gripped Matthew's arm painfully as he pointed mutely. Rising from the dead ground around the rim of the plain were row after row of warriors, a black wall of men that stretched for half a mile.

BOOK THREE

Eye for eye,
tooth for tooth,
hand for hand,
foot for foot,
burning for burning,
wound for wound,
stripe for stripe.

EXODUS 21: 23—25

1

The Matabele regiments were lined up in three phalanxes of a hundred men wide and ten men deep, standing side on to the hill. At Mkalipi's command, the front ranks stamped their feet and faced to the front, presenting their shields toward the laager. With this sudden movement the army seemed to double its size, blowing up like the threat posture of a frilled lizard. Under cover of the front wall of shields, the rear ranks streamed sideways and formed up on either side of the central body of the army. Again there was a great stamp of feet, and again the army doubled its length. To the east were the black shields of the Bees, in the center, the white shields of the Invincibles, and running to the west the pied shields of the Sticks.

A great shout went up. *"Bulala!"*

A pause, and the men in the second rank raised their shields above the heads of the front ranks and the army doubled its height.

"Bulala!"

"Kill," Klyn translated, chilled by the sight. Cord muttered an obscenity as Kit cleaned his sweating face with a dampened rag, her own expression dead and her movements automatic. Matthew loaded his smoothbore and his pistols with fragmentation balls and told Boie and Abba to follow suit. A wide spread of fire would be needed if they had to make a run for the laager through the encircling Matabele.

"At least Potgieter has chosen well," said Klyn. "He has the river at his back and the Matabele will be fighting uphill the whole time. They'll pay for every foot they advance."

Until the trekkers are swamped, thought Matthew, keeping his opinion to himself. He watched the Matabele as the warriors crashed spear haft against shield bar in concert. The grass plain seemed to ripple with each great crashing beat as the regiments gave voice to their battle calls, a rhythmic lowing that surfed out to roll over the circle of wagons. Impi champions came out of the wall of shields and mimed their previous victories, laying down challenges to single combat, each man backed by a regimental praise singer.

It was Boie who noticed a sudden flurry of movement inside the laager, and he drew Matthew's attention to it. The entrance wagon was being swung outward and a group of mounted men were filing out through the gap. They formed up in line abreast and rode down the slope of the hill toward the massed impi. There were sixteen of them.

"Madness," said Klyn.

Sheep scattered from before the mounted trekkers, milling in white rivers. The ranks of the Invincibles opened with several hard stamps to form a black corridor of men. A man mounted on a white stallion rode forward at a leisurely pace followed by four lesser indunas on foot, each carrying a long pole mounted with skulls and tails and topped out with carved symbols; the standards of the impi.

Klyn put his spyglass to his eye.

"Well," he said. "That's not Mzilikazi, the Great Elephant, that's Mkalipi, his chief induna. The King must think that sixty wagons are not worthy of his personal attention."

Mkalipi reined in some twenty yards in front of the Invincibles and watched the trekkers approach. Boie said something in his own tongue and extended his arm to the east. "See, Nkosi."

Rising from the long grass along the eastern flank of the plain, and stretching almost to the banks of the Vaal, were the lines of yet another impi, row after row of tan shields advancing in rows. The Ill-Tempered on the march, bent on flanking the sixteen trekkers.

"Can't Potgieter see what's happening?" said Matthew, realizing as he spoke that the Ill-Tempered were screened by the reeds and the rising ground.

Klyn was watching to the north, scanning the lower slopes of the hillock where they were formed up. Down in the folds and gullies and spare tree cover, another regiment was circling the skirt of the hill, using the broken ground to cover their advance. It was clear that it would only be a matter of minutes before the Snakes would have completed the encircling maneuver, completely surrounding the trekkers and cutting Klyn and Matthew off from the laager. The striped shields of the Snakes moved at incredible speed, as the warriors ran effortlessly and silently on their bare feet.

"Time for us to be gone," Klyn said quietly, his voice barely rising above the crescendo of drums and shouts. Matthew had already lifted Kit into her saddle and was mounting Gaika, the reins of the litter horses gathered in his left hand. Turning, he could make out the individual features of the nearest Snakes, the gleam of sweat on their shaven heads.

"All right, Matthew, take them down. Abba and I will cover you."

"Klyn...."

Klyn laid his quirt across Gaika's rump and she was down the hill, forcing the litter horses into a trot and then a gallop. Kit's roan leapt ahead of Matthew as she spurred its flanks, riding low over its neck and pulling the long gun from the saddle scabbard.

The boom of Klyn's gun followed Abba's and the advancing battle calls of the Snakes were counterpointed by the screams of wounded warriors.

Matthew allowed Gaika to set her own pace as he concentrated on the litter horses dragging behind him. The Snakes coming around the base of the hill had seen the breaking horses and were splitting into companies of twenty, running at angles calculated to cut across their path, closing fast on Kit's roan.

A sprinting warrior came up on her, reaching to pull her from the saddle as several more bunched in, yelling to spook the horse. Matthew had no way of making up ground to help her, for Gaika was still on the incline and hard put to keep her balance as she and Matthew pulled the bucking litter horses after them.

Kit swung and fired into the running warriors.

The closest lost shape as his torso spattered apart. Two others dropped and skidded on their faces as their shields bowled away. Another man spun in a complete circle with his face gone.

Gaika jumped the last ridge before the flat and Matthew bored her into the remaining warriors as they halted in confusion. A shower of throwing spears plumped into the ground around him as he swung Gaika toward the laager, then the litter horses found a matching pace and Matthew took them off toward the hill, leaving the Snakes behind. Cord was a sawing blur on the swinging litter and his screams pursued Gaika across the plain. Matthew pitched his hearing low to cut them out, twisting to look behind. *Where was Klyn?*

The party of Boers had wheeled away from the Matabele and were galloping full tilt for the laager, for Klyn's gunfire had awakened them to their danger. The entire front of the Invincibles were in pursuit. Incredibly to Matthew, the Boers reined in hard, reared their horses into a turn, and dashed back toward the Matabele. Matthew recognized Potgieter and Cilliers in the van of the charge, their muskets across rigid forearms. The horsemen galloped to within feet of the advancing warriors, reined in, and fired in concert, hiding themselves in their own smoke for a long moment. Then, whooping and calling, they were racing away from the hole they had torn in the shields behind them. The Invincibles closed their ranks and came on without pausing, trampling on their own dead and wounded.

Matthew swiveled in his saddle to see Klyn coming fast, blowing a ball into the muzzle of his smoothbore and ramming it home, controlling Pallas with his thighs and heels. Abba was beside him, hanging from his horse and spitting Snakes like so many running quintains, his arm and spear as red as a cavalry sleeve.

Klyn swept past Matthew, flashing him a broad wink. He set Pallas after Kit and urged her mount to stretch out with flicks of his quirt. The laager came closer and closer, and Matthew could pick out faces at the gunports, knowing they were going to make it.

The main group of the Snakes had curved in to join with the western flank of the Bees and had cut off the fleeing Boers; they were now between them and the advancing Invincibles. Matthew had to stop worrying about their welfare when he saw that six companies of the bachelor regiment were running across Kit's path. She looked neither left nor right, but kept her roan laboring for the bottom of the rise and the laager above it.

There were suddenly Snakes in Matthew's way. He drew off a bead one-handed and fired at point-blank range. Gaika leapt the fallen men and the lead rein bit into Matthew's wrist as the litter horses balked. Snakes seemed to be coming up out of the ground. Matthew scabbarded his long gun, drew a pistol, and shot a warrior from off his leg. Boie was covering his back with his short and deadly bow.

Matthew was almost wrenched from the saddle as he lost control of the litter horses. An *iKlwa* had slashed through one of the straps and Cord hung head down, his leg hanging at an odd angle as he was bobbed about between the shying horses. The horse that had lost its front strap was trying to run from the one responding to the lead rein.

Matthew freed the unmanageable horse with a slash of his knife and the animal ran straight for the Snakes. They cut it down with savage spearthrusts and gave Matthew the precious seconds he needed to tie the lead rein off to his pommel and to get enough purchase on the edge of the litter to support it with his hand. Unable now to defend himself in any way, Matthew set his spurs to Gaika and hoped her speed and his strong left arm would take them away from the warriors coming up swiftly behind him.

The Boers had scattered the circling Snakes with a volley and were making for the hill as they reloaded. Kit had reached the wagons and was hurtling through the gap with Klyn and Abba close behind. Boie had no more arrows and no time to reload the smoothbore as he tried to keep the running Snakes diverted from Matthew by rushing through them.

Furious, Matthew ordered him into the laager in his own language.

The Boers had turned and were making yet another dash through the broken ranks of Snakes, charging on toward the white shields of the Invincibles. Again their broadside ripped into the Matabele, and again the Boers were galloping out of their own smoke. This time they kept going toward the laager. The Matabele center was a rabble. The flanks were pressing in so hard that there was hardly room to wield a spear, and both well and wounded were trampled to death in the crush, so intent were the warriors to press the attack on the mounted trekkers.

"Come *on,* Boie!" Matthew wished he had a third arm to strike the Khoikhoi, willing the small man to cover ground and to pass him so that he could see that everybody was safely ahead of him. Boie and the foal streaked past him and Matthew urged him on with foul Dutch.

Then Matthew's vision was awash with red and singing pain. His fingers loosened on the litter, lost purchase, and gripped again. The flat of an *iKlwa* had opened his eyebrow. Stunned, his lifted his hat and jammed it down over the cut so that it bled inside the crown. His right eye was recording everything twice. Unsure of his direction, he did not know that Gaika had swerved toward the western flank of the Bees.

Klyn was dismounting when he saw the spear cut across Matthew's face. He was back into the saddle without thinking and pushing Pallas back down the bald slope. He saw Boie wheel about and take Gaika's rein, pulling the mare around toward the laager. Matthew was half out of his saddle, holding onto Cord's litter with all his strength, bringing the frightened litter horse around with him. But too slowly, Klyn knew, much too slowly. Let go, *boet,* let the bastard go, he's worth nothing and he's dying anyway. Then, as Pallas ate

179

ground, he thought: But you won't, you stubborn *rooinek*. You know you'd lose her if you gave him up to the kaffirs. Poor bastard, you lose both ways.

Klyn went through the nearest Snake company as if it had no substance. He fired sideways into the warriors with both pistols; there was no need to aim. He cannoned down a double row of Bees and cleared a way with his smoothbore, wheeling and reloading and drawing the rabble of Snakes and Bees to him, away from Matthew. He fired, loaded, and fired again. He was loading for the third time when Pallas fell.

His long gun flew in an eccentric arc, far out over the converging shields, and the shout from the Matabele was almost a physical thing.

Klyn struck the ground with his shoulder and he rolled to his feet, winded but unhurt. He cast about for Abba instinctively, and saw him running in, his arm out and ready to snatch him up onto the horse behind him. Klyn began running toward Abba. He did not have to spare a look for Pallas, the horse was dead from a broken neck.

Klyn set himself as Abba swept in.

Something punched him in the side, numbing and cold. Klyn stood stock-still, his outstretched fingers brushing Abba's as the Khoikhoi raced past and was gone.

A dark shaft grew from Klyn's ribs. He did not touch it. He knew that he was struck deep and finally, and it would all end here. Abba was bringing his horse around again and Klyn waved him off wearily; there was no pain, just a numbness below his waist and a growing lassitude he found comforting. Through fading eyes, he saw Boie lead Gaika and the litter horse into the laager with the last of the mounted Boers. The entrance wagon was swung closed behind them. Well, he thought, satisfied, at least Matthew is safe....

Klyn drew his pistols and cocked them as he faced the white shields. He smiled when Abba dismounted beside him and drove the horse away. All Khoikhois are fools, he thought with affection, and this one...

Klyn was still smiling when he was swamped and the *iKlwa* tore into him.

Abba was harder to kill as he defended the body. He took many Invincibles with him.

As soon as the Khoikhoi had brought Matthew and Cord inside the laager, two small boys whipped up the oxen and swung the entrance wagon in to complete the circle. They cut the animals free and shooed them away down the hill. Women rushed forward to pack bales of thorn under the wagon bed and nailed wooden gunports across the gaps between the wagons on either side. The canvas sails and the hides lashed to the wooden upperworks were doused with buckets of river water to guard against fire, and the work was done with speed and without hurry.

Johannes Krige had been one of the mounted party who had tried to parlay with Mkalipi and had come back without a scratch despite the many charges he and his companions had made. They had left scores of maimed and dead behind them on the plain. Krige handed his daughter Herrie his reins and his smoothbore and ran to where Matthew still slumped over Gaika's neck, and helped the big Englishman down. He had seen Klyn and Abba go down under the *iKlwa* of the Invincibles, and he recognized that he might have to restrain Matthew from going back out. He eased the bloody hat from Matthew's head and inspected his wound. It could have been worse. The bone showed clearly through the torn eyebrow, but the blade had missed the eye. He called for bandages.

Other trekkers were carrying Cord into the hospital kraal in the center of the compound where the children and the old women sheltered. Kit ran alongside supporting her husband's head.

When the bandage was tied around his head, Matthew shook himself free from Krige's supporting arm and took in his surroundings. The horses were being tethered inside a thorn *isango* roofed over with canvas, and the more skittish ones were blindfolded and hobbled. A small girl sat among them, singing a song that included all their names, a rag doll and a Bible in her lap.

Men stood at the gunports beside their wagons and held their fire as the Matabele re-formed at the base of the hill. Their womenfolk kneeled beside them, ready to reload, to give covering fire if needed, to dress wounds or douse any fires that might break out from the barrels of river water all around the perimeter. Sons stood ready to take their father's place should they fall. Potgieter and Cilliers went from wagon to wagon, giving courage and succor to all those who needed it. All the faces in the laager were fiercely calm, and it was as though they all felt they had been born for this struggle. Matthew was touched by their faith despite his own pressing personal concerns. His head wound pulsed in time to the Matabele's drumming shields.

Matthew stamped his heels to firm up his buckling legs and took his reloaded smoothbore from Boie, pleased to note that the Khoikhoi was unmarked. Matthew cast about for sight of Klyn, for the familiar booming laugh, the constant shadow that was Abba.

"Where's Klyn?" he asked Krige.

Krige shook his head and made no answer; he was working on how to frame his explanation of Klyn's death to Herrie.

Matthew looked wildly about him. "He's still out there. My horse."

"No!" Krige said harshly. "You must stay here, you're needed. You, your friend . . . you cannot help him. . . ."

"Where is he, Dutchman?" Matthew half-lifted Krige from his feet.

"Dead, *kerel*." There was no soft way to say it. Krige was lowered and he saw the big Englishman draw himself erect, expanding his torso as though he needed every ounce of flesh and bone to absorb the huge loss. His eyes glittered with more than mere tears.

"You're sure?"

"Sadly, yes."

"Then as God judges all men . . ." Matthew did not have to continue to make it clear that payment would be exacted. "Where should I stand?"

"I only have daughters, Matthew Eastman," said Krige, no apology in his voice. Herrie and her sisters would not hesitate to avenge their father if he fell, but it was traditionally fitting for a son to guard his father's back. Krige was offering that honor to Matthew, an honor not given lightly, and never to a stranger.

Matthew understood through his anger and anguish and thanked Krige formally. "And Abba, Menheer Krige?"

"Together."

"Here they come," somebody yelled. "Places, *kerels*."

Herrie watched Matthew and her father approach their wagon. She, her mother, and her sisters wore heavy leather aprons over their dresses, as much for protection as for cleanliness. Their faces were washed of all emotion and there was silence until Herrie asked formally, "May I load for you, Menheer Eastman?"

Then she walked slowly into his arms and held herself to him until their trembling had subsided, somehow finding solace together in their loss.

So, thought Krige, she saw Klyn's end and knows; he was glad of her ability to share her sadness with Matthew.

Matthew drew himself back and smiled down into the wan, round face.

"I should be honored, Mejevrou Krige. With your father's permission."

"Given gladly," said Krige, turning away to hide his own pricking eyes. The simple formality had helped them all.

Moments later, the first wave of the Invincibles surged in.

3

There was anger all around Jakot.

As the one with the luck, the one they all followed, he held himself aloof from it all and showed no expression.

The other warriors took their cue from him, they kept their lines dressed and watched for the induna's signal for the impi to advance across the thousand yards of open ground. The mounted corngrowers had savaged the Invincibles with their withering fire, each gun killed more than once each time it spat smoke, and the ranks to the east of Jakot's group had taken the worst of the whites' gunfire. The survivors were smeared with the blood of their dead, and the grass at their feet was red between the heaped corpses and the twitching wounded. Bands of herdboys moved about giving the death thrust to the mortally wounded before dragging them from the field.

Sihayo, Jakot noticed, had lost the lobe of his left ear and dark blood trailed down his chest. It was a lucky wound and could well be the sign that the old mud father was with them all. It had been Sihayo's thrust that had cut the life from the Khoikhoi who had come to fight with the dying white man. A good thrust that had opened him and finished him in one clean move. Jakot could not have done better himself, and he had let that show in his face for Sihayo to see.

The Bees had crowded in then, and had washed their spears like callow boys on their first pig hunt. Jakot had been pleased when Sihayo had shown his scorn, content to dip his

183

little finger in the slashed jugular of his enemy and touch it to his lips.

It was fitting and made the Bees ashamed.

The drums fell silent and all eyes turned to the great induna on his white stallion, for he was about to decide who was to make the first attack on the corngrowers. It must be us, Jakot decided, we are the ones who took the first fire as was fitting for the most senior of all the regiments here. We are owed blood.

There was a great sigh from around Jakot, and much stiffening of the limbs. Mkalipi had touched the induna who carried the totem of the Invincibles, and the standard was raised and turned sideways, the signal for them to advance.

Jakot struck his shield with the haft of his *iKlwa* and the men took up the beat until the whole regiment drummed out a walking pace. The induna drove the totem into the ground and the Invincibles moved forward, stepping in time to the beating spears; behind them, first the small drums and then the larger reinforced the march, accelerating the tempo until the walk became a trot and the trot a run.

The Invincibles swept up the hill.

There was no shooting and Jakot thought the whites could not have many bullets to waste; he saved his breath for running and let the other warriors shout for him. As he got closer to the circle of wagons the slope of the hill made them seem taller, and he saw the packed thorn and the hides lashed across all the gaps, realizing with sudden certainty that the fighting was not to be as easy as he had first thought. He began to run at an angle, looking for a gap in the defenses he could lead an assault against. There were none.

A bare six feet from the laager the guns opened up, and Jakot found himself choking in clouds of stinking sulphur. Invincibles were dropping all around him, thrown away by the impact of the fragmentation balls, ten here, a dozen there, and men became black ghosts illuminated by muzzle flashes.

Jakot was hurled to the ground when a dying man cannoned into him, and he sensed others dropping all around him. He was deafened by gunfire and his eyes streamed from the powder fumes. He scrambled in under a gunport, up to his waist in thorn, raised up and thrust a spear through a gunport, feeling it strike flesh.

A musket stabbed out at him and fired only inches from his face. Jakot was knocked down by the blast, his face burned and his eyebrows singed. A warrior stumbled over him and tore at the gun barrel. The hot metal burned through his palms and he withdrew with his skin hanging in shreds. He was still screaming when the next shot knocked him down.

Some fifty feet away, Sihayo was crushed against a wagon side, immobilized by the corpses piled around his legs and buffeted by charging warriors who cut at the hides and the wagon sails in an effort to breach the wall. Sihayo's spears and shield had been torn from his grasp, and all he could do was watch the slaughter. Every shot seemed to kill more men than he had fingers, and mutilated men screamed all around him with nobody to give them the death thrust. Sihayo turned his head into his shoulder to hide his tears of shame.

A long time later he found the strength to free himself. He crawled along the wall of wagons in search of a breach, and found Jakot, who was working to clear thorn. Feverishly, they worked together, ignoring the cuts and scratches they inflicted on themselves. They could hear the white women talking on the far side as they loaded muskets. To kill just one of them would be a considerable victory, for not a single Invincible had breached the laager, and they could feel the attack flagging.

A group of Invincibles near them had formed a tortoise of shields and were raising one of their number above the wagon sail. He began casting spears into the laager, and there were shouts of distress and warning from the whites. A corngrower fired through the canvas and blew the tortoise apart. The warrior was flung from the tottering shields and fell inside the laager, where a woman clubbed him to death with an iron pot.

Jakot crawled into the hole he and Sihayo had made, an *iKlwa* between his teeth. Sihayo watched him worm forward until only the soles of his feet could be seen. There was the sound of a blow and a grunt of pain. Jakot went limp and Sihayo grasped his ankles and hauled him backward. A musket angled down close to him and blew a crater in the ground next to his thigh, peppering his lower limbs with burning powder. Sihayo rolled himself and Jakot aside, barely avoiding a second blast. Jakot had a nasty head wound and the whites of his eyes were suffused with blood. Sihayo would not believe he was dead; he threw Jakot over his shoulder and ran back down the hill.

The whole impi was in retreat, the first time since they had been formed.

Let others do better, Sihayo thought bitterly.

4

Matthew fired steadily into the black and screaming wall of men.

He was deafened by the booming guns and his shoulder was bruised and swollen by the constant kick of his red-hot smoothbore. He sighted and fired like an automaton, as quickly and as regularly as he could, the press of men crowded so close together that aiming was unnecessary. With a fine instinct, Krige matched Matthew's shots so that their volleys had maximum effect. His pipe remained clamped and burning between his teeth, adding in its small way to the smoking pall that hung over the laager.

When an *iKlwa* took Krige in the thigh, he staggered away and pulled the blade out himself. His wife used a harness strap as a tourniquet and tied rags over the gash. Matthew fired into the face of the Invincible who had made the cast, and saw him fall away with his hair alight, huge teeth bared. Another warrior leaped in and bore down on Matthew's long gun, almost tearing it from his grasp. It was Herrie who killed him with a snap shot from the waist.

And still the Matabele came on, dying in rows as they clawed at the defenses with their bare hands.

Matthew knew he was killing bravery beyond anything he had ever known, and he was hard put to keeping the warriors away from his gunport without support. It was easier when Krige rejoined him, his leg strapped to a broomhandle.

Their eyes streamed and their clothes blackened. They snorted to clear sulphur and black powder from their nostrils, and when their guns grew too hot to handle, they steeped them in the water barrels to cool.

The Matabele threw themselves at the gunports as if seeking death, and their bodies piled up to form a second wall beyond the thorn.

Herrie's feet went from under her and she fell onto her elbow, kicking frantically, unable to cry out, for fear had made her mute. A black hand had gripped the edge of her apron and was drawing her beneath the wagon where a poised *iKlwa* sought to plunge itself into her throat.

Matthew stamped on the hand, rolled the girl away, and drove his gunbutt into the black face. The Matabele shook his head and thrust savagely up at him, slicing through the laces of his veldschoene. A second blow to the Invincible's

186

temple finished him and he was dragged from sight. Krige fired down through the gunport, depressing his gun as far as he could, trying to kill the man and his rescuer as they made good their escape. The two Matabele lost themselves in the rolling smoke.

A ragged cheering rose above the din of shots and cries, running rapidly around the peripheral defenses.

Krige fired a last time and then rested his smoothbore across the rim of the gunport where the hot barrel burned a black groove in the wood.

"They leave," he shouted incredulously. "God be praised, they leave!"

5

Matthew slumped against the wheel of the wagon and watched the smoke drifting away out over the river. Fumes clung to the ground around the wagons as though the very earth itself had burned. Herrie offered him a ladleful of water and it tasted sulphurous and wonderful.

"So, *rooinek,* you're back among us."

Matthew turned wearily and had his hand pumped by a man with both arms bandaged. His buckskin coat was stiff with powder and drying blood, and yet his smile was white and broad through the dirt and stubble.

"Dirk, it's good to see you." Matthew was surprised to find that he meant what he said. "Have we lost many?"

"None," Dirk sneer-smiled. "Just a few cuts here and there. God is with us, truly with us, neh? But your friend, that Klyn. Ach, he died bravely, that one. I would have made him my friend if he'd been spared."

Matthew nodded to save words. His grief was his own and he had no wish to share his loss. Not yet and not for a long time. Maybe never.

Dirk seemed to understand, for he did not press it. He drew Matthew to an open space where they could not be overheard. "Your woman calls for you, *vriend.* The man Laidler is badly off. The bone is smashed above the wound and the infection. One of our women laid an open Bible on the leg and your woman threw it aside. You'll have to calm her before the women...well, you know our women."

"Show me." Kit had been driven from Matthew's mind and decades could have passed since he had last seen her.

The air in the hospital enclosure was heavy and close, and

187

the stench of gangrene all too pervasive. Cord lay on a scrubbed tailboard supported by trestles. Kit held his head and defended them both with a butcher's knife watched by five matrons in black.

"Keep these witches away, Matthew," she said when she saw him. "They won't touch him. Where's the doctor?"

The matrons stiffened in concert, outraged by her charge against their piety. Matthew was overcome by a useless anger. He snatched the knife and pointed it over the Vaal River. "There's your doctor, woman," he snarled.

"Where?"

"Port Elizabeth."

Kit swore helplessly. "Help him, damn you."

Dirk shrugged and spat into the dirt. "Help him, how? That's a cutting job. A surgeon's work."

"No!" Kit surged in against Matthew, scrabbling for the knife.

Matthew took her clawing hand away from his face and doubled her arm up her back. "That leg has to come off. Listen to me. It comes off, or he dies. He might anyway."

Kit wriggled until the pain brought her up short. Matthew nodded to the matrons and they closed in around Kit. She was caught up by arms and legs and carried out of the enclosure, too exhausted to do more than whimper in their grip.

Dirk poured alcohol over his and Matthew's hands and handed over a surgical saw. Matthew hefted it and Dirk lashed Cord to the trestle table. Then they tipped the brandy bottle until it was empty.

Matthew began to saw through bone, muscle, and sinew. Cord's screams meant nothing to him.

6

Mkalipi called for the tally sticks when the first impi had fallen back and learned he had lost three hundred warriors to the corngrowers' guns. He ordered milk and dried meat for the surviving Invincibles and stood them down for a rest. He ordered water for the other regiments and sent his indunas among them to tell of the Invincibles' valor.

Then he sent for Sigwe of the Snakes.

The old man came trotting from the western flank of the army, as lissome as the bachelor youths he commanded. It was as if a seventy-year-old head had been grafted onto a boy's body.

Sigwe touched his forehead to Mkalipi's foot and remained kneeling. His knuckles were as proud as pebbles and the soles of his feet were as scarred as elephant hide. His oiled back shone in the hard afternoon light.

"Stand, old man," Mkalipi ordered. "Before your old joints knot."

Sigwe stood straight and showed his one black tooth, seeing that Mkalipi's frown had humor.

"How are you alive, old dog? Here." Mkalipi brushed flies from freshly roasted beef. "Eat from my platter. Meat to cover your old bones."

"With respect, eyes of the Great Elephant, I will only take what my impi takes. It would not be fitting for me to eat when they fast and wait to wash their spears for you. I would not be worthy to lead them."

Mkalipi knocked the meat into the dust.

"Only your extreme age saves you from a lashing for reminding me of honor."

"True, but I spoke with respect only, Lord. Forgive me, I shall receive your punishment with humility."

Mkalipi laughed aloud. The old man had never been kissed by the lash, his back was without blemish. He was lucky as well as brave. Mkalipi sent his other indunas and his servants out of earshot.

"Tell me with truth, Sigwe, what did you see today?"

"In truth, Lord, or what a lesser man would wish to hear?"

"In truth."

"There was bravery, Lord. You have counted the corn-growers' guns with the hearts of the Invincibles, which is as it should be. Next time all your men must show their chests. There are not enough guns in the world to pierce their hearts. I will gladly lead my impi there."

"You speak what I think, old man. And that is good. But I have a task for you first, Sigwe."

"Order me, Lord."

"Take your impatient young men and bring all the corn-growers' stock to me. Make show and noise. Have some of the rams among you go without loincloths with their manhood proud, have them present their buttocks and show how our men will treat the corngrowers' women when we take them."

"I have many who will do that with pleasure, Lord," Sigwe grinned. "Many whose parts are as sure as spears."

"Save such taunts for the Ill-Tempered," said Mkalipi, seeing the joke. "When you have the animals, you will
189

butcher a hundred cows where the guns cannot reach you. And make certain that the corngrowers see what you do. Make a great feast. It will tear their hearts and make them heavy."

"I will do these things."

"You will. But even before that, there is a matter of discipline to consider. You will remind the Snakes that they did not kill all those who came for the elephant teeth. And the one who led is now in the laager with his woman. There should be punishment for that."

"I will kill one in twenty, flay one in ten for you, Lord," Sigwe offered, knowing the punishment was too harsh. Mkalipi knew this too, just as he knew that Sigwe was giving him the opportunity to be merciful.

"Scald them with your tongue, Sigwe. It will be enough. I know how you can make a man a maiden with your words. If you must, name some cowards and send them to the guns with blunt *iKlwa*."

"Aye, Lord."

"Do these things now, before the sun moves the shadows. And Sigwe, see that roasted meat is thrown to the corngrowers; poison it first, then we will at least kill some of the dogs they keep. I understand these dogs are kept as members of their families. Will that not sadden them as the death of a son does?"

"Your wisdom is a great light, Lord."

"Go with Mwari, Sigwe." Mkalipi accepted the flattery and sent the old man back to his impi.

7

When Matthew had finished the cutting and stitching, Dirk seared Cord's stump with hot pitch, and one of the matrons took the severed limb away and buried it deep in the earth.

Matthew used a mirror to show that Cord still breathed, then he and Dirk left the women to bind the rough surgery and scour the marks of their work from the scrubbed tailboard. Others would be needing the table before the day was out.

Women and girls were gathering and stacking the spears that littered the compound, and the men were nailing *iKlwa* in rows above the gunports as a further defense. A Predikant went from wagon to wagon, offering prayers and solace, talking softly as the Matabele drums beat out monotonously. A single communal cooking fire heated soup and a team of boys wet the canvas sails with river water. So far the Matabele had not tried to deny them use of the Vaal.

Back at Krige's wagon, Matthew found Boie napping beside the smoothbores. They had been fitted with new flints and the Khoikhoi had lashed *iKlwa* to the barrels.

As the trekkers ate and cleaned their wounds, they watched the Matabele clear the plain of their precious stock animals and drive them to the rear of the army. When the Snakes began butchering some of the animals, all the trekkers were affected by the waste, both angry and sickened, for the bachelors had selected the fattest cows, the finest calves, the most handsome of the bulls. All the mindless slaughter was accompanied by obscene mime shows.

The trekkers held their fire and their tempers and waited for the next onslaught.

When it came, it would come from all three sides.

8

The earth shook as the Bees, the Ill-Tempered, the Snakes, and the Sticks stamped to the base of the hill.

An induna with a striped shield started a chant that was picked up by the other regiments and shouted in chorus.

"Bambani aba Thakathi! Bambani aba Thakathi!"

Kill the wizards! Kill the wizards!

The drumming stopped and a great silence fell over the massed impi, a silence so total and sudden that it seemed to crash around the trekkers and heighten their isolation. They could hear the wind in the brush and a warbler from across the river. A suckling child cried for a comforting breast and the cooking fire crackled.

All the indunas raised their totems and held them high. A cloud of spears rose from the front rows of the encircling army, flew high above the laager, converged at their summit, staggered, tipped, and plunged down into the circle of wagons. Warning shouts went up and the trekkers scattered for shelter, hugging the wagon sides and snatching up buckets and tubs to protect their heads. As the spears struck down in hacking clumps, a second multiple cast was in the air. There was confusion in the laager that stopped short of panic. Many fell wounded in the first few seconds, and there were cries for help.

191

With a great rolling bass roar, the impi ran in to throw their front rows against the laager with a great crash that rocked the circle on its springs. Those who were not cut down by the opening volley shouldered the wagons and slashed the sails from their hoops, pulling them down over the gunports and the thorn barriers. Some of the more daring Snakes had their friends catapult them over the barricades, dropping down on the defenders and stabbing out in all directions. The women used hoe and fork to pin the warriors where they fell and cut their throats with kitchen knives.

Wagons rocked and threatened to overturn.

A flaming brand ate the canvas from Krige's wagon in a huge gout of flame, and warriors tried to jump through the flames. The women from neighboring wagons helped beat at the smoldering ruin with brooms and wet blankets as the men fired around them in desperate attempts to defend them against the Matebele. Spears began to seek the women out and Krige had to order them down and out of sight.

From that point on, Matthew and Krige were forced to split their fire. Krige covered the gunports while Matthew fired across the wagon bed where the Snakes were scaling the thorn across a bridge of discarded Invincibles' shields. It was not too long before the fragmentation balls were exhausted and the trekkers were forced to aim at specific targets with normal ammunition.

Boie climbed into Krige's wagon, where he lay on his back and spitted Matabele with their own spears when they loomed out of the smoke.

Matthew was wounded in the upper arm and hip, then again as his chest was slashed and his jaw was laid open. He scarcely noticed. The palm of Krige's trigger hand was ripped open by an *iKlwa* and he had to shoot left-handed. An assegai pinned his hat to the tailgate and another buried itself into the broomhead tied to his wounded leg. He cursed around his pipe and fired each time a reloaded musket was placed in his grip.

The day began to dull into evening, and was made darker by the powder smoke and the fires burning all around the perimeter of the laager. When the boys who passed the ammunition dropped from exhaustion in mid-stride, the smaller children were pressed into service. Women put out their smoldering dresses and reloaded with rags wrapped around their burned hands.

The battle raged on without pause and time meant nothing.

9

Sigwe had watched his bachelor impi smash itself against the western flank of the ring of wagons. Row after row of Snakes had dropped and died, never to rise again, and in Sigwe's old heart was a deep sadness that was tempered with rightful pride. His Snakes were dying like the men he had made them.

Sigwe knew he would never raise another impi for the Great King Elephant, Mzilikazi, for he was now truly too old and his luck had been too good for too long. He vowed he would not face the final indignity of the slashed belly before giggling women and his enemies from the Ill-Tempered. He resolved to die with his regiment.

Sigwe had the impi totem dropped to signal withdrawal, then he ate a mouthful of dust to honor the old mud father and emptied his bladder on the ground. He then dictated his farewell to a praise singer and had him deliver it with his *mouti* bag to Mkalipi. Sigwe's personal guard saw these last rites and they made their own preparations.

The Snakes who still lived and could walk gathered about Sigwe and honored him by touching his feet with their faces and dedicating their spears to his memory.

Then Sigwe led them up the hill.

They drove in in a wedge and concentrated their attack on a wagon with a burned sail. They somehow managed to lever it out of line and fought their way through the gap, the only regiment who had breached the laager and died inside it.

Sigwe fought to die, but each time he exposed his chest to the guns, a Snake would shield him and take the shot himself. He fought into the clear ground and was at last alone as he wished to be. He was shot through the body four times, but with his dying thrust he killed a bearded corngrower, drawing him down into the shades of the old mud father's belly with him.

Mkalipi the induna, the eyes of the Great Elephant, was furious at the news of Sigwe's death. Beside himself with rage and grief, he had the praise singer executed and threw Sigwe's *mouti* bag into the witchman's fire. Then he relented and had it saved.

He wore it at his waist when he rode his white stallion out to urge his regiments to a final, victorious assault.

10

To Dirk de Villiers, there seemed no end to the pied shields.

The Sticks came again and again and yet again. Dirk fought in a raging stupor; twice he had run out of ammunition, and twice he had fought with an *iKlwa* in each hand. His coat was in tatters and wounds crisscrossed his matted chest.

His father Abraham had been stabbed through the right lung and could barely handle a pistol. The old man had had himself tied upright in a chair and he fought seated. At one point, he had held a Stick warrior by the ears as Dirk drove an *iKlwa* between the man's shoulder blades.

During a brief lull, Dirk had climbed the barricade to clear the corpses from before the gunports, for not only did they obscure his line of fire, they had begun to bloat and stink under a carpet of droning blowflies.

This day had seen a hatred born in Dirk, a towering thing that would consume him for the rest of his life. Up to that moment, Dirk had fought only when he had needed to fight. Raiding Xhosa kraals and hunting poachers were a natural part of his farmer's life; a risky game that had been born of necessity. Now it was different, changed out of all recognition and gone beyond all reasonable bounds. The black clans of Mzilikazi's impi were as many-headed as the mythical Hydra—sever one head and two more grew in its place, teeth snapping with voracious appetite for his blood.

Dirk no longer defended a part of the laager. He had declared a private war that would last all his days.

11

The third desperate assault by the last of the Snakes impi was the hardest to contain.

Matthew and the Krige family fell back from the wall when their wagon was lifted bodily out of line and the warriors streamed into the laager through the narrow gap. It seemed as if each warrior had to be killed more than once, for every man fought on after their spears were broken or lost, then they bit and clawed and punched, crawling into the

194

guns when they could no longer walk, dragging themselves when their legs had gone.

The Snakes had gathered themselves around an old induna and took their strength and lead from him. Matthew shot him full in the chest and still he thrust and parried. Men from other wagons joined in the fight, leaving their women and children to hold the line as best they could.

A second ball took the old induna's legs from under him, but he was up instantly, and without help from the warriors who rushed to help and to shield him. The trekkers fired into the shrinking knot of Snakes, clubbing and spearing the fallen Matabele when there was no time to reload.

To Matthew it was a blur of blood and smoke and noise and mindless heroism. He saw Nicholas Potgieter's weapon torn from his grasp, saw him grapple with a young Snake, taking the man around the middle and hugging the life from him.

The old induna took another ball in the body and still kept his feet, his eyes locked on the dying warrior. As Nicholas Potgieter threw the body from him and straightened up, the induna gutted him with a single sweep of his *iKlwa*.

A fourth ball blew the top of Sigwe's head away and his riddled corpse fell across the mortally wounded Dutchman.

The attack died with him.

12

There was barely an hour of daylight left when Abraham de Villiers said, more in hope than in confidence, "They cannot come again."

"They'll come." Dirk gave his sneer-smile. "They'll come for *me*." His mother watched him stalk away and shivered to see her son so changed...so animal. She had never been close to Dirk; he had always been a singular child and took the regular beatings his father was forced to impose upon him with less than a shrug. He seemed to have no tears in him, no kindness. She shook her head after him and wondered if her son would have been so had he been brought up in the lowlands of Holland, rather than here on the veldt. Despite her gentle sensibility, she thought it would have made no difference. She could picture him as a mercenary in the Flemish army too easily. She sighed and gave her attention to her husband, whose lips were blue from lack of oxygen. She got him some soup and kept her thoughts to herself. Abraham knew about Dirk, which was probably why he had such feeling for the Eastman boy. If any of them survived this battle she would pray for Dirk's soul above all others, for he was totally without grace in the eyes of the Almighty. If only prayers were enough....

Later, Matthew shook Dirk out of his doze.

"There's work to be done. Come."

It was dusk and Dirk wanted to sleep, ready to squabble seriously with Matthew. The Matabele had pulled back and did not seem to be forming up again for the moment. Matthew climbed a tailgate, hauled Dirk up beside him, and fired his smoothbore into the piled bodies outside the laager. A corpse jumped with the impact and disturbed flies rose in a dark cloud.

Dirk muttered in confusion. "Crazy, *rooinek.*"

"Think!" Matthew growled. "Dead men don't sweat."

The word was passed and sporadic firing broke out all around the laager. The noise woke Johannes Krige, who came hobbling to join Matthew and Dirk, scratching his beard with blackened fingers.

"You think they'll come again before nightfall, *kerels?*"

Matthew remembered what Klyn had told him. He pointed at the far figure of Mkalipi mounted on his stallion. "It's up to him. That's Mzilikazi's chief induna, and he'll have to kill us before he fills his belly on the King's meat. Mzilikazi doesn't like failure."

The Matabele were crisscrossing the plain to form into companies under their totems, the companies swelling into impi.

"That's a belly that would take some filling," said Dirk, testing the wind.

"How far would you say he was?" said Matthew, checking his backsight.

"Eight hundred yards?" Krige said, squinting over the plain.

"More like nine," said Dirk, using his rammer.

"A long shot."

"Too long. What are you...?" Krige saw what they meant to do.

"If we all fired together, one of us could get lucky. What can it cost us but a pinch of powder and twelve ounces of lead."

Krige shielded his eyes with his hat. "I would need a shoulder to lean on. I only have one hand, and the wrong one at that."

"Take mine," Matthew offered.

"No, I'll use Dirk's. We both will; you're the better shot."

"I don't think..."

"Shut up, Eastman. Krige knows," snapped Dirk. "You shoot, I support."

They leaned their long guns on Dirk's shoulders and snuggled in against their stocks, bearing on the distant target.

"I'll give the signal." Dirk breathed lightly to slow his heart and to give them a rigid rest. "Let him turn; see, he's pulling the horse around, he's wheeling, gently, gently. *Now!*"

The two guns roared and there was a long and breathless pause as echoes chased off toward the horizon.

Then, as though jerked by a lazy and invisible cord, Mkalipi, the eyes of the Great Elephant, bowed over his horse's neck and slid to the ground.

13

The day itself was dying.

Jakot had regained his wits enough to look around him, and he saw the re-forming impi off to the east and west of where he lay, the stark piles of dead that formed a black surf around the distant laager. His scalp smarted where it had been singed by the gunflash, and he thought his right eye socket was fractured under the swelling. His lungs felt as though he had chewed and swallowed burned wood. Sihayo made him drink some goat's milk and he vomited, unable to keep it down. Still, he lived, as did Sihayo, more than could be said of the Snakes impi or the rest of their company of the Invincibles. None of their company had survived the first rush, and more than half of their entire impi had been lost in the second assault.

The day had given little honor to any of the Matabele impi, and Jakot was chilled to learn of the loss of the entire Snakes regiment. All gone to the vulture and the jackal, including old Sigwe, who had been old when Jakot's uncles had been bachelors under his command. How many men had crawled away to die quietly and alone? Jakot wondered. Men who had no trusted friend at hand to make death come easily? Ayee, that was the hardest thing to face and one all warriors hated to contemplate.

Jakot coughed bile onto the grass as fireflies danced in his eyes. Sihayo was pulling him to his feet and giving him a shield to lean upon. Invincibles were standing all around him, making themselves as tall as they could, for the Lord Mkalipi was approaching on his sacred white horse. Even though it was an effort for Jakot to stand unaided, he did so, for he would rather die than dishonor his Lord by lying down in his presence. Drearily, Jakot noticed that only the Ill-Tempered, the Sticks, and the Bees were mustered in anything like regimental strength. The dead must be numbered like the days of several summers and there would be private grief in all the military kraals when the news reached the homeland.

Mkalipi saw and recognized Jakot, and he turned his horse toward him. Jakot held himself rigidly and concentrated on the top of the killing hill to help his balance, hearing the unshod hooves thump closer. If he was to be singled out, he must fight his wits and make them keen for any reply he must make to the Lord Mkalipi.

Two bright flashes winked from the corngrowers' hill and the shots racketed after, dashing away over the heads of the Invincibles' ranks. Jakot turned his head as a wail went up beside him, running down the lines and on to the other impi.

A ragged hole had appeared in the Lord Mkalipi's thigh, and a dark pucker bled down over his waistband. Mkalipi's eyes rolled and he slid forward from his horse to lie on his belly as still as death.

Nobody moved, for none of the warriors had the courage to lift or touch Mkalipi without his permission, and how was he to give it with two gaping wounds in him?

It was Jakot who had him placed on a litter of shields and borne out of the range of the corngrowers' guns. They took him to the witchmen's hill and laid him there for them to give him aid. The leg wound was gathered at the edges and closed with thorns before a herbal balm was spread to coagulate the blood and draw any poison. The mark on Mkalipi's belly was a ball burn. A skystone in Sigwe's *mouti* bag had turned the ball aside and saved Mkalipi from a terminal stomach wound. This meteorite had fallen on the night of Sigwe's birth and was said to have been the source of his lifelong luck.

The news leaked to the regiments and gave them heart. Sigwe and the Snakes had not died for nothing. So many deaths to ensure Mkalipi's lifeline meant that the induna was destined to survive for a greater greatness. Surely, the warriors argued, Mkalipi must follow Mzilikazi to the Matabele throne without treason.

Was it not true that lesser men must die so that the great might live?

It was so from the time from before the time of their father's father and his father's father. The impi settled themselves down for the night and posted their sentries. Tomorrow, if the Lord Mkalipi ordered it, they all resolved to take and destroy the ring of trekkers' wagons. Their hunger would be a strengthening fast to make them all strong and pure for the dawn.

14

In the gray time before the next true day began, Jakot was roused and brought before the Lord Mkalipi and his war council of chief indunas and witchmen.

Mkalipi lay on zebra skins over a pallet of soft grass, his wounds hidden by a green monkey kaross. His full face was drawn by pain but his eyes were clear and his voice was strong. He had heard the interpretations the warriors and the witchmen had put upon his escape from death and was amused by them. He was also determined to use it to his own advantage. He knew in his heart that the battle was lost and that he must withdraw, there being no real advantage in staying. The many cattle they had taken from the corngrowers were the biggest prize the Matabele had ever taken, and to press the battle further was to court disaster. He must make some token showing though, if only to keep the Boers from pressing farther into Matabele territory.

Mkalipi promoted Jakot to the rank of induna and gave him a rich gift of cattle, knowing that Jakot was his man for as long as he lived. Then he told the war council his will.

"I must go from this place," he said. "All men know my destiny lies in the north of the land of the Great King. The signs are clear."

The witchmen nodded sagely. It was true.

"I will take the Ill-Tempered impi with me to guard my person and to drive the cattle. We shall go before the Great King Mzilikazi and bring him our tribute." Mkalipi paused to let this point be digested, to allow the council time to recognize he was still loyal to Mzilikazi. Then he said, "You indunas will remain here to harry the wizards until you have

199

overcome. You will bring the wagons and the prisoners with you. Do not fail me in this. Do not dishonor me before our king!"

All the indunas save Jakot trembled as they bowed low. Mkalipi had just ordered them to die.

Mkalipi dismissed them and lay back on his soft pallet to think.

Mzilikazi would not like the huge losses his impi had sustained at the hands of the corngrowers, but he would have to put a good face on it when he saw the herd Mkalipi was bringing before him. Perhaps he would hide under his throne if he ever saw what the white men's guns could do from a fortified position. No tribe in Africa had seen such easy slaughter, and Mkalipi was not anxious to face the whites again; the knowledge that an enemy could strike a man down at will when he was a speck on a hillside turned Mkalipi's belly to water.

With an effort, he put the fear from him; with cunning and some cleverness, he should make certain he would never face the corngrowers again. But his paramount task now was to save himself from Mzilikazi's displeasure.

Mkalipi would go before the Great King with a great show of force. To be doubly certain of survival, he would send the witchmen on before him and the impi, to tell of the rivers of cattle and the magic of old Sigwe's *mouti* bag. The witchmen would embellish the tale with the telling, he knew, and all the better. By the time he arrived, Mzilikazi would be ready to welcome him with friendship and courtesy.

Mkalipi laughed with pleasure and called for food to break his fast.

15

The drums started solemnly and built up gradually to a hysterical and frenetic intensity.

The trekkers stumbled to their gunports and checked their arms and ammunition. The women calmed or scolded the children before herding them into the central reservation and relative safety.

Matthew jerked out of his own shallow sleep and watched the Matabele lines forming up across the plain. The Invincibles' shields were a wash of glaring white, the black roundels stark in the early morning light. The pied shields of the Sticks were on Dirk's side and facing the Kriges' wagon were rows of jogging black shields. Today, Matthew knew, he would be killing Bees. Or they would be killing him. He thought of finding Kit, of saying some sort of a goodbye, and rejected the notion. It would be a stumbling recital of apology, recrimination, and specious might-have-beens. He looked deeply into Herrie's shining face as she laid musket balls on the barrelhead before her. How she had managed to clean herself was beyond him. Even her hair had been brushed and was free of grass. She would have been so right for Klyn.

Biting his lip, Matthew turned away and stared out at the massing Matabele. There seemed to be just as many shields as ever, and he gave himself over to the more basic consideration of surviving the day. He patted Boie's shoulder and thanked him for the care he had lavished on their weapons. Without clean bores and sharp flints they were as good as dead. Boie looked solemn yet steady, and Matthew thanked God for him as he waited for the advance.

It was not long in coming.

The black shields started forward and the warriors' regimental song was a deep braying as they stamped upward, rattling spear against shield.

The first volleys cracked out and Matthew was lost in the smoke of the last battle.

16

Mkalipi heard the guns all through the morning as he was drawn away from the killing hill on a litter pulled by his personal guard. The meat and milk he had swallowed at dawn lay heavy on his stomach and made his bowels loose so that he was forced to stop many times to relieve himself behind a ring of shields.

Though fainter when he called a midday halt, they were still in his ears like troublesome insects and spoiled his appetite. When he resumed his journey north, he set himself at the head of the cattle so that their lowing covered the sounds of the battle.

Though he did not know it, and the rear guard had no intention of telling him, the final assault had failed by midmorning. Mkalipi drank milk and blood laced with the juice of the *kanna* bark to ease his pain, and had himself lulled to sleep by the praise singers. He dreamed of a night sky scored across by the constant fall of firestones as he was honored by all the great chiefs of the African nations.

The savaged Matabele fell back under cover of the fires they had set along the thorn barrier. The cover was luckily thickened by smoke from the burning wagon sails. The Bees had broken first and had abandoned all vestige of discipline as they ran away down the hill and into the cover of the trees to the west where they threw themselves down at the river's edge and slaked their thirst. Those indunas that had not died in the fight were speared in the withdrawal when they tried to use their flails. The impi had lost a third of its number, and the survivors were in no mood to be lashed back into the carnage.

The Sticks' retreat was more orderly, but they fell back into the eastern gullies all the same and filtered away to the north where they killed any stray animals they found and threw the quarters into hastily built fires, eating the meat before it was properly cooked, so great was their hunger.

Only the Invincibles were steady enough to cover the retreat in proper order with their shields presented in line to the enemy. Jakot steadied them, for he knew the corngrowers might follow on their horses and harry the stragglers. As they backed down the hill they gave the death thrust to any wounded they passed over, for there were too many for the exhausted herdboys and their blunted knives. When Jakot formed his impi up and checked the tally sticks, he had a bare one hundred and ninety-three Invincibles left out of one thousand, and not one of these was without a wound.

Jakot would have executed the other indunas had his impi been strong enough to prevail over the other regiments. Instead, he vowed he would name them all cowards when and if he survived to reach the royal kraal. He would see to it that they were ordered to fall upon their own spears and be buried in dung.

He took his survivors to a clear spot along the Vaal River and made proper camp for the night, resolved to keep good order while he commanded under the totem of the Invincibles. When he had named Sihayo his successor in the event that he fell during the withdrawal, he went alone to the high ground and made his peace with the Earth Mother.

17

The night had been without drums and had brought quiet darkness for the children to whimper into as they twitched in nervous, exhausted sleep. The men and women napped when they could between keeping watch and repairing their defenses. Ammunition was low and many of the guns no longer fired true. Matthew and Dirk shared a foot patrol together, and they walked outside the perimeter among the corpses, now and then clearing those bodies that crowded too close to the wagons and might have afforded cover for the Matabele.

They were relieved at dawn and went back to their wagons to rest, although both were beyond sleep and far too exhausted to eat the soup and cornbread that was pressed upon them by the women.

A faint eastern blush brought the first tentative birdsong, tiny trills that could well have been scout calls. River frogs boomed and a jackal gave its yapping laugh. Then the day was upon the trekkers, blooming as bright and as fresh as a sudden chrysanthemum. A breeze came off the sparkling Vaal and flights of birds whirred across the plain. There was dew on the heaped black corpses and mammals ran between the piled bodies. There were no waving spears or gesturing warriors, no calls or battle songs, just an abiding quiet. The trekkers gathered in groups and touched each other as though seeing their families and friends for the first time, all of them inhaling sudden notions of hope. Many kneeled together in impromptu prayer.

Boie ignored all this; he concentrated on Nkosi Matthew, who was buckling on his pistols and searching his chest for a Bible. Hefting his smoothbore and a shovel, Matthew climbed the barrier, dropped to the ground, and walked down the hill, looking neither right nor left. Boie scrambled after him and kept to his rear, watching for shamming Matabele. The plain began to shimmer with heat and flies droned in rising black clouds as they threaded through the corpses and skirted the fire pits where the Snakes had slaughtered and roasted the trekkers' steers. Smoke still rose from the embers and curled up around the Snakes' totem, stirring the strings of agate and feathers on the crosspiece below the carved and rearing snake.

The bodies here were no longer human. They were hideously bloated and disfigured, and not until the predators and the elements had reduced them to skeletons would they again resemble living men.

Matthew found the speared litter horse and struck off at an angle. Packs of hyenas had gathered and were worrying the corpses. Vultures coasted in on high, spiraling surveys

203

of the feeding ground, and smaller birds feasted on the many dead eyes. The plain swarmed and buzzed and stank. Matthew quartered the ground, oblivious to everything but his search, smelling and seeing only what he wanted to.

Boie spotted the gray and swollen curve of Pallas's belly and the rigidly pointing legs. He whistled a call and led Matthew to the spot, standing back so that Matthew could locate Klyn on his own as he would want to. Boie watched Matthew casting about in the huddles of Bees and Invincibles, moving more and more slowly until he finally stopped and lowered his head. He recognized Klyn from his size and his clothes. The white ants had taken what had been left of his features and still scurried in his beard. They knew Abba by the ocher markings on his torso.

Matthew gathered up first one body and then the other. Then, tightlipped and mourning, he strode away, cradling them as though they weighed nothing, making for a tall silver birch that stood alone, somehow untouched by and divorced from the carnage about it. He dug deep into the red earth and gathered large stones as a cairn to mark the spot, unaware of Boie guarding him against surprise.

When he had laid the bodies in the grave, filled it, and topped it out with stones, he made a rough cross from birch branches and tamped it home with the shovel. He said no words, content to lay the Bible below the cross and to swear to come back for the bones and lay them deep in a shaded spot on the land he chose for himself.

He stripped Pallas's saddle and bridle and carried them back to the laager with him, and when he climbed back inside he found Dirk waiting for him and realized he had been watching through a spyglass. Matthew pushed past him and threw the horse furniture into his wagon.

The elders were burying Nicholas Potgieter on the brow of the hill just outside the laager, and a Predikant read aloud in a carrying voice. Matthew lit a pipe and watched them dully, his thoughts elsewhere. He did not see Dirk until his view of the funeral was blocked by his body. Matthew looked at him with nothing in his face.

"You buried them together," Dirk accused.

"Just as they died together, de Villiers."

"It was fitting," Boie said in his own tongue, reading Dirk, seeing the reason for his bitter remark.

"So." Dirk ignored the Khoikhoi. "We all have our own ways."

"Say what's on your mind, man." Matthew's eyes and voice were cold.

Dirk hesitated, biting on the violent words he should have liked to spit at the Englishman. There was murder in the *rooinek's* face, and Dirk knew a wrong word would see him with his head twisted around. The raw agony had turned from mourning to consuming anger. Now was not the time to tell Matthew the truth of the world, the new world he, Dirk, now inhabited and saw in shades of light and dark.

"You'll hear from me, Eastman."

"I won't be hard to find." Matthew stood then and towered a full foot above the smaller Dutchman, his eyes lost in white glare.

Dirk stepped back and walked away. Up on the brow of the hill, the Predikant read from the 118th Psalm as clods of earth were dropped onto the shrouded body of Hendrik Potgieter's son. As the surface of the grave was smoothed over the Predikant raised his face to the sky and said forcibly:

"May God forgive the land."

Matthew gave a silent amen to that. They had all lost something.

18

The trekkers moved their laager from the top of the killing hill when they were certain the Matabele would not return, for the plain stank and was noisome from the countless unburied dead. Potgieter and Cilliers gathered their people together to give thanks to the Almighty and to plan for the future.

"The children of Israel have conquered the pagan hordes," said Potgieter, and was cheered for it.

Cilliers came forward and said, "Our children will inherit the land we have fought and died for. Each one of us will live doubly for those who have fallen. Our friend here," he indicated Potgieter, "does not grieve alone for his son. Nicholas Potgieter did not die in vain. Nor the other young men we have accepted into our midst with pride." The small mesmeric eyes swept the assembly. "They will be remembered and honored for all time."

Men nodded and women reached for ragged squares of linen. Standing beside Matthew, Herrie Krige wept into her hands. In the long waking hours of the night she still heard the taunting drums and the booming battle calls.

205

Hendrik Potgieter stepped forward and dwarfed his plump deputy.

"Now is the time to think of the living. We have our oxen and we have our horses. That is all and that is enough. The elders have decided to send one man to the Blesberg with news of our victory. He will return with as much livestock as he can manage, and bring those men and their families who may wish to join us. We need canvas for our wagons, and lead ingots to replenish our ammunition stores. We need medicines and harness. Until this happens, we will remain laagered here. Do the people agree?"

The trekkers did to a man and Sarel Cilliers led them in prayer.

Matthew slipped away to saddle Gaika and was tightening her cinch when Dirk laid a hand on his arm.

"You look ready to do something, *vriend.*"

Matthew shrugged the hand away. "What's it to you, *friend?*"

"I would join you," Dirk said slowly. The words came with difficulty, for he was not a man to ask a favor easily. "Another day in this place and I'd be ready to take on Mzilikazi single-handed."

"What's that to me?" Matthew knew what the other man was driving at, but could not bring himself to make things easy.

Dirk laughed and it sounded false. "So we think differently about men, you and I. Does that make us enemies?"

"It doesn't make us friends."

"Nou ja, but we can live that, neh? Now tell me, what're you going to do?"

"I'm moving out. Alone."

"Without a herd, without oxen?"

"All right, de Villiers. How many head of stock would you say we lost to the Matabele?"

Dirk pulled at the hair on his chin. "Thirty, maybe forty thousand according to my pa's reckoning."

"A big herd. And my guess is, it'll go direct to old Mzilikazi himself; it's the only way Mkalipi can sweeten his losses. Now, he's not going to run the fat off them, is he? He'll take his time and see they arrive at the royal kraal in good health."

Dirk was puzzled. "Why does this interest you?"

Matthew stared at the distant horizon where the blue mountains overhung the rolling veldt. "They'll move very slowly, as I said. Those herds will be spread out all over

206

creation, for miles. Have to be to see that they get enough pasture. They haven't got enough warriors to watch every cow and sheep. Some will stray, some will get lost."

Dirk grinned with pure pleasure. "And you plan to scoop them up, neh? Grab off the strays to the rear of the main herd? Man, I like it."

Matthew said nothing.

"We go after them? The two of us, Eastman?"

"I am. You must do as you will."

"As I always do. Look for me on the trail."

Matthew rode out of the laager within the hour, and Dirk was with him by nightfall.

Over the next three weeks the two men played a dangerous and competitive game. They had sighted Mkalipi's retreating army after just two days' hard riding. The regiments marched ahead of the dust pall thrown up by the massing animals, too proud to eat trail dust. Only the lowliest of herdboys moved through the choking mile-long cloud.

"You were right," admitted Dirk, as they watched the great progress from a kopje. *"Magtig,* if they spread out any more, they will fall into the sea on both sides."

So certain they were not followed, the Matabele scarcely bothered to protect the animals. Matthew sighted many herdboys but they were spread so thinly they were always out of earshot of each other.

Dirk culled straggling Matabele with as much fervor as Matthew gathered strays and hobbled them in kloofs along the way. As Dirk killed and boasted of his killing, Matthew became more introspective, thinking of Katherine Laidler and her husband. After the crude surgery and the cauterization of his stump, Cord barely breathed. He lay in Klyn's wagon, fever jerking his limbs in a macabre dance. In his rare lucid moments he said nothing; when the fever racked him he raved about things in the unknown and passing Doppers prayed for him as he reached for the empty place where his leg had been.

Kit never left his side, and with bald gracelessness rejected the help offered by the other women. Sometimes she allowed Boie to help her sponge Cord's body when he had to be strapped to his pallet, or when she wanted the Khoikhoi to prepare a tribal gruel of herbs and ground gamemeat. She hugged discomfort to herself like a penance, her unwashed hair scraped back and held by a rawhide thong, the sleeves of her one dress slit to the elbows, her skin peeled and dry.

Dirk knew better than to discuss the Laidlers when he and Matthew made cold night camp. They spoke little, as though words were as precious as water. They lived on biltong and rock-hard *vetkoekies,* moving when the Matabele moved, resting when the sprawling caravan of men and animals halted for the night. As Matthew's herd grew, Dirk's pickings grew less, and he did not always return with a trophy or a bloody story. Matthew would listen to him boast without comment; he needed Dirk for the drive home. On the nineteenth day, when the herd had grown to just over seven hundred animals, Matthew called a halt. The mixed herd of cattle, sheep, and horses were more than enough for the two men and their twelve boys.

"It's a beginning," said Matthew, exhaustion sapping his enthusiasm. "Krige will see that the sharing is equal and fair."

Dirk bit his tongue until they settled down to sleep. He had killed many men, but the last had stayed in his mind, a young warrior with crazy eyes who had no markings save the ocher Earth Mother symbol drawn beneath his loincloth. Dirk had worked on a suppurating wound in the man's side with his long filleting knife. The stoic Matabele had not uttered a sound although he lost consciousness from time to time.

Angered, Dirk had used the last of his precious water to wash away the sacred Earth Mother sign. The dying man had freed his hands from his bonds and taking a stone, had smashed his own skull with a single blow. Dirk laughed as he told the Englishman and watched the distaste twist Matthew's mouth.

It mattered little to Dirk. His own gratification was stimulus enough. There were no ghosts in his dreams.

19

Matthew made the Krige family a gift of Klyn's two wagons. Once the fresh herd from the Blesberg had arrived and were allocated among the more needy of the Voortrekker families it would be time to leave Vegkop, the killing hill.

Matthew gathered his and Klyn's boys together and told them they were free to go with him or to remain with the main body of the trek. Of the seventeen, only two wanted to stay with the Krige family.

"It is good, Nkosi," grinned Boie, hopping from one foot

to the other, a smoothbore over each shoulder, pride written all over him. His standing among the boys had increased tenfold since Nkosi Matthew had ridden in with the recaptured cattle and horses.

"Have you been with the Missie today?" Matthew asked.

"Two times, but the baas..." Boie's eyes rolled for effect.

"Bad?"

"His flesh falls away, Nkosi. He is like this." Boie held up a thin finger.

That night Matthew went to the wagon to see for himself and found Boie was right. The man lying on the fresh-grass bed was no more than vellum on a thin frame of bones. Only the eyes lived on, luminous and glaring from pallid sockets. His hair hung thick and drab around his reduced features and there was silver stubble on his hollow cheeks. Matthew's own size and health seemed an affront in the confines of the hooped canvas, his man's smell rich against the sweet and brackish odor that permeated the wagon.

Kit spooned a greenish mixture into Cord's mouth and did not look up as Matthew found room to hunker down beside her. He touched her shoulder and there was no response until Cord looked past her, spilling the herbal soup down his neck as he bared his teeth between wasted lips, glaring at Matthew from the cusp of the beyond.

"I'm leaving in the morning, Kit."

She turned to stare through a veil of red hair. "Leaving?"

"I'm going south with two wagons. As far as the Blesberg. If the land is as good as I remember it, I shall settle there."

"Settle?" she repeated stupidly. "What are you telling me?"

"Just that. You're free to stay here, the Kriges have said as much, or you can come with me."

Kit seemed to be a long way off, and she came back very slowly, seeing Matthew and the wagon as though for the first time. She stared with eyes that groped for clarity.

"And Cord?" she asked.

"He won't make the Cape or Blesberg. What difference does it make? He won't care which trail he dies on." Matthew watched Cord's eyes slew from his own and lose themselves in the shadows of the awning, full of knowing.

Kit raked her hair and her laugh was short and pained.

"Look at his eyes, Matthew. Look at his eyes and tell me he won't live."

Matthew stood, easing his knees and shrugging his shoulders.

"It's your choice," he said, already knowing what it would be.

"When Cord can travel we return to the Cape," whispered Kit, turning her back to ladle soup. "I'm sorry...for both of us."

Matthew stepped to the tailgate and dropped to the ground. The night air was as cold as his stomach and stung his brimming eyes. From the distance came the haunting sound of a child's reed pipe.

"Matthew?"

Kit knelt in the wagon and held the canvas flap aside, her face level with his own as he turned from the waist, not daring to turn fully.

"I'm sorry about Klyn. I know, I think I know what he meant to you...."

Matthew shook his head. There were no words, no clever phrases for the loss. He should have traveled alone from the beginning and not let anyone get close enough to take part of him when he left.

"A poor exchange," said Kit, swallowing nausea. Fat dripping from a roasting carcass turned her stomach. "Klyn for Cord," she forced herself to add, fighting sickness.

"There was no exchange. Understand that. If Klyn had wasted himself for that thing in there, I should have cut Cord's throat, not severed his leg." Matthew swiveled and walked away through the fires until he was lost in the night.

Kit drew back into the wagon and the world looped as her stomach tried to empty itself through her clamped mouth. Cord's dry claw of a hand closed around her ankle, drawing her to him.

"So, he's leaving you at last, is he?" Cord only spoke when they were alone, and his tainted breath bloomed in her face.

"Drink this." Kit kneeled up beside him, reaching for spoon and bowl.

"No more, bring me *brandewyn*."

Kit hesitated.

"What's the matter? Afraid I'll get drunk and ravish you?" Cord's laugh died in a spasm of coughing.

Kit found the black bottle and poured a small measure into a tin cup. Cord tipped the bottle so that brandy spilled onto his bedding and the cup brimmed. He pushed the cup against her mouth and the fumes clogged her throat.

"Have a *zoopje*," snarled Cord as she turned away, gagging.

"Not fancy enough for you, neh? You used to want it in the old days. You'd drink with *him* though, eh, bitch?"

"He gave us our lives, Cord," sighed Kit, thinking, please don't let me be sick.

"Yours, not mine, bitch. He gave me a cripple's future. He took my leg and he took you. I'll kill him for that."

"He took nothing."

"He took you. I saw him take you in the dirt like a dog, and I saw how you hated it, moaning under him as you did among the wine barrels with me. I *saw!*"

Kit paled and tried to move away from the bed but Cord caught her behind the knees and held her close with surprising strength. His voice alternated between bellows and whines.

"Aren't you going to deny it, Katherine? Lie to your husband?"

Kit found the strength to say, "That we made love or that I enjoyed it?"

"By God," Cord whined, one hand moving beneath her dress and along her trapped thighs. "That makes him a dead man twice over."

"Don't," Kit whispered as his fingers found her.

"Why not? He's gone, I'm here. It's not the first time I've eased you this way, my Katherine, my *wife*. At least I'll know if you've been with *him* or not."

Kit doubled up without a sound as the clawing fingers spread her labia and invaded her body. A welling nausea threatened to explode inside her head and her hand dropped protectively over her swelling belly. Then Cord's crudity did not matter any more.

The knowledge was her own.

When she stole out into the dawn to relieve her morning sickness, Matthew's wagons were far out on the bushveldt, lost in low mist.

BOOK FOUR

1

Mzilikazi had seen enough of white firepower. He took his people and cattle away to the north, where his tribe prospered and grew even more powerful.

The Voortrekkers' leaders could not agree in which direction they should go to settle, and their squabbles grew more heated, with the result that Hendrik Potgieter withdrew across the Vaal River into the Winburg district, labeled a coward by those he left behind. He blocked his ears, more interested in settling his people and establishing an overland trade route to the Portuguese fort at Delgoa Bay.

Gert Maritz and Pieter Retief were attracted by Natal and its port despite the sandbar at its entrance that allowed access only to ships with shallow draft, seeing that the lush open lands more than compensated for that single drawback. They too quarreled, for both wished to be recognized as supreme leader of their joint parties. The traders at Port Natal welcomed a Boer presence, seeing them as a buffer between themselves and Dingaan's Zulu nation, knowing too well how the despotic King vacillated between friendship and sudden threats.

Undaunted by Dingaan's treacherous disposition, Pieter Retief and his volunteer force met to treat with him, and were promised a grant of land if they could recover a body of cattle stolen from the royal kraals by the Tlokwa tribe.

With consummate ease and the use of a little trickery, Retief brought the cattle back to the Zulu King, who declared himself well pleased until Retief refused to give him the guns and horses he had also captured. Dingaan brooded during the two-day celebration he ordered, and although he put his mark to a land grant prepared by Retief he had no intention of honoring it, seeing the establishment of a white nation so close to his own as a threat to his security.

On the morning of Tuesday, February 6, 1838, Dingaan invited the unsuspecting Voortrekkers to a farewell drinking party. Retief, his English interpreter, his brother Commandos, and their many native servants were surrounded and seized as they watched the dancing. The entire party was dragged away to the execution hill, where they were impaled or clubbed to death watched by a horrified missionary who could do nothing to stop the systematic massacre.

This part of his plan accomplished, Dingaan sent his impi

to destroy those families who had already brought their wagons up between the Bushman's River and the Blaauwkrans River despite the fact that they had not received any guarantee of safe passage. Here the impi killed sixty-nine men and women, one hundred and eighty-five children, and in excess of two hundred native servants. The savagery of the attack so appalled the Voortrekkers they renamed the place Weenen, Weeping.

The impi commanded by Dingaan's brother Mpande fell upon Port Natal and razed the buildings to the ground, causing the inhabitants to take refuge aboard the only ship in the harbor.

Gert Maritz died the following September and left the Natalian Voortrekkers without a natural leader. The survivors sent for Andries Pretorius, who made the long and arduous overland trek to Natal at the head of his Commando and in the van of his followers' wagons. He was appointed Commander-General upon his arrival, and within days had taken the field against the Zulu with a combined Commando force of five hundred men, fifty-seven wagons, and a precious cannon.

Pretorius set up a strongly defended laager on the banks of the Ncome River and waited for Dingaan to come against him. And come he did, with an army of a hundred thousand men.

From dawn to dusk on December 16, 1838, the chest, loins, and horns of the Zulu threw themselves into massed musket and cannon fire, scrambling over the bodies of their slain and wounded to reach the men in the circled wagons. When the Voortrekkers made a mounted charge, the savaged Zulu were forced to retreat, leaving behind three thousand of their dead. Whatever their numerical superiority, the Zulu were unable to prevail against the white guns, armed as they were with only spears, shields, and raw courage. They had not managed to kill a single white.

The Voortrekkers renamed the Ncome Blood River, for it had run red during the battle. They had prevailed against the Zulu and considered themselves masters of their hard-won land by right of conquest. Some time later, they deliberately allowed themselves to be led into an ambush and killed over a thousand more of Dingaan's warriors in a series of skirmishes with the loss of only five of their own horsemen. Dingaan knew his power was slipping away, and ordered an assault on the Swazi to redeem himself in the eyes of his subjects. His regiments were beaten back and Dingaan fled, only to be murdered by the northern tribesmen. His brother Mpande ruled in his place as vassal to the Boers, who confiscated much of his lands for their own use.

The Voortrekkers had come to stay.

2

Matthew Eastman lay in the night grass and waited.

A light breeze stirred his beard and the low moon had set to leave a darkness so profound the high stars seemed to brush the crown of his hat. Insects trilled from the pastures and hyenas cackled hysterically from the high plains where they squabbled over fresh carrion, their laughing cries punctuated by nocturnal birdcalls. None of these sounds interested Matthew, who concentrated on the horsemeat lure he had nailed to the corral gate at last light. Although he could not see it, he kept his smoothbore trained toward the fresh haunch, knowing its smell would be carried toward the animal he waited for. He had lain without moving for over five hours and patiently hoped the animal would come before the sun rose.

A sawing cough came on the wind and he willed it closer, seeing in his mind's eye the high, spotted back and the lowered head of the foraging leopard skirting the compound and the smells of man, caution fighting his need to feed his empty belly.

Matthew waited, his trigger eased and his pan primed.

A muted grunt from beyond the long barn told him the animal had circled and was rounding in toward the lure. Matthew thought of the stillborn colt torn from his bloodstock mare only three nights before and his patience grew. There would only be one shot.

The spoor he and Boie had found showed a front pad twisted in against the right foreleg and suggested a badly healed shoulder break. The leopard was no longer swift enough to bring down veldt game, and made bold by hunger, it culled the herds of men.

Boie, his scent masked by mud, lay on the barn roof with a pitch torch, ready to light and throw it when the bell attached to the lure tolled. Dawn was close and time was rapidly running out. Matthew willed himself not to sweat or cough and prayed the wind would not change quarter and carry his fresh smell toward the approaching animal.

215

There was a scrape of claw against timber, the clap of bell metal against packed earth, the thump and skitter of the falling cat.

With a whirring rush, Boie's flaming torch spun in a high arc, hovered then fell, striking the ground in a shower of dislodged sparks. For a single, frozen moment, the animal was lit, his great head swinging at Matthew, the amber eyes full on him, the haunch of meat clamped between the scarred jaws as it growled deep in its chest. Then, with flattened ears and its tail swinging furiously, the leopard's back legs bunched and swiftly propelled the long body toward the great outer darkness beyond the spill of torchlight.

The stock bit at Matthew's shoulder as the smoothbore bucked and stinking smoke bloomed around a long spit of flame. The leopard squalled as it was punched back and away. It dropped the meat and worried its chest with its lower jaw, flecked by its own blood. Then, with a long, snarling roar it batted at the air with its forepaws, its muzzle peeled back from long yellow teeth as it backed away on failing legs, mad with pain and fear.

Matthew reprimed pan and barrel, spat a ball and a wad into the bore, and rammed them home, cocking the hammer with a swift thumb movement. There was no need for a second shot. The leopard stiffened and flopped onto its side, the tail gave a last quivering flick and shivered into stillness. Only then did Matthew rise, kick the circulation back into his legs, and approach the leopard, the gun aimed at its head. Boie was scrambling from the roof and torches gathered near the farmhouse as the Sotho herders came running to form a circle around the dead animal, gabbling in excited Sotho.

The leopard was old. One tooth was snapped off and a black and ragged scar ran the length of one shoulder where an ugly mound showed the crest of the badly set bone. In death the leopard seemed shrunken and pathetic.

"Wild pig, Nkosi," said Boie, tracing the shoulder scar with a finger. "Tusk cut bad."

The boys jostled and slapped their thighs as pitch from their torches dripped onto the carcass. By morning the leopard would have grown tenfold by their retelling, would have three massive heads and have killed and eaten a thousand horses.

Matthew passed the smoothbore to Boie and left them all there, somehow diminished by the death of the old cat and the ease with which he had accomplished it. He shivered as

216

he strode away, telling himself he was just tired. The long nights of waiting had tortured his nerves and gave him a distorted view of things. It was time to go to the high ground and take stock.

He saddled Gaika and rode out across the valley to the jut of a shelving kopje where he reined in and faced east, reaching for and filling his pipe.

It was drawing well when the first dull bloom fingered the lower stars and spread fanwise across the heavens to separate the Blesberg from the sky.

This was a ritual that never varied, for Matthew had become a creature of habit during the years since the battle of Vegkop. He liked to watch his farm grow from the night's shades; born again in the new dawn, pasteled, fresh and softly dewed. As his farm came alive he felt his own vitality grow with it; he and his property coming out of the dark together, in joint communion with the coming day.

Peach streamers lanced the paling skies, reaching to tint the high outcrops orange and buff, reaching farther to sculpt the undersides of high, massing cloud. The first red wedge of sun formed in a haze of bright pearl and cast shadows through the tree aloes, sansevieria, and bold stands of prickly pear.

Sheep on the high pasture glowed rose as a herd of fleet deer skipped through them, and in the valley below, the thatch of Matthew's house turned from tan to yellow, and smoke rose from the chimney in whipping strands and ran off toward the valley wall.

His home, by God. And all built in less than seven years.

There was no ambivalence in Matthew Eastman's heart for this place he had made from nothing in so short a time. He loved the place. His stockbred horses were considered to be the best in the territory and commanded top money from those knowing neighbors who came to haggle and eventually to pay his price. Even strangers sought him out to improve their stock.

Matthew tapped out his pipe and lost it in his pocket, suddenly soured.

He had brought Elise up to the high bluff on her bridal morning, but she had seen none of the beauty, none of the achievement, only the wildness and isolation and the far mountainous boundary of Mzilikazi's kingdom. The face she had turned to Matthew when he spoke to her had been a distorted mask of despair and antagonism, a cruel parody of

217

the loving one he had shared a pillow with the night before. After a long look of unhappy suffering she had spurred angrily down the hill, hair and tears streaming together.

Now she hardly left the house at all except when she rode the gray he had gentled for her, her seat ungainly, her rein hard on the soft, responsive mouth. She was ruining the animal as surely as she was turning from Matthew. Perhaps if there had been children it would have been different. Songs and children's laughter in the empty nursery instead of highly polished silence.

Gaika whinnied and pawed the ground. Matthew had tangled a fist in her mane and was pulling it hard, his face set and somber.

"Ach!" Matthew patted Gaika's neck and set her down the slope away from his thoughts.

There was too much to be done to brood.

3

The shot jolted Elise from her cozy Port Elizabeth bedroom with its stenciled walls, shutters and curtains and carpets, its sleek furniture with painted panels and upholstered seats, rudely waking her in the plain limewashed room with its bare wooden floor, steel chest, and the single *riempie* chair. Even the bed she lay in had been carved by native craftsmen and was neither painted nor varnished. She was thankful it was dark and she did not have to see the crude heathen symbolism of the uprights and headboard that wished fertility on those who slept in it.

Fertility indeed. The local women seemed to swell every second season and drop their offspring in the fields as though they were mild cases of hiccups, back to weeding and hoeing within the hour. She hated their solicitous looks as each moon phase passed, hated their sly presentations of barley dolls and ostrich eggs filled with bitter remedies for her eggless stomach. Her belly would never be fruitful while she had to stay in this rustic backwater with its storms and boredom and anvil heat that dried her skin should she even venture outside except on the coolest morning of a winter's day.

No dancing, no ballrooms, no *conversation*.

The talk here was of seeds and studs and mares and foals and feed and on and on and on....

Thinking of how she had come here still made her head spin. Matthew's first letter to her had been delivered at her

218

father's emporium by a hide salesman who had demanded four silver schillings for bringing it out of the interior. Elise had never really expected to hear from Matthew after he had stalked out on her, but reading his big, rounded characters had brought him back to her as surely as if he had walked in through the door and the years between had never passed. True, Matthew was no penman and his letter was written on thick wrapping paper that bore the imprint of an English steel mill, but it was all the more dear for that.

He had included careful drawings of his farm and the nearby town of Winburg, delicately tinted with watercolor and signed by the artist, a local doctor named Andries who had sounded a most cultured and gentle man if Matthew's pen portrait of him was anything to go by. With a liberal mixture of wishful thinking and self-deception, Elise began to build a picture of Matthew at the center of a small but cultured society where she could flourish as the first lady of Winburg whose influence could only grow as the community grew. Matthew's second and third letters arrived within a month of the first and before Elise had made up her mind to reply.

In them he described the battle of Vegkop as the final victory over the Matabele, opening up that part of the Central Plateau for the Boers to settle there in peace and implying that the amenities offered by the nearby town of Winburg rivaled even those of Port Elizabeth itself.

When Elise wrote back her letters were mere catalogues of questions. Matthew obliged as best he could and at length, and always included some small, rich gift of jewelry or lace. At that time, Elise had thought little of how he had managed to come by them, assuming reasonably that he had simply bought them in one of the many shops in Winburg. Now of course, she knew differently, knew he must have scoured the district and traded for the small heirlooms with families who needed seedcorn more than a hoarded gewgaw that had belonged to a better-placed forebear.

She had been foolish and Matthew must have lied, Elise told herself yet again, but how in the world was she to have known how things were here on the frontier? When Matthew had come for her to Port Elizabeth and stood beside those pale clerks and her father's portly trading partners she had felt herself responding to his maleness with unladylike flushes and the need to drink great drafts of cold lemon water. The desire to strip away the stiff store clothes and to explore the big brown body had stayed with her and made her impatient to marry and close the bedroom door behind them both. Martha's scolding fell on deaf ears. The banns were posted, flounces were sewn on white satin, women friends came and went in a whirl of petticoats and talk of seating, stitching, and table settings, excluding both Harry and Matthew, who slunk away from the constant bustle, too cowed to talk even to each other.

The wedding service had been a blur of floral displays and vibrant singing, of handshakes and kisses. The fiddles had struck up after toasts and Elise could still see the dancing couples in her mind's eye as she lay here on the rumpled bed in far Winburg.

She had so little here compared with her friends on the coast with their carriages and liveried blackamoors, churches where they sang in English, the socials where refined people of like minds met and exchanged invitation cards. Going back to Port Elizabeth for a while seemed so very little to ask of a husband.

Elise turned her face into the coarse pillow and ran a hand along the dip where Matthew slept when he wasn't brooding over a foaling mare or some silly boundary guard. Although cool, the sheet still smelled of his body warmth and tobacco. The shallow trench was wide at the shoulder and narrow at the hip, divided where his long legs sprawled as he lay on his back and slept like a dead man when she had convinced him she was unarousable. How many nights had she played that charade over the months, the weeks, the *years?* Anything to avoid impregnation and the loss of her figure before she was home where it was safe and clean. And *home*.

Oh, God in His mercy, how many times had she wanted his body over hers, his very life leaking into hers as the climaxes came and came and came? The long nights when, convinced she slept, he in turn slept and she waited for the dark hours to pass slowly into morning and to yet another dragging and useless day; passing from room to room, pretending to read or sew or supervise the cook. She had made early attempts at cookery with frills and wines, but Matthew would eat boiled hay if it were served with enough potatoes and dumplings.

Beer and dumplings and horses and bed.

If only he would take her back to Port Elizabeth for a visit, a mere four or five months, six. She could introduce him to so many nicely mannered people who knew horses as well as he, perhaps better. They hunted for pleasure, not for the pot. People with trimmed hair and polished shoes, not stale beards and rough veldschoene. Eating with the fingers required finger bowls, she had read so in a book on etiquette. All it took was reading and remembering; Matthew must be capable of that.

They could afford to go; Matthew must have enough money in the brass chest he had secreted beneath the floor. He had sold so many horses to the Dutch who came to his auctions. It was all cash, no scrip or paper, gold and silver coins in soft leather sacks; she had seen him count it each quarter when he marked up his accounts.

Matthew must be made to take her. She, Elise, must make him.

Elise kicked aside the mosquito netting Sergeant Coffee had brought the last time he visited, and went to the window to open the shutters, looking toward Matthew's favorite kopje. Yes, there he was, sitting on that mare of his, watching the day come up as though it could not be trusted to keep the appointment alone.

He talked of sunrises as though they were living things, describing them all individually as though each were as different as faces in a line; boring her over mounds of breakfast mealie cakes.

Elise frowned. But he *hadn't* been saying so much lately. He just ate up and left after pecking her cheek, gone all day and sometimes through the night. My God! How long had he been indifferent, and why hadn't she noticed before?

Elise thought back frantically, frightening herself with wild possibilities and wilder conjecture. He had taken a mistress in town, or one of the black women from the servants' compound. He no longer loved her, he had become impotent. Had Elise known there was such a thing as homosexuality, she would have considered that a possibility as well.

Badly frightened, she fled below and threw cold pump-water into her face until she gasped for breath, dabbing her face dry on the hem of her nightgown as she sat on the stoep, unmindful of the boys who still ringed the dead leopard and stared at her, marveling at the second wonder of the day.

The Missie up at dawn and outside in her sleeping robe. Had she not ordered a houseboy flogged for seeing her like that by mistake? And cried when Nkosi refused?

Ayee, perhaps a bad spirit had been released from the dead

221

beast, blown from the leopard's mouth by Mwari, who created all things.

More excited and fearful than the distraught Elise, the Sotho crept away to make peace with their ancestral gods.

Elise ordered her thoughts and was grateful the yard was empty.

She must contrive to leave the Blesberg. The town of Winburg was nothing but a row of two-story shacks, and every single item had to be carted in from the coast, costing eight or ten times as much as it should. The goods were shoddy and cheaply made, not a fashionable item among them. The dresses she had brought up-country had been ahead of the local fashionables by three years, and now they were just as passé as those her neighbors wore. She must go if only to buy a new wardrobe. And linen. Some silver, furniture....

Was it somebody in Winburg? Elise wondered. Somebody Matthew admired? The townswomen were so old and ordinary, weren't they? She pondered awhile and then dismissed the notion; it was too simple an answer for her convolute mind. No, it must be she herself who was to blame. She knew Matthew went to see Mrs. Hannie Gould, who ran that awful hotel, but that was to see her son. Matthew loved and wanted children, that was the reason for the frequent trips, not the woman herself; she was married and she must be over thirty....

Elise wandered back into the house and ordered hot water for the hipbath. As she soaped herself she made her plans to return home to Port Elizabeth, remembering that there had been some talk about Matthew and that woman from the Cape, Mrs. Laidler, but that she dismissed now as she had then, as malicious gossip. Matthew belonged to her and she would manipulate him as she always knew she could, *if* she was of a mind....

She would use her body to get her way. She would love her way home.

Matthew could not refuse her after she had warmed his bed as prettily as she planned to. The native women used some method to stop babies; she had enough Bantu to understand what they giggled about when they thought she didn't comprehend. She would bully one of them and find out.

Elise crushed mint between her breasts and thighs, dabbed precious perfume on her neck and shoulders and combed a little into her hair. She would make Matthew come to her instead of eating a mountainous breakfast and rushing off to see to his endless chores. She had seen him looking at her during the daylight hours, his eyes slack with inner heat. Hadn't he once wanted to make love out in the bush at full noon? Down on the ground where the sun would have glared in her eyes as the stony ground bruised her back? She had refused then, but she would not do so now. She would do it on Gaika's back if the thought ever crossed Matthew's mind. Perhaps she would see that it did.

Smiling broadly, she knew her scheme would work.

4

Boie brooded as he skinned the old leopard.

Until three days before, the real things of life had gone well since they had come to this place, he and Nkosi Matthew. There was game in the hills, the stock fattened, and the crops grew tall in the fields. Only rarely had they been molested by Sotho or Nguni, displaced from their traditional lands by the *lifaqane*, the killing time.

They had luck.

Many tribes had perished on the spears of Mantatisi and her Wild Cat people, Mpangazita's hordes, or the rabble who followed Matiwane; three great groups of mixed tribes who had been squeezed from the Central Plateau by the converging land-hungry regiments of the Zulu and the Matabele.

Living from the land as they fled, these starving multitudes massacred the tribes they met for their meat and grain, cannibalizing the clanspeople if they were destitute like themselves. Twenty-eight great Sotho clans had disappeared without a trace this way and many thousands had fled to the Kalahari Desert or into swampland where they and their cattle succumbed to the all-pervading tsetse fly.

Boie stripped the claws and pad from the foot, slashed the skin along the underside of the leg, and bared the raw meat with a run of the knife, exposing the torn musculature. The boar had done his work well and the leopard should not have lived to heal and hunt again. His spirit must have been strong and would live on again in another. Boie beat his forehead against the packed earth and asked the old mud father to make the spirit whole and good without a dark twist; to send its seed to a far land where it might hunt others' cattle when it was spawned again. For such seed could grow into a man of destiny just as well as a jackal or an elephant.

Boie sprinkled dust to the winds and struck his head on

the ground four more times to make the dispersal good. Then he resumed skinning, his thoughts darker than his skin.

The Missie had no seed, which was sad, for the Nkosi was a bull in his prime and would need sons, many sons, to hold this land when his body bent under the years. The aiwa who lived downstairs had said there were never creaks from the bed above, never the grunt and squall of boy-making. No flesh against flesh, no loin against loin. Boie had taken the girl off into the bush to beat her with a willow wand to stop her fly-buzz of gossip, and through her tears she had sworn on the Earth Mother and the Almighty Mwari that her words were true. That the bed had not shaken once in the six moon quarters she had carried water for the baas and Missie. When Boie let blood from her arm to cleanse her lies she swore it was true and would not be shaken.

Boie had then seen that it must be true. He had warned the girl he would abandon her to the hill lions if her mouth loosened again and released her, barely aware that she kissed his sandals before skipping away, more than gratitude in her eyes for him. He had a wife and a son already.

Two moons later the old leopard came and killed the pregnant mare, returning after three days more to die himself, on the edge of the dawn when the night spirits and the sun fought for the heavens. A bad time to die. In the confusion, the rising spirit could belong to both worlds, or to neither. Boie thought it was bad. Had not the Missie thrown water at herself until she almost drowned, and sat on the stoep to show her legs as she wiped her face?

Yes, a death on the cusp of day was very bad.

Boie slit the leopard's belly and pared the skin away from the stringy subcutaneous fat. He would bury the heart and the viscera in a deep kloof far away so that none could find them. Then any curse would be lost in the rotting.

He would watch the Missie closely and have the aiwa report to him in secret. No harm must come to the house of Nkosi.

5

Matthew was sweating freely when he arrived back at the farm. The dew had burned from the grass and there was summer lightning in the hills, invisible in the banking white thunderheads, where an electric storm lashed the far, high ground.

224

He found Boie stripping the last of the hide from the leopard's back and preparing to pare out the tail from above the anus, working as carefully as an army surgeon. Boie rose and bobbed his head as he usually did when he and Matthew met, but the usual smile was missing. Was he ill or tired? Matthew wondered as he halted Gaika and said:

"Which of the boys wants the head?"

Boie drew a line with his toe, silently shaking his head.

"None of them?" Matthew hardly believed it. "And the genitals?"

Again the silent shake of the head.

"Tell me?" Matthew commanded.

"This was a bad kill, baas. Bad luck to eat the parts."

Baas? thought Matthew. The Khoikhoi was using the form of address to distance himself, as though the subject should not be discussed between white and black. So be it. Matthew never interfered with his people's beliefs, however strange. They were free to keep to their myriad gods and demons and to safeguard themselves against witchcraft. He had seen too many marvels to deny them and although he knew he would never understand as Klyn had seemed to, he would continue to try.

"And the skin?" he asked.

Boie's grin grew like sudden light.

"Yours, Nkosi. It was a great kill. It will be a great trophy. I will cure it for you when..." Boie's voice faded as he turned his small head toward the far, high ground where the lightning hid in a green-blue haze.

"How long will it take?" asked Matthew, not adding "to make your medicine."

"Until the sun is here." Boie pointed straight upward to indicate high noon, his eyes still hooded and shy.

Matthew's scowl failed.

"No later," he said. Boie knew he meant to ride the twenty miles to Winburg and would want to be there before dark. It was always wise to avoid the banditti who roamed the bush at night.

"Yes, Nkosi." Boie ran for a sack, forgetting his dignity before the lesser boys; being one of Nkosi's *abenzansi*, he should always walk slowly with a high head. As it was, there was nobody to see anyway; the Sotho herders had left for the high pasture.

Matthew unsaddled Gaika in the barn, saw that she was rubbed down and released into the corral where there was shade, and walked back to the house with his stomach growling. He was hungry and tired.

The kitchen was empty and nothing bubbled on the stove. All that stood on the scrubbed table was a bowl of wild flowers. Matthew just stood there with his anger mounting. As he was called to the upper floor by Elise, the aiwa fled from the back door to find Boie.

Boie saw the girl coming when he was less than a hundred yards from the compound and he waited until she threw herself at his feet and gabbled in fast patois. He made her talk slower and was told that the Missie had demanded the fluid that stopped ovulation. Boie gripped the bloody sack tighter and wished he could kill the leopard a second time. Now, when the sun was up.

"You gave the Missie this thing, girl?"

"I had none, Lord." The girl shook. "The Missie pulled my hair when I told her where the cook kept hers."

Boie had not known the cook gave her favors, and he stored the information away. "What then?"

"The Missie found it and took it. She sent the cook . . . away."

"She drank?"

"There was very little. A few drops."

Boie watched dust swirl in the corral as the horses butted and reared, saw the sheep in broken white patches on the pasture. No eagles or vultures soared in the sky. He looked at the girl and raised her to her feet. She had good bones under the sweat and her eyes were pleasing when she did not roll them. Her name was Pyayo and she would soon be ready for her first fruiting.

"She has asked for more, Lord," whimpered Pyayo.

Boie grinned slowly, bobbing his head. There was a word for women like the Missie in his tribe where such things were not unknown. She feared the swelling and the pain of making boys.

"Pyayo," said Boie, "when the Missie asks again, you will give her the fluid. You will come to me and I will give it to you. Say nothing to anyone, remember the hill lions. If not to them, I will give you to Queen Mantatisi, who has a thousand breasts and suckles her warriors on her own milk. She would draw the marrow from your bones."

"My tongue is yours, Lord." Pyayo's shivering made it hard for her to keep her feet. "All my words will come to you."

Boie walked away without another word or a backward glance. In the high ground he would find roots and berries and grind them up with insects to make a potion that would make the Missie fertile. Nkosi would have his son.

6

Slow counting came to Matthew as he mounted the stairs, soft numbers rising to one hundred. He pushed open the bedroom door and stopped dead.

The window had been draped by a run of linen to cut down the hard morning light, reducing the room to soft shades. Matthew saw the white body against the whiter bedding of the dark ebony bed.

Naked except for house sandals, Elise sat on the counterpane and brushed her hair with long, languorous strokes, her right breast rising and rolling with the rise and fall of the silver brush. In the soft, borrowed light her skin glowed pale and her dangling legs seemed to go on forever. She frowned into a small mirror propped against the bedhead and changed hands at one hundred to brush the other side of her loose blond hair. Her left breast now moved with her arm, rhythmic and heart-stopping in its appeal.

Need punched Matthew in the groin and a new kind of perspiration broke out along his spine, a chill dew that quickened his entire system. Shocked to see the usually demure Elise making the simple domestic ceremony into something so naturally carnal, he balled his fists, confused by an honest surge of lust and the suddenness with which it flooded over him.

The slender roundness of her struck him as both new and oddly familiar.

Elise looked up at him from beneath her fringe and smiled the smile she smiled when she passed napkins, tea, and cake to other matrons, all of them clothed in modest black or gray.

The look, the smile, and the nakedness came at Matthew like an exploding fireball and he hardened inside his clothes, his swollen member backed by contracted muscle and raw, melting juices.

He reached for her but she swung her legs to the far side of the bed, rising and stretching her arms above her head, tossing her hair.

"Have Boie saddle my gray, will you?" she said, posing. "I thought we'd go riding before it gets too hot."

Smelling mint, Matthew had to puzzle out what she meant. Delighted with the effect she had caused, Elise made herself laugh at him as a shaft of light picked out the mound of her belly and the contours of her breasts. Matthew's face and neck were gorged and fiery.

"Hurry, you *dassie,* or the day will be gone," she said softly, mocking him. She reached for her chemise and covered herself.

Her laughter followed Matthew down the stairs and out of the house.

7

Boie was in the shadow of the mountain Nkosi called the Blesberg.

He had buried the leopard's parts in a deep and narrow kloof only he knew of, and had covered them with a cairn of rocks. Green mambas lived there, and Boie had sung his song of protection as he picked his way through them, knowing the risk to be worthwhile.

Then he had left the dark gully and climbed to another place that was his own where he collected young mulberry leaves and the small clusters of fruit that had not yet purpled. He gathered the leaves and flowers of the wild hemp, spurge gum from a tall euphorbia, the bitter leaves of the lilac, and the bark from a quiver tree. Then he dug white grubs from the roots of a tree aloe and trapped stinkbeetles, black moths and dug eggs from a termite hill.

He had all the other ingredients he needed in his hut, and would crush the insects in a monkey skull and soak them in fermenting beer laced with mamba venom. When he had added the boiled leaves and berries to the mess, he would distill the brew over a bed of charcoal and catch the slow drops from the green bamboo coil in a black pot that was old when his grandfather's father was old.

Boie shared his snuff with the four winds and started down to the farm. Far out beyond the pasturing where the land rippled into natural terraces and rose through broken Kopjes to the foothills of the mountain, two horses pecked up dust as they galloped south toward the waterfall that fed the river through a deep gray scar in the lower veldt. Boie squatted and squinted, making out the riders.

He hissed and grinned. Missie and Nkosi raced together; the mare and the gray stretched their necks on the straight and jumped the terrace walls as though wind demons snapped at their tails. They topped a long flat rise and ran down through the slopes to splash into the shallow river, where they turned east along the stony bed and lost themselves in the bowering trees and scrub of the high overhangs.

Boie watched the gap in the next bend to see if they went toward the hidden pool where Baas Klyn's stone monument rose above the sheer rock walls and guarded the source of the tumbling fall of water. Abba also rested there beneath a flat stone carved with his name and shadowed by a sweet myrtle. It was a fitting place for their bones to rest.

Boie and Matthew had worked through one spring to build the rubble core and wall it with dressed stone. Boie and his wife Ndala had come to this place for their first coupling and had made their son Josef over the three nights they had stayed, watched over by the brave dead of Vegkop. The boy had grown straight and slim and serious and was close to his fourth summer; another year and he would bend the bow his father had made for him.

The horses showed briefly at the far bend before cantering between the tall outcrops that guarded the entrance to the pool.

Boie's shout clattered through the buttresses of tumbled rock and disturbed quail rose all around him, their whipping calls chasing his echoes through the kloofs.

8

Gaika was gaining on the gray when they came in sight of the hushing falls of white water, but Elise swung her mount to balk the mare, forcing Matthew to rein in hard to avoid a collision. The gray went off through the shallows and took the far bank cleanly, stepping across the grass with lather spraying from his neck.

Matthew stayed in the river to let Gaika drink, and filling his hat with water, splashed it over his face and head, watching his wife rear the gray time and time again, its forelegs thrashing the air as she turned it in a graceful circle. Matthew searched his memory for the last time she had ridden a horse so well and realized it was back in Port Elizabeth before they had married. All her previous snapping misery seemed to have evaporated as though it had never been, and she was once more the girl he had brought here as a bride.

Matthew set Gaika up the stream at a slow gait, wondering at the startling change.

Elise flung herself from the saddle to sprawl breathless

229

in the turf, her boots and arms flung wide, a spreading damp patch on her waisted blouse. The world spun when she closed her eyes and perspiration gathered on her closed lids. She threw grass into the air and some of it fell into her opened mouth, the rest fluttering into the water to run off the stone shelf and drown in the slow race of the river.

Elise shielded her eyes from the dappled light and gazed up the sides of the water-carved bowl to the dark finger of Klyn's monument above the rim.

The air was filled with fine spray and her heart hammered less and less as her skin cooled. She filled her lungs with the fine scents of myrtle, bougainvillea, and wild herbs as the cataract roared and splashed down the sheer face to cascade into the deep green pool. For the first time in a long while she felt a part of the world.

She heard Gaika's hooves on the bank and she rose up to throw off her hat and her blouse, working at the buttons of her riding skirt. Matthew was dismounting when she plunged into the green water and sought to touch the bottom where the crayfish hid among the gray stones. Her fingers found a boulder and she caught at it, holding herself down. A dark shape scuttled and she snatched it up before bringing her feet down and launching herself to the surface. She exploded into sudden light and found Matthew staring from the bank. Elise drew back her arm and threw the crayfish at him. Without thinking, Matthew plucked it out of the air and laughed as a pincer trapped his thumb.

Elise rolled in the water and waited for him to join her.

As he pulled off his second boot, Elise jackknifed and dove again, hearing the dull boom as Matthew struck the water. Then he was down beside her in a cloud of bubbles and disturbed silt, his arms around her waist and his beard brushing her face as he sought her mouth. With pressure roaring in her ears, Elise kissed him back openmouthed and they rose up together in a slow spiral that went on and on and on....

Later, as they lay together on the turf with water dripping into her hair from Matthew's beard, she mentioned Port Elizabeth. When Matthew began to talk of next year or the year after, she found his soft manhood and stiffened it with strokes of her fingertips, eased him onto his back, and ran her tongue along his thighs until the tip rose up the huge column and she trapped the top between her teeth. As Matthew reared, bridging himself by his shoulders and feet, Elise brought her breasts down onto his loins and gave him a second, slower climb to a climax, bringing him into her at the last moment. All the time she whispered and exacted promises that he barely knew he gave.

As they rode home, hand in hand, she reminded him and he knew he had no way of going back on his word.

9

Matthew drowsed in the saddle as Gaika paced the wagon.

Winburg grew out of the middle air as an undulating line of smudges that melted and re-formed in constant dance above the shimmering ground. The green-blue northern horizon glowed above the sun-washed veldt, and thunder rolled through the brilliant skirts of cloud.

Far from being sated by Elise, Matthew's drive was merely revivified, and more than once he had thought of turning about to take her through several journeys on their big and ugly bed; each jogging hoof fall was a reminder of his awakened appetite.

He was concerned about this talk of an extended trip to Elise's parents in far Port Elizabeth. Harry and Martha had come up-country the previous summer and had itched to return to the coast from the moment they crossed his stoep. To Matthew it seemed that as fast as they accrued wealth from their several stores and warehouses, so their years had gathered faster, bowing Harry's shoulders and making his wife more shrewish, more fretful. Martha had seen Matabele behind every kopje, an assegai in every shadow. Matthew's honest assurances had convinced neither parent, and the two old people had gone away with solemn faces, unsettling Elise all the more, if that were at all possible.

When their quarterly letters came by packet from the Cape, Elise would shut herself away with each one and there would be days of sighing silences, headaches, and the savage rides across the veldt on the sweating gray; the usual nights of feigned sleep and the firmly turned back.

Until today, thought Matthew, realizing full well what Elise was doing and why. *Magtig*, if she took him for a fool, he would act the fool for her. He was tired of this doll he had married, this girl who thought of pretties and baubles instead of being wife and mother. He would make sweet promises and somehow delay this trip to Port Elizabeth and the prospect of weeks on end in the company of shopkeepers and their wives, those dullards with small minds and smaller talk, confined by narrow horizons, their faces as blank as their tablecloths. And the tight collars and tighter shoes.

Matthew took Gaika through the fringe of outer corrals where slaughter cattle waited for the auction hammer in their numbered pens. More beehive huts had sprung up in the sprawling native quarter, he noticed. More bare children romped in the dust and he recognized the facial marking and dress of the northern Sotho clans, all of them refugees from beyond the Drakensberg. A sure sign that the impi were on the march again. Matthew had heard of the great sickness that had struck the Matabele herds, decimating two thirds of Mzilikazi's prized cattle, more than enough reason for him to raid his neighbors to rebuild his dwindled stock. There was talk of slave-trading too, of Arabs and Americans who took whole villages into bondage and shipped them off to New Orleans and Virginia, where the few who survived the crossing were sold for high prices. If the Volksraad, the Boer Council, really did expel those natives who were surplus to their labor requirements from the territory, those same slavers would grow fatter on easy money.

Matthew forearmed sweat from his brow, shaking his head. He had argued with his Dutch neighbors, warned them of the folly of such an action. For his pains he had been called an Uitlander, as though he had not fought for his land as they had. Ach, they were unable to agree among themselves, let alone with an Englishman, and how they dearly loved to squabble. Matthew tried to stay aloof. If they wanted the British to annex Natal, they were going the right way about it. They knew what he felt and counseled; let them do what they must. Matthew had troubles of his own.

Leaving Boie to off-load the wagon and trade sheep for bridles and baling wire, Matthew rode down the main street to the hotel.

The Winburg Regency had two stories and a deep tiled verandah ran around three sides of it. To the rear of the building were the stables and the low bungalow where the Goulds lived with their son and daughter. The hotel foyer boasted a tiled floor and velvet furniture, and Matthew's veldschoene squeaked as he threaded through the crowds to the desk for his key. Knots of men argued in harsh Dutch and Matthew heard Potgieter's name mentioned more than once. So, it was the start of another of their interminable meetings and they would shout until dawn or the first fistfights broke out. There would be little peace in Winburg that night. Matthew ordered a jug of beer and went up to his room, where he stripped off and lay on the bed to cool off. A boy brought his beer and he was working on the second schooner when there was a scratch at the door and Mrs. Gould came in to look down at him sprawling naked on the rumpled counterpane.

She was slim-waisted and round-hipped and the long, severe black gown she wore did its best to hide her firm and generous proportions. Her butter-colored hair was scraped back in a severe bun and thick sidecurls hid the tops of her small lobeless ears. Her eyes were pale gray and her eyebrows dark gold. Her nose was slightly overlong with small nostrils and her mouth was wide and full-lipped, her teeth large and perfect. She had been considered a beauty in her youth and was now a handsome woman who avoided the potato with a fine instinct for her figure. She hardly drank except for a little wine at table, and rode every day to keep her muscles firm. She cocked her chin and planted a small fist on her hip. "Did you allow the boy to see you like that?" she said, her voice warm with mild censure.

Matthew grinned, belching beer gas, and slapped his hard belly.

"Ach, if he had no discretion he wouldn't work here. How are you, Hannie?"

"Need you ask, you *mal hond?* Didn't you just walk through the lobby? We haven't a single empty room. It's the Volksraad meeting, and you know talking makes them thirsty."

"I know. What's it about this time?"

"You don't know? They say the British are coming back to Port Natal."

Matthew leaned up on an elbow, spilling beer down his chest.

"When? How many?"

"Who knows, hundreds. They're marching in from the fort in Mpondoland, Chief Faku's territory. He asked for protection from the Cape when the Commando raided the Bhaca and took seventeen children as apprentices. He thinks the Volksraad want to push all the surplus kaffirs over the border into his territory. It seems the Volksraad didn't bother to tell Faku where the new boundaries are. As usual it's all talk and no *doing.*"

Matthew skimmed suds from his chest and swung his legs to the floor.

"Typical, no foresight. When they hit the Bhaca they shot first and didn't bother to ask whether the three thousand cattle they ran off were stolen from the Boers in the first place. Damn, you'd think Pretorius was trying to lose the Republic before it gets started. Are they planning to resist the soldiers, Hannie?"

"Yes, it seems like it. So far it's talk."

"Stupid, stupid." Matthew drank deeply.

"It's worse than that, Matthew." Hannie perched beside him. "They think they have the protection of the King of Holland."

Matthew's laugh died in his throat when he saw how serious Hannie was. He waited until she said:

"A man called Smellekamp came into Port Natal on the *Brazilia*, a Dutch trading ship, and he's convinced Andries Pretorius he has the blessing of the Dutch to offer us aid. The Voortrekkers will resist the British if it's true. Could it be, Matthew? It'd be wonderful...."

"It's a lie." Matthew almost spat, his color high. "The Dutch can't even protect themselves, let alone start a war with England. Pretorius should see that."

Hannie's head jerked to one side. "He believes what he wants to."

A roar went up in the street and several guns fired into the air.

Matthew went to the window and looked down into the crowds on the wooden sidewalks, their torches flaring in the dying light. A band of horsemen had reined in among them and Matthew recognized Henrik Potgieter as the lead rider before the massing crowd swamped in around him and he dismounted into the confusion. There could be no mistaking the mood of the mob, many of them women with torches and banners, all of them shouting slogans as loudly as their menfolk.

Matthew watched the milling crowds for some time in an effort to make out individual phrases or arguments and found it impossible. He had no idea Hannie had joined him until she snuggled into his side and spoke.

"They'll fight if they believe Holland is behind them. They'll implement their pass laws for blacks and they'll expel all the natives they don't need as farm labor. There are less than six thousand trekkers in the whole province and they're outnumbered twenty to one by the kaffirs. They're suddenly

234

very frightened people, Matthew. You know they don't like the way you run your holding."

"I've heard it said." Matthew sounded remote. His fingers found a stray curl on the nape of Hannie's neck and he teased it gently, barely noticing her shivering response. He could taste the defeat that must come for these people he admired so much in so many ways.

"You have more than five native families living on your place, Matthew. You know you should restrict the numbers to comply with the law," whispered Hannie.

"Their law, Hannie. Just how will they implement it? Most families haven't even occupied the farmland they claimed when we came here; they sit in groups waiting to see what will happen. Will they send the blacks across the river unarmed? They want to ban any kaffir from owning a horse or a gun. Boie's as free as all my people are, he follows me because he chooses to. Am I to tell him he has less right to be here on the high veldt than my horse? He carries a gun to defend *us,* our community. My God, I've been with the trekkers all these years, been one of them, and now I don't think I know them at all."

"I know, I know, but they..." Hannie's voice faded, her face in against Matthew's rigid deltoid.

"They," snapped Matthew, "have lost their reason. Don't they realize the British will happily annex Port Natal and St. Lucia Bay to safeguard their trading route to India? They don't give a damn about the interior so long as the Cape frontier isn't thrown into turmoil by these incessant Commando raids. We still have to administer ourselves and police the towns and frontiers. How will that be achieved if we can't or won't tax ourselves to pay for it? Apart from that, there aren't enough of us."

There was another flurry of gunfire in the street and a ragged cheer went up as Potgieter made his way into the hotel. Hannie pulled Matthew's arm. "Come away," she urged.

"You're right." Matthew plumped onto the bed and drew himself the last of the beer, his eyes on Hannie. "If they come to my farm to make me send my people away, I'll be waiting for them."

"They won't, Matthew. They won't."

"Best they don't." Matthew drained the beer in a long draft and lost the glass. "Will you come to me tonight?"

235

"If I can. With Martin and the children away...I do have a hotel to run."

Matthew frowned and said, "Away? Where?" He thought Martin Gould a dreamer whose charm and manners were outweighed by his love of books. Only Hannie's punishing capacity for work had saved them from losing the hotel a dozen times for the lack of any kind of effort on his part. Matthew had loaned her money, but not in the quantities he would have liked. He and Hannie never talked of love or even regard; their relationship was profound enough not to need words.

"They went on a trip up-country. Martin has been studying geology, and he thinks there might be gold in the rivers. You know how he likes to show the children the country, teach them the names of flowers and birds. He thinks that Cecile has a talent for drawing. And he says the boy—"

"Where up-country?" Matthew interrupted.

"Toward the Vet River."

"How many boys did he take with him?"

"Four. I insisted on that. Look, Matthew, I'm sure it's all right. Are you trying to frighten me?"

Matthew forced a hard, vague smile.

"No, Hannie. Pay no mind; you know how I care for those young *skelms*. It's just that I brought a few boiled sugar sticks in my saddlebag for them. Well, if I can't play with the children, I'll have to settle for their mother, neh? Come here."

Hannie thumbed froth from Matthew's mustache and avoided his hands as she stepped to the door.

"Later. *Perhaps*. Second choice indeed."

"Hannie."

"Haven't you got business down at the livery?"

"Some, why?"

"Then go and see to it." Hannie opened the door and stepped into the passage. "And put some clothes on." She blew a kiss from the back of her wrist and closed herself out.

Matthew grinned down at his naked lap until her steps had faded, then his face turned hard with worry. Martin Gould was a fool to take his children along the Vet toward the Vaal. The San tribes still raided there, as did the banditti and renegade Griquas. Any other man would have seen what had happened between Matthew and Hannie over the last two years, but not Gould. As he dressed, Matthew wondered how Gould had made two such fine children. Neither of them were dreamers like their father. If only they had been his....

236

10

The streets were filled with arguing groups of men and the saloons were doing capacity business; every mother's son seemed to have a thirst and something to say for himself. There was a prayer meeting beside the cattle chutes of the auctioneer's office and lights twinkled from the small laagers outspanned to the north of town. Every face was white and it was as if all the Africans had melted into the night.

Matthew made his way to the livery stable down the middle of the street; it was easier to avoid horses and carriages than the many drunken agitators who crowded the sidewalks and the saloon stoeps. Many of these were English or German migrants who were being discriminated against just as surely as the local tribesmen, for they were recent arrivals and only those who had come in the first year were allowed to settle, buy land, or farm without the written consent of a *landdrost* or two Dutch-speaking burghers. These permissions were hard to come by, for many impossible. These white immigrants were in many ways worse off than the clansmen, who could find employment even if it did mean servitude akin to slavery; their families did at least have food and shelter. It was no wonder to Matthew that many of the more desperate took to the high country to live by what they could steal.

Even though Matthew understood, he would shoot them as readily as he would any other thief. There was a limit to what a man could allow on his land.

What Matthew Eastman had taken he would keep.

He wove through a hand-clapping crowd who watched a clog dancer accompanied by a wizened fiddler, and walked down the side of the livery stable to Abraham de Villiers's office. The old man would not farm his huge holdings near Pietermaritzburg with only daughters to help him. With Dirk continually away on Commando duty, Abraham preferred to stay close to the towns and the volksraad. Sitting a horse for long periods exhausted him and aggravated his chest wound. He preferred to sit by a stove where coffee simmered and whittle bone animals as he argued politics. Although still big-framed and erect, he was breathless much of the time and spoke slowly with blue lips when the winter mists affected his weakened lungs.

"Rooinek," he bellowed when Matthew pushed inside the

237

office and took the big, gnarled fist in his own. Abraham's old blue gaze was as strong as his grip.

"Menheer."

"I expected you earlier. So, you'd rather buy your hospitality at the hotel than accept the little I can offer, neh?" Abraham turned to the men leaning around the walls. "You see how it is? I could forgive the *rooinek* for overcharging me for his palsied mules if he were Dutch. By God, he would be a true Hollander but for that red neck and temper to match."

Matthew helped himself to beer from a pitcher.

"You should be dead, old man. You know God made the English and the Dutch made themselves. What keeps you alive?"

"You see, *mense?* You see how he would steal my life as well as the few schillings I have in my purse. Anyway, who says I am still alive? You?"

"You'll outlive us all, menheer."

"Very probably," said Abraham. "So what have you brought to foist off on me, donkeys to be boiled down for glue? Or are you just here to goad me before you go to the meeting?"

"Neither. I lost the foal I was breeding for you to a leopard. The mare too. I shot the damned thing this morning. Had me up for two nights. I'm sorry, you'll have to wait until the other gray is ready in the autumn."

"Ach." Abraham's face and voice sobered. "That would have been a fine animal. Bad luck, neh?"

Matthew shrugged it away.

"It happens," he said. "I have some geldings you might want for the Commando. Five strong animals. Sturdy. That's of course so long as you haven't been replaced as purchasing officer, due to your great age."

"You see how he insults a patriarch?" Abraham asked the room, delighted with the news. "Only five? I need a hundred and five. I'll take them sight unseen." He offered his hand.

Matthew drew back.

"I don't do business that way. You must see them. I'll have Boie bring them in next week."

"Come, Matthew Eastman's word is good enough for me. Shake."

They spat on their hands and slapped them together.

"Good," beamed Abraham. "We'll get the silver and lodge the bills of sale at the Volksraad office tomorrow. We'd get no sense out of anybody tonight. They're all down at the Winburg Regency, brawling, cursing, crying for the impos-

238

sible.... I shall go down later, when they've shouted themselves hoarse and I can have my say. I'll time my entrance for the greatest effect. Will you come, Matthew?"

"To hear them vote to fight the British soldiers because they believe Holland will help them? No, menheer, let those from Natal fight for Natal. We on the high veldt should stay well out of it. You'll see, they'll have lost the port and will have to agree to British sovereignty. They've brought this on themselves. We're safe here, we have nothing the British want or need."

"Yet," said Abraham, taking the long view.

"Yet may never come."

"But if it does, Matthew Eastman?" The question was slyly put.

Matthew glared around to find the speaker, a farmer he did not like.

"If it does, ask me again then."

"You'll fight," said Abraham. "I know."

"Then you know more than I do."

"Age has its compensations." The old man smoothed his beard. "One of them is to know that tomorrow's bull is among today's calves. You were once a calf, Matthew."

The other men in the hot room watched the exchange with closed faces. None of them really trusted the big Englishman, but none of them wanted to fight him for the privilege of saying so. They, like Matthew, would wait and see, their memories as long as his legs.

Matthew tipped his hat.

"Gentlemen," he said generally. To Abraham he added, "Tomorrow morning then. Eight o'clock?"

"If the arguments are over by then."

"You'll see they will be, old man." Matthew's smile was as brilliant as it was sudden.

Abraham nodded, smiling, and Matthew left without another word.

As he walked back to the hotel he thought about the Gould children out on the veldt to the north and shivered as though a cold blade had run down his spine.

The night was hot and close.

There was no coolness in the wind that stirred the window net and the sporadic squalls of argument and laughter from the street were as heated as the night air.

As Matthew drowsed over a last pipe of tobacco he heard

239

the door open and close, saw Hannie's brief outline in the wedge of light before the rustle of silken skirts came toward the bed. He had long ago learned to leave the lamps unlit when Hannie came to him; even the barest tallow flame made her clumsy and unresponsive. Every sound had her tensed and rigid as she sought and analyzed the source, fearing discovery while naked and vulnerable, her desire leaving her like a fist when the fingers are opened and spread. It would then take all his patience and skill to bring her back to him.

How many fires of guilt she burned in when she contemplated giving herself to Matthew, or how she reconciled her passion for him after the event was beyond Matthew's comprehension. There were times as she lay with him in the dark when her tiny hand would steal into Matthew's and hold on as though she were poised over a precipice. She would whimper in her sleep and worry his chest with her face until he smoothed the fright away with his big and gentle hands, waiting for her to slide into the dreamless and unhaunted dark, untroubled and relaxed. Then the lines of her body would soften and her face would smooth and she would waken just before dawn to quicken with the day as his hands roused her. She would draw him to her and take the initiative, her responses languid and sure, her body generous, her mouth and hands clever. Those were the best times for both of them, and Matthew would pretend to sleep as she dressed herself, assuming her remote daytime persona with each hook and button, leaving the room without a smile or a backward glance.

Matthew had never directly asked Hannie about her relationship with her husband. He knew Martin Gould was ten years her senior and that the marriage had been arranged when she was barely seventeen. Gould's bearing and prospects had convinced the girl's parents of his worth as both suitor and husband much more than they had the girl herself, although Hannie had dutifully followed her father's wishes and kept her very real reservations to herself. At first she had hoped that love would come, but now after eight years with Martin she no longer wanted anything of the kind.

Hannie had found that Matthew could give her all her marriage lacked, and was content despite all the attendant guilt that plagued her religious sensibilities.

In public, Martin Gould seemed all a husband should be, but in private where it mattered, he was withdrawn and inattentive, and his rare attempts at lovemaking were dilatory and inept. With the arrival of the second child his ardor had completely withered away, and he sat long into the night with his books and specimens rather than share his pale body with his wife.

Matthew knew all these things without discussion. Hannie's driven sensuality told him more than words ever could, and there were times when she spoke in her sleep and he was able to piece the broken sentences into some kind of a whole. Then he would calm her without speaking, and never reminded her of her fears when she woke. Whereas Hannie loved Matthew without realizing it, Matthew knew his own feelings were less elevated. Something had died when the redheaded woman had left for the Cape, and he would never even think her name, let alone speak it.

A last petticoat sighed over a chairback and Hannie lowered her heavy breasts onto Matthew's chest as she buried her face in his hair, her breath warm against his scalp. He spread her thighs and came up into her with a skillful upward lunge, his hands lacing in the small of her back. Hannie bucked and her loose hair was flung about her shoulders as she settled in against the bunched thighs with vigorous circular butts of her hips. Her tiny, sipping cries punctuated the drone from the street and Matthew's hoarser breathing as her world turned into a giddy, liquid explosion, both too quickly and too late. Matthew lay beneath her while she slept, waiting to bring her awake when the window turned gray and he could pick out her slack contours in the grudging light.

Yes, he thought, that was the best time....

Two miles to the north, twelve horsemen primed their guns and made their final, careful plans as they too waited for first light.

11

The morning was brass and gold and breathless.

There were few loungers in the street and fewer horses at the rails. The town had finally gone to sleep during the last hour of darkness and most of the burghers snored in their rooms or their wagons. The less fortunate would have found shelter in the stables and warehouses on the edge of town.

Matthew tilted his hat against the sun and walked his long shadow down the wide main street. He would catch up on his sleep during the heat of the day and ride home during the cool of late afternoon. He could send Boie and the wagon on ahead, he decided, as he hammered on Abraham de Villiers's door and was told to enter.

The old man was in yesterday's clothes and sat low in his chair, his face pinched and his lips as blue as his eyes. He clawed the air weakly when he saw the flash of concern on Matthew's face.

"Politics and age don't make good brothers," he said. "And you do me no good when you show the grave in your face, Eastman. Just give me your shoulder as we walk. I'll live despite your mourner's look."

Matthew forced a laugh.

"Perhaps I should bring a shovel and save you the bother of coming back. Your old bones wouldn't need much of a cairn. The hyenas would find little meat on you—hardly worth their while digging you out."

"Better," Abraham said breathlessly. "An insult gives a man something to bite on. The women would have me on a diet of curdled milk and mealie pap like some old Zulu. Come." He pulled himself up Matthew's arm and swayed erect, panting.

"Just don't fall in the street, old mule. Or I'll leave you."

"Be sure it isn't the other way around, *rooinek*."

They walked slowly in the bald, hot morning, and Abraham's left foot dragged after his right much as though a recent stroke had affected his gait. He made himself talk as they went and his voice strengthened as they progressed, each step and sentence a small victory. Matthew asked him about the Volksraad meeting out of politeness.

"They squabbled, they punched noses. One of the women struck at Potgieter with a banner and accused him of cowardice. He quoted the Bible at her but nobody heard. They wouldn't even listen to me, and I waited until after three this morning to speak. We're alone so I can tell you you were right, Matthew. They want to believe Holland is still a great nation and will help them. They intend to march with the Natalians against the British. The Orange Commando under Jan Mocke have volunteered to a man to help Pretorius. Some of them brought their horses to the meeting and threatened to shoot any 'traitor' who tried to stop them. They all rode out at dawn."

"And what if the Zulu decided to turn on us again? Or Mzilikazi? Where would we be then, with our Commando gone?" asked Matthew, stepping aside as three horsemen came abreast out of the sun, almost brushing him and de Villiers aside. Matthew slapped the nearest horse's rump as it passed and the animal reared under its rider before it was roughly checked by rein and spur. The Griqua in the saddle turned and stared at Matthew until the man beside him told him to face front in San patois.

"After Blood River and Vegkop?" said Abraham. "They won't face us again, not here on the high veldt. Natal, perhaps."

"That's no comfort to me, old man." Matthew watched the riders join two others and wheel in toward the rails outside the volksraad office. There was something familiar about the Griqua that jibed in Matthew's memory. He knew better than to force his tired brain, it would come to him.

Abraham was saying, "...and Dirk's with the Commando along the Umkhomazi River. The Matabele always send spies before the impi. The Commando will spot anybody crossing to reconnoiter, and Dirk's a great one at interrogation."

Matthew wiped sweat from his mouth, knowing more about Dirk's methods than he was willing to share with the father.

Abraham stooped at a water trough to soak his handkerchief and he swabbed his face and neck, leaning heavily against Matthew, who supported him easily, saddened by his frailty. The old man was the last of a breed whose days were numbered, and he was all the more precious for it. Matthew eased him down so that he sat on the edge of the trough.

"Did I say I was tired?" snapped Abraham.

"I am, old man. You weigh more than ten plump virgins."

"Liar."

"We both are."

"*Ha!*" Abraham bared his teeth and drew breath through them.

Matthew saw that one of the saloons was opening across the street. A swamper had unlatched the shutters and was mopping the stoep as he yawned behind his hand.

"Is your stomach up to a beer, menheer?"

"For breakfast, you savage?"

"Ach, would you prefer curdled milk?"

"All right, beer. But only to keep you company."

"I'll bring them out here, wait for me."

"Like an old dog in the sun, neh?" Abraham squeezed water from his handkerchief. "Round it out with a little *brandewyn*."

243

"And I'm the savage?" said Matthew. He crossed the street as the five men dismounted, drawing their smoothbores from the saddle scabbards. One of the men gathered the horses as the others ducked beneath the rail and stepped up onto the sidewalk, where they stood in line while the Griqua looked at his fob watch, his long shadow touching de Villiers's foot. Something touched Matthew's memory and was gone. He waited at the bar for the swamper to shuffle back inside to serve him, watching the black hands pour slow beers and paddle the froth away before topping both glasses with generous shots of liquor. Matthew threw coins onto the bar and made for the door, where he stopped so abruptly he slopped suds onto the half-washed stoep. There had been other beers and other knuckles six years before when Miss Mattie had insisted he fight the Griqua.

Samuel, that was his name, *Samuel.*

He was thicker in the waist and had longer hair and a mustache that covered the permanently crooked smile, but it was him.

Matthew dropped the laced beers onto a side table. The four men had gone into the Volksraad office and the fifth watched the road and the horses. There had to be others.

Matthew vaulted the bar and pushed the swamper aside, looking for a pistol, a bar gun, anything that would shoot.

What would the likes of Samuel want with the Volksraad office except the huge safe where the community gold was kept? By God, but they'd chosen the perfect moment to make the raid, with just about every able-bodied man asleep or drunk. Matthew was just one man without a gun and no help. He had to think, to act. Mother of Christ, old Abraham was out in the street not fifteen feet from them.

Matthew found a short-barreled twelve-gauge ladies' gun hooked under a kegtree, and he broke it. It was loaded and primed. He snapped it closed and stopped the swamper from running away by tripping him and hauling him to his feet, holding the frightened black face close to his own.

"Where's your baas? Banditti are robbing the Volksraad office, neh? *Verstaan?*"

The swamper nodded, pointing through one of the walls.

"Verstaan. Baas sleeps. Just me. No baas."

"Damnation."

Matthew dragged the swamper to the shuttered front window and peered out. The horseminder and Abraham had the street to themselves.

"Listen," he told the swamper. "You go outside and work, eh? Swamp the stoep and tell me what you see."

"No."

"Yes. You look-see how many men on horses or on the roofs, eh?" Matthew pointed at the floor with the shotgun. "And you come back and tell me here. In here, *verstaan?*"

The swamper nodded and his "No" was firmer.

"All right. Here, see this schilling? You go to the Winburg Regency for help. Tell them to come here with guns. *Verstaan,* for Christ's sake?"

"Yes, baas." The swamper's smile was wide and full of gaps.

"There's another coin if you run both ways."

"Yes, baas." The swamper had almost darted out through the front door before Matthew pulled him back and threw him down the bar.

"The back way!"

"Yes, baas." And the swamper was gone.

Matthew loosened his belt and hung the shotgun down his right leg, most of it covered by his long coat, then, picking up the beers, he stepped outside and walked slowly back to old Abraham, his face hidden by the tilt of his hat. The heat from the baked road surface struck up at him and he squinted against the sudden glare as he kept his pace even. The road seemed to have widened by a factor of ten. More horsemen were coming from either end of the street and one look told Matthew they were not friends. The way they sat their horses with long stirrups, their guns across their saddles, was enough.

Matthew kept walking as they closed toward him.

Abraham seemed to have fallen asleep and his arms were crossed, his hands tucked inside his coat as he nodded over himself. Matthew wondered if he would have time to lift the old man and run into the cover of a narrow alley between a closed grain store and a hide merchant's. The only real cover there was the hard, black shadows. They might confuse the eye but they would not stop a bullet.

As Matthew reached Abraham he caught a flurry of movement from the corner of his left eye. Men were coming from the Volksraad office dragging heavy sacks of coin.

"Wake up," he said automatically. "Here's your beer, menheer."

Abraham's reply was soft and breathless.

"Who sleeps, *dassie?* I know what's going on." Then loudly

245

enough to carry: "Put them down and give me a cigar." Abraham's arms lifted the skirts of his coat to allow Matthew sight of his pistols.

"Just walk to the alley, old man. I'll cover you."

"Walk yourself."

With calm deliberation, Abraham rose with his pistols and fired across Matthew's bowed shoulders. Two men were flung from their horses and into the riders beside them. A horse threw its startled owner, a Kaffir with hide leggings and a pea jacket, and he flopped onto the back of his head as his horse backed over him.

Matthew heaved up into Abraham's middle and bore him over and down behind the trough as water gouted from the surface and bright scars tore the bleached wooden sides. Matthew felt splinters nick his face and arm before he rolled heavily and pulled at the short shotgun. As he freed it and bore down on Samuel, some of the tethered horses pulled away from the minder's grip and two jumped the stoep, hiding the Griqua. Matthew held fire and swung the shotgun at the group to the west, firing low. The blast cut at their horses and a gaunt black lost a kneecap as his gun spun from his grip.

A stray horse kicked its way over Matthew and a flailing hoof caught the side of his jaw. He fell with fireflies of pain roaring in his head and made a last supreme effort before the rushing shadows took his senses. Matthew fell across Abraham, covering him with his big, slack body.

Then there was a confused galloping that faded into a pit with no sides or top or bottom or any sensation Matthew could have recognized.

They were holding him down and too much water in his throat made Matthew vomit. One of his arms caught a solid midriff and heaved it away. A chair scraped and went over as a body struck the floor. A small hand slapped Matthew's face and more water smashed into his eyes, running into his nose and mouth. He heard springs squeal under him as he coughed black bile into a hastily placed bucket. Native drums boomed inside his skull and his eyes saw kaleidoscopes of color behind his closed lids.

"Where are you, old man?" he croaked, throwing himself back against plumped pillows and reaching for the floor with rubber legs. The small hands cupped his face and Hannie was

246

telling him to stay still. He nodded his head gingerly and worked on opening his eyes, recognizing Hannie's dress color before he could focus on her swimming features. Dr. Andries was picking himself up from the floor, holding his plump belly, and there were several people he recognized in the room, many of them still only partially dressed.

"Where's the old man?" he asked through rising nausea.

"In the next room. He's fine, which is more than I can say for myself." Dr. Andries unstopped a flask and drank deeply, coughed, and smoothed his rumpled waistcoat. "That's a devilish swing you have there, Eastman, and it will appear as extras on my account."

"You got four of them, menheer," said one of the hotel porters. "And one of the others carries your shot in him."

"Thomas!" cautioned Hannie in her hotelier's voice.

"Yes'm." Thomas grinned shyly at Matthew, who responded by batting one painful lid.

"Show me the old man."

"Now, Eastman..." said Dr. Andries.

"Now," said Matthew, trying for the floor again. He caught at the bedhead and tried to lever himself up, slid back, and tried again. One slack foot toed the polished boards and the room revolved both ways at once. Matthew lurched upright and elbowed his way along the corridor through the crowd and into the darkened room where Abraham de Villiers lay propped on cushions, his white beard above the sheets.

"Well, *rooinek*," he said weakly.

"Well, Abraham. They say we got four of them."

Abraham licked his mouth sleepily.

"Would have been more if I could have reloaded. Some fool of an elephant tried to crush me when he threw himself over me. Do you know who that could have been, Matthew?"

"No Dutchman would have done that, eh?"

Abraham moved his shoulders slightly.

"Who can say?"

Matthew felt relief and lassitude overwhelm him. He allowed Hannie and Dr. Andries to lead him back to his own bedroom, where he fell into something close to unconsciousness for eighteen hours. All that time Hannie and Boie never left his side. And when he awoke, Samuel's trail was already cold.

Samuel stood in the fork of the tall euphorbia and studied the far bank of the river.

The distant mountains seemed close enough to touch and sweat would not form in the mounting heat. The guns and metal parts of the harnesses were too hot to touch with the bare hands and the horses were spent from the hard riding.

Samuel and his men had reached the lower Vaal and rested beside the sluggish river to split up the money, each man responsible for his own share. The San with the leg wound lay against a kokerboom, and had made himself a splint from the river reeds. Nobody had offered to help him and he would not sleep for fear of having his throat slit. He kept his musket and gold close to hand and snarled at anybody who came close to him. Samuel knew the San would not be able to stay in the saddle if there was any pursuit, and was content to wait and see. If the San fell, Samuel meant to have the horse and leave the others to fight over the gold. The hyenas would take the San, and when he was gone there would be six left to follow the Griqua.

Samuel knew they must find fresh horses when they crossed into Dingaan's land. They must travel fast and light if they were to cross safely. Samuel would have liked to have struck west into Griqualand, but with Miss Mattie dead of the wasting fever, that was out of the question. The provisional Griqua government frowned on banditti bands now, and would hang them to a man as readily as the Boers, with whom they now had an uneasy alliance. The settlement had just broken up when Miss Mattie died, each man drifting away to fend for himself. There had been thirty who followed Samuel when he rode out, and now, less than a year later, he had lost most of them to the Zulu, private squabbles, and the black sickness when they had strayed into the Limpopo Valley.

Samuel had heard of a slaver in the east who gave good prices for young men and women with strong backs and sound lungs. He had heard the story many times so there must be some truth in it. If Samuel could find this man he would offer his services. The San tribes were drifting back into the Orange and the Central Plateau, and it would be easy to cull the small unarmed bands. Some of the lesser chiefs traded their people for grain or iron, and what Samuel could not take he would barter for, and either way would suit him. He was growing older and slower, and he must make enough to settle himself before someone younger left him for dead. The big Englishman had come close to finishing him in Winburg. If only he had been able to gut him when he came to the settlement to take Laidler and the woman out. One day, Samuel meant to settle that score... he knew where the *rooinek*'s farm lay.

Six years had not eased Samuel's hatred.

He was about to climb down when he picked out the wagon and horses following the south bank of the river. He took out his glass, opened it, and focused on the small group. He counted four mounted Khoikhoi and a white driving the ox team. He did not see the children asleep in the back of the wagon, and it would have made little difference if he had. All he cared about were the horses.

Samuel swarmed to the ground and got his men to their feet with silent kicks and hand signs, telling them to mount up and stay hidden. There would be plenty of time to set up the ambush.

Martin Gould was disappointed about the lack of blue clay along the riverbed; he had been so certain his theory would have been proven correct. There had not even been any pyrite deposits, and the Khoikhoi boys had grinned among themselves to see him scrabbling around taking bore samples from the riverbed. The children too had soon tired of the new game and had gone off to collect flowers and insects on their own. The heat and humidity along the river had made them petulant from lack of sleep; then Conrad had been bitten on the thigh by a stinging insect, and it was the Khoikhoi who found the right leaves to take the pain and swelling away, not their erudite master with all his learning from books. Now the children dozed under the canvas sail away from the flies and sticky atmosphere, glad to be going home at last. All in all, thought Gould, it had not been a good trip.

The few kaffirs they had seen were emaciated and starving, and the boys had to show their guns to stop the wretches from stealing food from the wagon. The hyenas came close at night, and came boldly into the firelight to show their teeth as they made fast dashes for the food pots. One of them had made off with a good blanket and the pack had torn it to shreds. Gunfire had not deterred them until one was gutshot and the others fought each other to feed on it.

Gould curled his whip out over the oxspan with a long, whistling snap. The damnable beasts were so slow and he was tired of smelling them, tired of the defeat he felt, tired of the children's constant whines for their mother and home. Gould had come close to raising his hand to them both before the Khoikhoi boys, something Conrad had instinctively known to be wrong. The boy had looked his father straight in the eye and grinned with fear. Gould had turned away and snapped at the nearest Khoikhoi for no other reason than he had to vent his feelings some way. It had proved to be a monumental mistake. From then on, the four boys did everything at half speed and had him clarify each order as though their senses were as addled as abandoned eggs. Gould had begun secretly to hate them.

The river was bending toward a great, ragged stand of reed above a hollow Gould had camped in on the way out. The boys had not liked the place because of all the dead ground surrounding it and its close proximity to the river, but he had insisted and he thought of doing so again for the pleasure of watching them cluck with concern. That would serve them back in some small measure. But no, there was still too much daylight left and he did not want them to think he had lost the initiative.

Gould decided to skirt the hollow and continue traveling until dusk. There were many good camping sites farther south, and he would have two of the boys ride ahead to start a fire and scout the way. Gould had no sense of direction. He kept the oxen parallel with the river, meaning to keep the reeds and the midges who swarmed there on his right, the river to his left, then to strike off at right angles for the open veldt beyond. Only then would he have to follow the boys' lead. He would salve just that little self-respect.

Gould turned on the driving box to call the lead Khoikhoi, and as he did so, yellow clouds banged from the outer reeds and something slapped at the air near his face, reminding him of a blundering stinging insect. Was he bitten? he wondered.

The lead Khoikhoi jumped from his horse without using his arms or legs, his chest ripped apart and most of his jaw blown away. The body threw up dust as it landed in a limp sprawl and the horse bounded off toward the reeds.

Gould stood straight up on the driving box, a hand to his face where a ball had burned it, his brain stunned by the sudden noise, staring anywhere but at the dead Khoikhoi. A white man was running for the horse, flagging it down with his hat.

A second boy threw up his long gun as he was punched from the saddle, one leg still in the stirrup. He was dragged away as the horse bolted into the river.

Gould was wondering where he had laid his own gun when he was knocked into a crouch and his right arm stopped being a part of him. Shock kept the pain at bay. He raised his whip and cracked it over the oxen. The animals were veering away from the shooting and the rapid puffs of gunsmoke. A front wheel slid on shale and ran through soft earth into a mudflat, slewing the wagon around and pulling the ox team with it. The lead bull floundered in the muddy shallows, trying to keep his feet, supporting the weight of the animal next to him as it slid in against him. The wagon tilted on the slope and as the rear wheels lost traction, Gould grabbed at the brake to keep his balance. The sky turned and Gould was flung out into the river. He landed awkwardly in the cold water and one boot sank in thick mud, holding him upright as the water around him reddened and weakness took his power of speech.

The wagon had turned over and the canvas sail was under water.

The children, thought Gould, the children.

He saw a hand scrabble against the inside of the ballooning canvas a moment before the wagon turned turtle and settled with only the wheel rims showing. A gout of air bubbled the surface, sent out lazy ripples, and the water became placid again.

Gould thrashed the water until he could move no more, too weak to do more than gulp air between sobs and stay upright.

There were men on the bank and one of them reined in to stare down at Gould, his mouth smiling crookedly under a thick mustache. Gould tried to talk to him, to tell him about the children and his specimens under the overturned wagon, pleading with his eyes when no words came, praying that the yellow-skinned man would save them and himself, not realizing that he thought of the children and the gathered ferns and flowers in the same way.

Gould was still pleading silently when Samuel shot him through the forehead.

* * *

Boie was a bare mile from the reeds when he heard the gunfire.

He had known he was close to the banditti because of their spoor, and had kept close to the ground for the previous two miles, finding cover like a lizard. Nkosi Matthew and he had caught up with the five burghers who had set out the day before them, and they were all now resting the string of Commando horses de Villiers had loaned them, and none of them could drink until they reached the river.

Boie wondered if Nkosi would have heard the shots where he was, for it would take a half sweep of the watch he carried to reach the reeds. Maybe a quarter sweep more because the horses were blown.

Boie squatted and sucked a stone, thinking the problem through.

Going back to Nkosi would take him twice as long as the tired horses, and if he went on alone, Nkosi may not know where to follow. Boie had made stone cairn sign as he went, but the afternoon would die soon and night would follow swiftly. Nkosi could not find sign at night, and the men ahead would have crossed the Vaal on their way into Mpande's land. A bad place to go after the Bastaard Samuel just to recover the yellow metal coins the whites valued so highly.

Boie did not think the Zulu had attacked the banditti, for the guns had all shot together and there would have been other volleys after the first if they fought Zulu. No, it must have been the banditti who had made the attack, probably an ambush.

A last shot clacked out and chased over the savannah to lose its last whispers in the far foothills.

Boie decided to take a chance.

He faced to the southeast where he knew Nkosi and the burghers were, and with the wind at his back, fired his smoothbore. The sound should carry and bring Nkosi to him. Boie reloaded and built a stone cairn pointing toward the reeds.

Then he trotted off toward the river alone.

Midges clouded in the reeds and made dark spirals over the dulling river as crane and duck skimmed out of a dying sun to roost on the mudflats and the tangled rafts of cane and uprooted trees on the northern bank where the big frogs boomed. The dusk was thick with the scents of flowering trees and river orchids, of wild lavender, peach, and myrtle, the vague bittersweetness of aloe and slack river water. Leopard and hyena told the coming night they were ready for it as cicadas brought the ground alive with their fiddling legs.

Boie heard the horses coming through the reeds, and he held his ground on the riverbank, his small brown face lacking any light, his forehead furrowed and his eyes dull, the smoothbore hanging from his arms. He stood sentinel over the bodies he had brought from the river and those he had found lying in the bush. He had cut most of the canvas from the overturned wagon and used it as a general shroud to cover the faces and torsos of the corpses. All that showed was a row of sandals, boots, tiny shoes, and one small outflung hand.

Boie had sung the death song as he cut the gallbladder from the dead oxen that had died in the traces, and had sprinkled the ground around the bodies as an act of purification. He had done this swiftly before the whites arrived for he knew they had different ways and would have frowned on his. To Boie, two gods were better than one, three deities better than two, and going to the old mud father with a eulogy from a praise singer was preferable to silence. He had done what he must, and the whites must speak their magic words from the paper bricks they called books.

Already the crocodiles were pulling at the dead animal, churning up the river with their tails, and soon it would be gone below the surface where it would rot enough for them to feast on it at leisure. Baas Gould had almost gone that way, and Boie had blinded two of the big saurians with his bow to keep them away as he pulled the body to the bank and covered it as the whites preferred. Now the burghers were coming with Nkosi Matthew in the lead, urging the tired horses through the reeds and fanning out into the broken, open ground where Boie waited for them.

Matthew brought his horse up close to the wagon and then turned the gelding away as he slowly took off his hat and bowed his head over the line of bodies. Somebody read quietly from Psalms as the horses whickered and smelled the water they wanted so badly. When the reading was over the men led their horses down the bank and let them drink as they filled their hats for themselves. The killings had affected them all and Boie knew there would be blood judgment made on the banditti and the Bastaard Samuel. There would be no prisoners taken for the rope in Winburg; the men would die as they ran and be left as carrion for the birds and the wild dogs. Boie hoped the burghers would not kill their horses by going on at once, and was glad to see Nkosi Matthew loosen his cinches and strip off his bedroll; he at least had not lost his reason. The others, though, were too quiet, too close-faced for the Khoikhoi to read their hearts. They were dead men who would only live again in the death of others. Boie kept apart from them and walked softly. Several had looked at him and the gun he carried and frowned among themselves, though none had spoken their disapproval to Nkosi, who would have roared and cracked skulls. But now they might, and Boie wanted no quarrels between the whites, for that meant one of his people would suffer. It was a new and bad thing that had happened since they came to the high country, something he did not understand. Something he knew by instinct and made no puzzle of. It was their way and Boie made certain he gave them no cause to take issue with his lord. Should that happen, Boie would have to kill in defense of Nkosi Matthew and himself, which would make them fugitives if they lived through the fight.

Boie quietly unsaddled the horse Nkosi had brought for him, and when it had drunk enough, he hobbled it and took biltong to Matthew, who ate it without enjoyment or comment as fuel to keep him strong for the hunt, fingering the blue bruise on his jaw as he stared at nothing with blank eyes.

Some of the men had found shovels in Gould's wagon and Boie slept lightly with the sound of digging in his ears.

Matthew lay looking at the stars for a long time before he dozed off. Bringing the news of her family's death to Hannie would be the hardest thing he had ever done, and yet he felt curiously ambivalent about the massacre. In some strange way he was neither shocked nor surprised by what had happened; it was as if he had known it was inevitable. The land took the soft, the tender, and the weak with equal dispassion, and would continue to do so until it was finally tamed. Only man seemed to care one way or the other, and then only when it was convenient to do so; otherwise he acted just as savagely as the country he fought to turn into productive acres.

Matthew wanted to get drunk, to make love, to find tears, or to punish something with his fists. To do anything that would ease away the great black stone he swallowed around. He could see no real difference between the men like himself who took what they wanted and the men like the Griquas who stole what they needed. Everybody in Africa, San, Zulu, Swazi, Xhosa, and burgher, wanted the same things; cattle, land, and wealth. The only difference was the manner in which they each sought to gain them, and that was only a difference of technique. It ended up with killing the least strong, the least quick.

Matthew slept, and when he awoke, the thought was still there and he made certain he rode apart from the rest of the burghers, wanting no part of their conversation; withdrawn and resolved to finish the thing as quickly and as cleanly as possible, and wondering if he had the willpower to take prisoners should the opportunity arise.

Boie rode at his back with peeled eyes. There was thunder in the air and a strong head wind was building.

The first kraal was small and poor and the outer *isango* hedge was gapped and sagging. There were no dogs and few chickens, the maize fields thinly planted and haphazardly marked out, the people stooped and round-bellied from a subsistence diet. An old chief and his sons stood at the entrance to the cattle fold, their spears and H-shaped shields ready. There were three white oxen in the *isibaya* behind them, all marked with the distinctive Gould brand, and they meant to hold them or die. A roasting pit was already being dug by the women, who brandished their hoes when the whites rode up.

Matthew discovered the chief had traded the beasts with a Griqua, a yellow man with a twisted mouth, for two mules, an elephant tooth, and a sack of maize cobs. Yes, it had been a bargain, but the clan was poor and the mules ate much, also the half-whites were armed with the long guns. Why change a bargain for a fight?

Matthew stopped the burghers from making an issue of it. There was no point in leaving an enemy at their backs, however poorly armed he might be; they could always round up the animals on their return. A vote was taken and carried to that effect, and the hunting party moved on into the wilderness of the upper Vaal and the elephant grounds.

The next kraal had not been so lucky and the thatch still smoldered. The villagers had scattered and the San with the ruined knee lay among beer pots and goat bones beside a dead cooking fire, a ball through his spine. The banditti had fought among themselves and had fired the kraal in their drunken rage. Boie calculated they followed ten horses, that six were mounted, three were heavily laden, and one was led unmounted.

The sign was less than two hours old and the country ahead was cut by deep kloofs and heavily wooded on the lower slopes of the high ground. Samuel's men must keep to the narrow strip of scrubland between the tall kopjes, riding single-file much of the way. There was no need for any discussion; the burghers looked to their primings and rode out at a brisk canter, knowing that luck had finally swung their way.

At a great dogleg of rock covered with vine, Boie read sign on the milled earth and pointed mutely north, holding back as the burghers spurred past him. He made finger sign and Matthew dropped back beside him.

"Two horses make that way, Nkosi." Boie ran an arm out and upward toward a narrow defile that rose through the rocks and shale to the east. "They separate here. Horses bite the grass and swing on their back legs as the banditti talked. Big argument. One man go away from the others, go up there. Leave them."

"You said two horses," said Matthew, watching the rising trail.

"One horse led."

Matthew nodded. Whoever had gone up the defile had shown good sense in realizing how vulnerable the band was, all bunched up together on the narrow trail. A man with two horses had a chance of outrunning any pursuit once he had cleared the maze of gullies and hills and had reached the open grassland to the east.

"Which way do we go, Nkosi?" asked the Khoikhoi. He had dismounted to clean lather from his horse with handfuls of grass.

Matthew followed a sudden instinct.

"Up there," he said, drawing his smoothbore and easing his pistols, hoping he was right. The burghers would catch the rest of the group and five against eighteen were no odds; he could afford to take the chance.

Samuel took a mouthful of precious water and spat the residue out.

The native beer had left his mouth furred and dehydrated, and his memory of the fight at the kraal was patchy although he remembered how uncontrollable the men had become, how suspicious of each other now they carried gold in their saddlebags. A fistfight between two of his Griquas over a piece of goat meat had become a general melee. Then one of the men had found a young native woman in the brush and a knife had flashed. A man had kicked the wounded San in the leg, he had reached for his pistol and been backshot. The black girl had escaped in the confusion as the men fought to divide his possessions and the kraal had caught fire when a firebrand was kicked against the thatch. They had all capered around the flames in a drunken dance....

Samuel hawked and spat as though the phlegm was a distasteful memory. They had not wanted him to leave the group, and had only half-believed his lie about scouting a route to the east. But they had let him go. If the Dutchmen did not catch up with the band, Samuel would circle and catch up with them again. Either way, as usual, it was all the same to him.

He had cleared the defile and was on a bald shelf of rock above the trail. The broken ground fell away sheer to the open savannah and he would have to find a way down through the shelving kloofs to reach the eastern grassland. He took the horses slowly over the tumble of rock and windswept scrub as though he rode on glass; a broken leg here would mean disaster, and Samuel had learned caution these last years.

When he reached the downslope he paused and watched the trail where his men threaded through the shadowed gorge, making their horses work too hard. Samuel shaded his eyes and frowned at their foolishness; then he saw why. A line of riders was closing fast, less than a hundred yards behind, their hat brims beaten back by the wind, their guns held along their horses' necks.

The first shots were distant pecks that grew in volume as they bounded up at him as clattering echoes, pricking his horse's ears and making him dance. The spare horse caught the fear and Samuel had to lead both animals in a circle before he got them quiet. When he looked down again, the burghers were in among his men, shooting them at point-blank range and shooting those on the ground a second or third time to make certain.

Samuel's fear made him sweat and shake. Those damned Bible-thumpers killed as though once was not enough. For all their piety they were as savage as anybody else. He saw one man running, his hat and gun gone, one arm flapping uselessly as he scrambled over the rocks. A rider went after him and knocked him down with a swing of his long gun. Then, turning on a copper coin, he galloped back to trample the Griqua, forcing his horse to rear and rear again until the screams stopped and the man was a limp, broken thing on the ground.

Samuel spat and found no saliva.

He knew he must leave as quickly as possible, but the thought of leaving the high ground turned him weak in the stomach and knees. The high rarefied air smelled good and his elevated position gave him the illusion of being divorced from what was happening far below him, as if going down to the plateau made him part of the hunters' world where he could only run and run until they caught him and nailed him to a board for children to spit upon. He had seen that done to an outlaw once, and people had stood beside the dying man to have their portraits drawn by a traveling artist for a schilling a time. He neither remembered the town or the year, but he had been young and had spat on the man like everybody else, jeering because he had allowed himself to be caught. Now Samuel knew what that man must have felt all those years before as he had waited for the sun to kill him.

The high ground was suddenly too exposed, too open, too light, and too windswept for Samuel. He wanted the shadowing trees and the shimmering distances to lose himself in. He took a last, long look at the burghers, who were rounding up the horses and opening the saddlebags, before setting his spurs to his horse.

The click of the cocking gun was loud and close to his face. Sweating hard, Samuel turned his head and looked into the huge bore of Matthew Eastman's gun, flinching away from the spit and flash of flame that he knew must kill his brain and end it all.

A small brown man was pulling his horse guns from their pommel holsters and taking his smoothbore from its scabbard. His knife was gone from his boot and the small pistol from the lanyard around his neck. Samuel dropped both reins and spread his hands in supplication as the man in the river had done, his crooked mouth jerking over his permanently bared teeth. In his mind he heard the chunk of nails driven through wrist and wood and wanted to die rather than face that agony. He grabbed at the gun barrel but it eluded him and cracked him across the shoulder, swung, and knocked him to the ground, where he scraped his face on the baked rock. He was sobbing when rawhide lashed his wrists together and crying aloud when he was hauled to his feet and led back down the defile.

Back down on the trail it took all of Matthew's persuasion,

backed by his gun, to save Samuel from summary execution right there. The Dutch had given lip service to the adoption of proper court procedures, he argued; now let them prove they had the will to live by that decision.

The burghers had watched Boie's leveled gun and had promised they would remember this moment, and the little Khoikhoi knew they would.

13

Winburg was in the grip of a rare dust storm when Matthew returned with his prisoner. It was an oppressive day whose blustering winds and mounting heat made Hannie Gould listless and sharp with her staff when she lined them up for morning inspection. They rolled their eyes and several pendulous lips jutted with vexation.

The Missie was hardly ever like this. There had been times in the past when she had given them the edge of her tongue, but that was before she and the Englishman shared a pallet, when the baas would not act the man for her and she tossed alone in the dark. Although they all knew these things about the Missie, none of them dreamed of gossiping with other indented blacks from other establishments. They knew their quarters were better than those of other houses, knew their food was superior, their treatment just. Several of their number had been offered their freedom on the advent of their twenty-first summer and had refused it, preferring to stay on with the Missie, who got them white medicine and put more than mealie pap in their bowls. Many of the married ones had brought their children into Hannie Gould's service when they were old enough to be of use to her and the hotel, training them early so there would be no mistakes and no dismissals. Perhaps her present mood was a combination of her moontime and the news from the coast which had made her pace the floor half the night.

A man had ridden in from Port Natal the previous evening with the news that the Boers meant to starve the British out and hold them as hostages against British recognition of their independence as a republic. There had been much shouting and shooting of guns by the whites, and drinking through the night, and further details had been lost in the general uproar. Many times the chiefs of the Hollander tribes had been toasted and a picture of the Dutch royals had been placed

259

over the long bar as the farmers and their wives sang their tribal song.

They were pleased when Hannie finally told them to start the day's work, for there were too many mysteries attached to her mood and the way all the whites were behaving.

Hannie drank coffee in her office and dabbed at her hot skin as she went through the motions of making up her ledgers, her thoughts divided between Natal and the high veldt where her family and Matthew Eastman were. If only they would all come back so she could feel herself again, embrace and spoil her children, and have Matthew comfort her when the night came. Even Martin at his books in another room was preferable to the completely empty bungalow.

Hannie had been brought up to believe in a free Boer republic. It was all her father and her uncles ever spoke of during her childhood on the Cape. She would still have believed in it without question as the Southern Americans believed in King Cotton and the plantation life, had it not been for the influence of the softly-spoken Englishman who brought her mind alive with new thoughts, her body to the awareness of greater physical subtleties than her strict Calvinist teachings had prepared her for.

Matthew never raised his voice in her presence, was never didactic as Martin Gould was, never dry or unemotional about his beliefs, his creed, his farm, or his people. His beliefs were founded in the life and realities around him, not on ancient philosophies whose probable meanings were lost with the civilizations that had fostered them. Books and their words meant nothing to Matthew Eastman unless he could adapt and apply them to his immediate environment, his present and ever-changing problems.

He was so like the cattle farmers around him, and yet so different. For him, people were nothing without the land, and the land was less without the people who made it work for them and for each other. He had no elitest views; a good farmer was better than a bad farmer, a good mule better than a badly spirited horse, whatever his bloodline, however eminent his sire or dam.

Matthew would rather spend patient hours with a bright San or Khoikhoi than minutes with a hidebound and stupid farmer.

For months his attitude and manner had confused and angered Hannie, had amused and bewildered her husband Martin, had alienated those burghers who followed the narrow mainstream of general thought. To Matthew, kaffirs were not *skepsels,* not creatures, as they were to those who believed the black tribes existed simply to serve the white conqueror; each individual was judged singly, each man, woman, and child assessed for their singular worth. Generalizations were for others. For Matthew, such concepts were worthless and unworkable. In this belief he was alone among his neighbors. Although some would have liked to have agreed with him and to have gone as far as following his example, they did not say so for fear of creating further divisions in the already badly divided embryo Republic.

Hannie would never again be able to slip back into her previous safe mold of thought after her two years with Matthew. Many of the innovations at her hotel had come about because of his influence, which was never directly aimed at changing her view of her kaffir apprentices, but which somehow precipitated subtle change and enlightenment and, to her delight and surprise, manifested itself as a new and cheerful vigor about the hotel and stables she would never have dreamed of. There was now a willingness on the part of her kaffir to do more than was asked of them, which sometimes meant she had to curb the more energetic from attempting too much.

Although Hannie had only once visited the Eastman farm at Elise's request, she had seen the same quiet efficiency there, felt the same accord that was growing around her own establishment. It had taken a good deal of restraint on her part not to blurt out as much as she watched Martin chivalrously respond to Elise's attempts at elevated conversation as Matthew fidgeted and pulled at his stiff collar, sipped sweetened tea from a tiny cup, his feet crammed into hard varnished boots.

Hannie had longed to pull them off for him and knead his cramped toes, only to find herself blushing as more basic thoughts warmed her cheeks and crested her nipples. She had seen Martin glance at her without comprehension, hoping to include her in the clever point he was making to the attentive Elise about the first triumvirate of Rome. Hannie had realized how little of what Martin spoke of was understood by Elise, much less than she herself did, how she was merely enjoying the surface flow of polite conversation rather than its deeper content, and Hannie had found herself despising the silly girl, who cared more for an embroidered

261

napkin than the welfare and interests of the remarkable man she had married.

That was when the first pang of jealousy had overwhelmed Hannie, had confounded her with its boiling intensity, causing her to start up and spill tea down her dress. After that she had avoided all invitations to the Eastman household and threw herself more and more into running the Winburg Regency—her children and Matthew's rare visits her only solace.

Wind rattled the shutters and fine red talcum found its way through the slats, dusting her pristine ledgers. Sighing heavily, her temples pounding from anxiety and lack of sleep, Hannie closed and locked them away, capping her inkwell and drying her quill. She usually never slept during the day, but she thought she might just nap for an hour. A little cologne on her neck and wrists might cool her and ease the drumming in her head.

She summoned Ham, her head boy, and told him to rouse her if she was not down by eleven-thirty, and left him to run things (something that would have been unthinkable only a year before), and climbed the stairs to Matthew's room. At least there she would not be haunted by the empty rooms of the bungalow, and could smell Matthew in the bedsheets.

She was lying there in the semidarkness when Matthew slipped through the door and told her the awful news in a halting and choked voice, his tears as genuine as her own. They had clung to each other through the long afternoon and into the evening when Dr. Andries decided to intervene. He slipped an opiate into a small pot of coffee and had Ham take it up to Hannie with instructions that she should drink it all, and to make certain Baas Eastman took none of it himself.

Matthew got roaring drunk that night and fought with anybody who would take him on, betting a hundred English guineas there was not a man in Winburg who could knock him down. Those who tried did not succeed and Dr. Andries was setting bones and treating cuts until Matthew was toppled by the third swallow from his fifth bottle of *brandewyn*. He smashed a table in falling and it took four men to drag his body upstairs to his room, where Dr. Andries took over, firmly barring the door against all comers. When he had laid Matthew beside Hannie he locked them both in and went next door to share a dram or two with old Abraham, who had kept the room despite his swift recovery, and both men, one old and the other corpulent and middle-aged, kept vigil as they passed their flasks, ears cocked for any sound, any cry from the bedroom next door.

"Matthew Eastman is a fool," observed old Abraham.

"True."

The flask passed from hand to mouth.

"He should not have brought the Griqua back."

"Again true, old friend." Dr. Andries drank deeply. "He should have left him for the crocodiles and be damned to the Bastaard's soul."

"Ach, he has forced the Volksraad to make the decision it has put off for too long. Will they build a jail and a gallows? Pay for a permanently appointed justice? Will they implement all the other laws they have so easily voted for? Will they?" de Villiers asked in a fierce whisper.

"Will they indeed," said Dr. Andries, loosening his waistcoat and putting his feet on the bed.

"We all like the notion of justice, but living with the fact is another matter. We have run away from rules and regulations for too many years to relish living under even those we approve of in principle."

"True, Abraham. But this must change."

"Not until it is too late. That is why Matthew Eastman is a fool. He has forced our noses into our own mess, and we don't like the stink, even if it is our own stink. We like to shoot first and expect God to give us absolution. We are ungoverned and ungovernable. The British have found that out to our cost."

"To theirs, surely?"

"No, to ours. They allowed us to leave the Cape when the law expressly forbade any citizen from doing so. They have stood back and have allowed Port Natal to be developed by private speculation and our blood. If they ever want to take it back, they will, and fight us for it into the bargain."

"But that's surely what the Natalians want, as well as some of our own people here, a chance to fight the British and show them they no longer rule us."

"Have they recognized our sovereignty here? They have not. Nor will they if there's open conflict. They'll send their soldiers, and if they're beaten, they'll send more. The British are slow to anger, and slower to spend silver on a military campaign. But I tell you, defeat them locally, and they'll come in strength. And they'll stay. That's something else that fool next door predicted. You think I couldn't hear him brawling

263

in the bar from here? His voice could drill holes through the Drakensberg."

Dr. Andries passed his flask with a question.

"If Eastman is such a fool, how is it he sees things so clearly?"

"Seeing is one thing, keeping one's mouth firmly shut is another. A smaller fool would know as much."

"Then you agree with the fool, Abraham."

Abraham belched around a long swig.

"Naturally, but I know when to speak, and when not to speak. I'm no Jeremiah. I say what needs to be said when the people are ready to hear it said. When the soldiers come, the politicians follow. When that day comes we'll have trekked for nothing. Alone, without a single friend in Africa. We're rich in land and cattle and poor in cash. Without modern guns we cannot hold our land. Have we foundries to cast cannon? We have not, and in order to fight the British seriously, we should have to buy our arms from them. The British are down every avenue we explore, and that's a truth that sticks in my craw, my friend."

"You paint a black portrait, Abraham."

"There's blacker to come. The fool has triggered a nerve, and we'll see blood on the streets of Winburg tonight or tomorrow."

An amber pearl hung from Dr. Andries's lower lip as he choked and dropped his flask. "Here, but why?"

"Because of the Griqua who killed a man and his two children and made a widow of Hannie Gould. A Bastaard, a half-caste, being held in my stables, supposedly to stand trial." Abraham got up from his bed and reached for his double holsters, strapping on the belt. "There won't be a trial, *vriend*. Unless..."

"Unless you too act the fool."

"Can you think of better company to be in, Doctor?" Abraham shrugged into his long coat and smoothed his black string tie. "Once they've thought of a rope and found a tall enough tree, they'll come to see justice done in their own fashion. I've sent for Krige and a few others; if they come we may see sense prevail."

Dr. Andries capped his flask and huffed to his feet, slapping his round belly as he heard himself say, "A doctor has to be a fool sometimes. I think I can still hold a musket to my shoulder, if you have one for me."

"There are two under the bed."

The two men walked to the stable through the quiet of the early morning and were met at the livery by Matthew's small Khoikhoi, Boie. He cradled two smoothbores and a pouch of ammunition in his wiry arms. They all went inside and waited for the mob to gather.

There were sounds in among the heaving uncertainties, sounds made by separate throats, both male and female, all of them surging together to make an alien whole, a beast that was bigger than any one of the individuals who made it up. A roaring, murmuring, and shouting thing that argued with itself with mounting ferocity, goading itself into a joint and mindless action no one person in that crowd would willingly do alone. Late arrivals shouted for information, for justice, for blood, surging in against the tightly packed center and forcing the more unwilling front to move closer to the source of their joint anger, shrillness counterpointing coarse baritone and the bully's shouts, an ugly disjointed thing made up of sounds that sought a common identity, a common courage.

Matthew was roused by the thing out in the street and came out of his stupor unwillingly, compelled by a part of him that sensed he must comprehend since it somehow concerned him and his actions over the previous days. He fought the alcohol and his need for more rest, his need for forgetfulness, and strove to rise through the wool inside his skull as pain split his mind like a cord of wood. He was holding Hannie's hand with its single gold band on the third finger, and he saw the dark rings around her sleeping eyes, the slow rise and fall of her breast as she slept her drugged sleep. He was tempted to fall back beside her and gather her to him to wait for the light before the dawn, the best time for them both, the time when she had no reserves and was giving and bold. But the sun was already up and pointing fingers of light into the room, dust motes dancing in the hard shafts. There was no time.

He worked his feet into veldschoene still caked with trail dust, and worked his trousers up his legs with rubber fingers, stumbling over the copper buttons. His hands shook and he wondered if he could hold a pistol, let alone aim and fire it, wondered if he had the will even if he could. He found a laundered shirt in a drawer and pushed his head and arms up into it, not bothering with the collar laces, getting most of the tail inside his trousers before he had to sit back down and gather himself. There was hot, popping sweat on his back, and his hands and face were cold to the touch. His stomach heaved and poked iron fingers into his throat. Why couldn't he leave this mess to others and go back to sleep with Hannie's musk and warmth beside him? He had done what he thought was right, hadn't he? Let others take their part, bear their share of the load. Matthew thought this and more as he found his horse guns and strapped them on, moving like a big, loose puppet, not knowing how much he staggered or how weak he really was. His scalp protested as he jammed on his hat and wove to the door to find it locked. He stood there, puzzled and stupefied for long moments, working the latch as quietly as he could, trying not to disturb the woman on the bed, knowing he would never be able to answer the inevitable questions she would throw at him.

Christ's shroud! He must be there. He had to get out of this tomb of a room with its warm, safe smells, its promise of rest. He thought of smashing the door with a chair and promptly rejected it. Hannie must sleep on.

The mob was louder now as a dozen impromptu speechmakers vied for supremacy, ugly sounds and uglier arguments.

Matthew staggered to the window, unhooked the shutter bars with shaking fingers, and the light crashed in around him, full of heat and noise. Hannie stirred and turned her face from the light, throwing a forearm across her eyes.

Sleep, thought Matthew, climbing out onto the verandah tiles, sleep. He closed the shutters and stood up, battered by shouts and his own nausea, swaying on watery legs and unseen by the massing people below. There were women in carriages who had come to see the show with wicker hampers and bottles of wine, their complexions shielded from the sun by large parasols. Burghers sat their bloodstock mares, farmers their mules, boys and youths packed into oxcarts waved down at those on foot, the whole sea of people pressing closer and closer to the livery stables for a sight of the murderous Griqua.

Matthew crossed the verandah roof toward the part that overhung the side street across from the next building. The gap between the Winburg Regency and the wooden canopy fronting the general store was less than four feet. Without thinking, Matthew launched himself into space and sprawled on the sloping wooden slats, barely catching at the carved cornice before sliding over the edge. He pulled himself onto his hands and knees and scrambled across the creaking surface to the far edge, swung clumsily over, and dropped in among buckets and tin baths, knocking a rack of besoms to the ground.

He was seen and recognized by those close to him and the word went through the crowd. Faces turned to stare, to shout his name, to spit expletives as he pushed through the hot press of bodies. Snatches of dialogue came at him like venomous fireflies.

...It's the *rooinek*....It's Eastman....He captured the Griqua...brought back the gold....All we *wanted* was the gold, not this Bastaard....Captured? He couldn't pull the trigger on the *skepsel*....Coward....Damned Englander, who wants him here with us?...You? Me?...Eastman and de Villiers took on twelve of them, man. *Twelve*....Hey, Eastman. Give us the Bastaard if you haven't the spine to finish it....Shoot the Griqua and hang him up as a warning to others....A trial, for what? We know he murdered the Gould children....Leave him for the ants with molasses on his face. Let him watch them eat out his eyes....They did that to my brother....Impale him like Dingaan did to Pieter Retief....We've all voted, Eastman....Give the Bastaard up or I swear...

Matthew pushed on, less and less gentle with his elbows and shoulders. A man, bearded and wild-eyed, his breath thick with brandy, tore at his shirtfront. Matthew drew his pistol and struck him between the eyes, dropping him in a heap at his feet, kicking his loose arm away from his shoe. The crowd leaned away from the naked gun, moving outward as those behind tried to press forward, falling away from the front of the livery. A mounted man reared his horse and scattered more of the crowd. People sprawled and fell and the shouts gave way to cries of pain and fear. The panicked horse bucked his rider away and more people were knocked to the ground. The clear circle around Matthew grew wider until ten feet separated him from the nearest men. The drunk Matthew had pistol-whipped snorted blood through his mashed nose, his eyes dazed and sobered. Matthew levered him to his feet and pushed him away, his own strength mounting, his temper rising to gorge his face with blood.

A silence spread until only those at the back still called questions and slogans.

Matthew wondered what he could say to the crowd, how he could make them see how badly they were acting, how insanely.... He shook his head and sweat spattered the dried ground to leave tiny holes in the dust. He heard de Villiers shout from inside the barred building, words that ought to make sense but did not. There were shouts and a rock struck the livery door. A bottle smashed against the shingles.

Then an elephant gun boomed and the crowd was looking away from Matthew, away from the livery, as horses came into town from the west, their dust swilling ahead of them in the hard breeze.

"The Commando," somebody yelled. "They'll see justice done."

"The Commando."

"Pray, Eastman."

"Say your prayers, *rooinek*."

Again the crowd parted, cheering now for the row upon row of horsemen who thundered in to halt in line across the width of the street, their mounts sweated, their clothes thick with dust, their guns and pistol butts catching the sun.

Matthew looked at them stupidly, picking out the faces he knew, hard put to know what to make of his position now that fifty fighting men might bear down on him and blow him to bloody ruin without so much as a hiccup. If these men had come to kill the Griqua he knew there was nothing to be done except to consider how he was to save his own neck. Was it really any of his business if these people chose the way of the Old Testament, using the same barbarism they so roundly condemned in others? Matthew holstered his pistol and stood slack-limbed, saving himself for any fight he might have to make if given the opportunity or the choice.

One of the Commando had pushed his lathered horse through the front line of riflemen and reined in, leaning on his pommel, lazily turning a bullwhip in his right hand as he sneer-smiled around with no show of looking at any person or thing directly. His quick eyes took in the crowd, the beaten drunk, the smashed bottle on the livery roof, the barred stable doors, and the swaying Matthew. When he saw the guns covering him and the crowd from the office and the loft his sneering smile widened and he hooked a lazy leg over his pommel and leaned on the crooked knee.

"You inside there, Pa?" he called, his light voice carrying without the need to shout.

"I'm here, Dirk, with the doctor," answered Abraham. "I'm coming out, boy."

Dirk? thought Matthew. But he's in the north, patrolling

the Umkhomazi River. He squinted against the sun and took in the wiry, unkempt figure and saw that it was indeed Dirk. The sight of him gave Matthew no feeling of relief or heightened fear; Dirk was just another factor to complicate an issue Matthew knew he could not control.

Dirk flicked at the ground with his whip.

"Stay where you are, Pa. You must have sold really short grain measures to rile up all these God-fearing neighbors of ours." He was looking at individual faces in the crowd now, playing with the situation, letting Matthew see he knew what was going on. "I swear," said Dirk. "It speaks badly of a town when a man can't ride out on Commando duty and leave his own father safe behind him. Neh, Eastman?"

Matthew had no time to reply. The drunk stepped out and caught at Dirk's bridle. "That's not how it is, de Villiers. Those men have got a murdering Bastaard inside, and by God—"

Dirk's whip cracked up a puff of dust and caressed the man's face.

"You'll talk when I tell you to, man. One of 'those men' is my father. He was a man before you learned to scrape your face or eat from a spoon. If I want speeches I'll go to a man, not his brindle bitch."

"I didn't mean any disresp—"

"If you don't *mean* anything, don't *say* anything." Dirk looked lazily at Matthew as his whip butted the drunk back into the people gathered around. "And you, Eastman. Have you been selling spavined horses to my pa, so he can resell them to these *dassies?* If you have, I'll hang you myself. That's the English way, *ja?*"

Matthew dredged up a grin from somewhere.

"It is, and I haven't," he said.

"You look terrible, Eastman."

"I shouldn't wonder."

"*Verdamn* it, *rooinek.* I can't trust you to wait until you can have my company to get drunk, so how can I trust you to care for my pa when I'm gone? Is this really about some damned Griqua?"

"As you well know."

"Maybe I do." Dirk sneered over the heads of the crowd, letting them see his very real anger. "And you want to kill this Bastaard, do you?" he asked.

"He murdered the Goulds...the children....Stake him out in the sun....He stole the Volksraad money...."

Dirk rose in the saddle and the whip cracked until there was a semblance of quiet again, his lazy voice cutting through the dying hubbub.

"And you'd hurt my father to get him, neh?"

More cries went up, conflicting and hateful cries for death, for justice, for *something*.

"My father!" bawled Dirk, then: "Muskets present. Fire directly into the crowd when I give the signal."

The rows of smoothbores cocked like firecrackers and the sound carried right down the street. The shouts died to murmurs, the murmurs to whispers, and the sudden silence allowed everybody to hear the creak of the wind in the hanging signs.

"By God, you'll fight both father and son then. Or clear the street. Decide very quickly, *mense.*"

There was some stirring in the mob but no real movement.

Abraham and the doctor came out of the livery with two muskets apiece as Boie guarded the open door. Dirk's sneer-smile narrowed and almost disappeared when he saw the armed Khoikhoi. He snapped a glance at Matthew, who stared back, their eyes locking for an instant of mutual antipathy.

"Wrong, Eastman," Dirk said, his voice deceptively soft. "Very, very wrong."

"Only because he's doing your job for you, de Villiers," Matthew answered evenly. "Now you're here, you can take over. I'll take my people out with pleasure. Have your father explain it all to you."

Dirk pointed his whip.

"If I see that kaffir armed in town again, I'll kill him. You know the law, Eastman."

It was Matthew's turn to sneer.

"The *law?*"

"That's what this is all about, Dirk," said Abraham, more breathless than ever. "The law. Our law. It took an Englishman, a black, and two old men to uphold that law. To make certain these fools didn't destroy our last chance to show we can operate by due process of that law. There will be no law unless we give that law teeth."

"These men are all the teeth we need, Pa," said Dirk, his eyes still on Boie.

"Then disperse this crowd," ordered Abraham.

"Are you all right, Pa?"

"Yes, yes. Will you give the order?"

270

"Yes, Pa," mocked Dirk, bringing the Commando to alert.

The Commando wheeled about, cantered off thirty yards, and wheeled about again, ready to gallop down the street at Dirk's signal.

"Well, *herrenvolk?*" asked Dirk, raising his whip. "The father has a son and the son has fifty cousins. What's it to be?"

The drunk picked up his hat and lost himself in the press of bodies with Dirk's laugh following him. After some initial hesitation women tugged at their men, men at their sons, wives at their daughters, and a general exodus began, interspersed with anonymous cries of "traitors" and the odd explosive curse.

Within minutes the streets were as empty as a Sunday during a *kerk* meeting.

Dirk brought his gray into a half circle to face Matthew directly, his smile gone, his mouth hidden in his ragged beard, wild heat in his slitted eyes.

"Always trouble, Eastman. Always complications. Kaffir is kaffir, and white is white. I should hang you alongside the Bastaard. You *and* your damned Khoikhoi. Do you think my men liked doing that to our own people? Do you think they would have done that for anybody but my father?"

Matthew smiled coldly, blood mounting in his face, asking, "Would you?"

Dirk snapped out an unequivocal "No."

"I thought not, de Villiers. Self for self as usual. That just makes me wonder what will happen to this country and your people when men like your father are gone."

"Boys, please," said Abraham. "You two should be friends, brothers. This talk is stupid."

"I'll tell you," said Dirk, ignoring his father, almost hissing. "Our people will be all the stronger once we bar all outsiders, all *skepsels,* all those who follow the British Jack. We're riding to Port Natal to clear them out for good. Then, Eastman, remember what I said about your boy there."

Matthew moved to shield Boie.

"You know my answer to that, Dirk. Don't even think it. Harm one of my people, just one, and I'll see you die in the only way that's fitting for a coward like you."

Dirk's sneer-smile was poisonous.

"You have pistols, *rooinek.* Let's finish it here."

Matthew spread his hands.

"That's not what I had in mind."

271

"And I'm the coward? Ha! Knives, whips, name it."

"No," said Matthew. "Nor billhooks or flails or cudgels. I won't kill you myself. I'll give you to the people you fear most. The Matabele."

"Matthew!" gasped Abraham as he and Dr. Andries turned pale.

Matthew kept his eyes on Dirk.

"I swear it on Klyn's memory, Dirk," he said.

Dirk had not moved, was a rigid and dark figure in the saddle, a nerve jogging the corner of one eye. His clenched teeth seemed to have locked all the air inside his throat.

"Matthew, Matthew, take it back," mourned Abraham, torn between ties of blood and those of emotion, seeing two sons fighting. He had seen Dirk grow black in the face with rage, but this transformed man that was his friend, this huge, resolved man, was a Matthew Eastman few had seen before.

Matthew's head did not turn, nor did his eyes stray from the silent Dirk.

"No, menheer. Now that it's been said it can't be unsaid. Dirk has his fifty 'cousins' as witnesses, so let it stay said in plain language. Anybody who comes onto my land and breaks a single ear of wheat or steals a pitcher of my milk or breaks one stick of my fence will look over his shoulder and find me there. And I swear, I'll kill him with a stone, with a stick, or with my bare hands. Whichever way I can, I'll kill that man. But you, Dirk de Villiers, I will find you wherever you go, and I'll give you to Mzilikazi." Matthew's words struck home all the more strongly for their lack of fury or bluster, and not a man there doubted his sincerity.

When he had walked away with Boie trotting behind him, everybody watched him go save one.

Dirk's inner vision was at the killing hill where he and his party had found Pieter Retief's Commando after Dingaan's torturers had finished with them. They knew them from their clothes, for their flesh had rotted about the stakes that had been driven into their rectums, their skulls still held the sharpened pegs that had been hammered up their nostrils and into their brains.

It was a sight he had tried to forget, and one he now knew he never could. When he came out of his trance there was no heat in the sun.

The first criminal session of the Volksraad court lasted less than twenty minutes. The Griqua was condemned to death by firing squad, the sentence to be carried out immediately by volunteer Commandos. There was no shortage of willing marksmen and they drew straws for the honor.

Samuel dug his own grave and smoked a pipeful of dagga to steady himself. He was releasing the last trickle of drugged smoke through his permanently exposed teeth when the order to fire was given and the heavy balls drove him backward into the shallow trench, dead before he struck the bottom. His hat flew from his head and the wind carried it away toward Griqualand.

Matthew was sponging Hannie's forehead when he heard the volley and the cheer from the mob of onlookers. He dabbed at the hot, flushed skin with the barest quiver in his hand, the slightest pucker between his brows. Hannie sighed in her sleep and her breathing became shallow and regular and less perspiration popped out on her face. The fever had broken.

BOOK FIVE

1

Elise wanted to scream when she heard the doctor's diagnosis.

Dr. Andries's plump hands had pressed her abdomen, he had noted her swelling breasts and listened to both heart and stomach with his eartube. He had asked her impertinent questions about her appetite and changes of taste, and more embarrassing ones about her monthly cycle. Then, beaming all over his cheeks and chins, his tiny black eyes quite disappearing into pink folds of merry flesh, he had patted her hand and told her she was pregnant.

Pregnant indeed.

Although the horror of the fact made her reel with deep-rooted despair, she thought the fat doctor indelicate in his choice of words; even the farmers did not use that word when they discussed their stock. Cows calved and horses... she did not know what horses did, but she knew they were never *pregnant*. He could have said "you are with child, Mrs. Eastman," or, "Matthew is to be a father"; anything but *that* word.

Elise heard him talk of diet and rest and all the things that had applied to other silly geese who wanted children, fat thighs, and gross bodies. None of these things should have anything to do with her. She was Elise and she had other plans. She was going home. Her mother had sent her traveling dresses that showed off her slender figure, a lovely gown for her first receiving night at Father's new house. If only she had some curses of her own that were not as basically profane as those Matthew used when he thought she was out of earshot. It was so unfair, men could do what they wanted, could live to a double standard. They never had to lie in confinement as their ankles swelled and their bodies changed shape. Her tiny sixteen-inch waist would be gone and she would not be able to damp her petticoat to make her skirts cling, nor wear a low-fronted basque when the milk came to distort her bosom. She would be forced to wear those awful shapeless oversmocks the Dutch women favored and tie her petticoats higher and higher as her belly pushed forward.

It was all spoiled, all ruined.

How could she take to the social scene of Port Elizabeth in her delicate condition? Expectant mothers were expected to keep to their houses until the squalling infant had been weaned enough to be handed to a nursemaid. Then they could emerge again, but to what? To take the backseats at recitals with the other matrons, to sit out all the dances unless one's husband or male relatives marked one's card, to talk babies and fish prices to other boring elder women. She would not even be allowed to sit with the unmarried girls in their brilliant gowns, for she would be too old and be dressed in demure black. She could not dance with eligible young men or flirt over a lace fan.

Tears stung Elise's eyes.

She would go home, she would. She should never have listened to those stupid kaffir women and their barbaric notions of herbal safety. By heaven, she would take a besom to both the cook and that skinny child, Pyayo. Everybody knew kaffir were different from whites, the other wives said so, they were constructed differently, their skulls were thicker and they needed less food. They could live on dust and water and still bear fat black babies every year. Elise would have needed some potion a good deal more sophisticated than any they could have supplied. She should have thought of that, Elise told herself. She should have.

And now this fat Dutch doctor who smelled of brandy and black tobacco was telling her she must rest because her hips were narrow and she was a trifle too thin to take any foolish chances during these crucial early weeks. Rest, meat, and vegetables. And three glasses of fortified wine each day; and then, as though it were a hilarious joke, he had warned her against hard liquor of any description. As if she had even tasted the brandy Dr. Andries reeked of. Was the man truly sober? Was this the man who was to be her sole medical counselor through this trying time? If only she could scream and drum her heels and rake his silly face with her long nails.

And Matthew, oh God, what would he say?

Of course the ninny would be delighted. He would grin and shuffle his feet and probably drink far too much of that awful sorghum beer the kaffir made so much of, boasting of his coming son, making Boie's chest swell along with his own as though they had somehow achieved a joint conception. As if men made babies and women were merely the vessels, the ovens where the things baked like so much gingerbread. It was intolerable...it was *savage*.

But then she had married a savage. Elise had seen Matthew dance with the San as though he were one of them, singing their strange clicking songs without stumbling over the words. He went off with them for days at a time and gave vague reasons for his absences. He talked to his kaffir like equals and took their advice, and worse, he had impregnated her despite her elaborate precautions to avoid such a foul thing happening.

How *could* she have taken such a man as a husband when she could have had her pick of the beaux at Port Elizabeth? Elise asked herself miserably. Matthew had seemed so big and bronzed and *healthy* beside the other men she danced and flirted with at the box socials. Those clerks, storekeepers, and bankers' sons who hardly ever walked or rode and whose bellies strained the lie of their waistcoats.

Oh, it was all so unfair, so undignified.

Of course Matthew was not here, now when she needed him, not that she even wanted to see him, she thought perversely. She hoped he would not come home before Dr. Andries had gone back to Winburg. At least then she could keep the news to herself for a little while longer, make him sorry for his absence. The last thing she wanted was backslapping and cigar-passing and the pair of them drinking heavily at table as she fumed and felt herself getting fat. Turning gross before their eyes. And Matthew talking of the son he would ride everywhere with, teach animal husbandry and all the barbaric tongues of the tribes of Ham. It would be insufferable. Why, Matthew would alienate the child before she got to know the brat, not that she wanted anything to do with any child of Matthew Eastman's, or any man's, come to that. She wanted to dance and be pretty and admired and...anything but *this*.

She would rather die than bear a son who knew nothing of the society she sought to be a part of. A son who would know crops and animals and the tongues of the savage, who would ride before he could toddle, would grow whiskers before he had learned to bow and shake hands, who would learn his tables counting fat-tailed sheep.

There must be some way she could stop this. Doctors knew how to stop things, didn't they? Elise watched Dr. Andries pack his instruments away and snap his black bag closed with a sinking heart, realizing he would not raise a finger to help her. Elise knew there were doctors who could terminate pregnancies, but they were on the Cape or in Port Elizabeth and they were only whispered about by parents whose daughters had shamed them. These were shadowy men who came after nightfall and were paid in advance, men whose names were never mentioned even if things went wrong. Merciful heavens, hadn't one of the girls suffered a breakdown and died in a hospital? Elise shuddered; she could not bear pain and the very thought of a stranger touching her private places...No, there must be another way. There had to be, there just had to....

Elise made no goodbyes when Dr. Andries closed himself out of the bedroom, content to retreat under the tent of her hair with her shocked misery, her mood too inverted to make polite responses.

Pyayo barely made the well of the stairs before the Baas Doctor came out of the Missie's bedroom and paused on the landing to pull at his lower lip, his face serious. Pyayo had listened at the door, and now as she stared up through the banisters, she saw the Baas Doctor with a straight mouth and knew things were not good with the Missie. His cheeks were usually as fat as peaches when he smiled at the children in the huts and told their mothers to drink more milk, to oil their babies every day, to burn bricks of dried flowers to keep the mosquitoes away. The straight mouth meant bad things for the Missie and Pyayo was frightened for her.

She was also frightened for herself, for now that Lord Boie's black soup had worked its magic on the Missie's belly, she must hide the besom and the fly-whisk before they were laid across her back and buttocks. The Missie's rages made her strong and quick and her blows cut hard. Her temper had been uncertain from the time she had noticed the blue veins in her breasts and counted fingers back to her last moontime. But now she knew for certain she would be worse, much worse, and Pyayo wished Nkosi Matthew was back from the horse auction. There were never any beatings when he was in the house.

Dr. Andries found her crouched on the stairs, too scared to cry, her eyes big with fright. She would not speak until he took her out into the walled vegetable garden where she was not overlooked from the house, for the walls were windowless and the gunports were covered by wooden shutters.

Dr. Andries sat on a bench and gently bullied Pyayo until she told her story in her own tongue, managing to understand the gist of what she was saying despite the ragged delivery. His cheeks turned to peaches and his stifled laughter made Pyayo laugh without understanding why. Pyayo only knew the Baas Doctor was a great witchman who cared for babies and women even though they were not first cattle wives or the seed of the royal kraal. He did not smell out spirits or burn feathers. He smelled the breath and peeled back eyelids to see into the brain itself. He read tongues and fresh excreta as the witchmen augured from goat's entrails. When he failed to cure an ailment he shed tears with a straight mouth, which was strange for a man with the power of healing. Tears were for chiefs or princes of powerful tribes, not commoners' babies and their mothers. In others who had no magic cunning, such shows of emotion would be looked upon as weakness of the spirit and they would have been stoned for their leaking eyes.

Dr. Andries sent Pyayo to Ndala, Boie's wife, with instructions to stay there until he came along. His sharp eyes had seen the faint stripes on the girl's thin shoulders and although he suspected some wives of beating their apprentice girls, this was the first time he had seen physical evidence of it. He was saddened at the sight. Matthew Eastman would have been appalled, he knew, if he were told, and Andries did not wish to be the one to point out Elise's intemperate cruelty. There were rifts enough in this family without adding another to the lengthening list, but just how he was to stop Elise from using her servants so badly escaped him for the moment, and he determined to give the matter some serious consideration after he had pondered the more immediate problem of the naked distaste she had shown when he told her of her impending motherhood.

There was nothing physically wrong with the woman, no reason at all why she could not bear a child with ease. She was young and strong and motherhood could be the making of her. She had been the doll-wife for too long and had lifted her nose far too often among the local wives. God knows the women had been more than patient with her. Many of them had wealthier husbands than Elise Eastman, quite a few were a good deal less well off, but here on the high veldt that was not what counted. Without the goodwill of one's neighbors, and their generous help, a small calamity could swiftly become high tragedy. They had all learned that lesson during the long trek and were reminded of it every day in one way or another, but Elise had not trekked, had not learned to share or to accept the generosity of others. For all Matthew's differences of opinion with his Afrikaner neighbors, his was always the first gift of seed or stock to any family struck by pest or raiders. His plow was always on loan to anybody who needed one, for he knew the reverse could apply at any time and when he least expected it. He knew better than most just how isolated were the people of the Central Plateau, and how

279

much they must succor each other simply to survive. But Elise...Elise knew none of this, would have none of it. Her aspirations were elsewhere, her loyalty and devotion, such as they were, were to the people of a society she had barely sniffed the periphery of, a society she had certainly never been accepted by for all her airs and ideas above her station. Even if she ever went back to Port Elizabeth or on to the Cape, she could hardly expect to find the elegant drawing rooms open to her. Not even if she did clank back with all her wealth pinned to her bodice and hanging from her wrists. Ostentatious display of wealth softened no patrician heart, guaranteed no place at table above the salt. Better for her to dream here as she nursed her children than to go back to a rude awakening with doors crashing closed in her face.

Andries had had his fill of that very attitude himself. Even as a professional man with degrees from the Sorbonne and Utrecht, he was required to attend the sick of the big houses by entering through the servants' and tradesmen's entrances. He who could discourse wittily and at length on philosophy and the humanities found no seat within the inner circle, found no acceptance with those whose money was older than the colony itself. To them, Dr. Andries and dreamers like Elise were of a like kind, upstarts with neither breeding nor background, he a Dutch Breakbones whose harsh accent grated on their ears, and she a trader's daughter only one generation away from the plows of the Home Counties; a foreigner and a rustic with nothing to recommend them but their patently gauche self-seeking.

Only the Laidlers of the world could break convention by the sheer weight of their influence in trade and politics. The fat doctor and the newly pregnant girl could hardly aspire to those dizzy heights. No, they were better off in the high veldt, where dreams cost nothing but the dreaming, where soaring palaces formed themselves in the clouds of the big sky and in the flames of the evening fire, the former to be ripped apart by the winds, the latter to burn to white ash in the grate.

Nothing lost and nothing gained, save in the imagination.

Sighing heavily, Dr. Andries sat in the drowsing garden with his thoughts and his silver flask, more concerned about the hurt Elise might cause to those around her than any she might inflict upon herself, although if he had known just how finely balanced her mind was on the cutting edge of self-interest and the fear of rejection, he might have revised his views somewhat. His main concern was with the damage Elise could work if she were allowed to follow her ambitions. He barely registered the chink and bob of bit and bridle above the whispering quiet of the fruit trees, and nothing penetrated his musings until the horses were well into the yard, where the houseboys tumbled from the stoep to offer the hospitality of the farm to the riders.

Dr. Andries hurried through to the front of the house, hoping against hope that Matthew had returned home so that the matter in hand could be discussed and dealt with before he returned to Winburg. Whatever happened he must impress Matthew with the importance of keeping Elise on the farm during her confinement and he promised himself he would pursue the fiction of her delicacy until both husband and wife believed it as gospel. To allow her to travel to Port Elizabeth now would probably result in her showing the farm and Matthew a clean pair of heels. A healthy baby would settle her down and bring an end to this futile dreaming of hers, would bring her closer to her husband, to the farm, to the community at large.

Her willfulness was based on childish petulance, not on an inner committed strength of one who has tempered her ego with experience and the humility that comes from self-knowledge. Learning to care for a suckling would give her some of that simple responsibility, a start toward an understanding of others' needs, others' views; from that would come some understanding of herself.

Dr. Andries crossed the stoep and leaned against the upright at the stairhead, peering from the hard shadow into the light.

The horsemen were all strangers to him, and had a hard-ridden look. Two were white men and their servants and attendants were a mixture of races, and Andries thought there must be thirty packhorses drinking at the corral trough. They could have been traders, hunters, or slavers for all Andries knew, alarm rising within him; and Matthew not here, nor Boie or any of the senior boys. Andries realized just how vulnerable any holding was when the men were away, mentally calling Matthew a fool for not making reasonable provision for such an event, then dimly remembering some arrangement the Englishman had once mentioned. By the matriarch's beard, what was it? he wondered wildly, what should he have remembered?

One of the white men had grizzled red and salt hair and

a mustache that would have been stiffly waxed in any other climate. Now it drooped under a freckled nose and two alert blue eyes. He sat his horse like a cavalryman and his spurs were of British make with small roundels, although his clothes seemed to have been selected for their anonymity and looseness. He was amused by the doctor's obvious fluster and gave Andries the impression he knew full well they were both visitors although the reasons for their separate presence there were wildly different. His quick eyes had counted the Sotho, noted the number of horses in the corral, and knew to within a nailhead how many of the natives were armed and could use those arms effectively. He doffed his shapeless hat and bowed in the saddle, speaking with the soft burr of the English west country coarsened by time spent in the capital.

"Rest easy, menheer. I have been here before and know about the Baralong in the hills. We are here on business with Matthew Eastman, and you'll see we've left our arms at the barn with the Tottie. I believe there's a signal to stop the tribesmen from coming down to slaughter us, and I wish you'd have the flag run up, or the fire lit, or whatever it is that has to be done. We've been seeing Baralong all the morning, and I'd hate to die for a mistake."

Signal? thought Andries, seeing the neatly stacked weapons guarded by one of Matthew's armed Sotho, noting other men on the barn roof, several more deploying themselves along the corral fence. They might have come out of the ground for all Andries knew. And he knew nothing about any signal either. He wanted to reach for his flask and take a swallow for his heart's sake.

"Shall I speak in Dutch, menheer?"

"No, I beg you, sir, and your friends." Andries hurried to make amends for his reticence. "May I on behalf of Menheer Eastman welcome you, and invite you to step down to refresh yourselves," he said, thinking that his English form of address was not halfway bad for a Dutchman, clipping his words at the graying redheaded man as if he had been one of those who had rejected him on the Cape all those years before. "Step down and honor this house by coming inside. I am Dr. Marcus Andries; may I have the honor of knowing you gentlemen?"

The second mounted white man made an aside in faultless Portuguese and his companion answered him in the same language, his accent less fluid. Neither of them seemed to want to identify themselves. Dr. Andries saw that the second man was huge where Matthew Eastman was, in his opinion, big. His great torso strained the fabric of his naval jacket and his thighs bulged inside his white canvas trousers. His untrimmed beard was a wild, black mat that hid his chin and cheeks, and his eyes and hooked nose formed a brown triangle beneath his heavy brows. The black marble eyes held little light as they regarded the doctor with suspicion.

"Not while the Baralong clans breath down our necks," said the Englishman directly and sharply, drawing Andries's attention back to himself.

"Ah," said Andries, not knowing what else to say. "Ah."

A slight black figure scurried through the men and horses to tug at his sleeve, another taller one following more sedately. The first was Pyayo and the second was Boie's wife, Ndala.

"Baaswitch," said Pyayo. "We know this baas with the burned hair." She pointed shyly at the Englishman. "He is a friend of Nkosi Matthew. Baaswitch, you must make the boys light the torch. It makes black smoke for the chief's men to see. Quickly, baaswitch, or the warriors will come and make killing on these men."

Andries looked to Ndala for confirmation.

"It is true, baaswitch," she said. "They will come with their assegais if they do not see the smoke. My man usually does this thing, but he travels with Nkosi to guard his back."

"Then see to it, girl," said Andries, relieved to find that one of the men was known to Matthew.

Ndala shook her head. "It is for the man to do, baaswitch. You must use the tinder."

"Must I? Where is it, Ndala?"

"There," said Ndala, and Andries followed her arm as it rose to point at the spire above the barn, a good fifty feet above the ground. Andries had no head for heights and it showed in his face. The huge man said something in an amused voice and Andries looked at him, sensing himself to be the subject of the remark.

"Our friend here," explained the Englishman, "wagers twenty schillings you won't make the climb, Doctor."

"Twenty schillings?" Andries clasped his pulsing stomach. "But I'm only a poor doctor."

The huge bearded man laughed. "Then now's your chance to be a rich one," he said in honest Dutch.

2

The auction had gone well and all of Matthew's horses had been sold at high prices. There might be a good deal of feeling running against him as a man, but as a horse-breeder he had no peer in the Blesberg, and those same hotheads who maligned him and dreamed of dashing Commando raids against the red soldiers needed his horses to ride off to their hoped-for war.

Matthew had idly wondered how well the Voortrekkers would acquit themselves against a British square and always concluded that it would prove to be a closely contested duel. Matthew did not want to think about the aftermath of such an encounter should the Natalians be victorious, for he knew there would be more in the air than after the proverbial apple fell into the fresh cow chip and spattered the farmer. The British might well be slow to react when any news of a military reverse finally filtered through to the Cape, but react they would, and come in force to bloody every Natalian nose, or worse, to take away their hard-won independence.

Still, for him there were very real compensations. Every one of the Commando would need to ride a steady horse, and that was where his profits lay. For the animals' sakes, Matthew hoped they would not be charged into batteries of British cannon. A naval captain had once described what grapeshot could do to men and oak bulwarks, and it took little imagination to realize how a horse would fare in a broadside of iron splinters.

Ach, there was no point in him even thinking of selecting whom he did or did not sell to. If the Commando meant to go against all the Queen's soldiers in the Empire, there was not a single farmer who would not gladly give up a spare horse and saddle to the cause. Even the most cautious and peaceful of his neighbors would cheer the others on and donate a horse to a braver neighbor.

Hannie had done that much for those who recently followed Jan Mocke and his Commando into Natal, for several of her hire geldings had gone east. Matthew had learned that from her stableboys although he had never questioned her about it. She was too frail yet for conversations of that kind. She ran the hotel like a sleepwalker, the core of her in black mourning, a state she was likely to stay in for some considerable time.

Four months had passed since Martin Gould had got himself and the children killed, and still she seemed to listen for them to tumble in from their play, for Martin's quiet, studious voice to call for books or a cool drink. Hannie did not associate any blame with her dead husband, rather she took all that upon herself, as though she were at fault for simply allowing any of them out of her sight. She spoke of Martin as though he had been a child himself and had died as a result of her preoccupation with her own affairs.

Matthew had in the early days tried to talk her out of such a nonsensical notion, but she would have none of it and would withdraw within herself, leaving him isolated and unable to follow after. Dr. Andries had told him the only medicine was time and Matthew had avoided the subject from that time onward, steering Hannie away from it when he could. During daylight he had no difficulty, but at night the dreams would come and he would be forced to shake her awake brutally and kiss the screams away.

Hannie had moved herself out of the haunted bungalow and into a suite at the Winburg Regency and it was Ham's daughter who slept on a pallet at the bottom of her bed when Matthew was not there and woke Hannie before her screams roused the entire hotel.

Hannie's hair had whitened over the first weeks and her lack of appetite reduced her to a thinness she would have been pleased with in happier times. Ham's daughter Jesse sneaked her mistress's dresses out to the seamstress, who took them in at the waist and hips more than once. They need not have bothered with the secrecy; Hannie would not have noticed if the work of restitching had been done under her very nose accompanied by fife and drum. She forgot to comb her hair and would only eat for Matthew, who fed her from his own plate when she refused one of her own. In order to be in town as often as possible, Matthew had split his herd and brought the horses in a few at a time, staying overnight whenever he could, making Hannie eat, helping her to sleep, and patiently waiting for her to want to make love again. That appetite had withered like the others and Dr. Andries said time, Matthew, time and care. Patience, old friend, patience....

Matthew had found wells of that commodity within himself and was as tender with Hannie as he was cautious and merely physical with Elise, whose whole being revolved about going home to Port Elizabeth. Matthew had not yet been obliged to search for excuses to delay the trip; there were too many real reasons for not going. Not least of all was the situation in Natal. If the frontier did explode into open conflict, he could hardly leave his farm to take Elise to tea on the coast while his barn burned and his horses were run off. He would watch the situation closely and keep Elise encouraged.

Some of the Natalians had already abandoned their holdings in the eastern province and had trekked back into the high veldt in search of land. They could dispossess the dispirited natives, who were drifting back to their hereditary lands after years of hiding in the deserts and swamps, but Matthew wanted none of them adjoining his twelve thousand acres. There was still land and distance for a man to lose himself in, but if they all came the picture could change radically.

Matthew brought Gaika up short.

Boie had reined in and stood in the saddle, shielding his eyes from the sun as he stared toward the southeast, where black smoke rose in a vertical plume. There were strangers at the farm.

Both men spurred their horses forward and drew their smoothbores.

Elise had opened her shutters in time to see Dr. Andries fire the signal torch a moment before he looked down and lost his nerve. The men in the yard watched him clutch at the ladderhead and lie along the rungs, unable to move.

There were so many men, Elise observed, so many races, all of them laughing, giving advice, and generally enjoying the doctor's distress. Elise could subscribe to that, and for a moment forgot her own misery at the sight of the loathed Andries so close to breaking his short, pompous neck. It would be only right if he did fall to the ground and burst like a sack of melons to pay him back for the manner in which he had informed her of her condition. He certainly was not as comfortably pleased with himself now, Elise was glad to see. God's justice, he was as white as a sheep.

Two men in flowing robes were swarming up the ladder and one of them had a rope coiled over his shoulder, both of them moving with swift assurance, their faces wreathed in smiles. They came up on either side of Andries and Elise heard him whimper as they tied the rope around him and prised his fingers from the top rung. Then they had him over the edge and were lowering him to the ground, his face ashen under his shielding hands. All too soon he was at the bottom, where he was surrounded and released from the rope with a good deal of jostling and jokes about his courage, his weight, and his trembling jowls. His belly was patted and his tousled hair rumpled. Once his feet touched the ground, his good humor instantly restored itself and Andries shook all the hands that were offered him, beaming and making jokes at his own expense in both Dutch and English.

The blacks in robes took Andries to where the bearded man sat his gray, and the doctor made a leg and bowed with a flourish. The bearded man took a pouch of coins and threw it to the doctor, who caught it clumsily, his thanks breathless.

"You earned it," said the bearded man in Dutch. "It takes a brave man to carry his fear with him. I've seen men who were good for a fight with pin, knife, or pistol shy from a climb to the top spar. But *magtig,* Doctor, where did you learn to make a leg like a Bond Street popinjay? Ach, I'm no maiden in skirts to be impressed by such."

Elise turned from the window to check her hair and gown in the mirror and missed Andries's reply. She wished she had a full-length glass, wished Andries had turned an ankle, wished herself a thousand miles away from the rough horse-play. She supposed she must greet these men as the lady of the house in Matthew's absence, even if they did scuff her floors and ruck her carpets with their spurs. They would probably drink noisily and pick their teeth, break wind at table and light cigars without so much as a "By your leave, madam?" And with the house full she could hardly take a besom to that scrawny nincompoop Pyayo, but that one could wait and the waiting would add spice to the reckoning that must come.

Elise went below and found feverish activity in the kitchen. At least the cook had been aware enough to have got the houseboys setting out beer and brandy, and was making up side dishes of cold meat and yams. Pyayo scurried through the back door with horn mugs of beer for the strangers' servants, and a houseboy carried a platter of biltong. The long table had been spread with linen and laid with silver, and bowls of freshly cut flowers were being set about the room. As usual, there was little for Elise to do and less to worry about. The house had learned to run without her since the moment her indifference had made itself apparent, adding yet another thorn to Elise's discontent with her lot.

She crossed the room and went out onto the stoep, shading her eyes with a rattan fan.

The Englishman had dismounted and climbed the stoep to greet her, sweeping off his hat as he did so, his eyes finding Elise as he made a formal bow. Elise lost the martyred look she had decided she would wear through what she had promised herself would be a painfully rustic encounter and grasped the man's hands with a sudden surge of pleasure.

"Sergeant Coffee," she said. "Is that you? But why in the world are you dressed so..."

"Like a Bristol tinker, eh?" Coffee said bluntly, spreading the tails of his tattered coat after kissing her hand. "A red coat is likely to draw gunfire, Mrs. Eastman. And there's no general army issue of *mouti* I know of that'd turn a ball from my heart."

"You've come from Natal?" Elise could scarcely believe it.

Coffee spoke lightly, but there was a strain underlying his manner.

"And glad to be here, lass."

Elise was plagued by a dozen questions she needed to ask, vaguely realizing that Coffee's presence on the veldt could be dangerous for Matthew, and more importantly, be placing her life in jeopardy. Coffee had always proved to be an amenable guest in the past, and his stories of his service life in India had always fascinated her, even though she doubted the veracity of some of them and the delicacy of most of the others. But these past pleasures and his generous gifts counted for little under the present circumstances. Coffee could be a threat to their very existence here on the high veldt, and although Elise cared little if they were forced to leave the farm, the thought of losing everything and having to return home with nothing but the clothes on her back appalled her. If the Commando knew a serving British soldier was beneath their roof they would come and burn them out; worse, they might bring ropes....

Coffee saw Elise's face change, saw the raw self-interest under the empty mask of prettiness, and he pitied Matthew Eastman rather more than he worried for himself. God help Matthew if he sickened or required her shoulder for support. She would lift her skirts and flee any sickbed with an alacrity that would leave any onlooker breathless. For Elise there could be no stained bandages or internal disorders, no sickness or weakness in others she could or would cope with. For her all blooms must be freshly picked and unrusted by blight, all furniture must be unscarred and shining like glass, and all mirrors must reflect only beauty and rich youthfulness; shining images that were ageless and permanent and therefore without pain or hardship.

"But why?" blurted Elise. "Why did you come and put us all at risk? The doctor..." That damned Dutch doctor, she thought. He might smile and be bluff, but he was one of *them* after all. One of those stiff-necked Afrikaners who stuck so closely together and who in their innermost hearts thought of her and Matthew as Uitlanders, outsiders separated by religion and nationality. If only Matthew could see that and leave....

Andries had joined them before Elise realized he had overheard.

"And what risk is that?" he asked, holding his bag of schillings like a boy with a windfall of bonbons. "Why are you so distressed, missie?" He turned to Coffee, frowning. "I trust you have not made some unfortunate remark, sir. Mrs. Eastman's condition is delicate."

Elise's alarm rose to near hysteria. Please don't let him tell the world. Had he no subtlety or breeding?

"I hope not, Dr. Andries." Coffee was firmly dismissive.

"Then what's this risk she spoke of?"

"I'm a British soldier." Coffee watched for a reaction, a hand on his concealed pistol. Andries's smile disarmed him.

"Indeed? I hear your troops are still smarting from Pretorius's attentions. You seem to have lost your uniform as well as control of Port Natal."

"Temporarily I think."

"That could be argued, neh?" Andries squinted up at the sun. "But not in this heat. Will you invite us inside, Mrs. Eastman?"

"You are welcome in this house." Elise gave the automatic response, thinking she wished Andries would go back to Winburg, realizing that if he did and wanted to make mischief there, he could bring the Commando back with him. Wouldn't that be doubly ironic? He had confirmed her unwanted pregnancy and now had the power to lose her her unloved home. Was she to be both swollen with child and destitute? She could see that Coffee was puzzled by her changes of expression, none of which totally mastered her face. Elise held onto the stoep rail, her face in turmoil and her legs turned to water, wanting and hating Matthew in equal and searing proportions.

Coffee was introducing the big Dutchman and she was inviting them to pass inside the house, her head and lashes lowered as she played the demure wife, unable to meet either man's direct gaze as they went through the door.

Coffee took Elise's arm and closed the door behind them, seeing the other men were seated and placing Elise in her favorite chair beside the fireplace where there was always a cool draft when the fire was unlit. The houseboys were serving drinks, dishes of marinated fruit, and fresh biscuits, grinning and anxious to please, glad to see company, especially strangers. They were somewhat cautious with the huge Dutchman, for he said little with dark, watchful eyes and made his chair creak under his weight, answering Dr. Andries's questions in High Dutch, which although guttural was elegant beside the doctor's simplistic Afrikaans.

Elise sipped and nibbled what was handed to her and kept silent, almost unnoticed by everyone but Coffee, who stood beside her waiting for her crisis either to pass or to degenerate into a faint or a screaming fit. Neither happened before there were horses in the yard and veldschoene thumped on the stoep, the door was flung open, and Matthew was there with drawn pistols fanning for a target, while Boie came more quietly from the back of the house with a leveled smoothbore.

Elise almost rose from her chair. Coffee came close to laughing and the Dutchman moved nothing but his eyes. Coffee sobered when he saw the sudden stunned look on Matthew's face as he stared at the Dutchman as though he were the only person in the room. Matthew's arms dropped and the pistols hung forgotten from the ends of his arms.

"Great God," he said in a strangled whisper. "Klyn...."

The Dutchman stood slowly as though he were used to armed men crashing in on him, and he looked Matthew up and down calmly. After a long moment he said:

"And you are Matthew Eastman. We have much to talk about, you and I, I think."

"A drink for your master," ordered Coffee, and a mug of *brandewyn* was pressed on Matthew, who allowed his pistols to be taken, his head moving from side to side. Coffee tilted the mug until Matthew swallowed a good half of it.

"Klyn?" Matthew repeated.

"I am Klyn. You knew my brother, *ja?*"

Matthew draped a ham over an armrest and leaned his elbow on the carved chairback. "Oh yes. I knew him," he said faintly. "Very well."

"I expected a reaction," said Coffee, "but this beats all. Matthew Eastman speechless."

Silently and unnoticed, Elise had begun to weep.

They were lighting their green cigars when Elise excused herself with a convenient headache, fearing that Dr. Andries would congratulate Matthew on the coming birth. She locked herself into the bedroom and stifled her sobs in the pillow, unheard by the men below.

They had eaten hot spiced beef and mountains of vegetables washed down with young local wine. During the conversation it was established the big Dutchman had been the first mate aboard the very ship that had brought the Dutch troublemaker Smellekamp to Port Natal. Klyn had not taken to Smellekamp, and was troubled when he realized that the French captain who brought the ship from Amsterdam clearly agreed with the man's cynical intent to sow discontent among the Natalian Voortrekkers with promises of aid for their embryo Republic from Holland, seeing such an action as a way to bolster their joint attempts to trade in Natal.

Pieter Klyn had held his tongue and temper for as long as he could, confiding his disgust to nobody. Klyn knew full well that Dutch sea power was a thing of the past, and it was the navies of Her Imperial Majesty Queen Victoria that commanded the seas. The Pax Britannica was the order of the day, and where it was true that that control had been in dispute when the Voortrekkers had been on the Cape, a series of crushing defeats had taken place during the period they had taken to the hinterland and cut themselves off from the mainstream of European affairs, so they knew nothing of Holland's reduced state, and would therefore be amenable to any suggestion of aid from that quarter, however baseless it might be in reality.

When the ship had finally sailed over the bar into Port Natal, Klyn had jumped ship with an Egyptian dealer's party, losing himself in the melee of disembarking horses and men. The French captain's intention to take on ivory at Port Natal and to return to Delgoa Bay where he planned to fill his holds with slaves was the last straw for the outraged Pieter Klyn. He had been on one crossing to the Americas aboard a slaver, and had sworn he would never expose himself to such barbarity again. Of the seven hundred men and women they had started with, a bare seventy-two finished the voyage alive, and the ship had never lost its accompanying sharks. The big

Dutchman almost spat when he mentioned the methods used by the Portuguese agent who acted for Cord Laidler, and the way he raided the upper reaches of the Crocodile and the Sabie rivers for healthy youths and maidens.

Matthew tensed when he heard Laidler's name, and he bombarded Pieter with questions, his forgotten cigar dying between his whitened knuckles.

It became clear that Laidler had been dealing with the Portuguese and American slavers for years, underwriting their ships and their forays into the interior, trading his ivory and wine to finance his trade in guns and slaves, holding a virtual monopoly on all such transactions along the western coast. He had consolidated his position so firmly that there was talk of him controlling much of the political life of the Cape Colony as well as much of the trade. As his physical stature had shrunk, so his power had grown until he was almost unassailable.

The sudden death of Katherine's father, Colonel Spenser, had left the opposition headless and divided among themselves, and those who were not drawn within Laidler's sphere of influence went to the wall or quietly left the Cape Colony.

There had been several clandestine petitions to the Governor, Sir George Napier, but although he publicly frowned upon Laidler's activities and quietly compiled a dossier on the man, his other duties and the constant turmoil on the Cape frontier kept him fully occupied. Napier had few Imperial troops at his disposal and they were committed to keeping the peace along the Fish River boundary. The money-grubbing of Cord Laidler and the like was of secondary importance to his primary role of holding the Cape and its ports open for the maritime trade plying between India and Great Britain. So long as Laidler's slaving was carried on outside British territory, there was little that could be done about it, however repugnant it might be to his administration and the ministers of his youthful Queen.

Laidler's ships left the Cape loaded with wine and returned empty; he was far too clever and cautious to have the Excise men find slaves aboard any of his vessels, so that there was more guesswork than proof in any of the allegations made against him. But the whispers grew and left him untouched in his villa, where he lived in splendid solitude with his wife and child. Laidler played the recluse except for two occasions every year when he opened his villa to the public. These balls were attended by everybody of any note since most of Cape society was indebted to Cord Laidler in one way or another and dared not return their invitations with a curt refusal however much they would have liked to do so. He had turned the tables on all of those who had rejected him during the early years, and held many of the older families in thrall as surely as if they were indented servants under the Boers or the Zulu.

He was never seen standing in public and preferred to be pushed about in a wheeled chair by Elias and attended by two strapping blacks who were known as the Praetorian Guard by the more outspoken wags.

All this came as news to Matthew although it was all well known to Coffee, who had deliberately withheld the information, seeing no point in bringing any further unhappiness to the Eastman farm. He knew Matthew would be full of questions about the boy and would not take long to work out the child's age and trace his inception back to the time before the battle of Vegkop. Luckily, the Dutchman had no idea of the boy's age, merely knowing of his existence and that he had been named James Spenser Laidler for his late grandfather.

Coffee ached to change the subject, to bring up his reason for coming to Matthew's farm, but Matthew himself kept on until he had all the information there was to be had repeated at least twice by both Klyn and himself. Coffee hoped he would be far away before Matthew realized there might be more he himself could add to what had already been said. He knew he would be hard put to lie or even pretend ignorance when Matthew started his relentless questions. Whatever Matthew Eastman might be, he was no fool and was capable of surprisingly penetrating insight in some matters, and Coffee did not have the stomach to face any such inquisition.

The heat of the middle of the day had passed and the veldt was stirred by faint breezes when Pieter Klyn asked about the circumstances of his brother's death. Matthew was surprised that Coffee had said nothing about the matter and his face showed it when he looked sharply at the sergeant.

"No, Matthew," said Coffee. "It's your place to tell Pieter, not mine. I've told him as little as seemed decent. Man, he was your closest friend, who could say otherwise?"

"Yes," said Matthew, and the Dutchman hissed softly.

"That's not what I heard on the trail from Natal, Eastman."

Matthew did not understand and said so.

"You know a man named de Villiers?" asked Pieter Klyn.

"Dirk de Villiers?"

"*Ja*. This man is no *vriend* of yours, I think."

Matthew's laugh was short and cold. "No."

Pieter nodded. "We met with his Commando on the trail, and your friend here," his eyes flicked at Coffee, "was not with me any more. I make no speech about that, I am a fugitive myself now. But this man, this de Villiers, had me share his fire and his food for news of the port before I left. I told him not to bother going on, the first of the reinforcements from Grahamstown had arrived. I did not tell him it was only one company of the 27th Foot; I had seen enough killing already, and I wanted them to turn back."

"And that's how you came there?" Matthew asked Coffee, interrupting.

"That's how," Coffee confirmed.

"But I don't understand...."

"Mercy on us, Matthew, let Pieter finish."

"Yes." Matthew ran fingers through his hair.

Pieter Klyn spoke on stolidly as though nothing had stopped his flow.

"There was argument then among the Commando. Man, everybody had an opinion. Should they go, should they go home. There was much drinking and this de Villiers drank much *brandewyn*. His talk was wild. There were others there who confirmed his story, though, all *kerels,* I think."

Matthew rose slowly and said, "Go on."

"He spoke of you and a woman. I use his words when I say she was a whore from Cape Town, a whore who belonged to another man. This man Laidler you have such a hunger to know about. I smell truth here, neh?"

"Matthew," said Coffee, "I swear I knew nothing of this."

"How could you? You were off in the bush where any sensible man would be when faced by a hostile patrol." Matthew's voice was deceptively soft although one fist was clenched and he was balanced on the balls of his feet.

"I tell you this in de Villiers's own words, Eastman, for that is how it came to me."

"You want me to deny this version of the truth, Klyn?"

"A brother is a brother, Eastman, and blood is blood. I saw little of Manfred or my parents when they came to Africa. I was at sea and preferred it that way. Now they are all dead and I am the last of the family. If nothing else, I'll have the truth and lay all the bones to one side with the past."

Manfred, thought Matthew, was that Klyn's name? He said: "De Villiers twists life to suit him. Klyn is dead and only he and I know the truth of how and why. I'll have it stay that way."

"You deny my right to *know?*"

Matthew pointed a finger over his fist.

"I deny you nothing that's yours. I'll only share what's mine when and if I decide to do so. I won't answer any charge Dirk de Villiers brings against me with words, Dutchman. There's only one way to answer him and the likes of him. Understand that."

Pieter Klyn sat in his chair for a long moment and said nothing. He seemed to be weighing worth with invisible scales. His eyes came up at Matthew's with slow deliberation. "If I had meant to kill you, Eastman, I should not have sat at your board and eaten your meat. I should have twisted your neck on an empty stomach. I came to know the truth, and know I will if I leave you nothing but your tongue."

"You threaten a man before his own hearth, menheer," said Andries.

"I will know," said Pieter Klyn. "I think you have enough honor to tell me. Reason says my brother would not have gone into bad country with an *idioot rakker.*"

Matthew searched for a rational reply and knew there was only one.

"There's nothing in words, menheer. Come with me."

"Where?"

"To the truth the only way I can tell it."

Neither man said another word until they were high up the terraces of the lower Blesberg and stood beneath the waterfall, smelling myrtle. When they came down from the stone monument with the night gathering at their backs it had all been said.

3

Katherine thought back to the green and gold room with a miserable shudder of self-contempt as she rehooked her dress in the darkness of her carriage.

She blamed herself for becoming involved with the young Lieutenant of Horse whose apartments overlooked both the bay and Table Mountain, and whose looks and charm covered an inner weakness that bordered on impotence. Katherine had thought she had chosen this current bedfellow with her usual discretion and care, and had hoped he would climax all her accumulated bitterness away, but how wrong she had been.

He had been gauche and brutal where tenderness and experience had been required, and Katherine still shook with rage. She had slapped his hands away and taunted him for his ineptitude and lack of virility, and had been astonished when the fool had wept and begged for her forgiveness and comfort as though she were some surrogate mother.

Katherine had left as quickly as she could with her hair and clothes in some disarray, ordering the startled Elias to drive slowly away through the darker back streets until she had made herself presentable. Since Colonel Spenser's death, Elias had been in Katherine's employ, and apart from these nocturnal excursions, he enjoyed being in her personal service, even if he did have to report Katherine's movements to Baas Laidler. Not that the baas did anything to stop his wife from spreading her skirts among the young blades of the community. Indeed, he seemed to take a perverse pleasure in the fact, and always used the intelligence to his own advantage. Elias did not need a great intellect to see that the baas threw his wife together with any young man whose family connections might be of use to him. More than one father had been faced with his heir's indiscretions by the outraged and cuckolded Laidler, who would demand the termination of the liaison, and, almost as an afterthought, would seek compensation in the form of a block vote swung in his favor, or the promise of a business tender at an advantageous rate. Few thought of refusing and secretly wished that they had been as fortunate with the beautiful Katherine as their errant sons or nephews.

The more the disillusioned Katherine tried to find some fleeting happiness, the more Cord used her affairs to his own advantage, first bringing a likely candidate to her attention, and then parting her from him when his purpose was fulfilled. Young men were abruptly sent up-country or posted on foreign duty with little or no time to make their goodbyes, and few of them suspected the reason for their sudden departure from the Cape Colony.

Katherine was sometimes puzzled by these sudden disappearances, but was soon distracted by the arrival of some fresh and appealing face. There was little gossip, and most of that was within the family circles of those men who preferred silent discretion to an open scandal. The moral climate had changed radically since Victoria had come to the throne, and the easier days of King George and those of his despised successor, William of Hanover, had been swept away by an upsurge of sobriety and decency. Like any other provincial society, the Cape Colonists rushed to ape the manners and mores of the Imperial Court. Bosoms were cut higher and skirts trailed the ground as more staid dance steps replaced the earlier more lively ones.

It was in this stifling atmosphere that Katherine was trapped, and despite the massive compensation of wealth and power, she found herself thinking back more and more to those hard, free months on the veldt before her son was born. Her memories had mellowed with time until she had refined them to days filled with sun and space and the ability to say and do whatever she had wanted to. She hardly ever allowed herself to think of Matthew Eastman or the life she might have shared with him had she not chosen to stay with Cord. Although she was still as self-willed and selfish as she always had been, she was devoted to her son, and was determined he should inherit both the Laidler name and fortune, and was careful not to alienate Cord entirely. She would not see Jamie start in the gutter like Cord, or scratch the dirt for a living like the man who had fathered him. She secretly believed that Matthew would have agreed with her about the boy's future had he known of Jamie's existence, and deluded herself by constant repetition until she had come to believe her own lies.

Katherine never expected to see or hear from Matthew again, and felt there was no danger of ever facing him with the son he must recognize as his own. Jamie was so like Matthew in temperament and looks that there were times when Katherine thought Cord must be blind not to see it. She had caught him contemplating the boy on occasion, but he was never anything but pleasant to the child, and generosity itself when the occasion demanded or warranted it, although there was never any real warmth in his manner. But then Cord was cool with everybody at all times, so it was hardly surprising that he treated Jamie in a like fashion. It was Cord's way and must be suffered by anybody who came in contact with him. Only with the Griquas and his black agents did he relax, and would laugh and drink through the night with them, exchanging reminiscences of earlier, wilder days only they had shared with him. Katherine always left the house on these occasions, and would return to find litter and chaos everywhere which would take the staff days to clear, making them rebellious and sulky in turn, for Cord's temper would be uncertain as the drink left him, and he would think nothing of ordering Elias or one of his two guards to whip a tardy servant.

Katherine could not imagine why Cord kept such men as the Griquas in his employ; none of them worked at any of the vineyards or warehouses on the Cape, but came and went at irregular intervals, full of talk of Delgoa Bay and hunting trips to the interior. What they hunted, Katherine could not imagine, and she had never had a satisfactory answer from Cord. He would grin his shrunken grin and talk of gryphons and camelopards, his eyes glittering in their hollows, his bony hands gripping and regripping themselves as though he were oiling his palms with money. His hair was honey streaked with silver and his skin was coarse-grained over jutting bone, for he ate little and drank much and stayed at his desk for long hours. His other appetites had also diminished and he only visited Katherine's boudoir on the first Monday of every month in a ritual claim of his conjugal rights, something he enjoyed little and something Katherine endured. Money-making was Cord's mistress and market manipulation was his wife.

Katherine smoothed the front of her dress and leaned back against the leather upholstery to stare at the back of Elias's thick, rolled neck. She would have dearly liked to have a confidant to share tea and gossip with, but there was nobody she either trusted or liked enough. She was grindingly lonely and desperately bored, for she found the men pompous and the women dull. Only when she discussed Jamie did her countenance lighten and her talk become animated; otherwise she might have been carved from soapstone when she attended any social function, preferring to sit apart as her husband did, accepting few dances even though her feet itched to tap and glide over the marble floor with a strong arm around her waist. To whirl and spin with somebody who admired her for herself and not as the alternative first lady of the Colony, second only in power and status to the Governor's wife herself. Katherine's prestigious position brought her little joy and less satisfaction. She was tired of the small affairs she had drummed up for herself, and the notion of taking another lover had palled. This last evening had left her soured and determined not to expose herself to anything of the kind ever again. All the secrecy and the attendant intrigue were just not worth a few moments of transient pleasure, and this last farcical evening would stay in her mind for many nights to come.

No, Katherine decided, no more, no more....

An overwhelming sense of isolation brought tears to her eyes and the night air became suffocating and close. The long years seemed to stretch before her in a long parade of dull sameness that would age and dry her until she too sat in line with the other sharp-tongued matrons who flowered the walls during the season, criticizing all that was young and fashionable from behind their black fans, taking revenge for their lost years by blanket disapproval of everyone and everything about them. When there were no other targets they turned on their own and none of them dared to leave the circle early for fear of becoming the butt of some cruel collective gossip.

A small raw flame burned in Katherine's throat and she mewed quietly without realizing she had uttered a sound. Elias heard, and his yellow eyes widened as he stole a look over his shoulder. Sure enough, Missie Katherine was crying like a lost kitten and Elias's mouth popped open at the sight. Ach, man, she was made from iron hoops and ship's timbers, she didn't cry for no small thing. She was tougher than the old Baas Colonel, and he had been a white lion that nobody barked back at.

Elias brought the carriage to a halt and lowered his big body to the ground, at a loss to know what to do. He could not take Missie Katherine home in this condition for all the houseboys to see. And if the baas saw, there would be a ring around the moon and rain on the sun. He would question Elias until his kinky hair straightened and fell over his eyes like a black waterfall. Elias hated the baas, and he had thought of running for the bush many times. But there was nowhere to go any more. Elias knew the Zulu would give him short shrift if he made for the high veldt. He leaned into the carriage and cleared his throat.

"Missie Katherine? You want Elias to run fetch some water, maybe a sip of wine? They's houses near who knows us. Just you tell Elias what you want."

Katherine raised her head and her eyes were luminous in the crisp moonlight. "What?"

"A sip of wine take the lump from your throat."

"Elias, you're a fool."

"Yaas, Missie. Thass true."

"And I am a bigger fool." Katherine dabbed at her eye with a fold of linen.

"Yaas, Missie. Except you ain't. Old Elias the fool round here." Elias was glad the Missie was showing some fire, and he praised the Christmas Christ and the all-seeing Mwari for it. Maybe that young baas soldier had been cruel bad to the Missie and done bad things with her, he thought, his lower lip jutting. Elias would twist his head off and give it to the jackals. The Missie should only go with the big chiefs of the red soldiers if she had to go with anyone at all, not waste herself on boys with no plumes to their helmets. Chiefs made big presents of horses and hard green beads to the women they bedded, and green was the Missie's favorite color.

"No, Elias," said Katherine, her voice stronger, her chin up. "You're just stupid. It takes a clever woman to be a fool."

Elias grinned happily. He understood insults.

"Yaas, Missie."

"You will not be taking me to that house again, Elias. In fact, you won't be taking me to any other houses at night. If I ask, you will refuse. Do you understand?"

"Yaas, Missie. Except you don't ever let me no you. You certain sure as positive you want old Elias t'do that?"

"Certain sure."

"Then you tell me again in the morning, Missie, when I knows there ain't no juju make you talk so. Then I'll know it's certain sure."

"Very well, you elephant. I'll tell you again in the morning."

Elias slapped his thigh, his opened mouth a pink tunnel in his black face.

"Elias can't be no elephant, Missie. Elephants is praise names of Zulu kings. You make a joke on Elias. You want I should drive around for a while?"

"Straight home. I'm very tired."

"Yaas, Missie Katherine. You set back and take your ease. I'll jog them horses real gentle so's you can nap."

Elias climbed back onto the driving box and gathered the lines, thinking the night was filled with miracles. First the Missie came away from her man early, then she cried tears, then she says she never going back. And she called Elias an elephant. It was a great compliment he would try to deserve. For once, he would not tell Baas Laidler what the Missie had done or say where she had been. Unwittingly, Katherine had gained an ally, and one who would stand her in good stead.

As Elias carried Katherine's sleeping form up the back stairs and along the deserted passages to her boudoir, the man in the green and gold room signed his name to the long, hysterical letter he had written, drained a last glass of brandy, and threw himself from the upper verandah to the rock garden below, killing himself instantly.

A gust of wind from the opened window caught the letter and blew it from the writing table, skimming it beneath the low chaise longue in the center of the room, where it was to lie hidden until the executors of the young man's estate had the furniture removed and sold at auction several weeks later.

4

The house was in darkness save for a single lamp, and the three men sat on the stoep, unwilling to leave the day behind. The cicadas and night birds filled the night with their chorusing and the cigar smoke rose into the thatch without a kink.

They had talked of many things in the balmy dusk, and only Coffee seemed to have little to say, as if he were shy of Dr. Andries's presence. For a while, this silence had puzzled Matthew, but he had soon realized the reason for Coffee's reticence when he pieced all the snippets together. Then he too wished that Andries's visit had not coincided with that of the two other men. He need not have worried, for Dr. Andries suddenly said:

"You will have seen the turmoil in Port Natal at first hand, Sergeant Coffee. I should be interested to hear your view of things as they stand at present. Some of our people on the high veldt would put a ball through your heart without a second's thought, but you have nothing to fear from me. I'll grind no ax on a borrowed stone. The Natalians have brought this fight upon their own heads, and wish to embroil us in this stand against the British. I'm for standing back to see how it goes, for as long as we of the Blesberg mind our own business, the British will leave us in peace."

"You sound convinced of that," Coffee said dryly.

"I am. Her Imperial Majesty won't squander her soldiers holding down a territory that can offer no wealth. There are never soldiers where there's no profit, neh?"

"That's politics, Doctor. I'm a simple soldier and don't understand these things. The 27th was sent into Durban to stop the constant upheaval within Natal."

Andries laughed. "That's a lie, a good lie, but a lie nonetheless. You're no simpleton and you know more than you admit to. You slipped out of Port Natal to see how things stand here among the British and the Dutch settlers, neh?"

"Slipping out isn't how I'd describe it," said Coffee. "But if I had, what would you tell me?"

"I'd tell you to travel with your collar up so the Commando can't see your red neck."

"Anything else?"

"Don't call Port Natal Durban. You British named it that to honor the last Cape Governor, a man who had never set foot there. To us it's Port Natal, and you calling it anything else shows you up as Uitlander."

"Well, that's plain speaking if you like."

"And here's plainer. Tell the British not to come to the high veldt unless they're prepared to kill us to a man. If the Natalians pull back from the coast and come here, we'll close ranks and be brothers again. A common enemy will always unite us and we'll never again submit to Cape law."

"You'd be cutting yourself off from the eastern seaboard."

"We'll use Delgoa Bay, and there's nothing you can do about that. The Portuguese flag flies there, and the Portuguese are your allies."

Coffee looked down at his cigar. "You're missing the point of what's happening at Port Natal. I got out of there by the skin of my teeth, and I don't think de Villiers or Jan Mocke would have let me live if they'd known I was within shooting distance of their camp. Ask Klyn here."

"It's true," Pieter affirmed. "They'd have nailed him up and shot him."

"And," said Coffee, "they're high-veldters, people from hereabouts. You're not as insular as you like to think. Give two Boers a watch apiece and they'll fight over whose has the louder tick without giving a damn whether they keep good time or not. You're your own worst enemies. You'll react before you think, and by heavens, now you'll have to think bloody hard."

Andries started to speak and Coffee talked over him.

"I was with a foraging party when Pretorius drove the British out of Congella. You know where that is, Matthew? Pretorius had forted up there and the British commander waltzed in to teach him a lesson. He got it back in spades and had to pull back to the camp at Port Natal. For all I know, he's still there with snipers all around him. The Boers ran off all the livestock and have left the garrison without meat or any means of transport. That's bad enough, but there are women and children inside the stockade. If too many of them die, you'll see more troop transports rounding the bar than you'd wish for."

Andries looked impatient. "Meaning, I suppose, that the British retaliation will be massive. We know about massacres, Sergeant. You should have seen what the Zulu did to our people at Weenen. Ten children cut to pieces in a single wagon, a fetus ripped from its mother's womb and dashed against a wheel. A baby speared and tossed onto its mother's hacked-off breasts. I know of a thirteen-year-old boy who survived thirteen separate *iKlwa* wounds. But I see your point, although you should make your speech to Pretorius. It's his problem, not ours."

"He's leading your people, Doctor. Damnation, you make him sound like the head of another nation. Don't you see you're holding two conflicting views? On the one hand you declare yourself a nation, and on the other, you take no responsibility for what Pretorius is doing."

"I don't. On this issue he's alone. Only one Commando group under Jan Mocke has gone to join Pretorius. We follow Hendrik Potgieter, and he was called a coward in public because he wouldn't advance into Zulu territory. Potgieter saw what taking Natal from the clans would lead to, and wisely stayed here. Let Natal save Natal."

"And you'll sit here and let them go to glory in their own sweet way. Man, you think like an ostrich. Out of sight, out of mind." Coffee's face had reddened, darker than his hair.

Andries lost the dimple in his smile. "Better sand in my eyes than defend a flag for a sovereign's shilling. Keep to the sea and leave us the land. You British'll annex any sandbar you can tie a skiff to, so long as it's in rowing distance of India. We took this land by our own force of arms and we'll keep it. Don't you realize you British also see the world with two sets of eyes? You jump to recognize any black despot who rules his clans with total disregard for human life. And yet we, who are Christians, are denied the right to govern our own kaffirs, even though we're more enlightened than any of the black kings your Queen sends gifts to."

"You're letting Pretorius bring you to war." Coffee showed disgust.

"What would you have us do, fight the Natalians for you?"

303

"You could have counseled them against attacking the garrison. That would have achieved something."

"For whom?" Andries looked puzzled and cross. "Nothing would suit you better than to see the Voortrekkers at one another's throats. Man, we may disagree, but open conflict? Never. Two hundred of our Commando went to help the Natalians. They ride horses supplied by neighbors who couldn't go, they eat victuals given by men who think them fools, and are armed by others who care nothing for their reasons. Whatever our internal squabbles, we're united against you or any other nation who tries to oppress us."

Coffee stared at Matthew. "And you?"

Matthew flung his cigar into the night with a straight forearm. "Take loaves and fishes to the British garrison, you mean?"

"Something like that."

"No," said Matthew shortly. "My barns would be burned before I'd loaded a wagon. I'd lose everything, and for what? I agree with Andries; if the British came here I'd fight them. We're all through running, there's nowhere else to go. We trekked here and took this land from the Matabele with no help from the Queen's soldiers, and Pretorius took Natal from the Zulu. Where were the red soldiers then, Coffee? I'll tell you, making and remaking treaties with the Xhosa along the Fish. Man, I don't agree with all my neighbors say and do, but they mean more to me than any soldier from Wales or Scotland. I've never even *seen* the old country. I was born here in Africa, and it's my home as much as it's the home of any kaffir you care to name. We took this land from Mzilikazi just as he took it from somebody else before me. Damn, I'll wager that's been going on forever on the veldt. If somebody thinks he's strong enough to kill me for my farm, he's welcome to try. But no foreign royal is going to dispossess me by slapping a seal on a decree."

"So you'll do nothing." Coffee seemed bitterly disappointed.

"What for? As you said, the British will probably come to Natal and stay. What could I do to stop that?"

"And your neighbors. Do they think the same?"

"Ask them." Matthew seemed to lose interest.

Andries laughed through smoke. "Such questions will earn you a ball in the ribs, Sergeant. And I'd have to cut it out." He looked thoughtful. "That's if they'd let me. It's academic anyway, they don't shoot to wound."

304

Coffee almost sneered. "The old cliché. You're all marksmen, and can ride a thousand miles a day on a sick horse. I've heard the boasts." Coffee lit a fresh cigar and swallowed smoke along with his brandy.

Andries touched Coffee's knee. "Cliché, *vriend*? D'you know how the Boers train their sons to hunt game? Each boy is given a musket and a single ball, and sent out on foot, charged with bringing back both his quarry and the ball he shot it with. To come back without either earns a serious switching. They learn not to miss very quickly." Andries leaned back comfortably.

Coffee found himself smiling. "A nice story, Doctor."

Matthew wiped his face clean when he flatly said, "Believe it."

Coffee became thoughtful. He had been told what he least wanted to hear, and he knew he had been mistaken about what he had supposed Matthew Eastman's view of the situation would be; perhaps more important, where Eastman's allegiance lay.

All he and the farmer really shared was a common language and no more. Coffee was a foreigner in a land he neither liked nor truly understood, and the polarity of views expressed by those on the Cape and these hinterlanders was as marked as the skins of black and white. It seemed they had never understood one another, and grew further apart as each year passed. Whoever was charged with bringing the two disparate cultures together would have more than tough mutton on his plate to chew. Coffee was glad he wouldn't be the one to do it, and fervently hoped he wouldn't be seconded to the staff of the man who was landed with the commission. He stretched himself and perched on the stoep rail, suddenly anxious to get some sleep.

"May I ask a favor, Matthew?" he said.

Matthew slapped his thigh. "Man, you sound like a man who's just walked away from a friend. My house is still yours, you'll never be a stranger here. What do you want? Name it."

"I still have to get back to Durban—sorry, Port Natal." Coffee winked tiredly at Andries. "I'll need to travel fast to avoid any patrols. Will you give me one of your boys as a guide? I'd like Boie, but I know you'll say no to that."

"And you'd be right. You'll have your guide. What will you do if you can't get through to Natal?"

"Swing south toward Grahamstown, I suppose. One of the

English settlers set off for there to get help from the garrison Let's hope he got through."

"We'll say amen to that, eh, Doctor?" asked Matthew.

Andries nodded slowly, too concerned to smile. "Make th British understand us, neh?"

Coffee yawned and said, "Politicians is politicians. An soldiers is soldiers. I've got more chance of explaining th innards of a steam engine to a Hottentot than of getting thos Civil Servants to see past the Fish River frontier. They think as different as you can imagine. But I'll do what I can. Now I'll take myself off to my bed in the barn. I've got to chec how my San are bedded."

Klyn rose to his full height and shrugged his huge shoul ders. He had been so quiet they had forgotten he was there

"To think that these Dutch terriers came from the lan of tulips and windmills. Ach, always it seems the hottes blood, like the finest wines, travels best. Maybe Holland ha lost the seas and has won a continent. It will be interestin to watch, I think."

"So, Pieter," Coffee said. "You do intend to stay here." I was a statement.

"It seems so, yes." Klyn sounded surprised by himself "These open lands are much like the ocean. The grass roll like the waves when the wind quarters. With a compass an the stars I may just navigate my way around." He smiled a slow smile that split his beard.

Matthew's chest was constricted by memories of th brother and the recognition of just how much he still misse his dead friend. Then, to make matters worse for him, ther came a poignant flash of long red hair and two intent viole eyes he damned for brushing so close to the present and open ing ancient wounds he thought had scarred over.

Matthew made his goodnights and climbed the stairs t bed. His sleep was deviled by visions of Kit's child, and mor strangely, by the sound of Elise crying close to his ear a though it were real and not a part of his dream.

5

Dirk watched the British fort through his spyglass.

A Union Jack snapped above the triangular stockade and the late afternoon sun picked out the howitzers and field-pieces guarding the flanks of the sloping earthworks. It was galling for Dirk to see how the soldiers were no longer keeping their heads down now that the relief ships were anchored off the treacherous harbor bar. Dirk lowered his glass and spat into the slack tidal water lapping the sandspit at his feet, remembering how different the situation had been a bare month before.

When Captain Thomas Charlton Smith had brought his weary column into Port Natal, his small mixed force had seemed to be no real threat to the republican cause at all. His infantry, engineers, and artillerymen numbered a mere 260 combatants, and were all but outnumbered by their many dependents and servants. Two of the officers' wives had been delivered of children during the hard journey, and the men were footsore from marching on the abrasive sand of the coastal strip. They had crossed more than a hundred rivers and had been forced to make inland detours around the many outcrops that barred the seashore. And to make matters worse on the journey, they had too few oxen to pull their sixty wagons effectively.

Smith had finally passed through Congella, which had been abandoned by Pretorius, and had set up his fortified position on the northern shore of the bay, where his guns could command the settlement of Durban a bare mile inland.

Smith's first and subsequent communications with the Boers made it clear he regarded them as rebellious British subjects who must submit to his authority. His reaction to the treaty of friendship drawn up for Pretorius and the Volksraad by the plainly mischievous Smellekamp was a haughty sniff of disdain. A dedicated though penniless career officer who had no chance of buying himself a promotion, Smith had seen action at Waterloo and was nobody's fool; he knew a specious document when he saw one. Pretorius went back to Congella and Smith sat tight in his overcrowded fort, both men seemingly convinced that time would make the other side see reason.

This situation began to change when a group of mounted Boers rode through the British ranks to insult the soldiers. Smith's short temper began to simmer dangerously, and he threatened to sweep the Boers from Congella if they did not mend their manners. The fact that his position weakened daily in direct contrast to Pretorius's, whose ranks had swelled to over six hundred fighting men, did nothing to deter him from his threatened course of action.

Several days later, two coastal trading vessels with shallow draft, the *Mazeppa* and the *Pilot,* cleared the bar and sailed into the port, bringing the British commander two more fieldpieces and badly needed provisions. To force Smith's hand, Pretorius ran off all the fort's oxen, setting the entire garrison afoot. In reply, Smith mounted a hasty night assault with most of his force and two howitzers. Unfortunately for him, the one mounted aboard a scow grounded on a sandbar, too far away to give him supporting fire, and he lost the other piece when the artillery oxen kicked their traces during the opening fusillades. His men were easy targets, lit as they were by a full May moon, and they were met by fierce fire from the Boers' massed musketry. The troops tried to reply, but their shooting was ineffective against men who were hidden by the crowding mangrove trees. Firmly repulsed, Smith fell back with a score dead and over thirty wounded, and was forced to bury his dead under a flag of truce.

Most of the British settlers had taken refuge aboard the two traders, and Smith summoned one of them, a young Zulu-speaking Briton named Dick King, and asked him to ride to Grahamstown for help. King agreed, and set out with two horses and his Zulu retainer, Ndongeni. Towing the horses behind them, the two men rowed to Salisbury Island, where they saddled up and waded across the narrow channel to the mainland, setting off for Grahamstown over six hundred miles to the south, and pursued by a Commando group led by Dirk.

Dirk and his group had only arrived the day before and their horses were not rested enough for hard pursuit. He lost King and Ndongeni and was reluctantly forced to turn back to Congella. What he and his Commando never knew was that a Zulu friendly to King had obliterated their spoor and laid a false trail. Pretorius had not been pleased when Dirk had brought his blown horses back with the news of King's escape, and he resolved to attack Smith's fort immediately. The Boers were beaten off, but Pretorius captured the stores off-loaded on the beach and still awaiting removal to the fort, and sent armed parties out across the bay to capture the *Pilot* and the *Mazeppa*. This was achieved and the Boers took the ship's officers prisoner, sending them off to Pietermaritzburg as hostages. The loss of the precious stores had been a blow to Smith; he had over five hundred people crammed inside his fort, and had to reduce his men to quarter rations.

Thinking he now had the whip hand, Pretorius offered to return the ships to Smith if he would employ them to evacuate his troops and leave Port Natal. Smith prevaricated but finally had his women and children placed aboard the ships, pinning all his hopes on King, who had made the ride to Grahamstown in an incredible nine days, a journey that usually took three times that. The military commander of Grahamstown sent a company of the 27th Foot, the only troops he had, to Natal aboard the *Conch,* and sent news of the insurrection to Cape Town.

The siege dragged on. Smith could not risk another assault, and the Boers were hamstrung by the lack of powder and ball to mount another major attack. The stalemate was beginning to favor Smith so long as he could hang on.

On June 10, one of the settlers made a run for the open sea. He boarded the *Mazeppa,* cut her cable, and took the schooner over the bar toward Delgoa Bay, where he hoped to find a patrolling naval frigate. The Boers set up a heavy fire but the *Mazeppa* made off out of range and then out of sight, carrying the women and children to safety. Pretorius had not posted guards aboard the ships, and was kicking himself for the oversight. Dirk would have liked to have used his boots on the Boer commander himself, and was not alone in that. Dirk could see the beginning of the end for the Republic, and only kept his Commando in the port to avoid being charged with cowardice.

Now, two weeks later, here were the relief ships in the bay. The tiny *Conch* had arrived first, followed by HMS *Southampton,* loaded to the gunwales with troops and artillery.

Dirk scuffed the sand and unearthed a brilliant pink shell. He picked it up and shied it out across the water, skipping it off the waves. The soldiers were climbing down into longboats ready to be ferried ashore. The frigates' gunports were open and the cannon had been run out to cover the landing. Dirk snorted; there was no real need, he had less than a dozen rounds and enough powder left to fire less than half that number. Despite himself, he thought of Matthew Eastman's remarks at the last Volksraad meeting they had both attended, when he had said there would be no arms without tax collection, no common policy without agreement among the United Laagers. United Nothing, thought Dirk. I'm tired of all this nonsense. I'd rather be up-country where a man can live his own life, make his own decisions, and not forever be waiting for a hundred other people to never make up their minds. I'll never go back to farming, back to the problems of rinderpest and drought, kicking black backsides to get a day's work done. Man, the old father was talking about cotton, *cotton,* rows and rows of grubby white fluff and hundreds of kaffirs to pick it and bale it. There was nothing *manly* in that. Fine for an old man to watch over the crops from a rocking chair, an old man like Abraham, but not for him, not for Dirk de Villiers. So what if they were growing millions of acres of the stuff in the Americas? So what if the British mills would take all a man could grow? Dirk would not deal with the bastard *rooineks,* take their silver and rot watching fields of fluff on stalks. The Americans were taking slaves out of Delgoa Bay every month for their cotton plantations, and the Portuguese and Arabs were coining money hand over fist, just for rounding up Kaffir. *Man, I could do that....*

Dirk felt sweat pop out all over his face as the thought struck a dark and hidden thing inside him. Man, he *could* do that. Why in the name of heaven hadn't he thought of it before? Beyond the Drakensbergs he could take what he wanted, whole kraals if he were of a mind. And who was there up-country to tell him no? The Portuguese didn't give a tinker's groat what a man did so long as they had their palms greased. There were no rules, no red soldiers or *kerks,* no Predikants and Bible stories. No law. None, save any Dirk wished to impose. He knew clan chiefs who would hand over half their tribes for a bolt of cloth and a rusty musket. He could have a seraglio bigger than old Mzilikazi himself.

Drenched now, his hands trembling, Dirk turned away and led his horse through the mangroves. The soldiers had come and the administrators wouldn't be far behind. They'd make Pretorius eat his damned Dutch treaty before they more than likely hanged him from his own tree. Jan Mocke would take his Commando back to the high veldt, and Mpande was wily enough to know his vassalage under the Natalians was at an end. He would fall in with the British and bring his impi over to them. The Zulu and the British together...the Voortrekkers had no way of standing up to them. Natal was finished, and the Blesberg meant cotton and being a dutiful son to old Abraham. Not while there was still some guts behind his navel, some iron in his craw, Dirk promised himself. He would live off the kaffir, just as the Old Testament meant he should. He would have the black tribes of Ham bend to his will and be rich off their backs.

When he had cleared the trees, Dirk mounted up and walked his gray into Congella. Men were already making plans to move out and to pull back to Pietermaritzburg. The horse corrals teemed with men and their saddles, and men hung over the rails, arguing about the future and what Pretorius meant to do. Just as always, thought Dirk, talk and more talk, men dividing into factions, ready to fight, ready to run, ready to chew a point to death just for the pleasure of making a point over the opposite view of one's neighbor. The waste and futility of it rubbed Dirk's temper raw.

He found most of his Commando group stowing their gear into their saddlepacks and giving their mounts a final curry before setting out for the journey back to the high veldt. The talk was that Mocke had already left for Pietermaritzburg to tell the Volksraad how to argue their case with the British. There was also talk of the British intent to ask for scapegoats to be handed over for their justice.

Talk, talk, talk....

"They'll more than likely want your hide, Dirk."

"What?" Dirk came out of his reverie to stare at a ring of grinning faces.

"Sure, man, you were there when we looted the *Pilot*'s stores. Man, they'll stretch your neck."

"And who'll be the man to hand me over?" Dirk snapped.

"None of us, man.... Ach, Dirk, the Volksraad, they'd be the ones...." The protests were many and jumbled.

"The question still stands, neh, *kerels?* Who'll be the one to act for the talkers in Pietermaritzburg? Who'll play the Judas goat for the Natalians? We fought for them, and you're saying they'd hand over a high-veldter to the *rooinek* hangman? *Kaffir.*" Dirk laid his whip over his forearm and stared the group down.

"Best we were gone, neh, Dirk?" It was Jan Mocke on a lathered chestnut. "Time we thought of our own people. This is finished here." His round, grizzled face was dark and angry. "They say the Volksraad will invite the English commissioner to address them and give him safe-conduct. They think they can talk for lack of powder. There's a rumor that Smellekamp was arrested before he got to the Cape with his treaty." He wiped his neck with a grimy neckerchief and his saddle creaked as he shifted his weight. "I don't know how true it is, but it's the word."

"If rumors were bullets, menheer," said Dirk.

"Ha, well said." Mocke blew dust from his nose. "Ride with me, Dirk. I have words for you." He wheeled about and rode off a way and waited for Dirk to walk his gray in beside him.

311

"Go straight home, Dirk. The Volksraad will give up anybody the English ask for now. Many are already leaving rather than be involved in a surrender to Cape rule. Be one of those. And, God help me for being the one to tell you, a kaffir runner came with a message from Winburg. It was so greasy I couldn't make out the words on the outside fold. It was for you, man. Your father...ach, read it for yourself." He held out the note for Dirk to take.

He read Matthew Eastman's big characters slowly, stumbling over them more than once, going back over the convolute sentences until he had boiled the flowery regrets into a simple message. Old Abraham had suffered a heart attack and was not expected to last too long. Dirk must come at once. The note was over fourteen days old. His father could have been under the ground for half that already. Dirk made a fist around the greasy paper and stared out at the troop transports, feeling more than hatred and less than sorrow.

"Eastman," he said quietly. Of all the people in the world, it had to be *him, Eastman,* who gave him the news of his father's death. There would be an accounting for that; it was as if the Englishman had stolen his father's last hours from him, denying Dirk his rights as a son.

"Ja," said Mocke, misunderstanding what Dirk had said. "You go east as fast as you can. Fly, *kerel.*"

Dirk did not answer. His fury was redder than the far uniforms in the ferryboats. He had begun to shake all over.

"Tell them," Dirk jerked his head at the mounting Commando, "to keep up. If they *can.*" And he set his spurs savagely, starting his horse toward the outskirts of town.

BOOK SIX

1

Elise sat herself in the stoep rocker and contemplated her swelling belly. She was halfway through her confinement and she felt as big and as clumsy as a calving mare. Her feet and ankles were swollen much of the time and her mounting appetite nagged at her all the day and half the night. Elise scowled and brushed a flying insect from her face.

Freak winds had brought an unseasonal influx of bright blue butterflies, and they were all over the compound and the garden, fluttering against the flyscreens and tangling themselves in hair and mane alike. Matthew had blinkered some of his more highly-strung horses to keep them calm.

At first the butterflies had seemed delightful, but like anything that went on for too long, their novelty had palled for Elise, and she suffered them with varying degrees of impatience, just as she bore the presence of the paralyzed old man in the nursery. Why did he have to collapse here of all places? If he had fallen from his horse on the trail from Winburg he should have been found far too late for medical attention, and should have been conveniently dead and buried by now, instead of being coddled here, turning her house into an infirmary.

It must be eight or nine weeks since old Abraham had laughed over a schooner of beer at the dinner table, choked, paled, and slumped forward with an ashen face. All these interminable weeks of playing nurse to an old man who only had the use of one hand and the right side of his mouth was adding depth to Elise's permanent frown. The old fool's legs were useless and he was disgustingly incontinent, and he should have died but for his unquenchable will to live. Why he held on she could not comprehend; he could barely speak and his mind dwelled in the past, drooling about people and events she knew nothing of and cared nothing for. How she hated the sound of the faltering voice and the keen blue eyes that looked inward most of the time and startled her when they snapped alive in his lucid moments. Elise hated him because he was close to the final darkness, reminding her of her own mortality and the transitory nature of her youthful beauty.

Matthew and Andries would sit at his bedside for hours, happy to let old Abraham ramble where his memories led him, content to sit in silence when he drifted into sleep; shifting him carefully when he felt cramped or his lungs became congested, bathing his wasted limbs with warm water and cleaning away his body waste, accepting his incontinence with patient solicitude. Elise thought she would rather die than have to be tended to in that way.

Surely it could not be true that the old man could not be removed back to town? He had jogged halfway across the continent during his time, and Elise was convinced the short and slow wagon journey to Winburg would not affect the old goat. His heart had sounded as strong as her own when she had listened to his chest as he slept. His chest bubbled a little, but sitting in the sun would clear that up if it was allowed, she thought. And what matter if it didn't? There could be no joy in his existence, lying in his own filth without a pillow beneath his head.

Elise recrossed her ankles and watched them blush under the swelling. Andries had said it was water retention or some such nonsense, quite normal of course, but she had been warned not to overdo things. Another conspiracy, she believed, designed to keep her here on the farm and away from the breezes and gentility of Port Elizabeth. How she ached to be with Mother and Pa. To sit and talk for the pleasure of it, to eat things that weren't just basic food. Towering things of cream and crystallized fruit, meringue and maraschino cherries, sugar icing and angelica. And tea that wasn't stewed. From porcelain cups. There had been no tea or coffee in Winburg for weeks. The Dutch drank some ersatz mixture made from cracked corn and flavoring, and it was quite disgusting.

Elise reminded herself not to frown so much; she would only deepen the tiny arrows that had appeared between her brows. She blamed the dry heat of the veldt for that—anybody would squint in the harsh sunlight that parched her skin of natural oil. Another year of such exposure and she would be as dark as any kaffir squatting in a furrow. What would her smart friends on the coast think of her then? She must make Matthew bring her some arsenical powders from Winburg when he next went there; a paste made up from them would whiten her skin and make it smooth again.

Elise was frowning without realizing she did so. Matthew had been to town only twice during the last several weeks, and always returned the same day, so concerned was he that Abraham de Villiers should have company. If she, his wife, were on the farm alone, then Matthew would have happily stayed overnight, she bet herself. As ever, she came second to his friends, his horses, and any damned kaffir with tooth-ache. It was intolerable, and more so now she carried his child.

Elise thought herself surrounded by enemies and indifference. The natives hated her and she felt only antipathy from the neighbors who rolled up with their noisy broods of children and dogs to see how old Abraham was faring.

Elise barely understood the vague world of politics that ruled the contradictory Boers on the high veldt. She had heard of the pass laws and the serious efforts that were being made to evict those clans who tried to reenter their traditional homelands now that Mzilikazi had retreated north. She sympathized with that action so far as it affected her; she neither trusted nor liked the kaffir, and she was puzzled by Matthew's stand when the subject was raised by their visitors. He seemed to believe there was room for more native families in the territory than the *landdrosts* or the Volksraad allowed. The neighbors would point to the lessons of Natal, where the massive influx of the clans saw the harassed Natalians outnumbered by many hundreds to one. That was not to be tolerated here in the Orange Free State, nor to the north in the Transvaal, and the evictions were being ruthlessly carried out by the Commando. There were times, and these were many, when it seemed to Elise that only Matthew's friendship with Abraham de Villiers saved him from more than harsh words. Matthew blithely gave his opinions and watched the tempers around him explode with something close to amused detachment.

Men came and talked of new crops, of flax, red bananas, cotton, tea and arrowroot, of coffee and pineapple. Matthew talked of horses and waited to watch these schemes fail, only advising against them when he thought his word might be heeded. Although he guarded his temper, Matthew did not care to mince his words, reasoning that an opinion stated clearly could not be twisted or misconstrued. He would rather be damned for what he said openly than be censored for what others thought he believed secretly. Elise did not know whether that view worked or not, but it did seem he had his neighbors' respect, however grudgingly given. The Boers recognized any man's right to believe what he wished on any secular subject, but when it came to matters of religious belief, they were less generous. That was one area of possible dispute in which Matthew thankfully did not hold contentious views. To him, God was God, and His works were all around him. Working in the fields was in itself an appreciation of His works. He needed no *kerk* or church to worship in. "Look around," he would say. "All this is God." And the burghers would nod and shake his hand and go away without understanding him, but respecting his eccentric piety all the same.

Elise watched a butterfly batter itself against the screen and sighed. She was hungry again and glumly realized she had eaten a substantial breakfast at daybreak, only ninety minutes before. She slept badly now at night and had taken to rising early, preferring to nap during the afternoon, one of the reasons being that she could avoid sitting with old Abraham through the heat of the day. She was doubly discomfited when she did her turn at his bedside, for apart from the experience itself, she hated the idea of his presence tainting the room where her unborn child would spend the first years of its life. She wondered if she would ever scrub and limewash his odor from the nursery, and toyed with the idea of working on Matthew to have another room built along the garden wall to the rear of the house. The thought of the energy needed to make him do so turned her sigh to an open-mouthed yawn. She had a sudden desire for watermelon smothered in syrup and iced black coffee, and curbed it by thinking of how mountainous she was likely to become.

Matthew was working in the corral, splitting timber for new palings, and he would come to the house for a midday meal, which was something, she supposed. She hated to eat alone, and she felt guilty when she ate too much. Matthew's appetite was so enormous that whatever she ate seemed insignificant beside his intake, which somehow made things easier for her. He would sit upstairs with Abraham too, which would save her plodding upstairs herself. Elise yawned again, and her head drooped onto her breast. Just a short nap....

2

The Commando came out of the sun and into the shadow of the Blesberg.

They had swung north and west at Dirk's order, and had been to the royal kraal of the paramount chief of the Baralong, where Moroko was ordered not to interfere with the action that was about to take place. The genial old chief concurred wisely; he knew what the whites' guns could do to his warriors. A squabble between the whites was their affair, and took precedence over any private treaty he might have

317

with one of their number. He thought of sending a runner to warn the Englishman of the approaching Commando, and decided against it. Not even his fleetest messenger could outpace the Boer horses. Moroko knew of the reputation of the small man who led the fifty Commando; his savagery had earned him the title "Burning Spear," and it would be expedient not to cross him. He also knew that it was a good thing for Dirk that he had fifty men at his back to go against the Englishman. Alone, he would be crushed like a dried old leaf.

Moroko also saw the Commando had a white prisoner tied to his horse. A man with burned hair and blue eyes. He had not been treated well and the rawhide strips that held his wrists had bitten into his flesh. He had been beaten too, and the marks were still on his face. A realist who recognized he would never understand the ways of the Boer, Moroko went back into his kraal and put the matter from his mind. The welfare of his clan came first.

Dirk had passed Winburg during the night and had camped far from the town, unwilling to have his presence on the high veldt known before he had done what he came to do. When that was accomplished, he would go to pay his respects at his father's graveside, and not before. He meant to arrive at the Eastman farm with the sun at his back, certain that no warning went ahead of him.

3

Matthew drove the wedge into the log with the heel of the ax and watched it split true. He enjoyed using his muscles and feeling the sun through his shirt. Every blow consolidated his place on the veldt, made his holding stronger, more permanent. Every stake he erected, every nail he drove, was for his son and perhaps for his son's son. It was a good thought, and Matthew was impatient for November, when the baby was due. Time and again he had made Andries promise to be on hand for the birth, trying out names on him and Abraham until their heads spun. Always they knew he would come back to his first choice, Jonathan.

Matthew cut the ax into the ground and took a long swallow from his waterskin. He had the best water for miles around, his horses were known throughout the territory, and the future seemed assured. For luck, he touched the log he was about to split. He had picked up the habit of never speak-

318

ing about his luck; the boys set great store by it, Boie particularly, although he always sought out a living tree to touch if his luck was mentioned. Trees stood in the earth and their roots were a part of the old mud father; a fence post was just a dead stick with no connection with the earth's heart.

Matthew envied Boie his son, impatient to hold his own and teach him all there was to know, from numbering his fingers to choosing the right bit for a soft-mouthed mare. He would see his farm with new eyes each time his son saw something fresh; would have to find the right words to explain, so the boy grew to respect what they had and learned how to make it work for him, working with the land rather than against it.

Even now, Boie had his boy off in the high ground, showing him how to recognize the edible roots, where the fattest berries grew, how to find an underground spring and draw it up with a hollow straw through a borehole. Things the boy needed to know in order to survive as his people had survived for a thousand centuries. Matthew wanted to do that so badly, he could almost taste it.

He rinsed water around his palate and spat it out.

Horses were coming out of the shimmering haze in line abreast and alarm set Matthew into motion. He dropped the waterskin and grabbed up his smoothbore from where it leaned against the fence, wondering why there had been no warning from any of his boys up on the high pasture. The riders were all around him and he had no chance to scan the slopes. There were at least twenty guns trained on him and he heard other horses coming in all around the compound. Matthew's heart knocked less when he saw they were Commando, but he wondered why they had taken so much care to come up on him with such secrecy. Somebody's damned silly idea of humor, he supposed; Boer jokes revolved about lower parts of the anatomy with a good deal of thigh-slapping thrown in. Basic and earthy.

Matthew looked for faces he might know, and saw one or two he knew vaguely, trying to place them alongside a family name. And why the drawn guns? They had come in as they did when clearing an illegal kraal. A gun prodded his back and a horse crowded him, breathing hotly against his face.

"Let the gun drop, man." The gun dug at Matthew's spine.

"On my own land?" Matthew roared, alarm turning to outrage. His head was butted and a hide whip cracked his cheek open. He staggered, took a step bowed forward, and

319

watched his own blood spatter his boots. Matthew swung at the nearest rider and hauled him from the saddle, driving a fist into the man's neck a moment before he was knocked to the ground and smothered by men. He smelled trail sweat and dust, tasted blood when a fist took him in the jaw, lost his breath when he was kicked in the lower chest. He was down on his knees, his arms twisted up his back, his head held savagely by the hair. There was grit in his eyes and taking breath hurt, forcing him to sip air through gritted teeth. He must clear his head and work this puzzle through to find the flaw in its senseless tangles.

And there through the film of dust was Dirk on his gray, leaning on his pommel and sneering his smile as he recoiled his whip, wiping Matthew's blood off on his trousers.

"The charge is treason, Eastman," he said. "Giving aid to an enemy of the state. You're a dead man."

Matthew knew that was not the answer. It just added to the conundrum. If he could swallow the dizziness and stop blood from leaking into his throat he might turn the bends into straight lines. He tried a laugh and a cough spattered more blood. "No," he said, wondering if that made any sense. He tried again. "You're crazy, de Villiers. All of you are."

"I can shoot you or hang you. But first you're going to admit your guilt to the Commando. We know you're guilty, *rooinek,* but the brothers would like to hear you say it." Dirk's whip snapped uncoiled and cut through Matthew's shirt, laying a rib bare. *"Talk,* bastard."

Matthew was lost in brilliant pain. Part of him made vigorous denials. Was Dirk going to cut him into pieces before he knew the way from the maze? He must talk. Think.

"Tell him what he wants to hear, man." The voice was close behind Matthew.

"Can't...." Matthew's left thigh burned cold as the whip cut at it. He was in mist and loops of darker fog, hanging on the arms that now supported him. He found a gap in his memory and realized he must have passed out. There was no strength in his limbs and he was beyond trying to use them. Both trouser legs were slashed open now, he noticed drearily. Dirk could cut the core from an apple with his whip, and Matthew wondered if he meant to blind him.

"Water," ordered Dirk, and it was dribbled over Matthew's head. "Bring up the prisoner."

Somebody else in the maze? Matthew made himself look outward and there was Sergeant Coffee beside Dirk, his face a bruised parody of itself. So that was it. Matthew wondered how Dirk would explain it, how much distortion there would be.

"You know this man, Eastman?"

"He knows me," mumbled Coffee bravely. "But only as a customer. He sold me horses. That's all, horses. He didn't know I was a British..."

Dirk forearmed Coffee from his horse and he fell awkwardly. His wrists were still tied to the saddle, and he hung from the horse, unable to straighten his legs to support himself. His cry was pure agony.

Dirk pointed his whip at Matthew.

"You sold this man horses for the British cause. I recognized your brand. This man came to you out of uniform; that makes him a spy, Eastman. We caught him three weeks ago. He had your horses and one of your kaffir was with him. I shot that bastard myself. His other blacks ran away into the bush." The sneer-smile flitted. "They took no tracking, Eastman, *verstaan?*"

Anger came back to Matthew and he choked on it.

"You understand," said Dirk. "You sold horses to us, and you sold them to the red soldiers. *This* red soldier. He doesn't look so much without his coat, eh?"

Matthew could not talk, something in his throat seemed broken.

"Before I hang the pair of you, I'm going to disperse your kaffirs, Eastman. They're illegals, all of them. And your property is confiscated. But that's not enough for you. I'm going to make you watch me burn you out, then I'll hang you. Him first, then you."

Matthew started to struggle, finding enormous strength from deep within him. He had to tell Dirk about Elise, the baby, old Abraham. *My God, Abraham.* "De Villiers," he bawled, throwing two men from him. "Your father, you have to know...."

"I *know* about my father!" Dirk bored his horse into Matthew and knocked him sprawling in the dust.

Matthew saw the foot swinging at him and tried to twist aside. It caught him on the point of the jaw and he felt his awareness fragment into singing colors. Still he tried to hold on and get to his feet. He almost made it before a second kick laid him unconscious. He did not see the first of the torches catch the bales in the barn, nor the brands that smashed through the house window. He knew nothing of how Elise was pulled out of her rocking chair, still half-asleep, and hurled down the stoep steps, her screams ignored by the Commando. She fell awkwardly and kneeled up clutching her stomach, her face contorted. There were flames in the house thatch before she was able to tell them about the old man on the bed in the back room. By then the fire had taken hold and the house was well alight and beyond saving. It was Dirk who got over his stupefaction first, plunging through the smoke rolling through the front door and finding his way up the stairs to the nursery. Two men followed him inside as the others made a bucket chain to the trough and damped down the passage and the stoep. Horses milled in the compound and the houseboys were running for the high ground, terrified by the madness of the whites. Pyayo and the cook left through the garden and hid themselves in a dry wash where Nkosi Matthew had told them to hide in case of a raid.

Boie's wife, Ndala, slipped away from the distracted whites who had bullied all the Khoikhoi from their huts, and taking her cooking pot, made swiftly for the stone finger where Boie had taken their son. She thought that Nkosi Matthew must be dead, for she had seen the way the whip had opened him to the bone so many times. She had only seen the one they called Burning Spear once; Boie had told her to remember him well. The Khoikhoi knew he looked upon native women like a boar in heat and took them to shame the men when he knew no other whites were near. Ndala had not understood why Boie had not told these things to Nkosi Matthew and forgot her place long enough to ask why. Boie had beaten her as he should when a wife forgets herself. Then he had held her and told her of Nkosi's promise to Burning Spear, explaining how bad it was for a white to kill another white. Ndala had understood then and was especially dutiful from that time on, for she knew Boie would kill Burning Spear if his eyes were cast her way, and that set Boie above other men of their people.

Dirk came out of the smoke, his shirt burned from his back and his father in his arms. They threw dust and a blanket over him as he laid Abraham on the ground, cradling the old man's head in his arms, calling his name, his eyes mad with remorse.

Abraham's eyes were open and he took in the burning buildings with slow blinks, staring when he saw Matthew sprawling in the corral, blinking again when he saw Elise holding her belly in the dust.

"Pa, I didn't know. I swear, I didn't know...."

Abraham licked his mouth and worked his lips together, finding saliva. Then, looking deep into Dirk's haunted eyes, he deliberately spat in his son's face.

"I didn't know, Pa," Dirk yelled, shaking the old man by the shoulders, willing him to understand.

"Stop it man." One of the Commando restrained Dirk.

"Remember," gasped Abraham, his eyes fluttering to white.

"What? What, Pa?"

Half a smile worked Abraham's twisted mouth.

"What, for God's sake?"

"Mzilikazi, Dirk," said Abraham, dying with a frozen grin.

Dirk released the old head and it thumped to the ground as he threw himself upright, retreating from the piercing dead eyes, drawing his pistol and pointing it at the corpse as if in self-defense. It was knocked from his hand and Dirk spun to face the wall of flame climbing the face of the house, feeling the heat singe his beard without caring.

Then he was running for his gray, had vaulted into the saddle and was spurring away toward the northern hills. One of the Commando moved to follow him and was held back by a friend.

"Let him go, man."

"What do we do now?" There were shaking heads; nobody knew.

Coffee hung from his horse and was trying to walk it toward Elise, calling to her, trying to give her comfort. He too believed Matthew must be dead. He came up on the Commando and halted after what had seemed an endlessly painful stumble.

"I'll tell you what you'll do," he croaked. "You'll ride for a doctor. You've not only killed the father, you've probably killed the mother and son. If that don't rate eternal flames, I don't know what does."

They looked at him, variously embarrassed and frightened.

"Get the doctor, *mense.*" Coffee looked as bleak as Satan. "Then you can come back and hang me."

A roof timber fell with a crash and blazing sparks flew all around them.

"Move, you filthy rabbits."

Coffee's paradeground roar moved them to their horses and in moments they were galloping for Winburg as the columns of black smoke climbed through the thousands of butterflies.

4

It was dark when Matthew drifted upward.

The night sky was shot through with lazy streamers of fire and the stars wobbled in the rising haze of heat. Whips still cracked in his ears and the ground under him was softer than goose down. He floated somewhere beyond the pain and the harsh smell of burning. There was whispered talk as oxen were harnessed to a wagon. Coffee asked for more speed as he spread hay on the wagon bed and covered it with canvas, making no more sense to Matthew than his lying outside when there was no light to split rails. His feet were remote and cold and he was grateful for the warmth from the dying fires. Dying moths of soot spiraled down to cover the ground like black lichen.

Then they were all around him and he was lifted and the screaming pain drove him away.

He drifted and came back to the stink of native remedies, the tensed faces of Boie and Ndala as they worked over him, the stars jogging past their heads. They spoke to him and he only understood their caring, beyond stringing words into logical progressions. Pain rolled the wagon away from under him.

He thought of Jonathan's coming between drifts of shivering and blankness. Elise might have been there, but he was never sure; most of him was lost in unconsciousness as he gabbled and tossed the cold compresses from his head.

There were burning days of coma and nights when he thought he waited to shoot the old leopard. Dirk rode in with the dawns and sipped from the same cup, sneering around the rim as he took more than his fair share of the warmed water. He lost days and nights when he lay in a cave high on the Blesberg where a banked fire sweated the fever from his system and lost its smoke up a natural chimney. He lost weight and chased the flickering shadows across the cave's roof with sunken eyes that saw nothing else.

Those thoughts he was capable of rode north with the man who had put him here. He thought out the route north and east like Dirk, unsaddled the gray and made dry camp like Dirk; drank at the same streams and crossed the same mountains by the same tracks, fooling the gray by smearing horse dung on the trail ahead to make the horse believe other mounts had passed that way.

He knew nothing of Boie's nocturnal hunts for edible mammals, or Coffee's daylight watches over the lower slopes and the savannah beyond for Commando or scouts sent to flush them out. Ndala sewed him into a blanket to stop him clawing his wounds and spooned soup into him even when he coughed most of it to waste. She washed him and warmed him with her body when the night winds struck cold, and taught her son Josef to keep the compresses damp and cold. She drained pus from his wounds with boiled straws as she had seen Baaswitch Andries do, and wanted to scold Missie Elise for taking no interest in their lord's welfare.

The Missie's baby was safe and she was unhurt but for a badly bruised hip and slight burns to her upper arms. Nothing for a strong young woman to overcome. There seemed to be no core to the Missie; she was whole on the outside, but she reminded Ndala of a tree whose healthy bark hid the fungus rot that had eaten all the green wood. Not that her appetite had diminished like her thoughts for others; she ate for the baby and three more. Ndala thought of suckling sows and hid her disgust from Boie. The red soldier with burned hair ate less and he was a mature warrior who had earned the white equivalent of a warrior's headring. He even made the Missie take more from his own plate and she always did without thanks.

The days and nights melted together and Matthew's crisis came. His temperature rose dangerously and Ndala could feel the heat coming off him a foot away. She baked stones in the fire and steeped them in water to make steam and bring on the sweating that must break the fever. Her ocher dress clung to her and her senses swam from the steaming humidity she had created, but she worked to keep life in Nkosi Matthew, reminding herself of her husband's devotion to him whenever she felt herself flagging. Nkosi must live for the sake of them all, and yet his wife made no effort to be of help.

The Missie merely fanned herself harder as the sticky heat intensified and made pointed sighs of complaint. Only when Matthew started to rave did she rouse herself from her self-imposed lassitude and draw closer to his bedside to listen.

Matthew was back on the trek and was reliving all his talks with Kit, word-perfect but out of sequence. He forced the arrow through her shoulder and killed Mfengu. He threw Kit down and took her on the ground while Klyn and the

325

boys tracked Miss Mattie. He remade his first farewell in Colesberg and the final goodbye after the battle of Vegkop. Elise showed nothing throughout the remembered exchanges, but she was in turmoil inside, consumed by the sick anger of betrayal. If she could have torn the embryo life from herself at that instant she would have done so, torn it out and thrown it into his dying face. Matthew was just a thing that resembled somebody she had once cared for; now she was cured, now she could do what she truly wanted. *Anything.*

Matthew was rounding up cattle in the wake of the retreating Matabele before Elise came back to herself.

Ndala watched her climb to her feet, drop the fan, and walk to the cave mouth, where she stared out at the night with quivering shoulders. Ndala would have liked to have run for Boie and the red soldier, but they were hunting the far terraces, and Matthew could not be left to thrash about alone, he would hurt himself. Ndala held Matthew as best she could as she strapped another belt around the blanket that restrained his arms, and did not see Elise gather up all their precious biltong and their only pistol and slip away to the hidden kloof where Boie's horse was tethered and hobbled. She pulled the sack of corn from its niche and scattered it over the ground. Then she broke the jars of fermented honey and threw the biltong into a crevice. When the dawn came up to show her the safe path, she saddled up and rode down from the mountain without a backward glance.

Back at the farm, she located the charred, loose board in the kitchen floor, prised it up, reached down into the gap below, and retrieved the steel box Matthew kept all his money in. When she had broken it open with a stone, she tore through all the promissory notes and account slips, tucked the roll of banknotes in her bodice, and hid the coins in a pocket beneath her apron.

A surge of hatred set her shaking so badly she could not move, and she fed herself on the devastation around her. The buildings were just black oblongs of burned earth and tumbled mud brick. The corrals were empty but for windswept sage. The thorn would soon come to claim the scars and turn the farm back into a wilderness fit for rabbits and kaffirs. The great dream was dead; no, the great *lie* was dead, Elise told herself. Just dead ashes. Deserted as she had been deserted, made ugly as she had been made ugly. Well, as for herself, there would be no more of it. She clutched at her breast and felt the crackle of the notes, working them together through the soiled cloth.

New clothes and all the luxuries she wanted.

Elise remounted and rode for Winburg, calculating she would be there before midafternoon. She would take Matthew's room and use all the hot water and scented soap the hotel could offer. The woman who ran the place, Mrs. Gould, could arrange for passage to the coast, where an Indiaman would take her to Port Elizabeth and home. Who knew? Perhaps Dirk de Villiers had done her a great service. She was free and she carried the only thing Matthew Eastman had left in the world, this lump in her belly. She would teach it to hate the very mention of its father.

5

The Drakensberg heights had been swept by cold winds and veiled by sudden white fogs that dropped without warning. They blotted out the precipitous trails and left Dirk with no option but to hobble his horse until the weather cleared. Hard flurries of snow stung his face and ice formed in his beard. He picked his way through myriad rivulets of source water that fell to feed the rivers on the plain below, and trailed through veils of vapor, soaked to the skin and shaking with ague. He had developed a hollow cough and the chill damp made him light-headed.

Dirk had slept little over the past weeks, for he could not control his dreams, and both Abraham and Matthew haunted him when he was at his lowest ebb. He talked to himself constantly, talked of anything that did not remind him of what lay behind him on the high veldt. Anything at all.

Many times he had been jerked out of sleep by the drum of pursuing horsemen, dead men who came to drag him before Mzilikazi. The hoof falls died the moment he opened his eyes, to be replaced by the insidious and persistent hack of knives on sycamore impaling stakes. Dirk would defy these shades with wild shouts that amplified themselves in the dark crags and towering peaks, but they came back to him as distorted echoes he could not answer.

In daylight, Dirk could live with what he had done, could even justify it. For every man must die to make room for those who came after, and none but suicides could choose the time and the manner of their ending. He had proved Eastman to be a traitor to his own satisfaction, and had killed him with the sure cuts of his bullwhip. The hanging would only have been a formality, and would only have saved Eastman from a lingering end. Dirk believed he might well have finished the woman and the brat she carried. So much for dynasties; Dirk had pulled down both houses with a single, violent tug. So what? Where his next meal was coming from concerned him more.

He was down to his last few husks of cracked corn and a small quid of smoking tobacco. He had about a hundred schillings and water was bountiful and fresh, but he must get food, ammunition, and at least one other horse. His gray must be rested and fed decent grain. Dirk suffered hunger cramps and chronic flatulence for want of decent meat. The rare antelope he had seen had been too fleet and shy for a safe shot, even if he had dared to chance one. He tightened his belt and resolved to save his ball and powder for kaffir; he was not about to die for the luxury of a full stomach.

Dirk fed the corn to his horse and starved. Each day lapped the day before and melted into the one after. Time and again he was forced to backtrack when he lost his way on his descent from the summit. He was afforded tantalizing glimpses of the plain of Natal when the cloud cleared, but most of the time he moved through walls of mist. He lost long periods when exhaustion muddled him and he fell a lot on the icy ridges.

The air warmed imperceptibly and the basalt was free of treacherous glazes of frost. Dirk could no longer control his gray on the rein; he was too weak. He tied himself to the horse's tail and allowed the animal to find its own way down to the savannah below. There were shivering nights under his blanket and he huddled against the gray's belly when the hooves and knives clopped and clashed all around him; others when he babbled and lost himself in fits of fever. Somehow he kept moving downward.

He vaguely remembered chewing the bark and leaves of a stunted tree and drinking from an outfall in a chasm, feeling sun on his back and steam rising from his clothes as he got into the saddle and let the horse carry him. Now there was mud under his face and his horse was drinking from a water hole scoured from the rocky plain, snorting at the hyenas on the far bank. A buffalo rolled in the mud near a salt lick and an eland tested the wind as it made a delicate sideways approach to the water.

Dirk was out of the mountains.

One of his feet was still hooked in a stirrup and he had no idea how far his horse had dragged him. Dirk took a lifetime to unsnag himself, another to pull himself upright, several eternities to unsheathe and load his smoothbore. Mercifully it had not worked loose from its scabbard and been lost.

His presence had spooked the game and he made himself skirt the water hole until the wind was in his face. Soon, zebra and wildebeest came to drink together, using the zebra's keen eyesight and the wildebeest's superior sense of smell as a joint safeguard against predators. They drank their fill in relay and butted around in a rare moment of relaxation, rolling ticks from their hides and sharpening their hooves on the rocks. Emboldened by the presence of other ruminants, the deer came in single file through the red mud to lap at the water's edge. Dirk spared the foals and the pregnant does. He dropped a fine young buck with a clean neck shot and the water hole was deserted before the dying animal had kicked its last.

Dirk skinned and quartered the carcass and ate the liver raw, too exhausted to cook. He stacked the meat beneath a stone cairn, hobbled his horse in a natural, shaded hollow, and fell into a deep sleep.

When he awoke it was dark. He built and lit a fire and roasted a venison haunch over the coals, on guard against the big cats who circled the outer darkness, attracted by the smell of meat and repelled by the smell of man. Dirk cleared the ground around his fire, scrupulously sweeping leaves and twigs away to dislodge any snakes or scorpions that might be hiding there before laying out his bedroll. He salted the rest of the meat prior to packing it into his saddlebag, planning to dry it in the sun the following day. When he had eaten until he could stuff no more into his mouth he slept with his smoothbore across his chest.

Twelve hours later he was shaken awake by Arab slavers. He tried to kneel up and found he was manacled and could not move. Exhausted and weakened by his arduous journey, he stared around him with rising and ineffectual fury. They had his gun and his horse and him, and there was nothing he could do about it.

Except perhaps die.

6

Table Mountain wore its mantle of cloud and the heights had turned an acid green, perfectly matching Katherine Laidler's bilious mood. A letter had arrived that morning, and now that she had read through it many times, she found herself more irritated than intrigued by the pages of careful green script. Although she recognized the name signed at the bottom of the third and final sheet, she also knew that the handwriting was in no way similar to that man's. Katherine was familiar with his written acceptances to her social invitations, and was certain that this letter had to be the work of a menial clerk or bookkeeper. It was ledger copperplate, and had none of the eccentric dash of a gentleman's hand. She also knew that that man had been dead for over two months, and the coy note pinned to the letter was of little help to her either; it simply read:

> Dear Madam,
> It is my earnest and humble belief that the enclosure will be of particular and peculiar interest to yourself. In the light of that certainty, I shall take the liberty of calling upon you at precisely three of the clock this very afternoon, in order that we may discuss any delicate matters arising thereto.
> Begging to remain yours faithfully,
> Your obedient servant,
> A. Bentley-Parsons.

Katherine stopped herself from tearing the pages across and eased the high collar of her dress instead. The new Victorian fashions were designed specifically for London and Bath and were highly unsuitable for the heat of the Cape. Rain threatened from the seaward side of the valley and would relieve the intense humidity if it did come, which Katherine thought unlikely. Elias was making what she hoped were discreet inquiries about this Bentley-Parsons person, and should be back with the information directly. Katherine despised this recent habit of hyphenating names by the middle classes. To conjoin the names of two illustrious houses was one thing—the Hanoverian royals were given to that sort of thing, mostly to perpetuate the female lines of their ancient lineage—but grocers and coopers should not aspire to such affectation.

By Gabriel's strumpet, Katherine thought, borrowing one of her late father's punning oaths, was she to be confronted by one of these *nouveaux arrivés* who hoped to spin out his pension or his remittance by a little blackmail? If so, he was in for a rude awakening.

Katherine rang for tea and was sipping it on the balcony when Elias rode into the courtyard below and dismounted ponderously. He did not ride well and much preferred driving four-in-hand, but as Katherine had reminded him, her carriage was too well known to allow him to take it off to the business section of Cape Town while he grubbed around for this hyphenated toad.

Elias loped up the stairs and looked pleased with himself despite the sweat soaking his livery. He ducked his head and said, "Done found him, Missie. Found him all the way down Fish Alley where they's offices for the likes of that man."

Katherine lost patience when he paused for breath.

"The likes of what man, you elephant?"

"Him got a room above a coffeeshop where them blades meet womens. That not for you to know about, Missie, that below the salt for chief wives like you. They's all kinds of wickeds going on down there, bad people all over. Mens go there when they lost their reputations, mens starts there when they just gets off the packets and got no money to get started away from they own country. Immigrants and such. . . ." Elias turned his hat in his huge hands and blew on the cockade, ruffling the feathers.

"I'm aware what goes on in Fish Alley, Elias, as you well know. Get to the point."

"I was clever, Missie Katherine. There was no way old Elias could just go aknocking at Bentley-Parsons' door and ask him polite, 'What you doing to my Missie?'"

"Obviously."

"I went to the back of the street where the stables is, where the ostlers and the messengers wait on they masters. There was this Kaffir girl boiling water for fine folk's laundry, and I got to talking to her about who she scrubbing all that linen for. She boasts on all the quality she washes for, and this Bentley-Parsons, he one of them. She don't think too much of him on account he ain't up with remittance men she likes best, and mostly because he don't pay fast like the young bucks. Seems he close with coin and don't like to part up with it." Elias paused for effect, but Katherine looked impatient so he hurried on. "She say he got money, Missie, lots of money, he just mean-fingered with it. She say he got companies he runs. That make sense, Missie Katherine?"

"Yes, go on."

"He moneylends to red soldiers and remittance men for the interest. This washer-gal say he charge five percent. I told her, 'Girl, that be contortion, I know mens who do the same for three percent.'"

"Extortion," Katherine corrected.

"Yaas, Missie, what I said, contortion. She say he lend to them as nobody else will lend to on account they bad risks. He buy bad debts too. And those that is bankrupted? He buy they effects and clothes, furniture and such. Then he auctions what's worth anything at all to those who wants quality and can't afford new. She say he foreclosed on more than one noble, even sold the effects back to the family to save them from scandal. Most families pays what he asks and don't make no fuss for him. He knows where the skeletons is hid in more than one fine house. You don't want no fuss with that man, Missie. You let old Elias turn his head around and drop him down some kloof."

Katherine ignored the brutish offer, nagged by worry.

"Did you catch sight of him, Elias?"

"No, Missie, him keep to his rooms. But that washer-gal say he all bones and skull and don't have enough meat on his frame to tempt a tickbird. She say he yellow like he got fly sickness and he cough blood when the dampness get to him. Track up all his handkerchiefs with all his spitting. That's all I get, Missie. You want I should go back and wait on him till dark? That Fish Alley bad lit, and he could fall on his stairs easy."

"No. Go to the gate and bring him here to me when he arrives."

"He coming *here?*" Elias's eyes rolled and showed a lot of white. "With Baas Laidler up-country? You been sleeping with a window open? The wind come and blowed your wits all over the veldt. You can't bring steerage trash like that in this house. Missie, he smell up the carpets like some damned kaffir who wipe his arse on his hand."

"You forget yourself," warned Katherine, touched by his concern but disapproving of the earthy way he expressed himself.

Elias crushed his hat out of shape.

"Yaas, Missie, and I about to do it again. I just got through telling you what kind of sewage he is, and here you is talking of having him come right in the house. He do you harm, Missie, sure as spit dry on a skillet."

"Hold your tongue."

"Can't. You know how Baas Laidler hear who comes and goes here. I swear he got the sparrows whispering who peck the berries from his hedge."

"Are you one of his sparrows, Elias?"

Elias shook his head and nodded.

"Yaas, Missie, once. Like all of us. You let this man come here, I got to go back to doing it again. I done the best by you I can, but the baas own us both as sure as beetles roll dung. We got no choice but to do what he says, you maybe more than me. Least I can run for the bush, but you, where you going to go without Master Jamie?"

"Run then, you impertinent elephant."

"Can't, Missie. Can't leave you." Elias looked miserable. "You got nobody but old Elias. You ain't a first cattle-wife raised up on Baas Laidler's right hand. He can put you out of his kraal and take another woman when he wants. Where'll that leave Master Jamie? He'll be named bastard and have no father to take his name from."

Katherine felt faint. "What do you mean?"

"Said too much."

"And not enough." Katherine sounded drowned. "This is no Zulu village and I am in no such danger."

"Yes, Missie, you is. This is truth I'm telling. The baas know all about the mens you laid with, except that last one. I made so he never knew about that one. But the others, he got that all writ down."

"You're trying to frighten me with nonsense."

"I wish you was frightened, Missie, then we could maybe make some sensible way of seeing this man off back to Fish Alley where he belongs."

Katherine opened and closed her fan, picked up the letter, staring from one to the other, her whole being in turmoil. Elias may be as loyal to her as he could afford, but he was most certainly not an ideal confidant. If only there were somebody she could turn to, somebody with enough power and discretion to help her. She could barely bring herself to consider whether Cord really did know about her indiscretions or not; if he did, her position was more precarious than the big Zulu could have realized.

333

What was to become of Jamie if Cord took it into his head to declare him the son of another man, an illegitimate? There was not a door in the Colony that would not slam in his face, not a friend who would dare to flaunt convention enough to offer mother and son sanctuary under his roof. And returning to England was out of the question. The news of her disgrace would go ahead of her, barring her from every withdrawing room in the twelve counties. France? Holland? She would die of boredom and loneliness in either country even if she should find a way of supporting herself and her son in the proper manner.

Katherine supposed she could pack and leave before Cord made any move to declare her an immoralist and disinherit Jamie. Could he prove Jamie was not his son, would he have to in law? Other men had disinherited wastrel sons with no problem, there being no need to supply burden of proof of unworthiness. A man could do what he wished with his lands, titles, and effects. There was no law to say what a man must leave his heirs or assigns. If only it were possible to have sight of Cord's will. That would gain her nothing, she realized; Cord could change it at any time he chose, and most certainly would if the mood struck him. Much as he would drag any divorce action through the courts in the full glare of public attention to humiliate her if she crossed him. Cord only cared for convention when it served his own purpose, and she could visualize the savage delight he would take in exposing proof of her affairs in open court. He would relish that and play the cuckold for all it was worth.

Katherine's temples pounded as she fought panic. Cord could divorce her and keep Jamie, barring her from any contact with the boy; separate mother and son with the full weight of the law behind him. She would be powerless to stop him. She would be forced into exile alone.

Elias was making her sip cooled water, supporting her as she sagged in her chair. Damn, she thought, pushing upright. There was no time to start vaporing like some silly Cape matron. She must think and act. There was too much at stake to rely on smelling salts.

A horse clattered onto the flags below the balcony and Katherine caught sight of a man reining in beside the gate. He was tall and as gaunt as the hack he rode. His black suit had shiny patches at the knee and elbows from long wear. It had to be Bentley-Parsons.

"That washer-gal 'scribe him good, Missie," growled Elias.

334

"Bring him to me," said Katherine, pinching her cheeks. "Missie...."

"Do as you are told!"

"By Mwari and that old mud father if I don't wish the old Colonel was still with us to crack a whip 'cross your skirts, Missie," blurted Elias, wishing he had bitten his tongue instead of showing Katherine too much of his heart. "All right, I'm going, I'm going." He stamped down the covered stairs into the garden, leaving Katherine with the ticking clocks and her drumming heart.

7

The Arab with a fishhook scar on his cheek prodded Dirk with his jezail and barked something in Portuguese.

Dirk gave a negative headshake and looked around. Stallions and mares drank at the water hole and a row of Sotho bearers squatted in the winter grass beside their loads. The Arabs had a fire going under their billies, and about twenty of them lolled about in their white robes, sipping from small cups. Griquas were posted on the high ground and a yellow wagon was outspanned in the shade of a towering baobab. From the number of oxen being led around the small bluff to a wallow below the water hole, Dirk calculated that these men were used to moving at speed and wondered if they outspanned fresh teams along their route. Only those who planned to poach game in Zululand usually came so well prepared. Somehow Dirk did not think these men were after hides.

The Arab tried English.

"You hunter?"

"No. You?"

The jezail butted Dirk to the ground.

"You speak what I ask, Hollander. Where you from, where you go?"

Dirk levered himself up and moved his manacled hands toward the Drakensbergs and swept them off toward the east. "I came from there, and I'm going there. To the coast. *Verstaan,* Arab?" he said, thinking, goat, his head spinning from weakness and the blow.

"Aiwa. Where you go on coast?"

"Delgoa Bay."

"Why you go Delgoa? Is Portogee there."

"Why not?" Dirk shrugged, his eyes busy.

The inlaid butt of the jezail knocked him onto his back again. Some of the Arabs laughed as Dirk got an elbow under him.

"Now you say why you go Delgoa."

Dirk spat blood and blinked spangles away. "Slaving, you *skepsel*."

"You? A Hollander?"

"I'm no Dutchman, Arab. I'm an Afrikaner. I was born here, just as you were. Supposing you were born of woman." Dirk muttered the last to avoid another blow from the jezail. His pockets had been turned out and his bag of schillings now hung from the scarred Arab's belt. One of the others played with his pistols.

"Where your timepiece, Afrikaner? Your watch?" asked scarface.

"I read the sun. It doesn't need winding," lied Dirk. His English half-hunter was wrapped in greaseproof under the game meat in his saddlebag. If they killed him they would find it, but then it would not matter. Dirk planned to keep his watch.

"You must be poor, you don't have watch."

Dirk glanced meaningfully at his bag of schillings. "I am now."

There was a man sitting beneath the awning attached to the sail of the yellow wagon, and Dirk's eyes were drawn to him. He was being served tea by a big buck in livery and white stockings as another held a map for him to study. The damned kaffirs were dressed in clothes better than any Dirk had ever owned and he was angered at the sight. He had heard such things happened in Cape Town, but had never thought to see such a thing up-country. He was being kicked around by heathens with goat stink on them and my lord was taking his ease at afternoon tea.

The scarred Arab said something Dirk did not catch, so distracted was he by the tableau by the wagon.

"What?"

The scarred Arab made as though to strike Dirk again.

"Touch me again, Arab," yelled Dirk, rearing up, "and I'll feed you and your toy musket to the baboons. Tell him I'll talk to *him*." Dirk rattled his chains at the yellow wagon. "Him, *verstaan*. Your effendi, or whatsoever you call your baas. Him."

"That man is nothing in your life."

Dirk needed to drink and make water badly. The mounting

336

stricture in his groin made him bold and his sneer was wider than the Arab's.

"Tell him Dirk de Villiers sends his compliments, and tell him..." Dirk fumbled with his fly as he rolled onto his side to urinate. "Tell him I know where his leg is buried."

The Arabs became voluble in their own language, arguing among themselves, leaving Dirk to relieve himself in peace. He buttoned up as best he could and watched the scarred Arab stalk off to the yellow wagon where he made a salaam and spoke urgently to the man in the shade. Both of them looked across at where Dirk lay, and when the seated man had made a short speech, the scarred Arab called orders to the men around Dirk. Dirk was hauled to his feet, dragged around the water hole, and thrown down before the awning, sprawling awkwardly with his manacled hands trapped beneath his body. He shook his head to disperse dizziness, blinking away the dancing liver spots. The sun was in his eyes when he craned upward, and the seated man was invisible in the shadows.

"Well met, menheer," grunted Dirk.

There was no answer.

"You take chances, I give you that, menheer," said Dirk. "I like that in a man. Most hunters who've been chopped up by the Matabele don't come this way twice. Man, I never expected to see you again. I thought you'd be taking your pleasure in Cape Town as others trod your grapes for you. Must be you want elephant teeth badly; with some men it's a sickness."

Again there was silence.

"Must be more than ivory then," guessed Dirk. "Only one thing worth more than ivory in Natal."

"How do you know me? We've never spoken before," came from the hard, black shadow. A dry and cynical voice from a hollow chest.

"Man, you were out of your head when we poured pitch on your stump at Vegkop. Ach, you missed a great battle."

There came the hoo of an alarmed monkey and a baboon screamed from the veldt. Dirk grinned into the shadow.

"They don't like you people being here. You're keeping the game from the water. They hate the stink of man worse than anything."

"So, you were there...." Dirk heard the tightening of the voice, the venom that made it slightly breathless. "What do you think that buys you? If anything."

337

Dirk held out his trapped wrists. "More than this, man. *Brandewyn* for the throat and a *riempie* chair for my rump would be a start."

The chuckle held no warmth. "You misread your position, Boer. You can make no bargains with me. You're an impediment, an embarrassment. You see, I planned to pass this way without being seen. You've rather spoiled that for me if I don't employ the only remedy that presents itself."

"Dead men speak no lies, neh? I see that, it's how I think myself. But you'd lose a lot if you leave me for the vultures. Listen, man, you're after slaves—stands out a full league on a moonless night—and I'm the man to make that easier for you. Take the risk out of it. But that's nothing to what I *could* do for you."

"Ha, you think too much of yourself, de Villiers. Like all the plains Dutch. Look about you, these men have been culling the coastal clans for centuries. Their ancestors raided here a thousand years ago; they filled the galleys, mines, and arenas of the Roman Empire when your people were living in caves on raw meat. Their great-grandfathers supplied the Turkish navy with oarsmen when the Ottoman Empire stretched from the Black Sea to the Pillars of Hercules. Their fathers supplied cane cutters for the British West Indies, and they now supply slaves for the American cotton plantations. Theirs is an ancient brotherhood that dates back to the building of the pyramids. There's nothing you could teach these men about slaving; to think otherwise is arrogance based on massive ignorance."

Dirk showed contempt and wished he could smoke.

"And I'll wager they haven't changed their ways since the lost tribes ate manna in the wilderness. Look at them with a fresh eye, man. Those smokestacks they call guns, the way they track up a water hole and foul it for the game. A man should leave things as he found them; there's always the possibility he may pass this way again. These men are spoilers, raiders, nothing more. What I'm getting at is this; they run in from the coast and take what they can from the nearest kraal, killing off anybody they can't take with them. How long do you think a farmer would last if he picked the best fruit from his trees and left nothing to feed the land between seasons? He'd starve inside a year."

"Is this a lesson, de Villiers?"

"Damned right, and you'd be sensible to listen. I know these Arabs; they like to buy protection from any chief and scoop up cheap, quick prizes. Any clan chief who comes cheaply can't be trusted. I'll bet you spend most of your time looking over your shoulder, wondering if some petty chieftain will keep his promise to leave you alone. Man, pay groundnuts and you'll get monkeys."

"You know better, I suppose?"

"Ach, yes." Dirk wiped off a stone to suck. His mouth was drying fast. "And maybe we'll talk further when we've talked over what's really sticking in your craw."

"And that is...?"

"Matthew Eastman."

There was no response. The silent shadows said more than a gasp or a sudden, sharp intake of breath. Dirk sucked his stone and grinned at the dust he trickled through his fingers.

"Come on, Laidler. It's not me you should be dangling on the edge of eternity, it's him you want dead."

"And why would I want that?" The question was as light as a sigh.

Dirk hid his face under his hat. He had skipped the outer rings and had struck the gold.

"Then," he drawled, "you could call your wife and son your own... neh?" Dirk raised his head with a sudden jerk to catch Cord's face as he leaned forward into the sunlight with white, pinched nostrils. God's mercy, thought Dirk, he's a death's-head with eyes like boiling blue ice. The man was all hatred. Man, he's powered by it. Nothing else could keep his heart and brain alive in that wasted frame. He was just knuckle and sinew. Dirk made himself say, "So we both know something that's worth nothing," not daring to show the uneasy compassion he felt for such naked agony. The jezails might be smokestacks but there were at least half a dozen trained on his spine.

"Nothing is worthless, de Villiers," said Laidler, sighting along his pistol. "The first lesson of the trader."

"Then we'll trade," Dirk said evenly. "If that's your style. My life for Eastman's."

"Plus a few golden guineas and a fast horse? I'd never see the money or the horse again. You have no collateral and your time has run out."

"Man, you're a fool. I can give guarantees without leaving here."

"How?"

"Trade and I'll tell you. What can it cost either of us, unless

339

your word isn't worth what I've heard? I'll take your handshake."

Laidler hesitated, then nodded. "You have my word, so long as you can deliver your end of the bargain."

"I can do that. What about these irons?"

Laidler gave a handsign. "Release him. It doesn't matter to me if you die with your hands free or not."

Released, Dirk chafed his cramped wrists. "Put that from your mind, menheer, and settle yourself. Matthew Eastman is already dead."

Shock drained Laidler's face of the last vestiges of color. "The circumstances, man. How?"

"That, menheer, is a long story," said Dirk, reaching for a waterskin.

8

Although Hannie Gould had slept deeply for the first time in many days, she felt drugged and slow rather than clearheaded. Perhaps, she thought, she had slept too deeply. Her office was a clutter of dusty papers and the hotel records were wildly out of date. The staff had done their best to keep the hotel going without her guidance, but standards had slipped badly in her absence. She wished she had more vitality to bring her business back up to its former excellence.

The weary days she had spent combing the hills around the Eastman farm had been fruitless and enervating. There had been no sign of Matthew or his wife, none of the houseboys or herders could be found, and only Pyayo had been discovered hiding in a dry wash, half-starved and totally inarticulate. It was as if Matthew had never existed at all. His stock was scattered and the search party had only been able to gather less than a dozen thoroughbred horses. Hannie had found Gaika herself, and had brought the mare back to stable with her own mares.

After ten days, Johannes Krige had called off the search and had brought Hannie back to town. In his direct way he had told her she must accept that Matthew was dead and she must mourn him any way she felt was fitting. He had made no sign of disapproval of her obvious attachment to Matthew, despite his rigid adherence to his Calvinist beliefs; he also felt the Englishman's passing deeply. Pieter Klyn and Dr. Andries believed Matthew to be dead, but Hannie could not.

Nothing could induce her to until she had buried his bones herself. Life without him was too dark a place.

The Volksraad had been divided by the factions who argued for or against Dirk de Villiers's actions. It was the manner of old Abraham's death that swayed the meeting to pass a motion of censure against Dirk and the Commando under him, however toothless such a declaration was to prove. The Commando could not be dispersed or stood down, it was too badly needed to keep the district secure against outside incursions or internal dispute. The move to declare Dirk an outlaw was no more than a salve for the collective conscience should he dare to return to the high veldt. Then, and only then, would any burgher shoot him on sight without a second thought. The crime of patricide was the more abhorrent for its biblical precedence, and far outweighed any consideration of what was considered the lesser charge of possible manslaughter. What he had done to Matthew Eastman had no real bearing on the Volksraad decision to banish Dirk; at best, the raid was considered rash and unfortunate. There was no question of mounting a manhunt to bring Dirk to justice; it was hoped he would go north and keep going, never to return.

The news had filtered through to Hannie and she had taken it in stoic silence. How soon, it seemed to her, these men forgot what so many of them owed to Matthew Eastman. From those who owed her money or goods she demanded immediate payment; it was little enough, but it did show her clear disapproval. Surprisingly it did her business little harm; the Boers admired and recognized the right of any individual to take a stance, however vainglorious. What Pretorius would do now that the British had consolidated their position in Port Natal interested them much more.

Hannie was checking available rooms against the hotel register when there was a disturbance at the door. The lobby was usually buzzing with business gossip during the heat of the early afternoon. Buyers and stock sellers sat over slow beers out of the hot wind, whiling away the time until it was cool enough to walk the stockpens. The conversation stumbled and ceased, making Hannie look up. There in the doorway was a woman in a ragged dress smeared with dried mud. Her hair was tangled and windblown and her shoes were broken at the heel, causing her to walk on her toes. As she approached the desk she raised the hem of her dress to save it from brushing against the floor, and she held her head on

341

one side, defying anyone not to see what a superior creature she was. She was in the middle months of pregnancy and there were burrs adhering to her soiled apron.

She inclined her head at Hannie and said into the quiet, "The keys to my husband's room if you please, Mrs. Gould."

Hannie rang the bell for Thomas the lobby porter, swung the hotel register automatically, and proffered a pen, watching the small black scurry from his cubbyhole from the corner of her eye. "Where . . . ," she said shakily, "where *is* your husband, Mrs. Eastman? Is he . . . is he with you?"

Elise looked through her.

"I shall require the boys to draw me a hot bath, of course. Send out for the best soaps they have at the store, scented naturally. Hotel soap is so clinging, I find. My horse is to be curried, given fresh straw and a dry stall. Have him walked before he's given water and grain."

"Mrs. Eastman . . . Elise. . . ." Hannie broke off; she was making no impression on the singsong voice or the calculating, overbright eyes that regarded her so dispassionately. Elise reminded her of a willful child playing queen. The veldt had done its work well.

"Also," Elise raised a finger. "You will inform your seamstress that she is to attend me when I call. I shall require a number of dresses. You may also tell Mr. Whatever-his-name-is at the ladies' emporium to bring me a selection of his latest styles. Traveling clothes, tell him. Something fit for sea travel."

Hannie wanted to slap and shake her.

"Matthew, Elise, where is *Matthew?*"

"Matthew?" Elise frowned and smiled. "Matthew is dead, did I tell you? They can't hang him now, even if they wanted to. And bonnets, tell him bonnets, and none of that awful gingham. Too much sun is not good for the hair. Oh yes." Elise dimpled prettily. "Sell the horse for a good price. I shall not be needing it again."

Men were gathering around now, curious and cautious. Elise glowed. She patted a tangled curl and ignored them.

"I shall need shoes too. Nothing in black or in bright colors. Pastels if you please. My key?"

The men muttered in wondering Dutch and Hannie felt hot chills bind her head in a clamp. She found the key and laid it on the register. Thomas had backed to the end of the counter as though he were smelling out witches in a kraal.

342

Confound the boy, thought Hannie, why did he have to act the savage now when he should be running for Dr. Andries? Did she have to do everything herself?

"There," she said. "But where is Matthew, Mrs. Eastman? Where is Boie ... and the English sergeant?"

"He's dead, I'm afraid." Elise laughed in high register. It stopped too suddenly and she looked crafty. "The others?" She seemed to be questioning herself and the frown came back momentarily. "The others?"

"Yes, Elise. The others."

Elise became confidential, whispering loudly.

"They're catching hares on the Blesberg. Now isn't that silly? I wouldn't, you know. And that silly kaffir girl with her hot stones and steam. I told her she couldn't save him...." The frown was there again. "At least ... I *think* I told her that." Elise brightened. "What does it matter? I thought it, which is just as good."

"Elise, where on the Blesberg?" Thinking: *tell me, you mad sow.*

"In a cave. I hate caves, don't you? Almost as much as I hate Matthew. He's dead, you know. That means nobody will ever have to trust him again. There was somebody else." Elise went back to being imperious.

"I'll go up now. Just you hurry those boys with the hot water."

Elise scooped up the key and swept away toward the stairs, leaving Hannie wondering if she knew about her affair with Matthew. No, she would have said more, shown it in her manner; however unbalanced Elise might be because of her recent ordeal, she wouldn't have let the opportunity pass. God, why was she standing here with her thumb in her mouth when Matthew might well be lying in a cave desperately wounded and in need of help? He must be alive, and Ndala and Boie must be with him. No wonder they couldn't be found. Boie knew the mountain better than anyone, and he would have made certain no white man found their retreat. He would have no reason to trust any European after the attack on the farm.

Hannie caught Thomas by the arm and shook him sensible.

"Fetch Dr. Andries," she ordered. "And Baas Klyn. Find Johannes Krige if you can. And hurry, you *skelm.*"

Thomas ran.

9

Boie straddled the sleeping mamba and held his breath for a long moment as stones he had dislodged rattled down around him. The snake lay coiled in a fall of leaves and many of its scales were gray. After its intermittent winter sleep it would cast its skin and emerge into the spring sunlight, greener than young grass. There were females and many young ones tucked away in the warm crevices, all of them as lethargic as the large, sleeping male. Boie waited for the clatters to die before he passed between the drowsing snakes to the cleft where he had buried the leopard's heart and entrails under a pile of rock.

The stones had been disturbed and shreds of dried offal showed through the torn leather sack. Boie's heart lurched; all the bad luck was explained. The bad spirit had been freed and had caused Nkosi Matthew to be struck down by his enemies. Like all men who are close to the earth, Boie saw why the Commando had come to kill the old baas and Nkosi Matthew. The leopard lived again in another form; his spirit had eaten into the inner clay of the man he called Burning Spear. Boie had looked long upon Dirk de Villiers in the past and had seen the space behind his eyes where nothing lived. Burning Spear and the leopard had conjoined to become a demon who walked inside a manshape. He would be harder to track and kill now, for he had two hearts and two minds, doubly strong limbs, and the night cunning of both man and cat.

Boie did not touch the mummified remains, nor did he recover them with the tumbled stones. The place was now a shrine and must be left open and ready for the spirit to return when it was time.

Boie sprinkled precious snuff around the broken cairn to stop any bold and hungry rat from chewing on the remains—one might come now that the mambas were torpid. But no rat had thrown down the rocks and ripped open the bag, they were much too heavy. Blaming himself for not burying the parts deeper, Boie returned the way he had come. His oversight may well have caused Nkosi Matthew more days of sickness than his wounds had warranted, but now he should leave the shades and begin to regain his strength.

Boie climbed the rock chimney to the surface where he had left his son on watch. Josef sat on the lip of a rock where

344

the shadow broke up his outline, just as his father had taught him. The boy acknowledged Boie's presence by putting a hand over his mouth and pointed off down the mountainside. He did not speak as any European child might; he already knew that silence was his best friend and that handsigns made points more readily than unnecessary words. Living on the mountain had been good for him; much of the compound fat had burned away from his round belly, and he had become lean. Soon he would start building proper muscle over his green bones.

Boie edged out along a rockspur and peered downward. Mounted whites were emerging from the shimmering plain and setting their horses at the trail to the lower slopes of the Blesberg. If they came on without stopping they would be at the secondary crest where he lay before nightfall. Boie studied the riders and knew with a sick certainty that they came on with the steady purpose of men who knew their way. They were not casting about for sign as he had seen the other patrols do, and they had no guides with them; they knew their way to the summit and knew what they would find there.

Boie sucked his teeth and hissed. There must have been more than one demon loose on the mountain. The Missie must have told the whites where Nkosi lay, and Boie feared for the child in her belly; would he be marked by her mad disloyalty? First she had shown her legs to the boys, now she had betrayed her lord and husband. For once, Boie wished he were a Zulu, for they would have broken the Missie's limbs and buried her alive under a polished dung floor.

He smelled the wind for weather changes. There was little turbulence in the upper thermals and the rising, warmer air from the plain reached him as a chill updraft. There would be ground mist before evening and Boie planned to use it to his own advantage. During his weeks on the mountain he had made rockfalls to guard the trail and had dug hidden pits, designed to break a horse's legs and a rider's back. He grunted deep in his chest. The hard labor had not been wasted and he thanked the old mud father for giving him foresight and cunning.

Boie pressed the tips of his fingers against the corners of his eyes to give him longer, clearer vision, a jealously guarded trick his people had learned from the Bushmen, and studied the riders. He knew Baaswitch Andries from his fatness, and recognized Missie Gould from her yellow hair. She rode as well as any of the men and helped her horse in the bad places with the instinct of a born rider. Baas Krige was there too, and the sight of the three saddened Boie. Their motives for leading the Commando to Nkosi did not concern him; he only had one loyalty, and had long given up trying to understand these other whites. It would be bad if any of them died in his traps, for their luck had been part of Nkosi's luck, and their paths had twined with his on the tree of life for so long. Now the tree would no longer bear their weight and some vines must fall.

Boie handed his smoothbore to Josef and led the way back to the cave along the rocks where they would leave no spoor. When Josef was strong enough to take the recoil, Boie meant to teach him to shoot the long gun, and carrying it was a constant reminder of the honor to come. There was a lesson in all things.

Sergeant Coffee showed himself when they were almost at the cave, separating himself from the camouflaging outcrop with an ease he had not possessed six short weeks before. He too had learned from the Khoikhoi, and Boie was pleased with the way he had traded his soldier's stride for the sure glide of the hunter. His beard had grown and he had less middle.

"You saw," he said, flicking the fingers of both hands twice. "I counted twenty men."

"Twenty horses, baas. Only twelve riders. Rest packhorses." Boie did not identify the three people he had recognized, nor did he say what had to be done; they had all planned against the possibility of this day long before. It would be easier now that Matthew could walk.

Ndala saw how things were by the way the two men and the boy came into the cave. She killed the fire with soil and set about making ready to move, knowing they must not be caught on the crest in daylight and that speed was everything.

Matthew leaned against a folded pallet, his long, naked legs splayed before him. The scars on his thighs were still tender and the flesh had knitted in puckered ridges. Although he was still mentally and physically slow, he worked at strengthening his arm muscles by constantly exercising with heavy stones until he fell back exhausted, streaming with perspiration. He ate ravenously to fill out his wasted frame even when he had little appetite, knowing it was the only way to regain his strength and keen reflexes. He said little and thought much.

Nobody had told him that Elise had gone in so many words; he had simply come out of his long coma and known it. How this was so caused Coffee to wonder aloud, but the two Khoikhoi had not understood his concern, accepting it as nothing extraordinary. Things of the mind and spirit were to be noted as the work of natural forces without wonder. Nkosi Matthew had been on a long journey through the shades where all things met and merged into dreams, where thoughts were stronger than the mountain they lived on, more elemental than the sun's fire. It was strange to them that the clever and powerful whites, for all their iron machines and guns on wheels that set the earth alight, could not see things the same way.

When Ndala had packed dried food into her cooking pot, she draped a blanket around Matthew's shoulders and made a kaross of a second one to hide his nakedness. She had made sandals for him, and she tied the thongs firmly before helping him to stand and make his first faltering steps toward the cave mouth. Josef took some of his weight too, trailing the loaded smoothbore behind him.

Matthew emerged into the sunlight, and screwing up his eyes against the unaccustomed glare, took a draft of clear air into his lungs. He resisted Ndala when she tried to guide him to the southwest, away from the search party.

"No," he said, the act of speaking making him shake with effort. "We go north. North, girl."

"Come, Nkosi," Ndala coaxed. "Come, Lord." She called softly to the men and they came back toward them, adding their voices to hers.

"North," Matthew demanded in a cracked voice. "North.... Dirk is in the north."

"Soon, Lord. Truly ... soon."

"Come on, Matthew, old chap."

The first slide and tear of falling rock rolled up at them. The faint scream of a frightened horse and the bawl of a dismounted man. Matthew's hand closed around Ndala's wrist and he glared into Boie's face. "Swear it," he said.

Boie covered his heart to make the promise binding, watching the sweat of exertion turn Matthew's hair into damp ropes.

"Good," said Matthew, falling forward.

Coffee saved his head from slapping the ground and Boie

caught him by the waist. Between them they carried him down the trail as fast as they could travel with his dead weight slung between them, and they were long gone when Johannes Krige brought Hannie into the cave to rest her twisted ankle.

Pieter Klyn followed them in and lit one of the wattle torches Ndala had left behind. As the feeble glow illuminated the far reaches of the cave, Hannie saw the dead fire and the abandoned pallets.

"They were here," she said, "and Matthew is alive." She said it with such certainty that it caused the men to exchange glances. It was clear where her heart lay.

"You are right, Mrs. Gould," said Klyn, throwing down his saddle. His horse had been killed by a rockfall. "And I think we won't see that man again. Why should he trust any of us again? If he's wise, he'll quit this territory and never come back. What has anybody shown him but disregard, eh? Ach, I am ashamed of my own people."

"Not all of us, menheer." Krige sucked his grazed hand. "He has friends among us."

"Some, true. But he deserves more than *this*." Klyn's outspread arms embraced the cave. "Lying up here like a wounded *skepsel*, and Dirk de Villiers? He rides where he chooses with no man's hand against him. Where is the justice in that?"

They heard Andries complaining outside and wind mourned in the natural chimney.

"We must find him," said Hannie. "Please try, some of you?"

"You ask too much of men with nothing to give." Klyn sat himself on a rock and stood again almost immediately. His quiet rage was close to spilling over into physical violence. He snatched up his gun and his saddle. "Will you give me your horse to ride, Krige?"

"If that's what you want." Krige wanted no fight with the big Dutchman, saw no point in a confrontation over a matter he agreed on.

"It's what I want. I'll take one of the packhorses too. I'll find your Englishman for you, Mrs. Gould. If he shoots me I won't blame him. He deserves to shoot somebody. And Krige, tell these people that if one of them so much as plants a potato on Eastman's land, I will kill him for it. That farm is his whether he wants it or not. I will guard it and my brother's tomb with my life. No fat burgher will build his house on that land and live to draw water from his well. Tell them that."

"Take my horses, Menheer Klyn. I'll ride double with Krige. You won't mind, will you, Johannes? Matthew will be afoot; take him my horses and tell him I have Gaika." Hannie was crying and did not know.

Andries came in mopping his face with a red handkerchief. "Is he here, is Matthew Eastman here?"

Nobody answered him as Pieter Klyn pushed past him and walked away through the dusk.

"That man makes a bad enemy, I think," said Krige. "If I didn't have daughters, I think I would have done the same."

"You would," said Hannie. "I know it."

"But do I?" asked Krige stiffly.

10

The man who called himself Bentley-Parsons sat without being invited to and studied Katherine with no show of the deference she was used to, causing her to frown and Elias to growl deep in his throat. He smelled like bitter aloes and did not cover his rank body stink with perfume. His linen, Katherine noticed, was far from clean, and there was grease under the trail dust on his clothes. He crossed a leg and showed an inch of patched hose.

"Let us to business, ma'am. I'm sure neither of us wishes to prolong this interview. I hold something you wish to have destroyed and I have set a price on it. Is your kaffir to stay, or are we going to afford ourselves decent privacy for what must pass between us?"

"Do not speak to me of decency, sir," Katherine flared. "Elias most certainly stays. I have no intention of being unchaperoned. Get to your business."

Bentley-Parsons shrugged and folded his arms. "As you wish, ma'am. Let us hope he has more discretion than he demonstrated when playing the spy for you. The laundress in Fish Alley earns extra schillings by keeping me informed of any clandestine inquiries. You cannot blackguard me, ma'am, nor can I be compromised. I am impervious to such..." He dabbed the corner of his mouth with a grubby handkerchief, stifling a cough. "...such sensibilities. A poor man cannot afford such feelings of delicacy."

"Then state your business."

"You have it in your hand, ma'am. That is the facsimile

of an original letter that came into my hands by chance. I have a price in mind and don't plan to haggle with you. Any prolonged dickering will only raise the asking price."

"At least you do not claim to be the agent for another in this matter," said Katherine, looking down her nose.

"No, ma'am. I leave such subterfuges to those who enjoy them. Direct is direct, I say."

"You realize, don't you, that my husband can destroy you with no effort? If you are not aware of that fact, you are a fool as well as a mountebank."

Bentley-Parsons' dry cough became a laugh. "Look to your own security before you threaten mine, ma'am. I shall deal directly with your husband if you prove not to be amenable. He will pay to keep your reputation stainless if you will not. I want eight hundred guineas for that letter, a small sum for you, you probably spend that on fripperies in a single month. On receipt of that sum I will save you further embarrassment and guarantee you will never see me again."

"And I have your word for that, I take it." Katherine's scorn made her shake.

"No, ma'am, you will have the letter."

"You may as well ask for ten times that sum. I have no fortune. Perhaps you had better deal with my husband."

Bentley-Parsons wiped scum from his lips. "I should have done, but he is up-country, is he not? Had he been here I should have gone to him at once. Don't delude yourself, ma'am. I do not usually deal with women."

"You surprise me." Katherine stood and moved around the long table. "I should have thought any gentleman would have wrung your neck when faced by such a proposition."

"Be as surprised as you wish, ma'am. They usually pay. I told you, bluster and prevarication sends the price up. I'll give you until noon two days from now to find the money. Gold or silver coins. No scrip and no banker's drafts. Each day you delay will cost a further fifty guineas. Think of that, ma'am, and send your kaffir when you have the money." His mouth could have been smiling. "He knows where to find me. Your servant, ma'am." Bentley-Parsons bowed from the waist and got to his feet.

"I tell you I cannot find that sort of money even if I believed that this letter was worth anything of the sort. Perhaps you had better deal with Mr. Laidler after all."

"Eight hundred and fifty guineas," said the tall, thin, and

ugly man, wiping his mouth. "You must have jewelry to sell. The baubles on your wrist should command half that sum."

"You would drive me into the hands of the moneylenders?"

"It's of no consequence to me, ma'am. And forget any thoughts you may have of letting your kaffir lay for me. If I should die, my boxes would be opened and your precious letter would be the first item that is appraised by my banking executors. The instructions I left them are very clear. Come, ma'am, did you think I would not make such an arrangement?"

Katherine stepped in and raked his face with her nails. Bentley-Parsons made no move except to lick his mouth. Blood ran down his face and dropped onto the carpet.

"That will cost you another hundred guineas and twenty-four hours. Nine hundred and fifty guineas by noon tomorrow, ma'am. Or I deal with your husband."

"I . . . can't . . . there is no possible way. . . ."

"Then I must deal elsewhere." Bentley-Parsons bowed again and left the room. He was whistling when he rode out of the courtyard.

Katherine stared at Elias without seeing him.

Within three weeks Cord would be back on the Cape if the weather held along the eastern coast. She began to pray for storms.

BOOK SEVEN

1

White horses rolled in from Madagascar and turned the American trader on its cable before tumbling into the shores of Delgoa Bay.

Dirk picked shreds of meat from between his teeth and sipped his wine, his thoughts lost in the broken blue sprawl. Full of food and self-satisfaction, he lolled in the shade of the fort wall and paid no attention to the mustered slaves in the compound below him. He was long used to the sound of the whip on bared flesh. The Arabs could snap a man into submission without breaking the skin. A marked slave was worth less in the marketplace.

The Portuguese breakbones had been lancing and cauterizing boils all morning, purging both the men and women with senna gruel whether they were regular or not, and his assistants oiled the slaves from head to foot to keep their skins lustrous. So long as they showed no signs of hookworm or bad teeth and could walk when they boarded the American ship they would hold their price. What happened to them once they were at sea was not Dirk's affair.

The trip had gone well for Dirk and Laidler. Dirk had proved his worth with the chiefs they bargained with, and they had only been forced to flog and hang one buck to discourage the others from thoughts of escape, arriving in Delgoa Bay with a hundred and two sound slaves. Sixty-four bucks and thirty-eight women, only five of whom were in the early stages of pregnancy. Any babies born aboard the slave ships were thrown overboard at once, and some captains would not take women in that condition, for experience had taught them there were too many deaths among the suckling mothers to be profitable. Laidler had a special compound where wet nurses kept the babies alive when the younger, prettier mothers were shipped out. There was no room for sentiment when profit was involved.

Dirk was learning the finer points of trading quickly, from aging slaves by the condition of their teeth, to dosing a buck for internal worms with lye and potash mixed with molasses. It was pretty much like doctoring horses, he found.

So far, Laidler had kept him at arm's length when it came to bargaining with the buyers—that was something he kept to himself—but Dirk feigned patience and waited for an opportunity to present itself. He wanted more than the one-fifth share he had been offered, and meant to have much more. If not this next trip, then on the next, and it was only a question of how he braced Laidler when the time came.

The squeak of an unoiled wheel brought Dirk out of his reverie and he turned in time to see the two liveried blacks wheeling Laidler up the ramp toward him. There had been a subtle change in the shrunken man since he had received the news of Eastman's death. He was no less abrasive and forceful, but he was less inclined to the dark introspective moods that had marked their early days as they pushed into the hard northern territories. He slept more, and his light did not burn through the small hours. Dirk envied him that; his own nightmares still plagued his sleep.

Laidler snapped his fingers and one of his blacks dropped a chamois sack onto the table before Dirk. "Your share less expenses, de Villiers," said Cord. "A trader must always expect to be surprised by the unexpected and profit from it. I've profited from you and intend to do so again, that's if you have the will to continue in my employ. Wine," he snapped at his blacks. One of them poured a measure from Dirk's bottle into a clean glass and tasted it before giving it to Laidler.

Dirk grinned. "You take no chances, man."

"I pay others to do that. You, for instance." Cord sipped and made a face. "Disgusting. These Portuguese are barbarians." He looked through the wine as he held it up to the sun. "Their vines are good enough; they don't take their cellarage seriously."

"It's good enough to swallow, man." Dirk filled his mouth, gargled, and gulped his own draft down, reaching for the bottle again.

"The man who ran this post before me thought that and died in agony from a stomach full of ground glass. There are times when a man should take precautions, even a man like yourself."

"Is that how you took over," said Dirk, pushing back.

Cord almost smiled. "No, one of the slave women he had abused got to his decanter and his stewpot. He took three days to die. She died more quickly. I simply picked up the pieces where he left off. The fool had gone native and let things slide. One very rarely gets something for nothing. I had much to do to make the post efficient."

"And profitable?"

"And profitable." Cord threw his wine over the parapet

354

"There is good advice in what I'm telling you, de Villiers; take note."

"I may make a poor gentleman, Laidler, but some things get through the bone." Dirk tapped his forehead. "Only a man used to the soft things of life loses himself in this country. I sleep better on the ground than in a goose-down bed, and a knife and fork get between a man and his meat. I'll take an honest saddle horse to a carriage and I'll walk in preference to both if I feel myself getting soft. Maybe when I'm rich I'll worry about losing what I have, but I tell you, I won't have others take care of it for me like some."

Cord ignored the taunt with a hard blink. "Only a fool doesn't guard against poison. A man accrues jealousy along with his wealth."

"That point I'll take," said Dirk.

"Then we're gratified," sneered Cord, including his blacks. They both showed their teeth in a dutiful smile, the humor beyond them. "If everything goes to schedule we'll be loading the slaves at low tide tomorrow. They're easier to handle when there's no swell. Let them learn seasickness when they're safely chained below decks. I hate the stink of nigger vomit in the longboats. If the weather holds fair, another ship will be making the point about the same time. In that event, I shall be boarding her to take passage to the Cape. You will stay here with my Griquas and the Arabs. And, de Villiers, take their advice when they offer it. Where you're going, you'll need it."

"Along the Sabie? Why?"

"Not along the Sabie. Farther to the northwest. I have an order for thirty tall men; such men are found in that territory, and none of us have traveled that far before."

"Why tall men? They only have farther to stoop to reach the cotton."

"There is a man who shows curiosities to the nobility and quality folk. He has such novelties as two-headed dogs and malformed creatures in bottles. I hear he has two girl children joined at the shoulder preserved in alcohol. He wants thirty tall men to fight with forest-bred lions in an arena. Ordinarily I don't oblige such people, but in this case it suits my purpose." Cord produced a rolled map and had it spread on the table. "That is where you will be going," he said, tracing a route with his finger.

Dirk forgot to swallow wine.

"Something troubling you, de Villiers?"

"There," said Dirk. "With a few Arabs and Bastaards."

"Yes."

"Christ in heaven, man. That's Mzilikazi's territory and beyond."

"And that daunts you?" Cord sounded amused.

"It would frighten anybody without cow turds in his head."

"I see I must look elsewhere. You are obviously not the man I supposed you to be."

"Let me think, damn you." Dirk had paled under his tan. "You don't just walk in on Mzilikazi with a couple of bolts of cloth, some Sheffield knives, and spit on your hand before shaking his." Dirk stared pointedly at the dip in Cord's lap blanket where his leg used to be. "You know that, man. It could take weeks of sending gifts and messages. That's one tough old buffalo even you can't buy with beads and sweet words."

Cord's open smile did not reach his burning eyes.

"Ah, but I have something he wants badly. Come with me." Cord spun his chair and his blacks jumped to wheel him down the ramp. Dirk roused himself and followed more slowly, making it clear he jumped for no man.

They went down into the compound where the slaves were being segregated into separate pens. Soldiers who had been watching the fun sat along a parapet making coarse gestures at the women. Some of them remembered the days before Laidler when they had the pick of prettier ones for themselves. Laidler allowed no one to maul his property, and had the power to have any man flogged by the fort commandant if he should try. Dirk knew that embargo embraced himself while Laidler remained in the bay, but after that, well, he would see....

He followed Cord through the steel gates that guarded the soldiers' barracks and passed the blockhouse where the officers quartered, down winding stairways and into the labyrinth beneath. Dirk had not been down there before and was confused by the intersecting tunnels and walkways, but that did not stop him from realizing the potential of the cells and vaulted cellars for housing slaves when the compound was filled. Twenty percent of a thousand slaves would buy him half the farms in the Transvaal. His fear of Mzilikazi began to recede to manageable proportions.

Soldiers unlocked two grilled doors and relocked them after Cord and Dirk had passed into the passage beyond. Cord unlocked a door with his own key and wheeled inside a darkened room where he lit a pitch torch set in the wall. Long wooden crates took up most of the space and bore pokered marks between the roped handles. Cord pointed out an opened one and told Dirk to look inside. Dirk lifted out a long gun that had been cleaned of factory grease and assembled. The stock and butt were heavily carved and inlaid with mother-of-pearl and ebony. The filigree work around the sights and stockplates was gilded. He tested it for balance and it snuggled in against his shoulder and cheek as if it were made for him. The leaf sights were marked for eight hundred yards and he looked at Cord with disbelief.

"Is this a lie, or is this a gun for shooting angels?"

"It's true, de Villiers. It has a rifled barrel and will shoot with accuracy for about five rounds, then it's just a pretty club. The Hanoverian and Russians have equipped their rifle brigades with them, as have the British, although they have changed the ammunition issue. It takes a strong man to ram a patched ball home and causes his hand to shake so badly his aim is impaired. Also, its kick can dislocate the shoulder if held wrongly."

"Sounds like you can't give them away," said Dirk. "I'll keep to my smoothbore." The fine workmanship was lost on him. If a gun was not efficient, a Boer had no time for it.

"It also suffers from powder fouling, but it makes an impressive bang when it goes off."

"Only a kaffir would care about that," shrugged Dirk, puzzled by this frankness.

"Exactly my point, de Villiers."

Dirk suddenly saw what Cord was driving at. "Mzilikazi?"

"The very same. He wants guns, we give him guns. Shoot a cow for him, impress him. Blow holes in a row of shields for him. Kill an induna or two if it will make the point. He has no way of maintaining or servicing such weapons anyway, but giving him guns will buy his goodwill, I would say."

Dirk nodded, thinking ahead. "That it would."

"Take him twenty and offer him a hundred more. If we can open up Mzilikazi's territory, we'll be ahead of all Europe. The ivory alone is enough to make ten men richer than the Pope himself." Cord sounded strangled by the prospect and his face was all hollows in the torchlight.

"And all for twenty percent, neh?"

"Open up that kingdom, de Villiers, and I'll make you a full partner in the enterprise. That by any standard is generous."

Dirk was not taken in. "It'll be more than worth it."

"So, the Boer begins to think like a trader. Bravo."

"I learn fast, Laidler. Very fast when the first lesson saw me with a pistol at my head." He was referring to their encounter at the water hole.

"You stayed my hand then, de Villiers, but can you do as well with the Matabele?"

Dirk slid the rifle back into its box. "When do I start?"

"As soon as you wish."

"Draw up the papers," said Dirk, sweating in the close, foul air.

2

Boie did not like the rain forest.

The towering trees were taller than any thirty men and thicker around than any ten more. Their trunks were as withered as the knuckles of old warriors, and thickly hung with birdweed and climbing saffron. They crowded together and banished the sun from the secret places held sacred by the Zulu. There was no quiet. Even the silence rustled.

Unseen bush pigs rooted in the mulch and vervet monkeys squabbled in the invisible upper canopy. Blue duikers, delicate antelope the size of hares, nibbled the ferns and herbs among the fallen branches, moving along their trails like dainty ghosts, falling to Boie's snares too easily for his liking. He thought of them as trapped spirits who could only leave the forest by dying.

The dawn came more slowly to the forest than to the open savannah, and came less honestly. First light was a spreading blue gloom that writhed close to the eye, blinding it more than the true darkness. High pinpricks threw down thin shafts that streamed outward into thick, misty beams, deepening the shadows and highlighting irrelevant licks of bole and fern. Early flitting birds cut the beams and spread a thousand diffused shadows in all directions. The forest floor steamed where the light struck it and smelled of decaying mold. It was with good reason the Zulu had named this place Ngoye: Place of Seclusion.

Boie slung the three gutted duikers from his waist and made his way back to the glade where Nkosi had chosen to camp. He was learning where the boomslang snake liked to hide and where the big spiders hunted fledglings. He now knew the cry of the bulbul and no longer started when flycatchers darted past at head height. It was as well to know what was not dangerous as well as what he should be wary of; a man can use too much energy on the commonplace. All the same, he would be glad when it was time to go on toward the north. He could not live without the sun all around him.

Boie went toward the camp by a circuitous route, careful not to mark a single trail for any enemy to find. It also served to keep his son's wits sharp as he watched for his father's return. Boie skirted a bog humming with treeflies, keeping to the harder ground. He ducked under a fall of white alder covered in red pepper and false dodder and went up into the glade through long drapes of monkey rope, concealing himself until the last moment. Josef saw him immediately and clicked his tongue against the roof of his mouth to warn his mother of Boie's approach. Sergeant Coffee came out of sleep with his smoothbore raised and aimed, eyes wide and awake. He yawned when he saw it was the Khoikhoi and waved a lazy hand. Nkosi Matthew's sleeping mat was empty.

Boie patted his son's head and handed him the game to clean, wondering where Matthew was. Although the long journey across the Drakensbergs and the plain of Natal had strengthened him, he should not have gone off alone. He was still not as he should be. He was slow in waking and quick to sleep at night camp, sometimes dropping off before his plate was empty. When they had walked to save the horses he tired quickly and was unsteady on his feet after an hour's march. In the saddle he used the spur rather than his thigh to guide his horse, and was too free with rein and bit. His brain was quicker than his reflexes and his previous quickness would not return for some time yet, even though he ate for two and slept for two more.

Without seeming to, Boie toed Matthew's bedroll, feeling for body heat. There was enough to tell him Nkosi was no more than a quarter sweep of a clock away. He had gone out of the camp at first light toward the open ground to the west. Boie squatted on his haunches to think.

There had been easier routes across the great blue Drakensbergs than the one Matthew had taken, but he seemed to know it had to be that particular pass they used. It had been hard for them all, but hardest for Matthew, who felt the cold in his wounds despite the extra blankets Sergeant Coffee had bought in Pietermaritzburg at great risk. He had bought horses there too, and for little cost; the Boers seemed to have a surfeit of animals after the withdrawal from Congella. Only ammunition seemed to be scarce, although he had brought back a hundred rounds of ball in a British ammunition box with the foil intact. He had said that no soldier worth his salt could survive a campaign if he could not scavenge. He had said that with a broad wink and ruffled Boie's hair. Nkosi had said he should have been hanged if he had been caught and that had made Boie see a new strength in the Sergeant.

On the plain of Natal, Nkosi had backtracked to a water hole and made everyone stay back when he went down to the water's edge. Through the glass, Boie had seen him turn stones and rake the ground under a baobab, kick about above a salt lick in the embers of old fires. When he had come back he had said nothing, pointing north to show the way they must travel. Later that night at dry camp he had said Burning Spear traveled with Arabs and a *kakebeen* wagon drawn by twelve pairs of oxen. His face could have been worn by someone nobody knew and Ndala had forgotten herself enough to remark on it. Boie had been too distracted to beat her for it. Even Josef, who sat as close to Nkosi as he was allowed to, sometimes curling up to sleep in his lap, stayed on the other side of the fire that night.

Many times Boie had lost the spoor they followed on the rough ground, but Nkosi just looked at the sun and the lie of the land and pointed his horse the way he meant to go, and always they cut the trail of Burning Spear. Boie did not question this magic but he was in awe of it.

Only when they had crossed the Tugela River and the high savannah beyond had Nkosi faltered. He had made early camp and had shouted in his sleep as he burned with recurrent fever. They had not been able to travel for several days until the sickness had passed. After that, Matthew's eyes had been clearer and he was gentle with Josef again. They had cut sharply toward the coast and come to Ngoye Forest. Many times Matthew had turned in his saddle to watch behind him as they rode, and Boie had backtracked without being asked to. His senses jangled like Nkosi's yet he never saw any sign of pursuit, saw no fires in the night, no dust from horses or impi. Nothing but the many bald kopjes and the shimmering horizons, massing game herds, and flights of birds that numbered in the thousands.

Now they were in the rain forest waiting as Nkosi waited, patiently and without knowing why.

Boie alerted his son to keep vigil and slipped from the

camp with his bow. It was surer than the long gun in the forest. And silent. He kept his pace steady, even in the rare open spaces; nothing was worth blundering into trouble with ears dulled by pounding blood. Nkosi's trail was still fresh and plainly marked where he had brushed through the thick, pliable vegetation and scuffed the leafmold with his weaker left leg. The hardwoods gave way to the elegant stands of ivory palm and fleshy bouquets of lala vegetable and the open places were more frequent, the ground harder underfoot. The downland was a brilliant golden haze beyond the trees, rising in saffron ridges to cut up into a cornflower sky dusted with puffball clouds. After the subdued hues of the forest the savannah beat at the senses like dried flame.

Nkosi lay in the lea of a kopje watching the plain to the southwest, his legs and elbows spread, his musket at his shoulder and held there by one hand. He was using the glass despite the haze rippling over the plain, distorting the far saddles of ground. Boie shaded his eyes to scan the rolling land and saw nothing but stunted trees and the smudges that marked a straggle of rhinoceros. Seeing nothing meant nothing. An entire impi could be out there and remain invisible unless they flushed game or groundbirds. Looking at nothing and everything by ignoring his central vision, Boie angled down the slope toward Nkosi.

When he was about a hundred feet from him, Boie notched an arrow and fired past Nkosi's face, close enough for him to hear the whir and feel the wind of its passing. It was a signal they had practiced but never used.

Matthew lowered the glass and raised his hat without turning his head. He was glad that Boie had come but he was not about to take his eyes off a ridge he had been watching. It was about three gunshots away, just over two thousand yards. A hint of dust and the sharp gleam of light on bared metal had shown about twenty minutes before, and a crane planing in from the north had swung away and circled to the east before resuming its flight to the south. He knew somebody was out there. His spine and his neck hair had prickled constantly. Now, with the forest at his back, he could afford to find out who it was. He had the high ground and five miles of cover if the opposition proved too strong. There was a deep kloof guarding his right flank and the forest was at his back and ran into broken ground to his left. Whoever was coming must advance right into the muzzle of his gun.

A bird whickered and fled upward in spiraling flight.

361

Matthew ignored a maverick nerve that jerked in his leg and wiped his hands on the grass. He wanted no sweat on the gunstock.

Boie had gone down into the rough ground to his left and was making a flanking movement to bring his short bow into effective range.

The sun climbed and turned the sky white.

Matthew sweated and the best part of an hour crawled by.

His straining ears picked up the chink of a bit and the creak of saddle leather beyond the raw scrape of ground that marked the mouth of a shallow, open gully directly below him, the sides just deep enough to cover a mounted man. Matthew swung his gun to cover the approach to his right, easing back the hammer and setting the stock into his shoulder, his finger down the side of the trigger.

A hoof skipped on a stone and a hat passed between a cleft in the gully rim. Boie came up out of the bald crown of the upper gully wall well to the rear of the lone rider and made a hand signal for one man and four horses. He sank down and lost himself again.

Then the man was there, setting his horse at the slope, hanging forward over the animal's neck, standing on the stirrups. His black clothes were white with dust and his beard could have been any color. He was too big to be Dirk.

He reined in on the crest and mopped his face, squinting up at the forest above Matthew's head as Boie came up around behind him, his bow drawn back to full stretch. Although the Khoikhoi made no sound the rider jerked around at him, drawing his smoothbore from its scabbard.

Matthew blew the hat from his head.

The horses reared and the man lost his stirrups, falling heavily. Boie held his arrow and stayed where he was, shouting something Matthew did not catch. The big man stayed on the ground and growled back. The disturbed dust drifted away and the horses stopped dancing to nibble at the thin grass.

The man on the ground had started to swear in High Dutch. He made a fist at Boie and lambasted him roundly, his language becoming saltier the more the Khoikhoi grinned. When Matthew showed himself the big man rounded on him, hurling a stream of abuse at him as he came down from the kopje to stand over him.

"Blood on my head, you scrofulous anteater. I should withdraw your entrails, plait myself a larboard sheet, and sail

362

myself back to Holland in a coracle, damning myself for wasting effort on your worthless arse. Kick me for a kaffir if I don't. And stop your gibbering monkey from capering and showing his teeth. I thought he was going to stick me with that poisoned arrow, enough to soil my trousers. I've broken my back trailing you Bastaards halfway across this parched midden of a country the good Lord made for His scorpions. God rot you, Matthew Eastman." There was more of the same without a pause for breath.

Matthew reloaded as though he had the veldt to himself. He felt drained and wanted to lie down and sleep. This anticlimax to the strain of waiting left him completely enervated.

"You track well for a sailor, Klyn," he said.

Pieter Klyn wiped spittle from his dried lips and slapped dust from his trousers with a punch to the thigh.

"Well!" he roared. "Better than well. Like an Afrikaner emperor. Ach, man. Who else but an ignorant man would cross the Drakensbergs alone? Eh, eh? And for what? To be set upon by the very footpads he sought to bring horses to in the name of friendship. I withdraw my hand and offer you my fist." Klyn caught the waterskin Matthew threw him and unstoppered it to swill out his mouth. "At least your water is sweet. Which is more than I can say for your bloody disposition."

"You came alone?" Matthew was scanning the southern vista for movement. His scalp still crawled with concern for their safety.

"Of course alone. How else? If I had hired a guide I should have had to trust a stranger."

"You were lucky," said Matthew. "Why did you come?"

"You ask that, you ingrate? To kick your arse, why else? Why, he asks me." Klyn took more water and spat out the residue. "If I hadn't kept my ears open in Pietermaritzburg I should have lost you entirely. As it was I was stuck in that dustbowl Bible class for almost a full week." Matthew was looking at him now, studying him. Klyn scowled to stop a grin. "Ha, that means something to you, does it? I was in a hovel where I could buy beer. They were talking about a raid on their ammunition store. Who else but an Englander would steal British ammunition in preference to Boer-made ball, eh? That's how I reasoned. They told me they had made a Commando sweep toward Natal and picked up nothing. So, figuring they had narrowed the field for me, I came north toward Delgoa Bay."

"You followed our spoor?" Matthew could hardly believe it.

"Ach, no, man. A map of the coastline and dead reckoning got me here. I wouldn't know lion dung from a snowflake. You follow footprints and I'll rely on a sextant. The sun and the compass never laid a false trail as far as I know."

"See anything, Boie?" asked Matthew.

"Only the land."

Klyn retrieved his hat and held it out.

"Look at that. You took most of the crown out of it. That could have been my head."

"It wasn't. Time we were getting away from here. There may be someone behind, but they'll be at least two days behind us."

"Nobody follows you, man," snapped Klyn. "Nobody. You can come back to the Blesberg anytime you like. Your land is still yours, your friends are still your friends. They'll hang de Villiers if he ever comes back. The Volksraad scolded the Commando and condemned him. You are no outcast, Matthew."

"They came up the mountain," said Matthew, close to hissing.

"That was us, your friends. The Commando were helping us to search for you. My God, did you think—" Klyn broke off and nodded solemnly. "My God, you did. And I see why now."

Matthew nodded back. "Shall we go? Get your horse, you'll have to walk from here." Matthew began to turn away.

"Hannie Gould is well. She has Gaika safe," said Pieter Klyn, watching for a reaction that might mean he could tell Matthew his wife had gone to Port Natal where she hoped to take passage for Port Elizabeth aboard the *Mazeppa*. There was no response. "Doesn't that mean anything to you?" Klyn was angry again.

Matthew would not be drawn. He limped off up the rising ground, favoring his left foot. Boie fell in beside Klyn, his smile shy.

"It is good you are here, baas. The red soldier will show it."

Klyn gathered reins and set his ruined hat firmly. "Somebody should," he grunted, stealing a glance over his shoulder at the burning plain. "Why doesn't he turn back south, Boie? The land north of here falls off the map."

"His way is there, baas. My way is there."

"And so is mine, it seems," grumbled Klyn.

They went up into the forest and were swallowed by cool shades.

3

The country Dirk led his party through was a lush woman with no name.

In ancient times a powerful black clan had ruled her mountains and intersecting rivers from their stone city of Zimbabwe, had traded on an equal footing with Phoenician and Carthaginian alike; had supplied animals and men for the Imperial Roman Circus and exchanged gifts with three successive Caesars. How that once great dynasty had fallen was not recorded. The city itself was overgrown and forgotten along with its past glories by the scattered descendants of its founders. What man had thrown up, the land had reclaimed.

The winters were milder than on the Cape, the springs more fruitful, and the summers crackled with heat. Water and game were plentiful and crops grew for anyone with the will to scratch a furrow and plow in his seed; a land for hunter and farmer alike. A land that had fallen to the impi of Mzilikazi after his headlong withdrawal from the superior firepower of the Boers, consolidating his hold on this territory that would be known as Rhodesia a half century in the future.

Dirk had crossed many rivers and followed the Shangani until he branched north toward Lake Kariba. Stopping a hundred miles short of the great water, he had drawn up his four *kakebeen* wagons in a square and outspanned his ox teams inside a stoutly constructed thorn corral. The Griquas and Arabs had grumbled at the unaccustomed labor, but Dirk was taking no chances; none of them had dealt with the Matabele as he had. He had seen sign of passing impi, great swaths of flattened grass that showed the passage of men on the march. A bare day after he had established his small laager, a group of scouts bearing the white shields of the Invincibles came out of the trees to warn him he trespassed on the ground of the Great Bull Elephant, Father of a Thousand Impi, Lord of the Crocodile and the Vulture, Guardian of the Hills and the Thundering Waters, Whose Stamping Armies Made the Earth Shake and the Moon Hide from His Shining Face.

Dirk ordered his men to mill about to make their numbers seem greater and went out to talk to the Matabele across a white truce shield, his gun inverted and his hands empty.

When he had tricked the Matabele into announcing their
names he handed them a rifle wrapped in red cloth and called
upon the old mud father to witness the fact that these warriors bore his gift to Mzilikazi, begging the deity to spurn
their bones if they dishonored his trust in them by stealing
it. It was a powerful and insulting prayer, both enraging and
impressing the warriors in turn. Dirk had made enemies of
them as well as ensuring the rifle would reach Mzilikazi; for
before trying to kill the corngrower they must keep faith with
the King and the god, and by that time, Dirk hoped his gift
would have gained him the King's protection, putting him
beyond their reach. If he had not, Mzilikazi would order his
impi to wipe out Dirk's party anyway.

Taking one of the warriors inside the laager with him,
Dirk showed him the boxes of rifles and gave him a tally stick
with a hundred and twenty notches in it, telling him to take
it with the rifle to the King to show Mzilikazi how many guns
he wished to trade.

The Invincibles accepted Dirk's gift of snuff and stalked
away, their backs stiff with injured dignity. Only one of them
had not allowed the massive slight to his honesty to fire his
temper or to slow his wits. He had carefully tallied the men,
counted their horses and weapons, and noted the condition
of the oxen inside the *isango* hedge. He looked long upon the
face of the white who spoke his language fluently, saw the
iKlwa scars on his forearms, and was interested in the way
he had drawn up his wagons. It was eight years since he had
survived the great fight on the Vaal River and it was still
fresh in his mind.

His name was Sihayo and he had good cause to remember.

Saying nothing to the other younger warriors, who had
not faced the laagered wagons, Sihayo led the patrol back to
the Great King's kraal and asked to be allowed into Mzilikazi's presence. Over the three days he awaited the King's
pleasure, Sihayo prayed to the Earth Mother for dead Jakot's
luck and banged his forehead raw on the baked ground as he
looked for a skysign that would show he had been heard.

Because he was cattle-poor, he could not afford the minis-
trations of the witchmen, which was just as well, for they
kept no secrets from Mzilikazi if such intelligence could be
used to their own advantage. Sihayo waited outside the
King's enclosure during the day and drew off into the bush
at night, where he slept under his shield surrounded and
guarded by the other Invincibles in his patrol. They would

have preferred to have slept in the military kraal, but they could not let Sihayo and the corngrower's gift out of their sight.

The word was that the Great King was purifying himself before taking a young girl to wife prior to her first fruiting, which was against tradition. There were whispers within the seraglio itself, but none of the subjects outside the King's kraal dared to voice an opinion either way, for Mzilikazi's spies were everywhere, and to be accused of disloyalty was enough to be dragged from the ranks by the witchsmellers and disemboweled on the spot. If the King wished to bed an unripe girl then so be it. That was a matter for him, his witchmen and indunas, and not a matter for Sihayo and his brothers. The King's wrath reached beyond the offending individual to embrace his whole family, and if the crime was great enough, his entire clan.

Sihayo was oiling himself when he was ordered before the royal throne. Several regiments were drawn up around the inner kraal, two women's guilds kneeling before them. The throne was empty, and Sihayo was ordered to hand the gift to the indunas, to prostrate himself and wait. Sihayo threw himself down but refused to part with the corngrower's gift however much they threatened him with punishment. Any one of them could have ordered him to be slowly strangled for disobeying, but they knew the King wished to hear what Sihayo had to tell him about the intruders. The indunas talked fiercely in low voices and drew off, leaving Sihayo alone in the dust.

The King came out with his women and made the throne creak when he lowered himself onto it. Sihayo had not seen the King for four seasons and the size of him made the Invincible blink rapidly. Mzilikazi's belly was fuller than any two women with child and his thighs were as thick and glossy as brown crocodiles. His eyes were lost in rolls of fat and his chins hid his neck in their folds. His feet were swollen but his hands were still broad and long-fingered. Only the eyes had retained their hardness and missed nothing. He was still the Great King of the Matabele.

Sihayo lay still and trembled.

The impi made obeisance and stamped out the royal salute as the women counterpointed with their ululating cries of homage.

The pick of the white cattle from the King's corral were paraded and several felons were executed. A woman accused

of adultery by her husband was slashed open, and when no
fetus was found in her womb, she was declared innocent post-
humously. Her husband was strangled and his cattle given
to her family as compensation. The indunas applauded Mzilikazi's sagacity and the praise singer added another verse to
the King's anthem, an ongoing song that charted his reign
and acted as a rough calendar.

During all this, Mzilikazi's beer gourd was never empty;
his women kept it filled and wiped him off when he dribbled
down his belly. Sihayo marveled at how much he could drink
and how little it seemed to affect him. His eyes and hands
were steady and his voice was strong when he pronounced
judgment.

The sun was high when Sihayo was called. He crawled to
the King and handed him the gift, glad to be rid of it. Feigning
disinterest, Mzilikazi unwrapped the cloth and bared the gun
to the general gaze. The filigreed metal caught the sun and
light flared on the polished walnut stock. There was a buzz
of wonder that died away when the King glared around him.
If he was not impressed nobody else had the right to be.
Inside, Mzilikazi shivered. He had a recurring dream where
whole impi were armed with such weapons and they advanced
on their enemies, blowing them away in rolling white clouds
of greasy smoke. All that differentiated his warriors from the
whites were guns such as these, flaming sticks that could
reach beyond a long spearcast and make enemies dead, killing
anywhere a man looked when he pressed the little dagger on
the underside of the steel pole. There were golden animals
in the metal, dogs and birds and horses running inside a
border of twining leaves. None of his ironworkers could work
such magic for him; their best was the crude blades they cast
for the *iKlwas*. He must have the help of the corngrowers.
They must teach his men to make such marvels, show him
where the burning powder hid in the earth, give him the
magic boxes that made the gray balls round.

The whites who had come to his land professed ignorance
of such things and talked of a god who required a man to die
before he lived. Talked of eating the flesh of this god, of drinking his blood in order to be like him. No man was fat enough
to feed all of Mzilikazi's tribe, and eating human flesh was
for lesser men than the Matabele. None of his warriors would
serve with a man who ate human meat. In the early days of
his reign when he was not so strong, Mzilikazi had been
forced to impress such men into the ranks of his regiments,

but that was in the time of the great famine and was necessary. But to eat another man for the sake of a white god was barbaric. Such white holy men were liars. All whites had guns, all whites must know how to make and shoot them.

Mzilikazi promised himself that if any more missionaries came to his land he would cut off their parts, cook them over a fire, and see if the holy men could make themselves live again by eating their own flesh. That would show the lie, he thought. He must have guns.

Mzilikazi found himself staring at Sihayo. This dog had faced the guns on the Vaal, one of the very few of his warriors who had. He still had the marks of the burning powder on his face and shoulders. His back was smooth and unpunctured, though; he had not run away in panic but had retreated facing the enemy.

"Look at your king, dog," Mzilikazi ordered. "You have seen this gun fire?"

"No, Lord." Sihayo wished he could wet his mouth. "I have seen others shoot. One bit me...here." He pointed at the rib of scar tissue on his temple.

"At the killing hill."

"Aye, Lord. There."

"Your king exchanged many children for the bounty of cattle that enriched his kraal."

"As is fitting," said Sihayo, knowing he sounded too bold.

"Wrong, dog. Death should come to the King's enemies, not his children." Mzilikazi knew his remark would get to Mkalipi's ears as he meant it to. No induna should set himself higher than his king, even one who lost his regiments and brought back more cattle than the King had in all his kraals. The story of Mkalipi's skystone still rankled Mzilikazi and he kept his eye on the strength of the impi the induna counted loyal to himself. He had traded on his popularity too long for Mzilikazi's taste, and once an opportunity presented itself, the Great King meant to act swiftly and decisively. Nobody but a natural son named by himself would mount the throne after his death.

"I only meant to express loyalty, Lord." Sihayo stumbled over his words, expecting a spear through his neck any second.

"The King knows that as he knows all things," said Mzilikazi, considering assassins with a corner of his mind. If he had an impi armed with guns, of course, Mkalipi could not prevail against it. Then it would not matter how many regiments stood with him. Their spears would only be good for falling on. "Would you like such a gun, dog?" he asked.

"I, Lord? I am not worthy."

"True, unless I say otherwise. Will this one shoot?"

"The corngrower said so. The blunt hook must be pulled back and..." Sihayo was lecturing the King, who knew all things.

Mzilikazi sounded careless. "I know this, but you will make the gun shoot. Stand up."

Sihayo climbed reluctantly to his feet and took the rifle.

"Where shall I shoot, Lord?"

"At one of the women," said Mzilikazi. "Stand one up," he told the induna in charge of the women's guilds. "One who has displeased you."

Sihayo cocked the piece as a woman was pulled from the ranks and stood in the open. He jammed the butt into his belly and crouched to sight down the barrel, trying to make the metal twig line up in the V backsight. The trigger depressed under his finger before he was braced and the world upended as his stomach lost all feeling. He skidded along the ground and was brought up short against a mud wall. The roar of the gun made his head buzz and he gasped for breath. All his ribs seemed caved in and white smoke wreathed the royal throne, drifting across the kraal in thick coils. There was no sign of the woman he had fired at and all the warriors had lain down under their shields. Sihayo's eyes rolled and he passed out.

He was slapped and pummeled and water smashed over his head. He was dragged back to the Great King only half-aware of what was happening. Sound came and went and he wondered why the Great King was laughing. Flesh quivered as he slapped his huge thighs, pointing off in the direction Sihayo had fired. Sihayo turned his head and saw the woman twitching on the ground, her shoulders a red ruin. Her head was a body length beyond, propped up on the severed neck, eyes wide with shock. Sihayo tried to laugh and was sick instead, which made Mzilikazi laugh all the harder. Shame-faced warriors were climbing to their feet and grinning foolishly, slapping each other on the shoulder. Truly, it was a formidable weapon.

Frightened and proud, Sihayo tried to stay on his feet as he accepted Mzilikazi's congratulations.

Later, Mzilikazi told him what he must do.

That night, Sihayo saw a skystone fall and knew it was the sign he had waited for.

4

For the first several days of the voyage, Elise kept to her tiny cabin in the forecastle and did not know who her fellow passengers were. Most of them had boarded at Delgoa Bay and were already installed when she came aboard at Port Natal. The fresh swell and her own sickness made the passage a constant misery. The food was badly prepared salt pork mixed with hard scoops of biscuit meal that ran with weevils.

The captain had assigned a man to guard her door for a consideration, and had invited her to sit at table with him on three separate occasions. His food was only marginally better than her own ration, but she found his talk about Port Elizabeth diverting if scant and confined to the waterfront.

The second time she had accepted the captain's invitation to dine there had been another guest, a man confined to a wheelchair who questioned her closely about her life on the Blesberg once he had learned her name. He commiserated with her new state of widowhood and her pregnant condition, referring to it with an oblique gentility she found flattering. She was not as happy about his morbid interest in the details of Matthew's death, however, but he made amends by sending small delicacies to her cabin each evening.

She never spoke to him again, although she glimpsed him taking the air when she slipped up on deck to watch the stars. The day she disembarked she sent a polite note of thanks for his many kindnesses but received no reply, and it was not until she had taken a carriage out of the port that she realized she had never learned his name. But it was not something to fret her for any length of time; she was too much interested in meeting with her parents again and planning for the future.

By the time she had reached her father's emporium she had quite forgotten Cord Laidler.

Rounding the Cape of Good Hope had been done in worsening weather and took the *Mazeppa* ten long days.

She had lost her mizzen in a thunderstorm and the mountainous seas running against the gale-force winds had made running repairs impossible. Two deckhands had been swept away while cutting away the wreckage, and the small coastal trader had been forced to lay off on half-canvas until the winds blew themselves out.

Cord Laidler was a good sailor but he wisely remained below decks, preferring the swill of the stinking bilges and the press of stale humanity to braving the waves that smashed over the upperworks. His two blacks were prostrated by chronic mal de mer and he was forced to fend for himself, living on raisins and hardtack soaked in wine.

More than once he thought the ship would not survive the breaking sea and was about to take him to the bottom. Although he did not relish dying in such a manner, he experienced a feeling of distaste rather than of fear, and occupied himself by systematically putting his affairs in order.

Confirmation of Matthew Eastman's death by his widow had lifted a weight from Cord's shoulders, for now there was nobody who threatened his claim to his son and the woman he had married. He prepared a detailed and comprehensive will naming Jamie as his sole heir, stipulating that the boy should take control of the estate upon gaining his majority. Until that time the executors Cord named would administer it within the guidelines Cord painstakingly laid out. After due deliberation, Cord made a substantial allowance for Katherine, which was to last until her death or until she remarried, at which point all payments must cease along with her use of his name.

This was the first time Cord had seriously considered his own mortality, or for that matter, the continuance of his name through his son and the generations that might follow. Now that the specter of Matthew Eastman no longer clouded his judgment, Cord found he wanted that very badly. He also recognized he must show more affection for, and a greater interest in, his son's welfare and education. Jamie was at an age where he should be ready to be shown the extent of his father's holdings and to learn the rudiments of business. The boy already demonstrated resilience and a quick mind. The previous summer a mamba had dropped onto his bed, coiled and ready to strike. Jamie had sat rigidly until the snake had calmed, then he had thrown the counterpane over it and called for a houseboy. Had he cried out or moved suddenly, the snake would have undoubtedly struck him full in the face, killing him instantly.

Cord had wanted to gather up the boy and cover him in praise, but as always, he had drawn back and said nothing. But now, if he survived, he meant to change all that. He had won an empire, so how much more difficult could it be to win the heart of a small boy? Cord would show him both the ballroom and the wilderness, make him equally at home in either.

The weather broke as quickly as it had come. The skies cleared to a high and hard blue, and the seas rolled green with a following breeze. Tacking around the point, the *Mazeppa* made good time up the coast and into the anchorage of Table Bay. Word had gone ahead from the lookouts stationed at the Twelve Apostles station, and as the longboats pulled for the shore, Cord saw that Elias awaited him with the carriage and a baggage wagon. He also noticed that the contractors had finished roofing his new warehouse and that a man was painting his name in tall white letters on the shingles. Several Indiamen lay off in the deep water and lading boats were ferrying barrels from his private jetty under the eye of the Customs men. Cord took his last breath of salty air as he was lifted onto the quay, where the baking stones made him sweat along with the kaffir dockers who labored around him. He should have liked to have taken a further turn around the bay to prolong his enjoyment of the clean ozone, but there was much to be done and he was still unused to this newly rediscovered appreciation of his surroundings.

For years, he realized, he had thought of nothing save money and business, of manipulating others in the pursuit of wealth. He scarcely remembered the last time he had watched an eagle in a thermal or bees collecting pollen in a garden of brilliant blooms. He could walk with the aid of a cane if he wished to, with the aid of a false wooden limb he could be seen standing in public if he chose. He smiled at the novelty of sitting a horse again, riding out with Jamie at his side, through the thousands of acres of vines heavy with thick-skinned grapes. There was no such smell in the world as the first pressing of a vintage. He must share that with the boy.

As he was being helped up into the carriage the waterproofed bundle of papers inside his coat crackled under his hand. His sudden laugh startled Elias as he climbed onto the driving box. Cord found Elias's expression as amusing as the thought that had just crossed his mind.

"Damn the chariots of hell," Cord said aloud. "If I *had* gone to the bottom, my son's birthright would have drowned with me. A waste of labor through and through." He prodded Elias with his cane. "*You*. Take me to my solicitor's chambers in Fish Alley. Hurry now."

Elias flinched, knowing he must find a way of diverting Cord. If the baas went to Fish Alley that man Bentley-Parsons would come slithering up on his belly and make trouble for the Missie. Christmas Christ, his office was only two doors along from the baas's legal man's office. He would be certain sure to see the carriage and recognize it.

"But baas, you ain't even off the boat yet. You don't want to go down there with them stink smells. Your legal man usually comes up to the house, that's fitting with your dignity. You send one of them lazy boys running there, baas. I get you away home out of this heat. It cooler there. The Missie waitin' too."

"Fish Alley," ordered Cord, sitting back and closing the subject. His blacks had climbed up behind and wore their tall hats. Elias gave up and set the horses forward, thinking out a circuitous route. He decided against that ploy immediately; Baas Laidler would notice and beat him until he told him his reasons. Then the whole story would come out and he could not save himself or the Missie. His hands slippery on the reins, Elias made the journey last fifteen minutes, driving as though the horses had glass legs.

When Cord had been carried up to his solicitor's rooms he sent his bodyguards downstairs to wait with the carriage; he wanted no eavesdroppers.

To pass the time, the two men described the sea voyage to Elias in graphic detail, each pointing up the weakness in the other during the worst part of the stormy passage. Elias could not concentrate on anything they told him, certain that their raised voices would attract the attention of the thin, cadaverous man who threatened the Missie. He should have cracked their heads together if he could have been sure the brawl would not have attracted just as much attention. Miserable and fretful, he crouched on the driving box and watched the upper windows for the hated sallow face.

Elias did not notice the middle-aged clerk emerge from the building until his sleeve was tugged and his name called.

"Baas," said Elias, looking down into mild brown eyes enlarged by thick eyeglasses. "I'm Elias."

"You are to come with me at once at your master's request. Hurry now, and bring your, er, companions." There was a slick of perspiration on the pink jowls and the clerk's hands washed themselves until Elias dropped down beside him.

Then they locked onto Elias's thick wrist and he was dragged down the street with the other two blacks trailing along behind. When they turned into a narrow doorway and mounted a dusty flight of wooden stairs, an awful realization dawned on Elias and he tried to hang back. The clerk would have none of it; he pulled Elias along with him, giving instructions in a nervous, breathless stream.

"Your master charges you to do as I tell you. On the next floor is an office. If it is locked you are to break it down. The man inside is to be restrained if he tries to...abscond. All highly irregular, I admit, but one must do as one is bid. When you have hold of the man he is to be brought back to your master in chambers. You are charged not to lose him. And, most importantly, you are not to harm him in any way. Is that clear?"

"Yaas, baas," Elias said miserably, clumping onto the landing outside an office.

"Go to it then," said the clerk, elbowing the small of Elias's back.

"Watch out, mans," yelled Elias, hoping the warning would be heeded. He shouldered the door from its hinges without trying the handle and stumbled into the room after it. The door fell across the corner of a desk and a man in rusty black started out of his chair, spilling ink over documents.

"Him?" bawled Elias, holding back as the others crowded in around him.

"That is the man," said the clerk, pointing at Bentley-Parsons.

"Oh, mans," groaned Elias, walking up the door onto the desktop. "Why din't you run out the window? Now you got to come." He dug a fist into the soiled shirtfront and lifted Bentley-Parsons up to his face. "Mans, now we all dead mens. You going to meet the mans who show you what you really is. And mans, you make one bad say about the Missie, me and these bad kaffirs twist off your whole head."

Bentley-Parsons sagged in terror as Elias took him up around the waist and hauled him out and down the stairs, knocking the man's head on every finial and buttress that presented itself. Out in the alley, more to waste time than for the pleasure of it, Elias dropped Bentley-Parsons into a heap of horse dung. Then, hefting him effortlessly, Elias took him up to the solicitor's chambers, where he dropped him at Cord's feet, all the time wishing he had squeezed his windpipe enough to keep him silent, seeing himself spread-eagled under the lash with flies feeding on his blood.

Bentley-Parsons began to bluster until he saw the look on Cord Laidler's face and realized that Mr. Hollings the solicitor was not about to protest on his behalf. Just how much power Laidler wielded within the Colony was suddenly clear to him, for here was an honest lawyer with some real standing in the community being a party to what amounted to a blatant case of criminal abduction.

Bentley-Parsons coughed into his filthy handkerchief, working on ways to make these men pay for the indignity he suffered at their hands. He wiped off his mouth and said, "I protest. You have no right...."

Elias hit him in the back of the neck at a signal from Cord, who waited until a second coughing fit came and went before speaking, his voice a menacing monotone.

"You have no right of protest here, my unwashed manikin. You forfeited that right when you thought to sell me this letter." Cord held the facsimile Bentley-Parsons had left in Mr. Hollings's care to await Cord's return to Cape Town. The solicitor still had no idea what it contained, and had no curiosity about it. Cord Laidler was worth over five thousand guineas a year to his practice and he was not about to jeopardize that business or the other benefits Laidler's patronage brought him over the mistreatment of a dealer in secondhand furniture.

"You should have thought a second and a third time before attempting to sell me something that has no value to me. The original of this sordid ramble is worthless."

"All reputations have a price," said Bentley-Parsons with a show of vicious spirit. "You'll pay for every line, word by word. And for this indignity."

"Wrong, my Irish cockerel. I have no reputation in the social sense. I have nothing to lose, whereas you have lost everything. I make it my business to know about people, you see, and I know all there is to know about you, Samuel Arthur Taggart."

The man on the floor could not speak. He had badly judged his approach to Cord Laidler.

Cord's sneer was like a tear in white paper.

"I keep files on every mother's son in this colony. Mr. Hollings here keeps these files for me. See, I have yours open before me. You came here from Dublin Town a skip-and-jump ahead of the sheriff's bailiffs, wanted for fraudulent extortion.

I know to within a schilling what your banking balance is, and I know where you keep your records. I have copies of those too, just in case you thought to embarrass any of my own friends. You see, only I expect that privilege. And according to this note you left with Hollings, you thought to extort money from my wife during my absence." Cord threw a cold glance at Elias and started him sweating again. "There are no secrets in this colony I am not privy to. As my people know and you are about to discover."

"A claim is a boast until proven," said Bentley-Parsons.

"Then I shall take the trouble to show you that proof," said Cord, playing with a purse heavy with coins. "You aren't even a good thief; you trade on the fears of those who have only the barest grasp on the petticoats of society. You should have stayed feeding on suchlike pathetics instead of coming at me. I have something more abiding than reputation. I have power." Cord threw a handful of sovereigns into Bentley-Parsons's face. They struck down all around him and chimed off into the dark corners. "You wanted money; there is your money. It will afford you a steerage passage away from Cape Town, and if you're sensible, from Africa."

"I have no intention..." Bentley-Parsons gasped as Elias's fist clamped around his neck, forcing him to hold Cord's icy stare.

"A messenger is on his way to your bankers with orders to bring your deed boxes here to me. When they arrive, you will sign for them and assign them to me. All your other assets are frozen and will remain so until your business has been thoroughly investigated by officers of that bank. It is clear that there are serious irregularities in the manner you have conducted your affairs during your time here among us."

"Bluff, damn you, Laidler. No bank would act in such a fashion, not even for the high and mighty Cord Laidler."

"I own the bank and I own you. A correct statement, Hollings?"

Hollings confined himself to a nod and Bentley-Parsons coughed into his handkerchief.

"There's an Indiaman leaving on the evening tide. You will be on it. The boys will see to that. If you ever try to return I shall kill you. Not that I think you will; your physician tells me you have the coughing sickness and less than a year to live. Time enough to make landfall and get yourself decently buried."

377

"It's a mistake to leave a man with nothing, Laidler."

"Nothing?" Cord raised an eyebrow over one hollow eye. "Fifty guineas and your life? I consider that generous." He tapped Hollings's desk with an immaculate nail. "See that my orders are carried out. I'll expect to receive the documents at my home later today. I'll leave the boys with you; Elias can take me home. We have much to discuss, don't we, Missie's elephant?"

"Yaas, baas." Gas bubbled in Elias's stomach.

"You can leave it all safely in my hands, Mr. Laidler," said Hollings, rising and offering his hand.

Cord ignored it, pushing himself toward the door. He was anxious to see his son and the expression on Katherine's face when he handed her the original suicide note. On the way home he bought a box of lead grenadiers for Jamie and a finely wrought silver box, just large enough to take the folded sheets of paper, planning to present the gifts at the dinner table that evening.

On the open road he gave Elias the edge of his tongue and a bag of silver schillings, confusing and frightening the big black in equal proportion. For him, there was no understanding the baas and the open smile he had never seen before.

5

Pieter Klyn watched the fat Portuguese caporal trying to work out what had happened to him when he had ducked inside the hut in search of the old chief who sold him women to spend his furlough with.

Caporal Hernandez had never truly lost consciousness, but the blow to the back of his head had stopped him caring too much about being trussed up and searched. Because discordant bugles blared inside his head when he moved he lay still and tried to work backward from the brief and total blackness that had swallowed him.

He had left the Delgoa Bay fort on a borrowed horse and made the kraal of the old chief and his many "daughters" within two hours. Apart from the dogs and scrawny chickens there was no sign of life among the huts. Caporal Hernandez had not been unduly alarmed; the old chief sometimes took his people off into the bush for some obscure aborigine rite or other when the mood took him, but he was never gone for more than a day. Dismounting and hobbling his horse, Hernandez had found himself some kaffir beer and gone to the chief's hut, where the world had caved in on him.

Why was another matter. He had been there many times since Senhor Laidler had barred the soldiers from seeking comfort in the slave compound. A little initiative had found him this place, and a few copper buttons gained him the female company he sought. Today he had brought a mirror and he wondered if it had broken when he fell.

Caporal Hernandez opened an eye and saw Pieter Klyn eating mealie pap from a wooden spoon, washing it down with kaffir beer. Another man with red-gray hair drew a cleaning rod through a smoothbore and a big, rawboned man who looked to have been ill recently whetted a knife on a stone. A small kaffir from the southlands squatted in the hut doorway, dipping arrows into a jar of venom and laying them in the sun to dry.

Caporal Hernandez thought he had seen the man who ate mealie pap before, and he puzzled over it as his head thumped. Had he not been aboard a slaver with a Dutch captain? Earlier in the year when the man who boasted of being an agent of the Hollander King had said he meant to rouse patriotic feelings among the Boer trekkers down the coast in Natal? Yes, this was the first officer who had avoided any contact with the slaves the captain was buying to be boarded when he came back north.

With sudden insight, Caporal Hernandez saw that these men were antislavers, enemies of Senhor Laidler and the new Hollander who had gone up-country to the land of Mzilikazi. None of them looked like missionaries, quite the opposite in fact. They wore their weapons like extensions to themselves and used their ears without thinking about it. They were men of the bush and as unpredictable as the wild pigs or the big cats Hernandez hated so much. Even the sailor looked down at him as if he were raw meat fit for the lure. Hernandez knew he would give them whatever they wanted, including the secret way into the fort if they needed that intelligence.

The one who had been ill said something in English, a language Hernandez understood little and spoke less. He shook his head.

"I do not understand, senhor," he mumbled. "You talk Portogee?"

Pieter Klyn licked off his spoon and wagged it.

"I do. Who, apart from the soldiers, is at the fort?"

"You speak it well, senhor," said Hernandez, ingratiating

379

himself. "Very few now that the Yankee traders have gone. Just a few Griquas and the agent for the slavers."

"No Dutch?"

"No, senhor."

"You're sure?"

"All are gone. Some one way, some another."

"If your tongue lies it goes to the wild dogs, neh?"

"As God's mother loves me I tell the truth. Senhor, with Christ's Calvary nails through my own palms I could not speak truer." Hernandez listened for horses and the sounds of other men outside. If these men meant to waylay a slave train they would need many more men and guns than he had seen, for soldiers would be sent from the fort if the commandant lost his slave bounty. Capitão Valques meant to go home a rich man who could afford to buy back his long-lost family estates. Old pride was worthless without new money, and Valques would fight all the Kaffir in the world to ensure an escudo of profit.

Klyn, Coffee, and Matthew spoke together, ignoring their prisoner.

"What do you want from me?" asked Hernandez wearily. "I will tell you anything to keep my life. All Africa knows Senhor Laidler runs the slaving here, hand in hand with Capitão Valques. As close as two fingers in a fist. Together, they are one giant with arms that reach far."

"He favors the bastinado as I remember," said Klyn.

"You have seen it as I saw you, Senhor Klyn," said Hernandez. "Forgive me, I recognize you now. We talked, you and I, after such a punishment. That man still does not walk well." A thought struck Hernandez. "Ah, my loose tongue. I told you of this place, didn't I? I told you. That is how..."

Pieter Klyn nodded. "That's how we're here, Caporal."

"Please, senhor, forget your plans to take their slaves. You will die, I will die. I have little to live for, but it is more than I wish to lose. Believe me, the soldiers will come. The Arabs and the Griquas will come and we will die."

"Perhaps." Klyn tamped tobacco into his pipe.

"Not perhaps, *certainly*. How can I go back without taking you as my prisoners? Capitão Valques will expect it. We both know that is not possible, but he will hang me if I do not. What am I to do, senhor?"

Klyn translated that for the others and Coffee smiled.

"I have the answer," said Hernandez. "If I haven't seen

380

you, you haven't seen me. You go your way and I go mine, you see? Let us be strangers and live."

"Ask him about de Villiers," rapped Matthew.

Hernandez recognized the name and nodded himself nauseous.

"I know this Hollander. He has gone from the fort, you are too late. Four, five weeks ago. The day after Senhor Laidler went back to the Cape aboard the *Mazeppa*. He is gone and I thank the blessed virgin for it. There is no way of finding him."

Again, Klyn translated for Matthew and Coffee.

"Ask him where he went," said Matthew, splitting straws with his keen knife.

Klyn did so and listened to a stream of rapid Portuguese before saying, "I don't think he knows. He says Dirk went north of the Sabie into land where nobody goes. The natives there are not so docile as in this immediate territory. They're bad, he says."

Matthew's knife buried itself to the handle in the dirt between Hernandez's thighs, pinching out a wedge of flesh from his left leg.

"Matthew!" said Coffee. "Damn it, this is going too far. I won't stand for torture. God, we'll be as bad as the kaffir if we resort to that. D'you hear me?"

Matthew ignored him. "Klyn, tell him I want all he knows or I cover him with molasses and leave him over an anthill."

"When your knife is in its sheath, man. I'm with Coffee on this. Don't make me fight you now, you can't go on without us. You'd try, of course, but the outcome would be the same. Dirk de Villiers would evade you and you will die for nothing."

Matthew stared at Klyn before he pulled his knife from the earth, wiped it off, and lost it under his coat. "Just tell him about the anthill. The threat's enough; I'm not going to cut him into strips if that's what you thought. And Pieter, make sure he doesn't tell you any more than he really does know." He turned away abruptly and sat back in the shadows.

Hernandez whimpered, drawing Klyn's eyes to his own.

"Senhor, I know nothing of the country the Hollander travels in. It is Mzilikazi the Matabele's kingdom. He goes there to trade guns for ivory and slaves."

Matthew was back, towering over the Portuguese caporal.

"Mzilikazi? You said Mzilikazi?"

"Sim, senhor," flinched Hernandez.

381

"He trades guns with the Matabele? How many guns?" asked Klyn, and when Hernandez told him he told Matthew, who was gathering up the contents of his saddlebag, muttering Mzilikazi's name over and over again. Coffee and Klyn exchanged glances. Boie had come erect in the doorway, a rigid and incensed figure whose grin was as hard as a bite.

"The leopard and the spear go to the elephant, Nkosi," Boie said in his own tongue so that only Matthew understood.

Klyn looked down at Hernandez. "What about the caporal?"

"Leave him and take his horse," said Matthew, making for the entrance in a ducking stride. "He'd rather be afoot than dead, neh?" He scattered chickens as he made for his horse. Having an extra horse meant that Ndala and Josef could ride separately and not share the overworked bathorse. Now they would make better time, he thought, trying to remember what the Kommissie Trek had told him about the land ahead when they had scouted it for van Rensburg all those years before.

He was mounted when Hernandez came blinking into the light, gingerly holding his breeches away from his cut thigh. "Klyn, ask him if de Villiers had wagons with him, and how many."

Klyn did and held out four mute fingers.

"And ox teams?"

"Twelve pairs to each wagon."

Matthew made a swift calculation. "Then his five-week lead is cut by half. We'll be on him in about ten days, by God. Think of that!" He spurred his horse for the *isango* wall and cleared it, whooping and waving his hat.

Coffee waited for Ndala and Josef to mount. "What then, Klyn?" he asked.

Klyn had no ready answer.

6

The Great King Mzilikazi had called a Great Assembly.

Wild rumors swept the kraals of the Matabele as the impi hurried to the new royal kraal set between two hills that rose and separated themselves from the plain of sweet grass as softly as a reclining woman's breasts. All the King's indunas were to attend without exception, bringing with them all their herds to be recorded on the royal tally sticks, all outstanding tribute and suitable gifts. The women's guilds built temporary kraals to house the incoming regiments and the granaries were opened for beermaking. All the King's zebu bulls, cows, and calves were gathered on the flat western pastures, and the royal herdboys plaited the tails of all Mzilikazi's favorite white cattle for a parade that was to last all day and shake the earth for miles. The impi were to dance for the King and to pit their champions against those of other regiments, the surviving supreme champion to be given the honor of raising a new impi for the King.

The Matabele knew something of true import had taken place, for such Great Assemblies of all the clans traditionally coincided with the first green shoots of spring and were not called in the heat of November when the land lazed and slumbered.

The rumors were many and varied. It was said that a double-headed calf with the gift of tongues had been born, that at last Mzilikazi meant to name his successor. There was talk of a golden stranger among the clans, the one of ancient legend who was to bring a new king from the upper skies, one who would make the Matabele the rulers of all Africa.

Only Sihayo and his patrol moved against this flood. Charged with bringing the corngrower and his small train to the King, they made their way back to Dirk's laager. On the third day they came upon the massed impi who followed Mkalipi, the six regiments camped in battle order, head, horns, and loins spread out over a quarter mile of veldt. The discipline of these six thousand men was reputed to be the finest, matched only by the King's elite, the Invincibles. Rivalry between the regiments was keen and fighting between the groups was a common thing when they chanced to meet without their indunas.

Sihayo would have skirted the huge army but he remembered Mzilikazi's orders and trotted his men into the heart of the bull's head where he knew Mkalipi would be resting behind his men's shields. There was jeering when Sihayo drew closer and stones were thrown until the warriors saw the King's bloodmark on his shield. To injure or abuse a king's personal messenger was to court a lingering and painful end; killing one meant the death of the entire offending impi and their families.

Sihayo was brought before Mkalipi and they exchanged compliments and greetings. Mkalipi wore his *umuTsha* low on his hips to display his lucky scars and the skystone from old Sigwe's *mouti* bag hung from his neck. His belly was slightly bigger, but his limbs and chest were still trimly muscled. It was said he could lift a warrior by the ankle with one hand even though he had seen forty summers. He asked Sihayo why he had honored him by seeking him out in Mzilikazi's name.

"Lord," said Sihayo. "I take a gift from the Great Elephant to a corngrower who camps a day from here. I tell you this in the King's name, for this corngrower is not be harmed, but is to be brought safely to the King's kraal to look upon Mzilikazi's face."

Mkalipi hid his fired curiosity. His scouts should have found this corngrower and brought his head to him on a pole. Backs would be lashed to the bone for it. He had to know why the King wanted to see this corngrower alive rather than headless. "Then you must do this thing, messenger," he said. "I will send men to protect your shield."

Sihayo pretended the insult was an honor.

"I thank you, Lord, but Mzilikazi wishes me to go alone. There are words I must speak to the white no other must hear."

"We are all the King's subjects. Does this corngrower come into these lands alone and by the invitation of the King?"

"He comes with half-men and others who buy slaves, Lord. He has the King's protection. If my Lord would tell all those he meets this, he will have served Mzilikazi well."

"My men will thunder it," Mkalipi said easily. Sihayo was giving nothing away and Mkalipi wondered how he could bring him over to his standard. "The corngrower would have sent a gift to the Great King. It must have been of some magnificence. Did you see what it was?"

"Aye, Lord. A gun banded with yellow metal."

Mkalipi's face was too smooth. He looked out over the ranks of his impi and patted his horse's neck. The short white hair under his hand was comforting. What kind of a corngrower gives a gun to the Matabele? he wondered, half-guessing the answer. He killed his other thoughts and said pleasantly, "Sihayo, messenger to the Great King we all serve, you must take meat and milk from my own plate before you travel on. I insist as I would for the King himself were he here in my camp. Take your ease and go in peace in your own time."

Dismissed, Sihayo bowed and moved away, not daring to refuse the induna's hospitality, although he knew he should be on his way as rapidly as possible. Only dead fools trusted Mkalipi when they served the true King of the Matabele.

Mzilikazi had said the induna would delay Sihayo in order to organize his own spies, and had warned him to leave the confines of the camp while the sun was still high.

Sihayo gobbled down the beef he was served, swallowed some curdled milk, and belched loudly out of respect for his host. When he had bowed before Mkalipi's totem he took his patrol south at a leisurely pace until he was out of sight of the camped impi.

In a gully he forced himself to vomit for fear of poison, swilled out his mouth from a stream, and led his men to the southeast at a dead run, laying a false trail through the kloofs and kopjes.

Sihayo did not expect to lose Mkalipi's trailing spies, but Mzilikazi had warned him he should be seen to try just hard enough for appearance's sake. Alternately running and walking, Sihayo changed direction many times, drawing his overzealous pursuers into the open more than once. When he swung west by south onto his true course, he and his men counted three separate parties on their trail.

For the sport of the chase, Sihayo's group rested at the mouth of a wide pass where lions liked to lie up between hunts, forcing Mkalipi's men to hide in the thorn thickets until they moved again. Just before dusk, Sihayo ran his men down into the pass and brought them out on the other side just as the sun died. Those who came after had a bad time of it.

Sihayo and his men ran on through the night and dry-camped in sight of Dirk's fires, sleeping under their shields until first light. They spent the morning dressing their hair, oiling their limbs, and painting ocher onto their faces. Then, watched by Mkalipi's spies, they walked to within musket range of the wagons and hailed the men inside, calling Dirk out to talk.

Squatting in the sun, Sihayo thought Mzilikazi would be pleased with the way things had gone. By the time Sihayo had delivered the King's message to the corngrower the day would be spent and the wagons would not set out for the Great Kraal until the following morning. That would put Mkalipi a day closer to Mzilikazi and his spies a day farther from him. Even if they traveled day and night, his spies would not catch up with Mkalipi until he was on the point of entering the King's presence. Their intelligence would be of little use by that time and the arrival of the wagons a day later could be staged just as Mzilikazi wanted.

Sihayo concentrated on what he was to say to the corngrower on behalf of the King as Dirk walked toward him, suppressing his own feelings in order to do so.

Only time would give Sihayo what he wanted for himself. He and Dirk spat on their palms and clasped hands.

"I see you, corngrower," said Sihayo, bowing his head.

"And I see you," said Dirk.

"I see you with the eyes of the Great King, for I am his messenger. He asks if your father and his father are well, if your sons are strong and your uncles and nephews are honored in your eyes. He asks these things for he wishes to honor them as he would honor his own clan."

"They are honored as I humbly honor all Mzilikazi's ancestors, his wives, his sons, and his own person," Dirk answered, using the polite language of the Zulu fluently. He went on to honor all the King's relatives, his cattle, and his personal strength and wisdom. The speech was half through when there was a shout from the laager in hoarse Arabic.

Dirk turned to see the front ranks of a Matabele regiment stream out of the trees to encircle the wagons. Sihayo had started up and his men rose with him, automatically forming a defensive ring around both men.

"Sihayo, they are the Bees, Mkalipi's men," said a Matabele.

"I see them," said Sihayo, realizing that he and Mzilikazi had been outmaneuvered. Mkalipi had obviously sent an entire impi to his rear to take the corngrower for his own glory, which meant that Sihayo's messenger's shield would not protect him. "We are betrayed, corngrower," he said simply.

Dirk was not listening. He pulled a horse pistol from under his shirt and slammed it against Sihayo's temple, dropping the Matabele where he stood. He shouldered out of the ring of Invincibles and ran for the laager, intending to die with his back against a wagon. He would not be taken alive. Stealing a look over his shoulder he stumbled and almost fell, twisting his ankle painfully. Warriors were already hacking at the Invincibles as they stood their ground around Sihayo's body.

Dirk ducked under the stab of a *iKlwa* and shot the Bee through his shield, throwing him back against the men behind him. Thin firing came from the wagons and there were already Matabele inside the *isango* corral. A shield slammed Dirk to the ground and he rolled onto his back, kicking for a crotch and scrabbling for the stabbing spear when his heel went home. He was kneed in the neck and the flat of an *iKlwa* cracked against his skull.

Screaming with demented rage, Dirk threw himself in among the muscular black legs, punching and kicking at crotch and groin until a hardwood club smashed down onto his head. The ring of spears came in at him and he fell into a darkness, knowing he was dead.

A Bee took his hat and capered with it on his head until an induna's lash cut his back. A last shot rapped from the wagons and it was all over.

Following Mkalipi's orders to the letter, the warriors broke up the laager and inspanned the oxen for the journey to the Great Kraal where Mkalipi would be waiting impatiently.

They left the Invincibles where they fell without honoring them by opening their bellies, relying on the jackals to dispose of their corpses. To add contempt to their dishonor, the bodies of the Arabs and the Griquas were thrown on top of them so that the predators would eat unclean flesh before picking their bones.

By the evening the Matabele were gone and the lions came.

BOOK EIGHT

1

The Bees impi force-marched through the second night and came up to the outskirts of the Great Kraal as the morning fires were being lit. They had cut the oxen from Dirk's wagons and hauled them in by hand to save time. They halted in the military kraal assigned to Mkalipi's forces and reported their success to the induna, who praised them and killed cattle from his own herd to feed them. As the Bees broke their fast with meat and beer, the oxen were brought up and yoked to the wagons again. Mkalipi sent word to Mzilikazi, informing him that he and his loyal regiments were ready to parade before their King and to bring him their poor tribute.

The answer came back swiftly. Mkalipi, most beloved of all the King's subjects, was to come to the throne at once, for Mzilikazi was anxious to look upon the induna who had brought more wealth to the Matabele than all the other generals put together.

Mkalipi dressed himself in a long kaross of green monkey fur with a collar of leopard skin fringed with black civet tails, a new *umuTsha,* and old Sigwe's lucky skystone. Mounting his white horse, he sent his regiments ahead to stamp the ground flat, singing his praises all the way up to the very entrance of the Great Kraal. Only when the impi had passed inside did their chant change to one that honored Mzilikazi.

The six regiments lined up behind their totems and found that the massed impi of the Invincibles, the Ill-Tempered, the Coiled Ones, the Mists, the Haze, the Jackal-Baiters, the Earth-Shakers, and the powerful triple regiment of the Matchless Ones were there ahead of them, flanking the throne and facing out at them. Mkalipi's regiments grounded their shields with a crash and fell as silent as the ten thousand men facing them.

When Mkalipi rode in to make obeisance before the King he found to his fury that Mzilikazi was nowhere to be seen. Sitting on the throne was a tame baboon that had been taught to clap and show its fangs in a parody of a welcoming smile. It was a fine joke and Mkalipi forced himself to laugh as loudly as the other Matabele, even when the beast showed its multicolored buttocks and directed a stream of urine in his direction.

When the laughter had died away, Mkalipi approached

the throne and bowed low before the baboon. "Your loyal dog greets you, Lord of a Thousand Impi. All honor to your illustrious and celebrated self. Come, handmaidens, you should be whipped for your tardiness. The King thirsts. Beer for his majesty."

There was a roar of appreciation from the impi at this daring show of humor at Mzilikazi's expense, many laughing despite their disquiet. It was clear that something was coming to head this day, something they could all tell their grandchildren if they survived the King's witchsmellers who might be called out if the King was displeased by Mkalipi's sharp clowning.

Mkalipi handed a calabash of beer to the baboon and the animal drank deeply. Spears applauded, rattling against the many thousands of shields.

Then Mzilikazi was there and silence fell.

He wore a purple velvet robe and a wide red sash worked with golden thread. His face was impassive as he stared around the kraal, seeming to see every face, read every treasonable thought. He walked in a slow, wide circle, inspecting all the totems and greeting indunas he favored, remembering the names of men he may not have seen for years. When he returned to stand before his throne he made a show of seeing Mkalipi for the first time, touching him lightly on the chest with his horsehair flyswitch.

"I see you, Mkalipi," he said, his voice carrying easily.

"And I see you, Lord Elephant."

"Can that be?" asked Mzilikazi. "My general grows old if he cannot tell a king from a baboon. Perhaps he should retire with his blindness. Sit with his children and let others till his fields."

The laughter was long and savage. The joke was against Mkalipi again.

"Not while I can serve my King," said Mkalipi. He snatched up an *iKlwa* and drove it through the baboon, pinning it to the ground. "See," he sneered. "The impostor is dead. Mount your throne in safety, Lord Elephant."

The shocked silence was as hard as mica.

Mzilikazi acted as though he had seen nothing untoward. He had one of his women drag the small corpse away and sprinkle earth over the dribbles of blood. Then, with a great show of ease, he mounted the throne and spread his robe comfortably.

"It is good to see how quick you are to wash your spear for

your true king, Mkalipi. But induna, kill enemies for me, not baby monkeys."

"Forgive me, Lord Elephant. I could not bear to see the high throne of the Matabele so debased before its subjects. You yourself taught me to honor that seat so highly. I am jealous of its majesty on your behalf."

Mzilikazi snapped his fingers for beer. "I forgive you your overzealousness, induna. I did teach you to honor my throne. But who is to decide what is right for the Matabele, the rightful King or his favorite dog? You forgot yourself in your anxiety to please me, which I understand. We will not talk of this again."

Mkalipi inclined his head and kept it down, fighting to control his burning face. From where the impi stood, he seemed to be showing tacit and dutiful acceptance of the King's will.

Mzilikazi drained the first gourd of beer and had it filled again.

"I see the dogs you command for me, induna," he said. "But there was talk of tribute. I would see these 'poor' gifts you speak of. I know they must be truly rich if they come from you. You are too self-effacing, Mkalipi." He called sharply over his shoulder, all humor gone. "The tally sticks."

Mkalipi signaled two Bees with baskets. They ran forward and knelt, holding the covered baskets out.

"Behold, Lord Elephant," said Mkalipi, whipping away the covers. "You asked me to kill enemies. I have done so, not two days' march from this place." The severed heads of the Griquas and Arabs were already bloated and covered in flies.

Mzilikazi forced himself to drink beer as the heads were tumbled out before him, counting twenty-three in all. The corngrower Sihayo had described was not among them, he noticed, thinking furiously. Mkalipi had fallen into his trap. In order to take the laager he would have had to kill Mzilikazi's messenger, the height of treason. He wanted to roar aloud and throw beer into the air, to drive an *iKlwa* up into Mkalipi's rectum immediately. He did none of these things; instead he drank down his beer and wiped off his mouth and said:

"This seems well done. These are more heads than were taken at the killing hill. Remind me, induna, how many did you take for your king that time?"

"Very few," Mkalipi said quickly, worried by the lack of

reaction. Whatever he had expected from Mzilikazi, this blandness was not it.

"Shall I call for the tally sticks to remind both of us?"

"Nay, Lord. There were no heads."

"And you brought me great tribute then." Mzilikazi jerked his head up and the massed impi crashed spear against shield, crying, "True!" in concert.

"That day will be remembered so long as the Matabele abide," said Mzilikazi, and another great shout went up. "You took no heads on that day and yet you brought me herds so vast it took a whole season for them to be tallied. I tell you, induna, I can hardly breathe with the wonder of that and the thoughts I have now. If you have taken all these heads, then the cattle tribute you must have brought me this time must be that much greater. Our kingdom will thunder from the hooves of all these beasts. Is this not true?"

Mkalipi bit his mouth until he tasted blood, seeing the pit he was being buried in and hating Mzilikazi for his quickness of mind.

"Sadly no, Lord Elephant. That day at the killing hill was a time of miracles as the witchmen know and still speak of. I bring you these poor things instead." Mkalipi clapped his hands and Dirk's wagons were brought into the kraal and halted in the open space where all the impi could see them clearly. Mkalipi swaggered around them, inviting Mzilikazi to note their unmarked condition. "This time, in your name, Lord Elephant, we prevailed by cunning and stealth, and only lost three times ten of our fighting dogs. See, Lord, we bring you four stout wagons, ox teams trained to the shafts, as many guns as there are heads at your feet. And..." Mkalipi paused for effect. "The murderer of your messenger, the one known as Sihayo, killed by treachery while in your service."

So, thought Mzilikazi, that is how Mkalipi wished to play his bones. The strategy was clever, but not clever enough. Nothing showed in his face and even his eyes were dull. "Go on," he said.

"We have no cause to trust the corngrowers when they talk of parlay with us, and I worried when Sihayo told me he meant to talk to these interlopers on your behalf. I could cut off my feet for not being as swift to protect him as I should have wished. Although my men ran all through the night to attack these whites and half-men, they were not in time to save Sihayo. The whites had killed the guard of the Invin-

392

ibles and murdered Sihayo as he sat in council with the leader of the whites."

"Your slowness saddens me too, induna." Mzilikazi sounded deceptively mild. "Point out the head of this treacherous white so that I may spit upon it."

"His head is not there, Lord."

"You let this corngrower escape? You dare to tell me that this white defiled my sacred shield and you let him go on his way? Was he a wizard who wrapped himself in cloud? Did he addle the wits of your men with magic words? Must I call the witchsmellers to sniff the ranks of the Bees for those who were bewitched by this demon? Speak, Mkalipi, and tell me true or I shall have you smelled out."

There was a stir in the long lines of warriors. This was the first direct threat the King had aimed at Mkalipi and could mean his execution and the purification of his warriors by a smelling out of wizards, against which there was no defense. If Mkalipi defended himself by force of arms it would mean civil war and the dead would be numbered in their many thousands. To make things worse, a pair of vultures sailed in over the assembly and settled on the poles on the execution hill, a clear sign that they expected corpses to feed on.

Mkalipi showed no fear as he sauntered to the rear of the nearest wagon and whipped aside the sail.

"No, Lord. He did not escape my vigilance. See for yourself. Bring the corngrower out."

Two Bees dropped from the tailboard and brought down a man bound by thongs, throwing him to the ground. He fell heavily and scattered the severed heads as he struggled to raise himself onto his knees. His beard was matted by dried blood and his naked torso bore many scars. From those alone, Mzilikazi knew he was the man Sihayo had described. The healed cuts on his forearms could only have been inflicted by the thrust of *iKlwas*. Mzilikazi knew he must save him from execution hill and knew it would not be easy.

"I thank you for the gift of this corngrower, induna," he said. "Wet his mouth with beer, I will talk to him. A man must know how he is to die and be given time to contemplate it."

Mkalipi kicked Dirk onto his side.

"He is a corngrower. He will have no knowledge of our tongue. I have questioned him and he makes pig grunts like all his kind."

"All the same, wet his mouth, induna."

Mkalipi was repelled. "I, Lord? To what purpose? We kill our own felons and give them no chance to speak. Why give our enemies more than we give those of our own blood?"

"Do not question *me*." Light flared in Mzilikazi's eyes and he threw down his gourd. "You fluff your feathers like a frightened hen ostrich. Do you fear what the corngrower might say?"

"No man's words can harm me," boasted Mkalipi. But he touched his skystone and made a fist of his free hand, actions that did not go unnoticed by the King.

"Only a wizard's words," Mzilikazi said with withering scorn. "Perhaps this man did bewitch your men and place the worm of fear into your heart."

"Could I have captured him if that were so? Here, I will quench his thirst." Mkalipi pulled Dirk up by his hair and slopped beer into his mouth. Dirk nuzzled the suds, swallowed deeply several times, and retained a last mouthful to moisten his dried tongue. It was his first drink since his capture.

"A wizard does not think and act as ordinary men, have you forgotten that? Have you thought that this white wizard may have wanted to come before your king to speak to him alone, Mkalipi?"

"If that were true, Lord Elephant, why did he kill your messenger and defile your shield? I brought you this man to be killed, knowing you would wish to give that order yourself. Give the order and let us be done with this clay man." Mkalipi was close to shouting and his eyes bulged with fury. The King's taunts had cut his pride too often.

"Calm yourself, induna. When the corngrower's tongue is softened we will ask him about his wizardry."

"The Great King is wise in all things, but I doubt that even he understands pig grunts."

"We will be patient and see," said Mzilikazi. "I will deliberate." He was handed a fresh gourd of beer and he settled his buttocks more comfortably on the hard throne. One of his women brought the gilded rifle and stood it at his side where Mkalipi and Dirk could see it. Mzilikazi let the flies buzz and the clouds roll as he feigned deep thought. He had learned long ago that a prolonged silence gave weight to his words when he finally did speak. He whispered with his witchmen and pretended to weigh their previous augurs against the one they had read for that day. The shadows had crawled an inch before he spoke to all the waiting Matabele, addressing Dirk on their behalf.

"You have come to my land unasked, corngrower. Strangers are forbidden here, as you should know. You sent me this gun as a gift. I in turn gave you a greater gift, my personal protection. And yet, because of your wizard's way, you killed the bearer of my sacred shield. That is a crime against the whole Matabele nation, one that a single death cannot wipe away. You must die many times to cleanse that stain of blood from my throne. This induna accuses you of this murder, and as all my warriors know, his word is as my own, for I have raised him above all others in this land. Is that not true, Mkalipi?"

"Your generosity humbles me, Lord," affirmed Mkalipi.

"And what is the punishment for treason?" asked Mzilikazi.

"The Long Road of Tears, Lord Elephant."

"And that is fitting for this dog of a wizard?"

"It is the longest way of dying."

Mzilikazi raised his voice. "And do the Matabele approve of that punishment for treason, for the killing of my personal messenger?"

The assembled warriors stamped and crashed spear against shield and the earth shook under Dirk's knees. His muscles knotted and he held onto his courage with everything he had.

Mzilikazi swung on Dirk, pointing his flyswitch.

"Listen well, wizard. This is how you are to die many times. The stings of bees will be planted into your skin until you bloat. The soles of your feet will be flayed with wands until they will not stand the touch of a feather. Your arms will be broken in two places and tied up your back with wet rawhide. Then you will be raised on a gibbet and lowered onto an impaling stake until your rectum is penetrated. You will be lowered a hand's length each day, until the shaft penetrates deep in your vitals. This will take time, as many days as you have fingers and thumbs. To keep tally of the days, one of your fingers will be cut off at the joint each morning at sunrise. On the day you have no fingers left, your eyes will be gouged out and pegs will be hammered up your nostrils into your brain. If you are not dead then, and I have known of men who have lingered past the eleventh day, your body will be coated in clay and you will be slowly roasted over a bed of hot coals. Only then will you die and be grateful for it. That is the decision of the Matabele, corngrower."

Throughout the long speech, Dirk fought panic by concentrating on the rifle and keeping the beer in his mouth. He wanted to scream and run and protest, but he said nothing, biding his time.

"He has courage, eh, Mkalipi?" said Mzilikazi.

"No, Lord, he makes no sign of hearing your words because he has no understanding of them. No man could hear that sentence and be brave."

"You think so," said Mzilikazi comfortably.

"Aye, Lord. With all my heart."

Dirk spat out the precious beer, swallowed, coughed, and said, "I heard your words, Mzilikazi. And I heard your induna's."

"He is a wizard," said a handmaiden. Another whimpered and made the sign of the evil eye. A witchman blew colored powder over the King, who was watching Dirk with what could have been relief. He called for silence and took a lash to his women until they broke and ran for the seraglio. Seating himself again, Mzilikazi said:

"You heard my sentence and understood it then?"

Dirk said he had and did. "But I am not guilty. Ask your induna. He is a liar."

Mkalipi tried to snatch up a spear but found himself surrounded by white shields. He raised his fists above his head and yelled, "I claim his head as my right of conquest."

"My claim is absolute," snapped Mzilikazi. Then to Dirk, "By what wizardry do you speak our tongue?"

"I learned it fighting you at the killing hill. I learned it killing your warriors when I took my cattle back. I learned it burning your kraal when you ran away to the north. I learned it when we were enemies, Mzilikazi. Now I speak it as one who would be your friend."

"There, Lord," shouted Mkalipi, struggling against the indunas who held him. "He admits he is our enemy. Kill the dog now."

Dirk sneer-grinned and stood up clumsily, swaying weakly.

"I call myself enemy because it was true. I do not act the friend like you, Mkalipi. Even your famous skystone is a lie. I know that better than anyone."

The ranks of the Bees were loud with protest and the other regiments shouted them down. The royal indunas lashed at their warriors, forcing them to redress their lines. At Mzilikazi's order the Invincibles streamed sideways to link up with the Ill-Tempered to form a defensive screen around the throne. Order came back slowly and became complete when the witchsmellers came out of their huts and walked along the front ranks of the impi. Mzilikazi stood on his throne.

"Now we will listen to this wizard. Mkalipi has said no words can harm him. Very well, let him prove that for all of us to see. There is talk of treason and lies. I will hear more of this. Speak, wizard."

"Send men to where my wagons were laagered. If the bodies of Sihayo and the Invincibles are still there you will find no bullet wounds. Only the cuts of spears. And by digging where I tell you, you will find my true gift to the Matabele. Guns like this one by the throne. In one hole there are nineteen. In another there are many more. Mkalipi meant to take them for himself."

Mzilikazi bared his teeth at Mkalipi. "Well, induna?"

"The wizard lies. I swear on my stone of destiny."

"If you trust your stone," challenged Dirk, "let me see it protect you from my gun. That scar on your belly is familiar to me. An old friend. I put it there."

Wind sent dust devils whirling across the kraal and the screech of the vultures was harsh in the silence.

"I would like to see that," said Mzilikazi. "But that cannot be. If Mkalipi died at your hand he would be guilty as you say. Only by traveling the Road of Tears will he pay for his treason if he is guilty. Listen, Matabele, we will go to this place where the wizard says these guns are. We will see these corpses and look upon their wounds. It is decided. And I tell all those who would set any man above me, your king, if this guilt is proved, you will all bow to me or draw off and fight all my loyal impi. I have gathered all my armies here and the *iKlwa* will decide who rules this land and the Matabele. Think on these things and remember my words. To demonstrate his loyalty to me, Mkalipi will stay at my side when we go from this place. The Bees regiment, who may share his guilt, will stay inside their military kraal until I return. Mkalipi will also tell them to do this for love of me. Tell them, induna."

"It will be as the Great Elephant says," said Mkalipi, biting his mouth raw. He had no choice with a dozen spears at his back, whereas on the trail an opportunity to swing things in his favor might present itself. Somehow he had to get a message to his impi.

Dirk stepped close to Mzilikazi to whisper.

"Send a man you can trust to see if any of the Bees bear

iKlwa wounds. The Invincibles must have wounded some before they died."

Mzilikazi liked the way the corngrower thought—a natural court intriguer. He took Dirk's arm and led him away to talk.

2

A white ant explored the corner of Labule's right eye and when he did not blink Sihayo knew he must be dead.

An *iKlwa* had gone clean through Labule's neck and had snapped off at the shaft. He stared down at Sihayo, smiling a dead smile that favored one side of his lopsided mouth. Sihayo envied Labule's quick end. The bodies piled over and around him made breathing difficult and moving impossible. Thirst plagued him and the carnivorous mammals that nibbled the corpses had bitten him many times. Sihayo hated the Bees for leaving him to die like worthless offal; he should have been honorably dead if they had opened up his belly to release his spirit. Sihayo lay still and saved his strength.

A crimson sunset burned into night and moonlight brought the bigger predators. Hyenas padded around, darting in to worry the topmost corpses, their need to feed on the freshly slaughtered meat at odds with their reluctance to approach mansmells. Their yipping laughter was all around Sihayo, and with luck, the hyenas would pull some of the corpses away and help him to free himself. If that happened, Sihayo planned to wait for daylight before making any further effort. He was too bloody to move at night when he would be at a disadvantage against the keener senses of the big cats. With an effort of will, Sihayo made himself sleep.

He was brought awake by the deeper rasp of a lioness. She had got in among the hyenas and one of them was sideswiped, scrabbling away over the corpses yelping with pain. Sweating hard, Sihayo heard the rest of the pride circling in to take the kill for themselves. He glimpsed hard amber eyes against the stars and Labule was lifted away from him in the jaws of a mature male. The lion held the corpse like a corndoll and looked around for a good place to feed. Walking stiffly, it went away and Sihayo found himself holding his breath instead of taking air into his aching lungs.

From the roars and grunts around him, Sihayo knew the pride was a big one. Pale yellow shapes passed over him and a huge pad stepped close to his face. More bodies were being taken and one of the Arabs was caught up between two lionesses, clamped by leg and shoulder. Snarling, they faced off, ears flattened, muzzles drawn back, batting the air with bared talons, tails lashing. One darted in and the other leaped high, biting down on the outstretched neck. They rolled away locked together, parted, and threatened a male who came between them. He cuffed them aside and came in for Sihayo with an easy lunge.

Yelling, Sihayo sat up and threw a headless Griqua into the lion's path. Disconcerted, the lion backed away and had his flank raked by the still squabbling lionesses. Turning on them, he bowled one away, and as the second retreated crabwise, followed her in a furious rush.

Sihayo squirmed onto his stomach and kicked his legs free, elbowing himself across the blood-soaked grass. He jumped to his feet and fell again almost immediately. Returning circulation stabbed him with a million knives and cramped his stomach. Forcing himself upright again, he hobbled toward the far trees and the rocks beyond, hoping to lose himself in one of the kloofs. He scattered some romping cubs and they mewed in alarm, calling their mother. Dragging his numbed right leg, Sihayo kept moving, not daring to look behind him.

The trees were a long way off.

The ground tilted under him and he was sprawling down a slope he had not seen. Thorn whipped him and rocks bit at his sliding back. He slammed onto a ledge, teetered, and went over the lip, catching at a branch to break his fall. It snapped in his hand and he fell in a loose sprawl onto a dirt bank. After a while he rolled onto his back and felt his arms and legs for breaks. To his relief there were none. Sihayo thanked Mwari for it and congratulated himself for his good fortune. He would stay where he was until daylight and then make his way back to the Great Kraal. He saw himself denouncing Mkalipi and the entire impi of the Bees before the Great Assembly, demanding the honor of executing them for the Invincibles. He would be made an induna at least, Mzilikazi must show his gratitude....

Falling shale made Sihayo look up.

All along the rim of the kloof were glittering, blinking almonds, the fret of sharp muzzles and tufted ears. The thwarted hyenas had found him and it would not be long before they found a way down to him.

Sihayo was reminded of Jakot's good advice, furious with

himself for forgetting that a man should not count his luck like beans in a furrow.

Sihayo began crawling for the sheer southern wall, hoping the hyenas would not get there before him.

3

Pieter Klyn and Matthew Eastman saw the running man in the same instant.

Matthew had split his party in two when he saw vultures feeding where the wagon tracks ended and a browned patch of ground marked the site of a recent laager. He and Klyn had made for the northern trees and Boie had swung south in company with Coffee, Ndala and Josef, both groups meaning to circle the plain and to re-form by what remained of the *isango* corral. In the event that any of them sighted Matabele, they were to fall back to the high, rocky eastern hills where they could more easily defend themselves and slip away at nightfall before they were surrounded and cut off.

They had seen no human life during the last several days, even though they had passed between two large military kraals. Both were deserted, and from the condition of the beehive huts and the cooking trenches, only recently. Whatever their reasons for leaving it was clear they meant to return, and soon, otherwise they would have emptied the granary pits and fired the huts.

Matthew and Klyn were on a humpbacked ridge with a view over sloping, broken ground cut through with deep, wandering kloofs. The running man was about two hundred yards below them, racing across a narrow, undulating saddle between two erratic crevices. He ran with the last of his strength, his head rolled with effort, and his legs were rubbery as he panted up a slope that flattened out to form the crest of a tumbled butte where the crevices conjoined. He was running toward a cliff that fell sheer into deep shadows.

Blotched, dun animals with long necks and coarse manes snapped at his heels, herding him irrevocably toward the point of no return, never getting too close, never giving him the chance to veer toward the gentler slopes at either side of him.

"Hyena," said Matthew, unslinging his smoothbore. "Watch them and learn, Pieter. They're smart and they're brave. Why they're called cowardly I'll never understand. It is they who will bring down a buck or a wildebeest, and it's the lazy old lion who'll take their kill away from them. Not the other way around. See how they're herding that kaffir? They've got him every which way, and I'll bet some of them have got down into that kloof ahead of him. If he falls or climbs down, they'll be waiting for him. He's dead meat for certain."

"Unless we help him," said Klyn. "Is he Matabele?"

"If he is or he isn't, it doesn't much matter. One shot could bring an impi down on us before we reload. I'll bet a bullet to a belch those vultures aren't eating cabbages."

"All the same." Klyn dismounted and deliberately handed his reins to Matthew. "Don't stop me, man. Or I'll fight you." He primed his pan and cocked his musket, stepping off and aiming down the slope.

Matthew swung down and found himself hesitating. With the stock cradled against his beard and his left eye open over the sights, Pieter Klyn could have been his brother. So similar and yet so very different. Matthew still did not clearly understand why the big Dutchman had come across half a continent to stand at his side. No real reason had been offered or asked for, and it was much the same with Coffee. The British Sergeant could have left them in Natal and gone back to his regiment at the port. But he was here, offering no advice unless pressed, patiently enduring hardship for Matthew's sake. Or was he? Wasn't his life just as scarred by Dirk's madness? De Villiers had murdered Coffee's native levies and had come close to hanging him in Matthew's yard. They all had a score to settle with Dirk, but without Matthew's own single-minded commitment none of them would have come this far alone. However Matthew rationalized the situation, it all boiled down to their commitment to him.

Klyn's musket roared and bucked in a snort of white smoke.

Dust kicked beyond the leading hyena and it jumped and died, sailing out over the edge of the kloof like an unraveled bundle. The man and the other hyenas ran on.

"Why the hell didn't they stop, man?" Klyn could not believe it.

Matthew picked a point in the middle of the pack, tracking with several hyenas running bunched together, squeezing off his shot unhurriedly. Several things happened at once. The running Matabele threw up his arms and fell on his face. Two hyenas folded their legs and bucked sideways together, biting at their flanks before they died. A third lost the use of his back legs and skidded to halt, jetting blood onto the ground

401

behind him. A fourth howled and limped into cover. The rest of the pack halted, turned away, and went to ground.

"That's how to stop a pack." Matthew reloaded fast, spitting a ball into the bore and ramming it home. "You wasted a shot going for one. You're loaded with fragmentation ball, man, use the spread next time. Congratulations anyway, you probably shot the first hyena in the territory."

"And brought Mzilikazi to us if he's out there," said Klyn.

"He's out there."

"What about him?" Klyn pointed at the Matabele.

"Stay with the horses and keep your eyes open, sureshot. I'll see to him."

"I will. And Matthew..."

"Yes."

"I had to do it."

"Hell, man, I know it." Matthew shrugged and made a tired smile. "One of us had to, neh?" He went down the hill and found a natural bridge that led to where the Matabele lay with a turned ankle, a rock in his hand.

Sihayo watched Matthew come, seeing his long gun and his pistols, the knives in his belt and in his boot, the way he used his right leg more than his left, the facial scar that ran down into his beard and turned the brown hair white. The way he saw all there was to see without looking.

Matthew offered Sihayo his waterskin. "Water for a friend."

"I see you, corngrower," said Sihayo, ready to use the rock.

"No trust, eh, Matabele. You were dead and now you live. The hyenas drove you toward a long drop. They should be cracking your bones for the marrow now. Drink and live to count a thousand grandchildren."

"You are an enemy, corngrower. I, Sihayo of the Invincibles, tell you you are in the land of the Great Bull Elephant."

"Yes."

"Accepting life from an enemy is a hard thing."

"Not for a real man, Sihayo. Drink and live."

"Do you come to bring gifts to the Great Elephant like the other corngrower?" asked Sihayo, wanting an answer as much as the water.

Matthew narrowed his eyes and shook his head. "No, I follow the corngrower who came here with Griquas. I saw the vultures where he camped. Is that what happens to those who bring gifts to Mzilikazi?"

"I will drink." Sihayo rinsed his mouth, careful not to

choke himself by swallowing too quickly. This corngrower was different from the one he hated and he did not know why. He threw the rock aside. "Why do you follow this man?" he asked, taking a shallow swallow.

"To kill him."

Sihayo saw a raw hatred akin to his own in Matthew. Although the white spoke mildly, muscles ground in his jaw and he caressed the wooden part of his gun.

"I thought the invisible god of the whites made killing each other unlawful."

"Not all men obey the god," said Matthew. "You are a king's man and I will tell you the truth. I came here to kill the corngrower who came with guns. He destroyed my kraal and drove all my animals into the wilderness. He killed his own father when he burned my huts. If he is with your king I must go there and kill him. If he is dead with his Griquas I must see his body. Mzilikazi would hold him dear because of the guns. I know why he would do this, I was at the killing hill when our guns killed his impi. If I were Mzilikazi I would do the same."

"I too was there." Sihayo drank more water and gnawed on the strip of biltong Matthew gave him.

"I see your powder burns, Sihayo." Matthew filled his pipe and lit it, sharing the smoke with Klyn. "But you have fought since then, eh? Is there war in the land of the Matabele, or is that the blood of slavers and Griquas?"

"The blood is the blood of many, corngrower. Some from my friends, some the blood of others." Sihayo told Matthew about the attack of the Bees on Mkalipi's orders, finishing with: "There was treachery and I must tell this to the King."

"So Mkalipi has the guns."

"Not the guns," said Sihayo. "But he will have the corngrower you want dead. Mkalipi will take him before the King for his pleasure."

Matthew looked and sounded strangled. "How?"

"I watched the laager through the night. They buried the boxes of guns in the *isango* corral and covered their digging by driving the cattle back and forth. Then they spread the ground with dung. All this I saw."

"Listen, warrior, what gift would make you help me?"

Sihayo spread his bloody palms. "Nothing, corngrower. We follow the same road in this. I will serve my king and myself by helping you. Come." He staggered to his feet and spat on his right hand, offering it to Matthew. "The burning skystone told me you would come," he said as they shook hands.

4

Sihayo heard the King's approach long before the first impi came into sight.

The sound of the Matabele armies emptied the land of game. The rhinoceros lost themselves in the bushveldt, the elephants withdrew into the wild banana groves, and the deer, wildebeests, and zebra made for the grazing along the Okovango Swampland. Leopards and lions took to the rocky fastnesses of the high kloofs and fasted patiently until the stamping columns had passed.

Mzilikazi rode in Dirk's wagon at the center of the bull's loins, the head guarding his front and the far-ranging horns sweeping out on both sides. It was the first time he had ventured from his kraal in many years and the traveling tired him. Despite the continual singing and chanting of his massed warriors, Mzilikazi napped much of the day and slept soundly at night. Upright and awake, he was never without a gourd of beer in his hand and a question on his lips. He grilled Dirk about his part in the sacking of Mkalipi's military kraal and the attack on his own Royal Kraal of eGabeni after the battle of Vegkop, discussing tactics with shrewd appreciation of a high order.

Dirk was forced to admit, however grudgingly at first, that Mzilikazi was not the fat and black avaricious rascal that he in his prejudice had always taken him for. Mzilikazi's people adored him despite his harsh and arbitrary treatment of those who balked him, and treated him with a reverence that had been earned by much more than the simple rule of fear. Under him the Matabele thought themselves to be a great people with a greater destiny. They were the only people in Africa who could match the might of the Zulu and had fought them to a standstill when Dingaan, the Hungry One, had thought to take advantage of their several rapid defeats at the hands of the Boers. Dingaan had boasted of a victory, but so badly mauled were his impi he never sent them north again.

Mzilikazi's curiosity was boundless and he would talk about anything that might be of use to him at some future time. Although he was quick to understand most things strange to his culture, his view of Christianity was so warped that it would have been laughable if it had not been so dangerously literal. Dirk always managed to guide him away from the quagmire of theological misunderstanding, a field he was ignorant of, being barely able to stumble through a simplistic outline of the Calvinism he had grown up with. Talk of guns was the certain way out of any corner. Guns were the one subject Mzilikazi never tired of. For muskets he would trade ivory, rare animal hides, and land (so long as it was somebody else's), and probably, if it were necessary, his overflowing seraglio of women. If Dirk wanted slaves he had only to point out the neighboring tribe he wanted and Mzilikazi would subjugate that people and hand them over to the Afrikaner without a second thought.

In this way Dirk and Mzilikazi passed the time between the Great Kraal and the site of Dirk's laager. Of Mkalipi, Dirk saw no sign, although he did witness the summary execution of a man who had tried to pass a message for the induna. Clubbed unconscious, the man was quickly skewered and left on the trail to die.

Dirk had not slept that night for fear of spectered dreams.

The great army swept onto the plain around the site of Dirk's laager and secured the boundaries. No Matabele was allowed near the site itself upon pain of death, and the Ill-Tempered impi were charged with that duty, being in favor with Mzilikazi at that time and as trusted as the Invincibles themselves, that impi forming a royal bodyguard. When Mzilikazi arrived during the afternoon of the fifth day, all his indunas, witchmen, advisers, augurs, and keepers of his Royal Kraal were already assembled and awaiting the King's pleasure.

Mzilikazi sat in state under the rush awning of the wagon and all the corpses that were in any way intact were gathered up on woven carpets and laid out for his inspection. When he had seen enough he had Mkalipi brought from the rear of the assembly and made him walk the lines of bodies with the other indunas. The evidence was inconclusive; most of the dead had already been reduced to skeletons and it was impossible to make out features or their original skin color, let alone discover the way they had died. It was much as Mzilikazi had thought it would be, and he ordered the remains taken away to be left for the jackals.

Now he could concentrate on the matter of the guns, and Mzilikazi had Dirk point out where he had buried them in the *isango* corral. Men armed with adzes and hoes moved in, and with the whole assembly's attention on the digging, nobody saw Boie drop from beneath Dirk's wagon where he had been hiding since the previous night. He made his way quickly into the rocks carrying the rifle Dirk had sent to Mzilikazi wrapped in a piece of matting, moving toward the high eastern ground where Nkosi Matthew and the others waited with the horses. On the way up the steep draw he met Sihayo, who was working his way downward in the opposite direction, carrying his messenger's shield. They sat together for a moment to exchange snuff.

"You have the rifle," said Sihayo, nodding at the bundle.

Boie grinned and nodded. "I have it, Matabele."

"Take it to your Nkosi with this small thing for me." Sihayo gave Boie a small skin *mouti* bag. "Tell him these magic things brought luck to another man before his sign of faith was washed from his loins by the corngrower who came with the guns. His name was Jakot, and he killed himself with a stone, and went to the Earth Mother consenting before the torture stole his wits and strength. Tell your Nkosi this. It is why I want the corngrower dead. If we do not meet again in this life, tell your lord I honor him."

"As he honors you, Matabele."

"May you reach your own land safely, Stutterer." Sihayo used the Zulu word for Hottentot, a literal translation of the imitative Dutch.

Boie saw the joke and laughed. "Go with Mwari and the Earth Mother."

Both men turned and went their separate ways, hoping that the god of all things thought well of them.

Sihayo chose a route that brought him down into the safety of the ranks of the Invincibles, where he was greeted with shouts of awe and respect. He was still crusted with dried blood and the open wound on his head made a red parting through his hair. The warriors opened a corridor for him and Sihayo walked out to stand in sight of Mzilikazi, raising his bloody shield in salute.

The last of Dirk's guncases had been unearthed and hauled unopened before Mzilikazi's throne, where Dirk was in the act of prising the lid from one of them. He stopped working and straightened up, jostling Mkalipi, who stood beside him, the crowbar squealing on a nail.

The induna hissed and paled, unable to look away from the gory apparition of Sihayo. Mkalipi truly believed he was seeing the dead walk. Cries of superstitious fear came from the regiments and only the whips of the indunas kept them formed up and steady. Mzilikazi too was affected. He stood up dribbling beer, his lips gray.

"Do you live, Sihayo?" he asked.

Sihayo bowed. "I live, Great Elephant," he said. "Protected from Mkalipi's treachery by magic and your sacred shield."

Mkalipi held his skystone with both hands. "The shade lies."

The witchsmellers moved around Sihayo and one of them touched him.

"He is a living man."

Mzilikazi recovered from his fright quickly. "Speak out, Sihayo, so that all the Matabele may hear how you are not killed."

"Great magic, Lord." Sihayo spaced his words so that they carried. "The Bees sent by Mkalipi attacked us here as I spoke with the corngrower. They ignored your sacred shield, Lord, gave no warning, but came silently like cowardly Fingo. Seeing this, the corngrower struck me with his enchanted pistol and I fell into a mist that hid me from your enemies' eyes. The Bees killed my guard and threw them over me. They did not treat the Invincibles as men who served their king, but left them with unopened bellies for the lions and jackals. I alone lived. The corngrower's mist stayed with me and I was able to walk through the beasts unharmed. In a dream I saw you would come and I have waited for you all these long days and nights."

Mzilikazi's belly shook with fury.

"Hold that man who was once my induna, this dog Mkalipi who ate my bread and has repaid me with treachery. All of you are witness to this and shall see this dog travel the Long Road of Tears for it. Know that this is doubly fitting, for it was he who named this punishment for his own crime. When he is dead, no man shall ever again speak his name. No man will ever remember he ever lived or stood at my right hand. All his cattle will die, all his fields shall lay untilled, all his clan will perish, and all those who followed him will be smelled out by the witchmen and fed to the crocodiles. I shall purge this land of traitors, and no man will ever again stand higher than my knee. The Bees impi are enemies in my land and will all die on my spears. Take this dog away and tell me when he is dead."

Four indunas threw Mkalipi to the ground and fitted a wooden halter around his neck. They tore off his headdress, his kaross, and his *umuTsha*, broke his spears, and tore the skystone from his neck. His totem was chopped into kindling and set alight, and his shield was burned on it.

When Mkalipi's arms were broken and tied up his back nobody made a move to save him.

Dirk watched him dragged away as adzes rang from the trees where timber was being cut for a gibbet. He had been unnerved by Sihayo's sudden appearance and the Matabele's odd belief in his magical powers. Dirk knew he could use that belief to his own advantage, given the time to think, but all he wanted now was to finish the business at hand and relax with the women Mzilikazi had promised him. The smell and press of the Matabele impi now oppressed him, and Mzilikazi's appetite for casual acts of brutality chafed even his calloused sensibilities. The absolute power of this one man over these hundreds of thousands of kaffirs made his nerves jump and his nightmares more vivid. So much so that he slept with his fist in his mouth to stop himself from crying out. The stink of the recently removed corpses still clung to the ground at his feet, permeating his hair and clothes so thoroughly that Dirk thought he would never be able to scrub himself clean again. He would always smell of this charnel house if he stayed in this part of Africa. Whatever he had fondly believed, the ways of the Matabele would never be his however much he deluded himself. He was lost in the drums and crash of spear and heel, the booming baritone sea of praise singing, the high, ululating cries of the women, all washing over him until he was part of it, and it was part of him.

The silence came as a loud absence of sound.

Mzilikazi had raised an arm and was looking at Dirk.

"Now, wizard," he said. "We will see these guns of yours."

Dirk jammed his crowbar under the loosened lid of the first box and prised it off with an easy wrench, watching the King's reaction, waiting for the buzz of wonder from the watching impi. Mzilikazi's face had stiffened and he gripped his huge thighs, his lips compressed. Dirk stared down at the rough cords of wood stacked inside the box with choked disbelief, unable to register the fact that the timbers were not gilded rifles, wondering why Cord Laidler had betrayed him in this way. It made no sense. There was no profit in such a move. It was also not possible. Laidler had been safely at sea when Dirk had had all the boxes opened before having them loaded aboard the wagons, and supervised the wagon beds nailed down over them. At no time had Dirk left them unattended, so the Arabs and Griquas had had no opportunity to spirit them away.

Spirit them...Dirk found Sihayo's blank face, suspicion dawning. The damned kaffir might have used his time digging up the guns and hiding them elsewhere. But no, the job would have been too much for one man.

"More wizard's tricks, corngrower?" asked Mzilikazi. "Do you mean to change these sticks into guns to show off your powers?"

Dirk smashed open a second box and a third, grunting with effort and blinding himself with sweat. They were all the same, all filled with useless balks of timber. He turned on Sihayo.

"Where are the guns, damn your eyes?" He had lapsed into Afrikaans, forgetting himself. "You damned kaffir, tell me or I'll twist your neck around."

Sihayo said nothing. Showed nothing.

Mzilikazi stirred on his throne. Dirk faced him, close to snapping.

"They are stolen, Mzilikazi. Question Mkalipi. He must have them."

Sihayo clicked his tongue against the roof of his mouth. "There was more to my dream, Lord Elephant. With your permission .."

"Speak."

"I saw Mkalipi on the impaling stake and he talked with the corngrower. The corngrower taunted Mkalipi and showed him a gun that became a stick. Then the stick tore itself from the wizard's hands and impaled him so that he and Mkalipi died side by side."

Mzilikazi became impatient. "What does this dream mean?"

Sihayo apologized and said he did not know. "But Lord, you have a gun. You saw it shoot. If that gun is still good, the dream is a lie sent by Mkalipi to confuse your messenger. If that is so, Great Elephant, Mkalipi will know where the guns are."

Mzilikazi conferred with his witchmen and Sihayo noticed that they looked across at him with fear and not a little jealousy. They rattled their fans and gourds and waited for Mzilikazi to show them how he wished to be advised.

"Bring the gun," ordered Mzilikazi. Then, trusting nobody but himself, he said, "No. I will fetch it myself." He climbed into the wagon, rooted around, and stepped back down with the long red bundle in his arms. "See the truth," he said, and let the cloth unravel.

A stick carved in the rough shape of a rifle fell to the ground and fetched up against Dirk's foot.

Dirk jumped away from it as though it were a striking mamba, hearing the hisses from the indunas and witchmen, knowing too well he was finished. He found Sihayo and caught the flare of satisfaction in the Matabele's eyes before the blood-caked face blanked. Mzilikazi's voice battered at him as he was seized and forced to his knees, held there by strong arms.

"Sihayo's dream was true. Bind the white wizard before he conjures mist to hide in. Listen, Matabele, we will never talk to whites if they come again to this land. You see how they try to cloud our eyes with lying magic. They would have us throw away our spears and go against our enemies with nothing but magic sticks."

"Wait," said Dirk. "Wait...."

"Make another gibbet," said Mzilikazi, walking away and calling for beer.

A rough wooden collar choked off Dirk's wail of terror before it had formed in his throat. Then they broke his arms.

5

Katherine struggled to encompass Matthew Eastman's death and her husband's reawakened sexuality.

She slipped from Cord's bed and stood quivering on the balcony, chilled by more than the night wind. The consuming cold came from within herself and would prevail on her spirit however many brazen noons she might live through, for something vital within her had died with Matthew on the far, high veldt. The loss seemed darker than the night itself.

Not seeing Matthew had been something she had learned to live with, for she had the trick of conjuring him at will, secretly sharing the milestones of Jamie's growth with her memory of him. The first tooth, the first staggering steps across the nursery floor, the beatific smile of wonder when his chubby fingers had reached for a Christmas toy, the pleasure of the suckling mouth against her breast when she had spurned the services of a wet nurse despite the warnings that her figure might suffer for it....

Just knowing that Matthew existed, was out there somewhere in the wilderness, had always been enough for her. A prowling, ageless image of him stayed with her, a fond and solid picture of him solving the problems that frontier farming constantly brought. Patient with his foaling mares and lambing ewes, striding about with the small Khoikhoi in his shadow, neither troubled by exhaustion or gathering years. Frozen and perfect.

But now Cord had acted the spoiler and brought the news of his sudden violent death. He had fed Katherine the story evening by evening, spinning it out as he enjoyed a cigar and an after-dinner brandy, watching for any reaction she might have made. Katherine had not given him that satisfaction. There had been times when her temples swam and silent screams blocked her throat. Times when she wanted to kill him with a fruit knife. But she had not. She had retained her outward composure and poisoned him with her hooded eyes, thinking of Jamie's future now that Cord had finally named him heir to his estate. For that alone she would have lost a dozen Matthews.

Cord's encounter with Elise aboard the *Mazeppa* had been the most agonizing point of the rambling narrative. The news that Matthew had married and sired a child had caused Katherine both jealousy and, incredibly, even to herself, a feeling of intense betrayal. Lying with another when he should have been saving himself for the reunion with Katherine, making a child with that cuckoo of a girl from Port Elizabeth. It was a betrayal of the worst kind, thought Katherine, conveniently forgetting that she had convinced Matthew he should forget her. Why, she would rather have had him share a pallet with a horde of Bantu doxies and fill the Central Plateau with café-au-lait bastards than to have to stomach him marrying and bedding some provincial minx. Had she retained more of her slight sense of humor, Katherine might have laughed at herself at that juncture. But she had done nothing other than have the houseboys pass Cord more coffee.

Katherine shivered and drew her gown around her.

Cord's musk seemed to permeate her flesh and her loins ached from his repeated hard penetration. It was as if he were trying to make up for six celibate years in a single week. As if a permanent erection could pump away the rift between them, could erase her memories of Matthew and reduce his face to a gray and unmemorable smudge with no meaning and less substance. He was wrong, Katherine told herself fiercely. The time with Matthew was all she had left for herself alone. She might not revolt against Cord's tyranny, might play the compliant and servile wife for Jamie's sake, but she would never put Matthew's memory from her. Never.

Matthew might be dead, but he lived on in her and her son.

Cord's dissipation had ensured he could not go on forever and Katherine meant to survive him by many years. Then she would take the boy up-country to see if he had any taste for that life, show him his roots and tell him something of his father without revealing all. If the boy had her vivacity, his grandfather's fire, and Matthew's strength of character, he would take to the land without a second thought. He must not be allowed to become one of those precious and snot-nosed youths who lounged about the colony with no thoughts save those of massive self-indulgence, falling into dissolution before they were thirty, fat in the girth and thick in the head. Jamie already had Matthew's eyes and his grave way of looking at the world. Pray God there was more.

But damn this other brat in Port Elizabeth.

Katherine's nails bit into her palms as she thought of the unborn child that should have been hers. If it turned out to be a daughter she thought she could forgive and forget, but the idea of Matthew's son being brought up by a woman of unsound mind and less backbone than a fairy shrimp filled Katherine with an intolerable fury. That she had no rights in the matter did not occur to her, so incensed was she, so consumed by this trespass on her domain; she felt herself the only proper person to have any proprietary interest in any issue of her dead lover's. In death as in life, Matthew was hers.

She had contacts enough in Port Elizabeth to glean intelligence about the Cuthbert girl, and enough wit to make her inquiries appear to be the exchange of social gossip. Cord may control Cape Town and its environs but he would have no interest in intercepting her letters to Port Elizabeth. She would start at dawn when there was enough light to put pen to paper. Calling for a lamp now would only arouse Cord's interest if he were to awake.

Katherine started when Cord's arm encircled her waist and pulled her back against him. She had been so deep in thought she had not heard the pad of his single, naked foot on the marble floors. He was so silent and agile when he wanted to be, she thought, swallowing bile. He had even mounted a horse that morning without allowing Elias to hold the rein. At luncheon he had talked of the false limb he had ordered and boasted of how he would be taking a hunter at the jumps within a month of its being fitted. His hand ran up her breast to massage her throat.

At that moment the sky was split by a falling stream of brilliant white light that streaked across the top of Table Mountain, gone as quickly as it had come.

Like Matthew, thought Katherine, forcing herself to lean back against Cord's naked chest. He had illuminated her life just as briefly and just as brightly. A fleeting stream of fire that stayed in the retina and the memory long after it had passed into oblivion. Searing the inner eye.

"A shooting star, Katherine," Cord said into her hair. "You must make a wish, my dear."

Blinking from the afterburn that spangled her vision, Katherine turned to face Cord, her hands going to his naked hips.

"I have, husband," she said, her thoughts far away from the distasteful physical encounter that was to come.

6

When Matthew told them they were to go on and that he would catch up with them within a day or two, they knew the screams had got to him. Coffee had tried to argue and Klyn had lied, saying it was fine with him. Boie thought of his wife and son, weighing their lives against Nkosi's safety, hating himself for obeying with a dumb nod.

They waited until Matthew slipped away during the dark of the moon, turning their horses east when they could no longer see him, all of them busy with their own thoughts, saying goodbye to him in their own ways.

Matthew rode down to the kloof where the hyenas had trapped Sihayo and hobbled his horse there, working his way down to the Matabele fires on foot with his smoothbore and the ornate rifle Boie had brought from Dirk's wagon. He took a long time over his descent, and longer over the selection of a vantage point, finally choosing a V of rock with a good view over the plain and backed by a long, covered draw he could lose himself in when the time came. He primed and loaded both guns, set their flints with care, and loaded up with four-ounce balls.

Then with the screams and shadows for company, he waited.

The false dawn came up at his back and threw no light

413

onto the plain ahead of him, but there was enough light to see that the Matabele had not thrown out a deep screen of guards, content to rely on those posted around their immediate perimeter, relying on their strength of numbers. Matthew's position was safer than he had hoped.

A trick of acoustics brought Dirk's moans to him as clearly as though he were at his side. Matthew heard him damn his father and rant against the British. Once he talked softly to a girl he had shared a slate with back on the Zuurfeld during a writing lesson. When he screamed the morning seemed a long way off.

The sky paled and oblique light stole over the Matabele camp, turning the warriors into gray wraiths as they moved through woodsmoke and groundmist. Herdboys trotted about with water jars and fresh kindling.

The far hills took on substance beyond the violet trees and finches darted in and out of the thorn around Matthew as if he were one of the rocks. When he lifted his smoothbore they exploded into motion and were gone.

The gibbets grew out of the haze like bald trees bearing strange fruit. The two broken men hung quietly, their bonds lost in their bloated flesh, foul and shocking parodies of what they had been only the day before.

Matthew ducked his head to wipe off his mouth, both repelled and attracted by the sight. He had known what would happen to Dirk de Villiers and he considered himself directly responsible for it. If he had gone before the screams started he might have learned to live with what he had caused to happen. But not when he had lingered to make certain the Matabele would kill him, not after a night of listening to those tortured cries, and certainly not now he had seen for himself what had been done to him. The sight of Dirk's impalement far outweighed the pain in his legs and would last longer in his memory than that of old Abraham lying dead in the smoldering ashes of his farm.

Finish it, Matthew told himself. You owe yourself that much.

Almost casually, Matthew aimed into the camp and shot Mkalipi through the chest. The induna kicked just once and hung motionless. Dirk came awake and began dancing like something wooden worked by strings.

Men were coming up from under their shields like reborn corpses, chasing the racketing echoes with swinging heads. Soon they would see Matthew's smoke and be coming for him.

414

Closing his eyes to the piercing screams, and overcome by sudden panic, Matthew brought the gilded rifle up to sight on the thing that capered on the pole beside Mkalipi. But his finger would not curve around the trigger and the blurring sights would not line up. He could not hold the rifle still.

Damning himself for this inexplicable weakness, Matthew tried again, fighting his rigid finger, making it pull against the cold metal spur. The rifle kicked and discharged without warning, bruising his shoulder and throwing him up out of his crouch. A second shot had cracked out almost in concert with his own, fired from close behind him. Matthew turned, dropping the smoking rifle, seeing Boie lowering his own long gun, knowing he had missed and the Khoikhoi had not.

Shaking uncontrollably, Matthew leaned against the kloof wall, unwilling and unable to move. He tried to speak and had nothing to say. He was empty and filled with an overwhelming sadness. Nothing meant anything any more.

Boie came down past him to retrieve Matthew's smooth-bore and to leave the rifle where it could easily be found. Then he took Matthew's arm and drew him away toward the east like a big, shambling child.

"It is done, Nkosi," he said. "Come home now."

Home? thought Matthew, was there such a place any more? Had he the strength to rebuild again? Clear the thorn and plant borrowed seed with no wife and no son at his side? Not knowing the answer, he followed Boie down the draw until they were lost in the thorn and the long morning shadows.

When the Matabele came and found the rifle they knew the wizard's magic had turned against him, and they ran back the way they had come without taking it with them.

And no Matabele went there again.

GREAT ADVENTURES IN READING